It Happened
One Christmas

Judy Babilon

It Happened
One Christmas

ReadersMagnet, LLC

ReadersMagnet, LLC
10620 Treena Street, Suite 230 | San Diego, California, 92131 USA
1.619.354.2643 | www.readersmagnet.com

Book design copyright © 2019 by ReadersMagnet, LLC. All rights reserved.
Cover design by Ericka Walker
Interior design by Shemaryl Evans

CHAPTER I

———※———

*I*t happened every year. Charlotte, known better as Charlie, dreamed of her fantasy Christmas. The kind of small-town, Thomas Kinkaid–type Christmas that everyone dreamed of, complete with carolers strolling from house to house, pausing briefly at old Miss Caroline's for a steaming cup of hot cocoa. A warm, friendly little town that celebrated Christmas the way it's supposed to be celebrated, with cookies baking in every oven, brightly colored lights twinkling from porch railings, and lawns seemingly alive with displays of Santa and his reindeer, lopsided snowmen, and life-sized manger scenes. Nearly every house had candles glowing from second-story windows and beautifully adorned Christmas trees standing regally inside bay windows, creating picture-perfect postcard scenes.

Downtown, lights intertwined with garlands of holly bordered both sides of Main Street and shone like welcome beacons for visitors to the small town—Charlie's town—where Christmas began the day after Thanksgiving and lasted until January first. A one-big-happy-family town where everyone knew everyone and neighbor helped neighbor.

A private domain where the only way in or out was by horse and buggy over an old covered bridge, Braxton, a tiny town in northern Vermont, was a wonderful place where joy and cheerfulness seemed to be the rule rather than the exception. It also meant that the job of raising your children in such a small town meant having no fear of letting them go off to the skating rink alone or meet at the church nearly every Wednesday night to practice for the Christmas play, a pageantry in which everyone, down to the smallest toddler, played a part.

It was a well-known fact that when folks came to visit or had perhaps lost their way and simply stopped for directions, they didn't want to leave. At least, that's how Charlie Faraday wanted Braxton to be, and she told anyone who would listen.

"You're dreaming!" Her stepfather called over his shoulder, snapping aside the newspaper he was reading. "You've been watching too many old movies if you ask me!"

His wife, DeeDee, never could figure out how he managed to read his newspaper, discuss verbatim everything he'd just read, and still hear any and all conversations going on around him.

"Please don't start, Pete," she said softly.

"Well, she'd better wake up and face reality, there's no place on this earth like she's describing, except in her own mind!"

"Just leave her alone," DeeDee said, walking toward the kitchen. "It doesn't hurt a girl to dream a little."

"That's right," Pete sneered, "Take her side like you always do! You should try to teach her a thing or two instead of humoring to her like you do, she'll never learn how to live in the real world!"

"Oh, for heaven's sake, Pete, she's twenty-five, not twelve! If she hasn't learned by now..."

"Fine, just forget I said anything!" Pete snorted, hiding behind his newspaper again. The subject, now considered closed, warned DeeDee that further discussion could possibly resurrect a sleeping lion.

"It's okay, Mom." Charlie's voice was hushed. "It's not worth getting into a fight over, he just doesn't understand. But—" She leaned closer to her mother and whispered, "He'll certainly understand after tomorrow!" Before her mother could ask what she meant, Charlie disappeared from the kitchen.

In the privacy of her room, Charlie lay on her bed staring up at the ceiling. She hated to admit it, but her stepfather was right: the special kind of Christmas Charlie dreamed of was just that—a dream. Instead of the beauty she imagined in her mind, she saw bare, undecorated storefronts, streets piled high at the curbs with dirty snow, and people in too much of a hurry to give you the time of day, let alone a "Merry Christmas!" Of course, baking cookies or carefully decorating a real Christmas tree had become outdated too; it seemed that buying stale cookies from dirty store shelves and artificial, pre-decorated trees from Lester's Emporium was the fashion of the day. To make matters worse, the Christmas carolers were gone too, save a few die-hards who thought the way Charlie did; though try as they may, bless them, most of them couldn't carry a tune if they had a wheelbarrow. Even the covered bridge she'd adored since she was old enough to reason was falling apart and had been closed to public transportation years ago. Now the only ones to use it were the willful youth; boom boxes slung over hunched shoulders, blaring with a force so loud it shook the entire bridge, not to mention causing severe hearing problems to anyone within a hundred-foot range.

And according to the majority of those kids, Braxton was a place they would rather *not* be, where ice skating was for sissies, singing in the streets was for lame-o's, and visiting your neighbors during the holidays was just plain weird. It was, however, an easy way to rip off the old folks by putting the five-finger discount on their priceless possessions.

What had happened? What had become of the old-fashioned Christmases of days gone by—the days of one special gift, hand-carved or crafted for that one special person? Now, the youth of today demanded CDs from Video Break-Out or exorbitantly priced preppy clothes from Abercrombie & Fitch and County Seat.

Where had all the love and warmth gone? The children's happy faces aglow with dreams of prancing and pawing hooves and setting out cookies and milk for the jolly old fellow in the red suit with his huge black sack filled with gifts and treasures? Were they really just dreams or something only found in books? Surely, the ideas for those books and happy times had to come from somewhere and not just from someone's vivid imagination.

Charlie refused to accept it. She not only wanted Christmas back in all its glory with bright lights and tinsel, she wanted to see those happy, smiling faces, and the very next day, she went after it, determined to change the town and everyone in it.

"But, Mayor Braxton," Charlie insisted at his office the very next morning. "The town was founded by your very own ancestors! How can you, in all good conscience, not carry on their traditions? I've been to the library. I know how much your family loved and adored Christmas! Wouldn't you like to have that feeling back again?"

"My dear Miss Faraday," the mayor began, folding his hands on his huge desk. "Times have changed, things aren't what they used to be. In the first place, we could not possibly afford the expense of paying the vast number of people we would need, the cost would be staggering. Why, to string even one set of lights along Main Street would cost a fortune not to mention paying an exorbitant price to purchase the lights *and* the expense of keeping them lit. Then, there is the cost of personal insurance protection, the materials needed, and the people to perform the work." He sighed heavily. "And in the second place, there is no way I will ever allow the pond to reopen, it's totally out of the question. You see, Miss Faraday, although it all sounds like a very nice little fairy tale, no one in this town would be interested. Some have tried, admittedly, but all have failed. More importantly, I would be the laughing stock of this entire town. I'm sorry, but you're simply not being realistic."

"But you wouldn't have to pay anyone. If you just explain what we plan to do, I'm sure people would volunteer. Just think of it, Mayor Braxton, an old-fashioned Christmas with skaters on the pond again and horse-drawn buggies, can't you just see it? The people would—"

"Call me an idiot and run me out of town on a rail!" The mayor scoffed. "Have you any idea what you're asking?"

Charlie bristled. She *had* done her homework at the library and was well aware of how seriously his family had viewed the holiday.

Their influence on the small town was unsurpassed when it came to the love and sharing of the season, and it was at that very moment that she realized where her own ideas originated. So how could a man whose very name was practically synonymous with Christmas be so cold and unfeeling about such an important event?

"Your parents viewed Christmas with a reverence, Mayor Braxton." Charlie reminded him. "And what does that say to your daughter and son-in-law or, more importantly, to your granddaughter? Have you taken their feelings into consideration?"

"Kindly leave my family out of this, Miss Faraday," he cautioned. "They have nothing whatsoever to do with how I run this town and they never will!"

Something in his tone spoke volumes to Charlie, but she refused to let his personal problems interfere. Not now, not when she'd already thrown caution to the wind by even approaching the mayor with her stepfather on the town Finance Committee. He had made his stand perfectly clear to the townspeople as well as his own family that the committee had already begun cutbacks to save money and that any major changes were out of the question. Charlie was skating on thin ice by even broaching the subject with the mayor, knowing Pete would hit the ceiling when he got wind of it. And lately, she hadn't been doing a whole lot to bring out his good side. However, since she'd already gone this far—

"Mayor Braxton," she coaxed sweetly, trying another approach, "You have been an *icon* in this town. Everyone likes and respects you, and they *listen* to you!" She lied. "Surely, you have to know that if you would just say the word—"

"Miss Faraday," he said, standing. "Spare yourself the humiliation of groveling, it doesn't suit you." He snatched his suit jacket from the back of his chair and the chair spun like the well-oiled machine that it was—the irony that he wouldn't justify spending a little money to wake up his sleepy town, but could spend hundreds of dollars on such a luxurious piece of furniture just to hold his big—

"I have an important meeting to attend to," he said, breaking into Charlie's thoughts, and she quickly rose to leave, though not before she scanned the plush office.

"Well, I certainly would like to thank you for taking time out from your busy day to see me." Her tone dripped with sarcasm after spying a box of clay pigeons and a rifle in the corner of the room. "I hope I haven't kept you from your meeting at the Sport's Club."

"As a matter of fact, I am a bit late, but I doubt that it will bother my skeet shooting partner. I'm sure he will be quite forgiving when I tell him the reason for my delay was due to an impromptu meeting with you."

"I'm very happy for you," Charlie said bitingly. "That certainly makes me feel a whole lot better."

"I was sure it would." He mused. "You see, my appointment is with your father, and I'm sure that our little meeting will make for interesting conversation on the shooting range!"

Charlie grimaced inwardly. It wasn't the first time she'd battled with the mayor over improvements for Braxton, but it was one of the major reasons she and her stepfather didn't see eye to eye. She also knew that the mayor was well aware of that fact, but she refused to show concern. "He's my *stepfather*, and I could less what you talk about."

"Well, that makes me feel a whole lot better too. I certainly wouldn't want to make things uncomfortable for you at home."

Charlie couldn't get out of the mayor's office and into the fresh air fast enough. Of all the people in the world, she should have known better than to approach the very man her stepfather worked for, but it had never occurred to her that they were buddies. She didn't think either of them had buddies.

She walked to her car parked at the curb, spied the familiar ticket, and snatched it from the windshield, ripping it to shreds and letting the pieces flutter to the ground. Once inside her car, she laid her head against the cold steering wheel.

Pete's gonna have a field day with this one, she thought, not thinking about herself but dreading how it would affect her mother.

He'll probably raise the roof and send it flying clear across Main Street! She looked up then and spied the car sitting in the spot marked Reserved for Mayor and moaned aloud. "And with my luck, it'll land right on top of the mayor's new Cadillac."

Charlie wasn't afraid of her stepfather, but he did have a habit of making her feel stupid—and that made her furious. He had a bad temper, and though he'd never laid a hand to Charlie or her mother, he did have the most annoying habit of raising his voice and repeating himself when he knew you didn't understand something he thought you should.

Pete Faraday had been Charlie's stepfather since he adopted her when she was seven. Her own father had passed away when she was just a baby, so Pete was the only father she'd ever known, but for some reason, they just couldn't get along. He was a good man but hadn't been the greatest at raising children, especially a girl, but he tried. It wasn't so bad when Charlie was younger, but as she grew up, she sensed a distance in him. Eventually, that distance began to put her off and cause her own distance to grow, and that's when their problems began. And while Charlie adored her mother, there were times when DeeDee Faraday naturally took her husband's side although she did work hard at being equally fair with both of them. She did, however, believe that her daughter missed the normal father-daughter closeness since she didn't know her real father, and Pete sometimes had a problem with that.

On the other hand, Charlie was a bit envious of the way her mother stuck up for Pete, and *she* sometimes had a problem with *that.*

When she pulled into the driveway later that day, she knew Pete wouldn't be there, but that it wouldn't be long before he would be home—after his nice little chat with the mayor—and though she knew it could cause still more trouble, she decided to explain it all to her mother before he had the chance. After all, she needed *someone* on her side.

"Charlie, you know how Pete feels about you going to the mayor without him knowing about it, how could you go behind his back like that?"

"Mom, I didn't go behind his back. I thought talking to the mayor would be the best place to start, I didn't even think about Pete." The minute her last remark came out, she knew it came out in the wrong way.

"Well, maybe that's the problem," DeeDee said sharply. "You rarely think about his feelings." She caught the look of disdain on Charlie's face and sighed. "Charlie, I do know how much this means to you, really I do, but you have to understand that Pete—"

"Likes things his way?" She finished for her. "Come on, Mom, he thinks Christmas is just another way everyone spends too much money. He makes more than enough, but he won't even put up a lousy string of lights around the window, for heaven's sake. Do you even realize that we're the only house on Shady Lane that's not lit up during Christmas?" She caught the second look of warning from her mother's face. "Mom, I'm not being disrespectful and I don't mean anything about the money, you know that, but what is so wrong with wanting to make Christmas something special? It would give everyone something to believe in again instead of being so stressed and miserable all the time."

Just then, the kitchen door swung open and Pete came charging through it.

"Pete, you're through with your meeting alrea—?" DeeDee began, but Pete never gave her a chance to finish.

"You had to do it, didn't you?" Charlie was his target. "You just had to go to the mayor—my boss—and make a laughing stock out of me?"

DeeDee lightly touched his arm. "Pete…"

"No, Dee." He shrugged her off. "You won't put me off this time. Charlotte deliberately went behind my back and…"

"Don't call me Charlotte." Charlie flared. "And I did not go behind your back, I just wanted to talk to him about Christmas and—"

"And horses pulling buggies, and lights lit all over town running the electric bill sky-high while people make damn fools of themselves walking through town singing stupid Christmas songs—oh, what fun it is!" He mocked. "Well, I won't have any daughter of mine acting like a moron. From now on—"

"I am not your daughter," Charlie interjected, her tone venomous. Her eyes, now a dark emerald, matched the darkness of her tone, and the color immediately drained from Pete's face.

"What did you say?"

Charlie lifted her head proudly and looked him squarely in the eyes. "I said I am not your daughter."

Pete stood there for several minutes, staring down at Charlie as though he'd been kicked in the stomach, and then he merely turned away from both of them and quietly left the kitchen. Everything was deathly quiet, except for the steady humming of the refrigerator.

DeeDee watched her husband, his shoulders slumped, walk into the other room, then she turned to her daughter. "That was a vicious thing to say, Charlotte. Pete has always thought of you as his real daughter and you know it. How could you say such a thing to him?"

"Mom, listen—" she began, but DeeDee held up her hand to silence her.

"I'm not interested in any explanation you might have. You've hurt him badly, and it isn't the first time. You seem to have this chip on your shoulder where Pete is concerned, but he's my husband and I love him. When you hurt him, you hurt me, and nothing you could say right now will change that."

She followed her husband, leaving Charlie alone with her thoughts—thoughts that didn't make her feel quite so proud anymore. She hadn't deliberately tried to hurt Pete, but she knew her mother was right; she did have a chip on her shoulder where he was concerned and she didn't really know why. At this point, she only knew that she had a sick feeling in the pit of her stomach and suddenly wished she could start the day over again—or at the very least take back what she had just said.

CHAPTER II

———※———

The rest of the day went by without any words spoken between Charlie and Pete, and though Charlie regretted her cruel remark, that's the way it had always been with them—both too stubborn to admit a mistake. Still, despite Pete's feelings, Charlie spent most of Saturday morning going door to door, trying to solicit help from anyone she could.

"But, Mrs. Daywood, you have children, wouldn't you like them to grow up in a town that celebrated Christmas the way it used to be? Besides, your husband is in construction, right? There is so much he could—"

"Charlie, we would love to help, really we would, but we have a hard enough time making it as it is. James's work is seasonal and he barely worked at all this winter. You must understand that—*Mason, stop pulling on your sister!*" She shouted into the other room. "Sorry about that—they seem to act up the most when anyone takes my attention away from them. Anyway, as I was saying, aside from being sick, and that hasn't always stopped him—" She hoisted the baby she was holding higher up on her hip, her huge belly making it impossible for her to hold him out in front of her. "James just isn't able to take off work. There are six of us you know, with another on the way and—"

"Oh, of course I understand!" Charlie interrupted. "I didn't mean to imply—"

"You didn't imply anything, dear." She smiled tiredly. "I'm just sorry we can't help. It sounds wonderful, really, but I'm afraid we can't even think about anything like that, we barely got through Christmas this year."

Charlie walked away from the modest little house, looking defeated. She had been to six homes and five businesses, and each one of them had one reason or another why they couldn't participate. Some of the people were downright rude, but many of them seemed genuinely sad that they had to turn her down. Although she had no doubt that their problems and busy schedules were legitimate, Charlie was disheartened that not one single person would even give her a maybe, and she looked totally defeated when she arrived home late that afternoon.

"Is something wrong, dear?" Her mother asked when Charlie plopped down in one of the kitchen chairs.

"Oh, you're talking to me again." Charlie sounded despondent.

"We had a disagreement, Charlie, it doesn't mean that I've stopped speaking to you."

"Pete has." Charlie reminded her, then caught her mother's stern look. "Sorry!" She sat quietly for a few seconds and then asked, "What is wrong with everyone? I've talked to so many people about Christmas, but no one seems to care. Either they don't have the time or the money or both. And when I did find a few who did, they weren't interested."

"Well, people do have their priorities, Charlie."

"I realize that, Mother, but I can't be the only one around here that believes in Christmas. All I'm trying to do is get everyone involved, but it seems they're all too busy and can't be bothered." She thumped her elbows down on the table and cupped her face in her hands like she did when she was small. "I can't believe that no one cares anymore."

"Well," her mother began, wiping her hands on a tea towel. "Maybe you'll just have to show them."

Charlie remained in her defeated position as her mother sat down on a chair across from her.

"Charlie, do you remember when you were little and you were afraid to go down the sliding board by yourself? You were so scared that I actually had to go down the slide myself before you would even go near it."

"Mom—"

"I'm just saying that some people have to be shown rather than told."

Charlie merely raised her eyes to look at her mother. "What can I do that I haven't already done? The point of all this was to get everyone involved."

"So get them involved! You work with people at the office, ask their opinions. Find out if anyone is interested. You said yourself that you can't be the only one who feels this way, right?"

Charlie slowly rose to a sitting position. "Well—" She looked thoughtful. "Actually, I have heard a lot of complaints from some of the lawyers about how commercialized Christmas has become and that they never seem to have enough time to spend with their families. Maybe they would like to get involved and try to help change things a little." She looked at her mother cautiously. "But what about Pete?"

"What about him?"

"He won't like you siding with me."

"There is absolutely nothing wrong with giving encouragement, Charlie, and I happen to like your idea." She stood up then and went back to the kitchen sink, mumbling, "Besides, what he doesn't know won't hurt him."

After spending Sunday comprising a list of pros and cons about her new Bring Back Christmas campaign, Charlie walked into her office on Monday morning with a renewed enthusiasm. "Good morning, all! What's new?"

Her three disgruntled coworkers merely groaned their protests in unison.

"It's Monday! How come you're so happy?" Helen Grouse piped up sarcastically. She was always sarcastic. Her name suited her.

"Yeah, you're never this cheerful, especially on Monday mornings." Mary Forsythe, the youngest and most naïve of the group called out. "You're usually grumbling about 'another crummy workweek' before you even get through the door."

"She must have met a fella!" Jean O'Donnell, the oldest of the group, teased from her desk in the corner. "Didja meet a fella, Charlie? Is that why you're so happy or is it because spring is just two months away? Ooh! Maybe it's early spring fever." She cooed, and the other girls snickered.

"Okay, you guys, knock it off." Charlie teased back. "Can't a person just be happy, without a reason?"

"No!" They all barked in unison.

"Well, I *am* happy—even though I must admit that I do have a reason. Now, before you start complaining," she said, raising her hand to shush them. "Maybe you'd better listen. This involves all of you, too, you know—especially you, Jean—you have kids, right?"

Jean groaned. "You know I do, eight of them."

"Well, maybe you more than the others," she admitted. "But, Helen, you have a son, and, Mary, well, if Tom Patterson knows what's good for him, he'd better pop the question so *you* can have the pitter-patter of little feet running all around the house, too."

"Okay, okay, what's this all about, anyway?" Helen insisted. "I have work to do and it'll probably take me til next Christmas to do it."

"Ahh! It's funny you happened to mention Christmas." Charlie took a deep breath.

"How would you guys like to be a part of my Bring Back Christmas campaign?"

"Uh, Charlie, where have you been? Christmas came and went or hadn't you noticed?" That was Helen, the grumpy one.

"Yeah, where *have* you been?" Jean grated. "I can show you the credit card bills to prove it, shoes for the kids and underwear and—"

"No! I'm not talking about *this* Christmas, you dummies, I'm talking about *next* Christmas, nearly a whole year away. I have this really great idea that you're gonna love."

"Come on, Charlie, it's the beginning of March, for Pete's sake. I'm still paying off bills from this Christmas and I'll probably still be paying them off next Christmas, so I don't even want to *hear* that word," Helen complained.

"Yeah!" Mary chimed in. "My parents are kind of complaining about how much they spent on my nieces and nephews, and—"

"Whoa!" Charlie yelled, catching them all with their mouths open. "Give me a chance, will you? Just hear me out and then you can talk, okay?"

The three of them looked at each other and then back at Charlie, grumbling.

"Okay, but hurry it up, will you?" Helen interjected. "The bosses will be in soon, and I haven't even started on that insurance fraud deposition yet."

Fifteen minutes later, Charlie finished and took a deep breath. "So what do you think?"

Helen, as usual, was the first to speak up. "Well, I for one think you've lost your mind. Besides not having enough time to do everything you're talking about, where are you going to find volunteers in *this* town or the money to pay for everything?"

"Yeah!" Mary jumped into the conversation just for the chance to be a part of it. "Just where in the hell—" She caught herself and promptly blushed. "I mean where in the heck are you going to find horses and buggies around here?"

"Oh, for crying out loud, Mary, that's not even worth talking about." Helen quipped, then to Charlie, "Do you have any idea how much money it would take to fix that dilapidated bridge? My Willy's in the construction business and I'm telling you right now, they would have to rebuild the whole damn thing!"

"Honey," Jean began again softly. "Your idea sounds terrific, but there is no way you can possibly get all those things accomplished. Besides, like Helen said, how in the world are you going to get the people to volunteer to do anything in a town run by John Braxton? They complain about working for him for money and you want them to volunteer? They won't even give him the time of day, let alone help him put his town on the map, and that's not the only problem. Everyone is trying to raise a family and make ends meet or plan for retirement or just survive—no one can afford to take time off from work. As a matter of fact, a lot of these people have been laid off and don't even have a job to go to, but they still have bills to pay and mouths to feed—"

"I know, Jean." Charlie said sympathetically. "But those who are out of work would have something to occupy their time until this project gets off the ground. All these people need is a chance, and once the revenue starts coming in, there'll be jobs enough to go around. Besides, just because John Braxton is the mayor doesn't mean he owns this town, it belongs to all of us. We pay our taxes and help run the school, and we should have some say about what goes on around here, including making Braxton a better place to live."

"Sure, and a dollar-twenty-five'll get you a cup of coffee." Helen snapped. "Wake up, Charlie, there's no way you can make something like this fly." She caught Charlie's look of disappointment. "Aw, look, kid, you're young and you have all these great ideas, but don't you get it? Nobody's gonna listen to you because nobody cares."

"Well, I do!" Charlie said hotly, dismissing Helen's attitude. "And no matter what you say, I intend to get off my duff and do something about it!" She slammed her purse onto her desk and sat down hard in her chair, a woman determined and with a purpose.

I can do this! she told herself, picking up one of the folders piled high on her desk. *Even if I have to do it myself!* She looked over at the grim faces in the office. *Uh huh, and a dollar-twenty-five—*

The day dragged on slowly, and by four o'clock, Charlie was more than ready to go home. She hadn't said much to the other girls since her explosion in the morning, and surprisingly, she'd gotten a lot accomplished—even though her mind was on more important things. She straightened her desk and shut down her computer, but before she had the chance to say her goodbyes, Mary appeared at her desk.

"Uh, Charlie? I was just thinking—"

"Uh oh, look out!" Helen shouted over at Jean. "Mary's thinking again—get the fire extinguisher, her brain's on overdrive!"

Jean just shook her head pathetically, and Mary totally ignored her.

"Well, *anyway*, I was thinking that maybe we could have a, you know, a fund-raiser or something." She fumbled awkwardly for the right words. "You know, to raise money for the Christmas thingee."

"What's this 'we' stuff, Mary?" Helen quipped. "Don't go getting *us* involved in your 'oh-let's-do-help-the-cause' routine, just leave me out of it."

Charlie frowned at Helen but looked at Mary with renewed interest. "You mean like holding bake sales or craft shows, something like that?"

"Yes, or maybe both, maybe a *lot* of craft shows!" Mary caught Charlie's look of approval and offered more. "I know Jean crochets, and I make potholders and little angels *and* the best peanut butter cookies in the county, if I do say so myself!" She added and then merely nodded in Helen's direction. "Even Helen over there could help because I know for a fact that she puts models together, like cars and boats and things, and she just sits them around her house. Heck! We could sell them! And maybe have a car wash, like they do in Montgomery and even do odd jobs around our neighborhood—" Her excitement waned then, and she looked a little sheepish. "That is, if you would *want* to do anything like that—I mean, it is your idea and all."

Charlie smiled. "Yes, but it's not just for me, Mary, it's for everybody, and those are fantastic ideas! All we have to do is…"

"Beg and bribe people to do it?" Helen merely shook her head, rolled her eyes, and went back to work.

Charlie continued to stare at her without saying a word, but she never looked up.

"Go ahead, Faraday—you can stare at me all you want, but I'm still not doing it! No way, no how am I getting hooked into that, huh uh, forget it!"

Now all the girls were staring at her, and she began to fidget in her chair. She pretended to concentrate on the deposition in front of her, then slammed the folder shut, and picked up a pile of papers. After shuffling them around, she moved them to the other side of her desk for the third time. A few seconds later, she picked up the telephone receiver, listened intently, then wiped it off and placed it back in its cradle, and when she couldn't stand it anymore, she gave up.

"All right, all right! So I'm in already, you satisfied now?"

Jean suddenly chimed in, catching the spirit. "Well, count me in, too. I've had an awful lot of practice crocheting booties and even scarves for my brood, and to tell you the truth, I sort of miss it. I think I can find some time for such a worthy cause, and having a Christmas like the old days sounds pretty good at that."

"Guys, you're great!" Charley gushed. "Listen, I figure we can have a meeting at my house this Thursday—it's Pete's late night, and we won't have to worry about him being there so bring all the people you can."

"Well, it sure seems like you've had this planned for a while." Helen sneered. "Just what made you so sure we'd all agree to your little Christmas thing, huh?"

Charlie grinned. "I know you guys pretty well, don't you think?"

"What about your mom?" Mary sounded concerned.

"Mom's with us all the way." Charlie dismissed her alarm. "So can you all be there by six? If we have a good crowd, it might be a little cramped, but I think it'll be okay. I really wanted to have a meeting in the town hall so we could invite everyone we could think of, but—" Visions of the mayor's face caused her to shudder. "*That's* totally out of the question."

"Well, I'll be there." Jean assured her. "Henry can watch the kids for one night—after all, I didn't have them alone!"

"Yeah, yeah, we'll be there!" Helen waved her off. "Now, get outta here so I can get some decent overtime! Somebody's gotta work and make money for this little project of yours."

"This little project of ours." Charlie corrected. "We're in this thing together, remember?"

"Yeah, yeah! Whatever." Helen waved her off again. "And please take *Little Mary Do-Good* there with you."

Thursday's meeting went much better than Charlie could have hoped, and the extra people that Jean had brought along, fifteen in all counting relatives were a tight fit in the small cottage-type home, but they managed, and it helped lift their spirits even more. It seemed there were quite a lot of people interested in Charlie's idea contrary to what she was led to believe in the beginning, and she found that many of them did want a change. Several of the younger married women came up with the idea for a car wash and even offered themselves and their husbands to help work it, and since they figured the sooner they all got things started, the better, they scheduled it to take place three weeks from Saturday, at the high school. It would begin at eight in the morning and last until two in the afternoon, with the girls guaranteeing their husbands would all be there, or else.

Zeke Thurman, owner of Thurman's Pizza Palace, offered to buy and donate a television set, raffling it off at his shop on Mother's Day, while Jenny Lindquist offered to put on a show featuring her fourth-grade dance troupe, "Little Butterflies," on Flag Day.

The biggest surprise was when Miss Eleanor Loganberry and her brother, Theodore, owners of Loganberry Dairy Farm, offered to sponsor a picnic barbeque on the Fourth of July. The two-hundred acre estate was not only the perfect location for holding such an event because of its size, but because of its close proximity to Braxton, so close in fact, that most of the people living in town could walk.

Eleanor also offered to have flyers printed up announcing the event, as well as making her renowned jellies and jams, which could be sold along with other's contributions. She suggested that it begin at two o'clock in the afternoon and last until ten o'clock at night—not too late for the children, of course—and stated that the cost for the entire day of fun and amusements would be only five dollars per family. She really didn't want to charge anything, but since it was a fund-raiser for the betterment of Braxton, she agreed.

Helen of course argued that they wouldn't make squat charging only five dollars a head, but Eleanor tactfully explained that there would be other events to raise money, and that this was actually a charity event created to bring the townspeople together and that there were, after all, more important things in life than money, to which Helen harrumphed her disapproval while everyone else applauded.

The day would include all you could eat and drink, rides for the children on their cherished horse, Joan of Arc, and hayrides for young and old alike, in addition to many other events too numerous to mention. And, as a special treat, Theodore Loganberry, once a world-famous pianist, offered to provide the entertainment.

Though there weren't many people who didn't know about the Loganberry fortune or that they had more money than the Braxtons and Donald Trump put together and could well afford to throw such a gala event; this was the very first time they had taken an interest in anything concerning Braxton.

Still others brought up ways to raise money, including Miss Creighton, the principal and second grade art teacher at the elementary school who humbly offered several of her own famous carousel paintings to be raffled off at the craft shows, which she generously suggested could be held in the cafeteria during August. She planned it for the ninth and would let them know for certain as soon as she cleared it with the school board.

Further discussions were offered regarding the planning and execution of the event before the meeting at Charlie's house ended—just minutes before Pete pulled into the driveway. He didn't say a word when he came in, but Charlie could see by the look on his face that he wasn't happy as he watched the last few cars pull away from the curb. She managed to slip upstairs before he could question her, but less than five minutes passed before she heard Pete and her mother battling it out downstairs.

"Then you admit that you knew about this?" Pete shouted.

"Of course I knew about it," DeeDee shouted right back.

"Well, why didn't you tell me?"

"This is why—you always lose your temper."

"Well, if you had any idea how much trouble she's causing, you wouldn't be so quick to take her side. The mayor heard about this meeting and actually threatened to replace me, Dee, doesn't that mean anything to you?"

"Of course it means something to me, but what would you like me to do?"

"Stop her."

"I will not! Charlie's doing a wonderful thing, you can't ask me to tell her to give up on something she wants so badly not just for herself but the town too—not after hearing me lecture her on never giving up for most of her life."

"Well, my job may be at stake, DeeDee, and I'm not asking you, I'm telling you!"

Charlie cringed at his last statement. *Uh oh! Big mistake, Pete—HUGE!*

Although it took an awful lot to get DeeDee Faraday to the fighting mad point, the one thing that could and usually did light a fire under her was someone telling her that she *had* to do something. She disliked ultimatums of any kind, and Charlie was sure that Pete had overstepped his bounds and she held her breath waiting for the bomb to drop.

"You're *telling* me to stop her?" DeeDee asked, incredulously, unleashed anger suspended in midair.

"Yes, I want you to stop her, and I want you to stop her *now.*" Pete lashed back, and Charlie closed her eyes, suddenly sorry for Pete. She had been on the receiving end of her mother's wrath only once and with good reason, but DeeDee Faraday had never really lost her temper with her husband during the entire seventeen years of their marriage.

Charlie feared the worst and for some unknown reason felt the strangest urge to run downstairs and stop Pete from doing more damage, but the feeling though real enough, was fleeting. But instead of hearing the bomb hit, everything became eerily quiet—right up until she heard the sound of her mother's footsteps on the stairs and the violent slamming of her bedroom door.

Charlie didn't sleep well believing that the argument the night before happened because of her, and she awakened with the personality of a Grizzly with an attitude. Still, hopeful to not wake anyone, she quietly padded down to the kitchen.

"Good morning, Charlie!" her mother called out, catching her daughter in the middle of a yawn.

"Mom, what are you doing here?"

"I live here, dear," her mother answered smoothly.

"You know what I mean, Mom." Charlie's tone matched her morning personality. "I didn't expect to see you here."

"Well, where did you think I would be?"

"I don't know," she retorted. "Just not here, I guess—after last night."

"You have a lot to learn about relationships, Charlie, not all arguments lead to divorce, you know."

"I didn't say that, but you were pretty mad."

"Yes, and I still am, but I don't run at the first sign of trouble, Charlie. I am quite capable of handling my own problems. I got along quite well in that area before I met your stepfather and nothing has changed that."

Charlie was skeptical. "Look, Mom, maybe I should get my own apartment like we talked about. I don't want to be the cause for a split between you two."

"This won't last and I certainly don't intend to end my marriage over it. I do intend to help you get your campaign going however, and I know from the meeting that a lot of things have been planned, so what can I do to help?"

"Well, if you're really sure—"

"I'm sure, now what do you have in mind?"

"Well, you know I spoke to the mayor, which obviously ended up a disaster in more ways than one, but the meeting did go well. We actually do have a lot planned thanks to many of Jean's relatives, and I'll fill you in on that later, but can you think of anything else we can do to get more people from Braxton involved? I mean, we do have Evelyn and Theodore Loganberry and quite a few people, but if you recall, I even tried going door to door to get them interested and that didn't work. Do you have any other suggestions?"

"Maybe." Her mother looked thoughtful. "You know, when you used to go shopping in Manchester, the music was playing in all the department stores and you were so excited to see all the bright lights and decorations. You loved Christmas, Charlie, and not because there were presents under the tree or that everything was centered on you, but even at a young age, you loved the *thought* of Christmas. You loved to watch them light the tree at the courthouse and you knew all the carols by heart—you even stayed awake for midnight service."

"Mom, I hear what you're saying and it sounds really sweet and all, but how can that possibly help the situation?"

"Reach out to the children, Charlie. Don't you see? If you get to the children, *they* will get to their parents. Children have always adored Santa Claus and the pure magic of Christmas, but with all the changes and the busyness of their parents, they've simply forgotten how wonderful it can be, and if you can bring back that magic to the children, how can their enthusiasm help but rub off on their parents?"

Charlie jumped up from the table and grabbed her mother by the arms. "Mom, you're a genius! You can tell your Sunday school class—it's fairly big—and there are all the kids you can reach when you sub at the junior high—I can't believe we didn't think of this…"

"Whoa, wait a minute, Charlie, what do you mean, all the kids *I* can reach, this is your idea, remember?"

"I know that, but it's a perfect place to start, and you did say you wanted to help, right?"

"Yes, I did, and of course I will help, but it's up to you to get the children involved."

Charlie looked indignant. "But it's your Sunday school class."

"That's right, but you've substituted for me before and you can do it again, only this time, you can talk to them about Christmas."

"What? Mom, you've got to be kidding. You had that whole lesson prepared, all I had to do was follow your instructions, and I was still scared to death to get up in front of the class!"

"Maybe so, but you did it. Besides, this isn't the same thing, you won't be teaching, you'll be talking."

"It's the same difference. I'll still be up in front of all those kids. I don't see why you just can't tell them, you're used to them. Oh, never mind, I have to get ready for work."

DeeDee Faraday looked displeased, but she spoke gently. "You still have time, Charlie, sit down for a minute." She patted the seat of the chair next to hers, and they both sat down. "Now, try not to take this in a critical way, but it seems to me that you want to go swimming, but you don't want to get your new suit wet."

Charlie rolled her eyes. "What's *that* supposed to mean?"

"It means that you want to reap the benefits of a wonderful, old-fashioned Christmas, but you don't want to work at creating one."

"You're not being fair, Mom. I've been—"

"No, Charlie, what isn't fair is that you want it to happen, but you aren't willing to do what it takes to make it happen." DeeDee watched her daughter's eyes darken slightly, as they always did when she got the least bit angry. "Charlie, listen to me. Anything worth having is worth fighting for, and though it may take a lot of hard work, if you want something badly enough, nothing can stop you." She watched her daughter's face soften a bit. "Did you really think it would be easy?"

"To tell the truth, I don't know if I even thought about the work involved. I guess I was just thinking about the end result."

"Well, maybe you haven't given this idea enough thought. Not only will you have to work hard, but you may have to fight to prove yourself and show these people that your main idea is to help this town. There will be those who will oppose you, saying you're wrongfully trying to influence their children, and you'll even find those who, like the mayor, don't want change at all and will fight you all the way. Unfortunately, the saddest part is that there are those who just don't believe in the excitement of Christmas anymore. But with a little hard work and a lot of effort, you can bring back that excitement back."

The very next week, Charlie found herself standing before the Sunday school class full of wide-eyed, eager children who were told only that there was going to be a friend coming to speak with them about something special. They were full of anticipation, and it took Charlie quite a while to get them to settle down in their seats.

"Good morning, children!"

"Good morning, Miss Faraday!" they all chimed in unison.

"Why are you here?" Little Billy Martin yelled out. "Are you going to teach us again?"

"Yeah, are you gonna tell us about the 'postles again?" Brian Scarfello called out. "I like hearing 'bout the 'postles!"

"It's 'apostles,' Brian, and no, I'm here for another reason." Charlie surveyed the classroom. *Their little faces are so innocent,* she thought, glancing at her mother skeptically, but DeeDee merely nodded, urging her on. The children were now silent and Charlie took a breath and let it out in a whoosh.

"All right, first question: do you all like Christmas?" she asked and a resounding "yeah!" confirmed her suspicions.

"Good! Now, how many of you believe in Santa Claus?" Charlie knew it was a rather dangerous question, knowing how most of the adults in town felt about Christmas in general, but she had to ask, and she was ecstatic when nearly every hand shot up into the air—every hand but three: Jeremy Knight, Mason Greene, and Christina Noelle Braxton.

"Mason?" Charlie called out to the little boy in the back row. "You don't believe in Santa Claus?"

"Heck, no!" Mason sneered. "There ain't no Santa Claus! My mommy and daddy buy us shoes and socks for Christmas! It ain't nuthin special, my daddy says it's just another dumb ole' day!"

Charlie frowned slightly. "Oh, that's too bad. Christmas isn't all toys and presents, you know."

"Yeah!" Janie Marlow shouted. "We have a real Christmas tree and sing songs and have punkin pie and negnog!"

"We have Christmas with my gramma," Amanda Daywood said excitedly, but the smile disappeared from her face as quickly as it had appeared. "Well, we *used* to go to Gramma's house every Christmas, but she lives kinda far away now and our car doesn't work too good. But she might take a bus and come to our house this year." She finished, her smile returning.

"Well, that's wonderful, Amanda, good for you—now, what about you, Jeremy?" She deliberately left Christina Braxton until last, fearing her answer the most. "Do you believe in Santa Claus?"

Jeremy looked up at Charlie shyly. "Yes, ma'am."

"Well, why didn't you raise your hand?"

"'Cause my mom doesn't like me to talk about Santa Claus. She says he's a fairy tale."

He looked up at her with mischievous brown eyes. "But I know there is a Santa 'cause I seen him!"

"You mean you 'saw' him," Charlie corrected.

"Sure I did—I seen him lots of times!"

"You did not, Jeremy Knight!" Melissa Brody stood up and shouted. Her hands were on her hips, making her look curiously like Margaret on the old *Dennis the Menace* television show, complete with pipe curls and dark-rimmed glasses. Unfortunately, she had her snotty personality as well. "You're just making that up. No one has ever seen Santa Claus, 'specially not you."

"Have too," Jeremy murmured.

"Have not." Melissa stuck out her tongue.

"Now, children." Charlie soothed. "We're not here to argue, we're just having a little talk, right?"

Melissa immediately crossed her arms, stuck her nose into the air, and plopped down in her chair while Jeremy slumped down further into his.

"Tina, I noticed that your hand wasn't raised—don't you believe in Santa Claus, either?" Charlie asked, quickly diverting the children's attention. She knew the danger but she had to ask.

The little girl slid out of her seat and stood erect.

"First of all, my name is Christina, and no, I do not believe in *Santa Claus*," she said, making his name sound like bad language. "He is a myth, a nonexistent figment of someone's overactive imagination. Someone simply made up the character because he or she needed something to make his or her life less dull. Christmas is just another day, like Mason said. My grandfather told me so, and since he is the mayor, he wouldn't lie." She looked directly into Charlie's eyes, mockingly. "Isn't that right, Miss Faraday?"

"Well, everyone is entitled to their own opinion, Christina." Charlie forced a smile, trying to remember that she was talking to a mere six-year-old child, a child who she was sure was repeating her grandfather's words verbatim. "But I do think it's interesting that someone who doesn't believe in Santa Claus or the holiday for that matter has a name that sounds a lot like Christmas. But of course, your grandfather probably didn't think about that when they picked your name." Charlie knew she must sound pathetically petty, but she so wanted to wipe that smug little smirk from Christina's face, and she even felt a childish sense of satisfaction when the confused little girl slid inconspicuously back into her chair.

"Now ," Charlie turned her focus back on the classroom. "I know it's a long way to Christmas, but we need lots of time to get ready for it so let's all try to think of some really neat things we can do here in Sunday school." She saw the snotty girl's little hand frantically wiggling in the air in the back of the room.

"Yes, Melissa?"

"We should have a party!"

"Yes, we could do that," Charlie agreed, rolling her eyes at her mother. "Good suggestion!"

Several more hands shot up into the air.

"Karen, do you have an idea?"

"We could make pictures with Baby Jesus with his mommy and hang them on the wall."

"That's a good idea, too, Megan?"

"We could make our very own *man-ger, mainager*—" Megan tried the word with effort, and then just gave up. "We could have a crib and *aminals* and put it right in front of the church so that all the people could see!"

"You mean a 'manger'? That's a super idea, Megan. Maybe we could even draw the three wise men and paste them on cardboard and make stands for them."

"And I would let you use one of my baby dolls for the baby Jesus and put it in the crib!"

"That's wonderful, Megan, thank you! Now, class, can you think of anything else we could do to make this special?"

One small hand rose timidly into the air.

"Thomas, you have an idea for us?" Charlie sounded surprised but pleased. Little Thomas Sullivan barely spoke in class, and coming out on his own was a first. Unfortunately, his voice was barely above a whisper and Charlie leaned forward.

"Did you say we could have a play, Thomas?"

Thomas nodded. "We could have Joseph and Marie's jury to Brethlem, and Baby Jesus bein' born in a barn."

"It's Joseph and Mary, an' they didn't 'jury' to Brethlem, stupid, they 'journeyed' to Bethlehem! And Jesus wasn't born in a barn, neither, he was born in a stable! Jeez, what a dope!" one of his classmates shouted out cruelly.

"That will be quite enough, Keith Winters!" Charlie scolded, shaking her finger at him. "I haven't heard any ideas at all come from you, and I happen to think Thomas's idea was one of the best ones yet. Now, I want you to apologize to him right this minute."

"Sorry, Thomas," Keith grumbled quietly, bowing his head.

"That's okay, Keith, I am a dope sometimes." He didn't look the least bit upset; as a matter of fact, his green eyes danced with mischief as if he'd discovered something good about himself, and he looked up at Charlie and smiled and Charlie smiled back and winked.

"Well, class, we have lots of work to do. We have to put on a play, create a manger set, and even have a party, all before next Christmas, do you think we can do it?"

"Yeah!" they all cried in unison, and Charlie glanced over at her mother, who nodded her approval.

"All right, since class is nearly over, I'm going to ask each one of you to think of something special you would like to do for the play or the manger scene or for the party and then you can tell us about it at our next Sunday school class, okay?"

"Yeah!" they all cried out again, all of them yelling and screaming at the same time.

Charlie raised her hand to shush them and then added one more thing. "So for now, we'll just keep this our little secret, okay? Then when the time is right, we'll surprise our moms and dads and everyone, okay? You can all go now, but remember, it's our secret, so lips zipped!"

All the children silently pretended to zip their lips, and Charlie looked over at her mother and crossed her fingers as all the children noisily filed out of the room. It was only when they had all gone that DeeDee spoke up.

"You do realize that it was unwise to tell the children to keep this a secret, don't you? They're better at telling them not keeping them. I smell trouble, Charlie."

"I know, Mom, but what else was I supposed to do? I can only hope that they'll keep it quiet at least until it gets closer to Christmas."

"Yes, but what about Christina? You know very well that she'll go straight to her grandfather and tell him what you're up to."

Charlie hadn't really thought about that, but she refused to let it dissuade her. "Well, let her tell him. We can still put on the play and make a manger, and we can still have a party. Besides, how is going to stop thirty kids from screaming and crying that they want to be in a play, especially at Sunday school? He'll be so swamped with visits and letters from the parents of those screaming kids that he'll have to give in."

"Don't be so sure, Charlie. I've seen him walk away from a woman who dropped her groceries in the street after he bumped into her and nearly knocked her down. He walked right past her, refusing to even acknowledge what he'd done or even help her pick up her groceries."

"Well, that certainly sounds like our wonderful mayor, doesn't it? I hope others were watching and did something about it!"

"You know the old saying, "You can't fight City Hall"? Well, one man made the mistake of berating him in front of everybody, and the next day he didn't have a job. He's a fighter, Charlie, and he doesn't care who he steps on or what the cause is—he has the power and the means to win no matter what the stakes."

"And your husband works for him, isn't that wonderful!" Charlie was thoroughly disgusted.

"Charlie." DeeDee warned. "One thing has nothing to do with the other."

"How can you say that? He works for the man, and he's not deaf, dumb, and blind, is he?" She second thought that one. "Well, maybe not deaf and blind —"

"All right, Charlotte, that's enough."

"Well, I'm sorry, Mom, it's just that I don't see how Pete can compromise himself like that. I thought he was at least a man of honor. The mayor is a jerk so why doesn't Pete just—"

"Just what, Charlie, quit? Just because Mayor Braxton feels a certain way does not mean that your stepfather agrees with him."

"Well, how do you think the people of Braxton feel?" Charlie bantered, and DeeDee Faraday looked at her daughter warningly.

"You don't know all the facts, Charlie, and I refuse to get into this discussion with you. Let's just drop it."

"Whatever." Charlie mumbled. "He's your husband." She turned and walked toward the door and tossed an arrogant, "See you at home, Mother," over her shoulder, and as DeeDee watched her only daughter angrily slam out the door, she shook her head, sensing that they might all be in for a very long and trying nine months.

CHAPTER III

———✦———

*A*fter making preparations for the coming events to raise money, Charlie spent a lot of time with the Sunday school children a half-hour each Sunday after class, and before she knew it, weeks had gone and the day of the car wash at Braxton High arrived.

Although there was no snow, it was still cold for April, and Charlie donned a sweatshirt, her down jacket, and piled her long auburn hair on top of her head, stuffing it under a baseball cap. Thinking she would get there before anyone else arrived, she went down to the high school at six-thirty in the morning and was shocked to see that the parking lot was full; quite a few cars had already gone through the line and were on their way out already.

She tried to count all the men and women busily washing, rinsing, drying, and buffing cars but lost count around thirty. Even her coworkers were there and Jean met her at the entrance gate.

"Grab a rag, honey, they're coming in droves!"

"Oh, isn't it wonderful, Charlie?" Mary gushed. "They've been coming in steadily for a whole hour, now.

"Yeah, ain't it great?" Helen grumbled, coming up behind Charlie. "I'm drenched from head to foot, I'm freezing, and Little Mary Sunshine there is thrilled to death. Whose stupid idea was this anyhow?"

"My friends came up with the idea, Mrs. Gloom and Doom, and it was not a stupid idea, it was a darn good one—look at all these people—have you ever seen so many cars in one place in all your life?"

"Yeah, right here." Helen griped. "Jeez! I'll never get these jeans clean again."

Charlie grabbed a rag from Jean's bucket. "Let's go, gang! Seven more cars just pulled in. Time is money!"

By noontime, the flow of cars began to slow down enough for the girls to take a break, and everyone but Mary took a seat in Jean's oversized van.

"I'm pooped!" Jean breathed heavily, plopping down into the driver's seat.

"I'm cold, wet, tired, and hungry! What a great way to spend my day off," Helen complained.

Mary was grinning from ear to ear. "I feel great!" she said, stretching her arms into the air and running in place. "I'm getting my exercise, I'm talking to old friends and making new ones, what a great day!"

"Now look, Mary Poppins!" Helen rounded on her, sticking her head out the window. "I've had about all I can take of your happy-to-be-alive, skipping-through-the-tulips routine! No one in their right mind would be happy washing cars on their day off in this kind of weather no matter what they say! And actually, now that I think about it, I don't know anyone on this earth who is as happy as you. You're happy when the sun shines, you're happy when it rains, you're even happy when you're unhappy—what are you, some kind of nutcase?"

Charlie held her breath, sensing a fight, but Mary surprised even her.

"You're just jealous, Helen Elizabeth Grouse," Mary said nonchalantly.

"Jealous?" Helen scoffed. "What in the world do I have to be jealous about? And don't *ever* call me Helen Elizabeth. I knew I should have hidden my resume."

"You're jealous because I can see the good in everything you see bad in, that's what. Maybe if you laughed at yourself once in a while, you wouldn't be so grouchy!"

Helen looked a little stunned, and for the first time, she couldn't think of a spicy comeback. "Oh, is that so?"

Mary looked her dead in the eyes. "Yes, that is so. You're so busy looking at the negative side of everything, that you don't even see the positive side!" She pointed at Helen's face. "What's that?" she asked, and then playfully flicked her cold nose before she turned and sauntered away, leaving a surprised Helen with her mouth hanging open.

"Hey, what's with Mary?" she asked, wiping at her nose. "Has she lost her marbles or what?"

Charlie smiled, secretly pleased. "No, I think Mary has finally found herself."

Helen sneered. "What was she, lost?" She jabbed Jean in the side, obviously pleased with her own joke.

"I think what Charlie is trying to say," Jean remarked, not finding Helen's comment amusing. "Is that Mary has always been an introvert and this Bring Back Christmas brigade is bringing out the *real* Mary. Jeez, Helen, you really can't see the good in anything, can you? You know, you could learn a thing or two from her," she added hotly, then slid out of the driver's seat, slammed the door shut, and walked toward Mary.

"Well, what's *her* problem? Has everyone lost their mind?" They both got out of the van. "You say one little thing, and—"

"They're just excited, Helen, haven't you ever been excited about something?"

Helen frowned. "Oh, what, are you on their side too?"

Charlie smiled knowingly. "There are no sides here, Helen, we're all just trying to make a difference, that's all. Didn't you like Christmas when you were a kid?"

"No!" Helen snapped. "We didn't have the time or the money to be happy at Christmas or any other holiday. We did what we had to do to get by, and that's it. Nothing was handed to us on a silver platter."

Charlie looked sympathetic. "Hmmm, now I think I understand why you've been against this whole Christmas campaign."

"Oh, now don't go getting all psychoanalytical on me, Charlie. So I'm Ebenezer Scrooge, what's the big deal? Not everyone believes in Christmas like you do."

Charlie grinned knowingly. "Then why are you here and why have you offered to help out?"

Helen shrugged her shoulders. "I'm a nice guy, what do you want from me?" She started to walk away.

"And you like us," Charlie shouted after her, and Helen merely waved her hand in the air, dismissingly.

It was nearly four o'clock before everyone began to clean up and get ready to go home, even though the girls had put up a Closed sign at the entrance gate around two o'clock to count the money.

"We made over six hundred dollars, girls," Jean shouted, waving the bills in the air, and Mary stood there with her mouth open.

"Wow! That means we washed over sixty cars today."

"No, it means that some people paid more than six dollars, oh, brilliant one," Helen chided, rolling her eyes and Mary blushed.

"Oh. I didn't think of that."

"I'm sure you didn't!" Helen agreed, shaking her head. "Come on, let's get outta here." She grabbed a bucket and some sponges, but just then a stretch limo with dark tinted glass drove up and stopped right in front of Charlie.

"I'm sorry, but you're a little late," she shouted through the glass unable to see inside. "We've closed up for the day."

Just then, the back window began to open slowly and Charlie was able to see the passenger.

"Mayor Braxton!" she exclaimed, happy to see he'd decided to participate in their campaign after all. "I'm sorry, I didn't realize—come on, girls, hook the hose back up and—"

"I do not wish to have *amateurs* washing my car, I have *men* specially trained to do that sort of thing."

Charlie stiffened at his tone. "Oh, of course you do. I forgot who I was speaking to for a minute."

"Apparently so, and it would behoove you to remember that in future," he said contemptibly. "And speaking of which, I need you to do something for me."

Charlie's frown deepened. "Oh, really, and what might that be?"

"Could you step closer to the car, please? I would rather no one overhear our conversation."

Charlie moved only a step closer and barely leaned down toward the window. She didn't want to get *too* close.

"Now, listen to me and listen well, you little twit!" He grated through clenched teeth. "If you don't stop this ridiculous Christmas quest of yours, you will be rue the day you were born."

"Why, Mayor Braxton," she said loudly. "Are you threatening me?" Charlie asked, unafraid.

"Keep your voice down." He cautioned. "You may call it whatever you wish, Miss Faraday, just do yourself a favor and stop it *now*, before you regret it."

"You are threatening me," Charlie said incredulously. "Just who do you think you are?

You have no right—"

"I am the mayor of this town, and I have every right and the power, I might add, to make you stop."

"Just try it, Mayor Braxton, and I'll splatter your name all over the newspapers and even the radio and television to make sure everyone knows about your threats."

"Oh, I don't think you'll do that." The mayor pretended to inspect his fingernails. "You see, there is more at stake here than your small pea-brain can handle and I do not intend to let your inane nostalgia ruin my reputation or my town." The mayor's tone was calm and more confident than ever, but Charlie sensed much more than a mere warning.

"Why, Mayor Braxton, surely the thought that your town could become renowned as one of the greatest little towns in Vermont is not a determent to you?" She began to count on her fingers. "Now, let's see: number one, the fact that tourists would come to your little town and hence, bring more revenue into it couldn't possibly be a problem—everyone knows that 'money' is your middle name. Number two, you would not only be a big hit with all the people living in Braxton, but you would be Christina's hero forever, and everyone knows that the sun rises and sets in your little granddaughter—after all, she is exactly like you. Number three, and the best one of all is that you would have all the respect and honor that you deserve as mayor—or rather, that you *believe* you deserve as mayor—so we know *that's* not the problem, either." She pretended to scratch her head in befuddlement. "Gee, Mayor Braxton, I can't think of a single reason why you of all people wouldn't want all those things so there really must be something else behind your mere hatred of Christmas." Charlie looked directly into his eyes, defiantly, and gave him a warning of her own. "Your first mistake was telling me that my Bring Back Christmas campaign was a stupid idea, claiming that it would make you the laughing stock of Braxton. That's when I began to wonder how a Christmas celebration could possibly ruin your reputation and that got me thinking—well, *suspicious* actually—that you just might be—oh, how *do* I ask this delicately—hiding something, perhaps?" Charlie's eyes grew wide with innocence.

"I warn you, Miss Faraday, do not try my patience!"

"And I warn you, Mayor Braxton, that I intend to find out exactly what it is you're hiding."

In an instant and to Charlie's shock and disbelief, the mayor's hideous look of warning was suddenly gone and replaced with a huge smile. Charlie couldn't believe her eyes, the change was incredible.

"All right, Ms. Faraday, all right you win," he said, now looking as serene and docile as a lamb. It was actually the most miraculous transformation she had ever seen. "I can't fight you on this anymore, you can have your Braxton Christmas or whatever you wish to call it." He sighed resignedly. "I know when I'm beate, and if there is anything I can do to help, you just need to ask, except for providing money and the pond, of course, the money is up to you to provide but the pond is definitely out of the question." He smiled musingly. "You know if I didn't know better, I would think that you were actually related to Pete Faraday and not just his stepdaughter, you certainly have his determination." He tapped his driver on the shoulder. "Proceed, Carlton." The smile on his face was the last thing Charlie saw before his window closed.

"Well, what was that all about?" Jean asked, as the stretch limo pulled away and out of the parking lot. "Was that the mayor?"

"Oh, yes! That was the mayor, all right," Charlie said, looking stunned.

"What did *he* want?" Helen asked sarcastically, "Your heart on a plate?"

"Actually, he gave us carte blanche, without benefit of money or the pond of course."

"He did?" Mary asked, wrinkling her nose, not sure exactly what that meant.

"It means he gave her free reign to do as she pleases, you dope!" Helen blasted Mary and then to Charlie, "So what gives? Did you threaten him or something?"

"Something like that," Charlie said evasively, staring off into space.

"Well, that's great, right?" Mary asked, concerned. "Isn't that what we wanted?"

Jean patted her on the shoulder. "Yes, of course it is, dear." Then to Charlie, "Is something wrong, Charlie?"

"He's hiding something," she said cautiously.

"Oh, jeez, she's going into 'detective mode' again." Helen moaned. "Charlie, I swear—"

"Shush, Helen! Let her talk!" Jean warned. "What do you mean, Charlie?"

"It means," Helen interjected, "that Charlie suspects everyone and everything, that's what it means. She can't just accept the fact that the man gave in and gave her what she wanted, she has to shroud it in mystery, like she always does."

"Not this time, Helen," Charlie said quietly and turned to face them. "When he first started talking, he literally threatened me if I didn't stop my campaign and warned me that he had the power to do it, and that's when I told him that I'd spread his name all over the place telling everyone he threatened me, but he acted like he could care less, and that's when I told him that I thought he must be hiding something."

"You didn't?" Mary gasped. "Boy, you sure are gutsy."

"No, she's not gutsy, Mary, stupid maybe, but not gutsy." Helen shook her head. "You can't see the forest for the trees, can you, Charlie! Don't you realize that if he was threatening you and he is hiding something, things could get ugly?"

"I don't care. I'm telling you he's hiding something, and I don't care if he gives me the keys to the entire town, I intend to find out what it is."

Sunday was a quiet day for Charlie, but since she was hell-bent on getting to the bottom of the mayor's weird behavior, she spent the better part of the morning looking up telephone numbers of people who might know him well enough to know something about him and his family—and were willing to talk. She knew it was no use trying to talk to his daughter, Cleo. She was naturally on her daddy's side and would have told him everything Charlie said down to the last hot little detail. So she continued to search through the local directory for familiar names and addresses, and though she found a few, they all led to a dead end. The Coxes, who lived next door to the Braxtons had moved to California with their daughter ten years ago, and the Straussers, who had lived across the street from them for over forty years, moved out of town just last year. There were more neighbors, but they had either moved away or didn't know anything and Charlie was more than just a little discouraged.

As she disgustedly flipped through the pages, she spied Matthew Torrance's name and let out a whoop of joy.

"Matthew! Of course, how could I forget Matthew?" she said to no one and picked up the receiver. "If anybody knows anything about anyone, it's Matthew!"

"Charlie, who in the world are you talking to?" her mother asked as she passed by the family room.

"Uh, no one." Charlie answered, hastily hanging up the receiver. She slammed the book shut and stuffed it under the telephone stand. "I'm just talking to myself again."

She decided not to tell anyone about her little investigation, especially her mother. Although she was sure she would understand, Charlie knew several other people who would be furious if they knew what she had in mind—and her mother was married to one of them.

"Going to Matthew's, Mom, see you later."

Matthew Torrance, a sprightly sixty year old who never minced words or held them back, had been on the courthouse payroll as far back as John Braxton's grandfather. He was on the Advisory Board then and was still somewhat active, serving as a consultant in various areas. He was a good, upstanding man—honest and outspoken to a fault at times—but a man you could count on in any given situation. Even Pete had nothing but good to say about Matthew, and though Pete and Charlie were rarely able to see eye to eye on a personal level, she knew that Pete was a fairly smart man and that he actually valued Matthew's opinion and trusted his quick instincts. The truth was Pete was one of the deciding factors in Charlie's decision to go and have a talk with Matthew—but not on and level could she ever tell him that.

Matthew lived fairly close to the perimeter of the mayor's estate, but since the property extended out and around for about seventeen acres in all directions, one couldn't say that he lived close by, but she decided a walk might clear her head. It would take a little more than an hour to walk to the modest little one-story house ranch even if she dared to cut through Braxton territory', but Charlie didn't mind. It was cool and brisk but not bone-chilling, and she did need the time alone to collect her thoughts.

Charlie loved Matthew, and as a little girl, she remembered scurrying off to visit him even though she had been warned repeatedly never to walk that far alone. However, her mother secretly knew of her daughter's little jaunts to Matthew's house, and they had both set up a system between them where DeeDee would call and tell Matthew that Charlie was on her way, and he would walk out to the end of his property and watch her coming from far off. Then he would call DeeDee and tell her Charlie had arrived safely and drive her home after supper and everything was smoothed over.

Charlie had always thought of Matthew as the grandfather she never had, and she was suddenly hit with a pang of guilt. It had been well over a year since she had seen him last, and now she was only going to get information out of him. Well, this time, she would make it a personal visit, then she would get down to the dirt on John Braxton.

Matthew, outside splitting wood, saw Charlie coming long before she saw him, and he let out a wild Indian whoop. He tossed his axe on top of the woodpile, ran the fifty yards to meet her, then grabbed her up in his arms and twirled her around as though she weighed nothing, just like he always did.

"Charlie! By God, it is you!" He set her down on the ground gently, not even breathing heavily. "Ahh, let me look at you!" He held her out at arm's length and twirled her like a pirouette doll. "Darlin', you sure are a sight for sore eyes! And you've grown an inch or two, haven't you?"

"Maybe around the middle is all." Charlie grinned mischievously. "It's wonderful to see you, Matthew! I'm sorry I didn't come sooner, but—"

"But you're here now and that's all that counts! Come in! Come in! Do you still drink your tea like the English?" He draped his arm around her shoulders and they walked toward the house.

"Yep, still do! I guess some things never change."

"Well, you sure haven't, you're still as bright and pretty as ever! You must have gotten that part from your mother, you sure as heck didn't get it from your dad!"

"You knew my dad pretty well, didn't you, Matthew?" she asked after they had gone inside. She took a sip of tea from the cup he'd handed her. "What was he like? We never did talk about him much."

"You were just a baby, there was no need to talk. Besides, you couldn't understand us anyway." He laughed like he'd said the funniest thing ever, and Charlie laughed right along with him.

"It's sure good to laugh!" He stopped laughing on a dime, and Charlie just shook her head and grinned. "So where was I, oh yeah, your dad. He worked hard, Charley did, too hard, and that's why he went sooner that he should have, but he loved you that's for sure. He used to bring you with him when he could pull himself away from that damn repair shop of his. He'd work way into the night on those tractors trying to finish them so the farmers could have them back to work their fields—gone from sun-up to sun-down. Your poor mother barely saw him. And then he had to go and have that damn heart attack and, well, no use rehashing old news," he said, noticing Charlie's watery eyes. "Anyway, when you were about five or six I'd say, your mom met Pete." He sat down at the table across from Charlie. "Then they got married and he became your daddy, and that's about it."

Charlie's smile disappeared. "He is not my father, Matthew." Her green eyes blazed, and Matthew held up his hand as if in defeat.

"Okay, little darlin', okay! I didn't mean to step on your toes. I just meant—"

"No, no, it's all right, Matthew," she said, her anger immediately dissipating. "It's me who's sorry. I guess I'm still kind of mad that I didn't have my dad around when I was growing up instead of Pete, please forgive me."

"There's nothing to forgive, darlin', you feel how you feel, that's all. And truth be known, you never were keen on Pete from the first day he stepped into that house. I thought things might have changed after some years went by, but I see they haven't and that's okay, too, we don't see eye to eye with everybody in this world."

Charlie looked pensive. "I don't think I would have minded so much if he hadn't come in all pushy and taking over. 'I'm your father now, and the sooner you learn that what I say goes around here, the better we'll get along!'" She mocked, in a deep throaty voice, and then, "Funny thing is, that was kind of the beginning of the end. I mean, even though I was really young, I remember getting mad when he insisted I call him Dad, and well, we never did get along after that." She took another sip of tea, while Matthew looked on sympathetically.

"He just didn't know how to talk to kids, Charlie, that's all. He talked to you like you were an adult instead of six years old."

"I know. Mom didn't see it, I guess, but I did. I suppose when you're in love though, you don't see all the flaws."

Just then, they both heard the back screen door slam, and heavy footsteps coming down the hall toward the kitchen.

"Paul?" Matthew called out without turning around. "What brings you out here on a Sunday?"

Charlie stared up at the tall stranger now standing in the kitchen doorway and instantly knew he had to be related to Matthew. He resembled the older man as he might have looked thirty or so years ago—startlingly handsome, with intense eyes. And they were fixed on Charlie.

"Paul, this here's Charlie, the little darlin' I told you about. Charlie, meet my grandson, Paul."

"Hello, Paul," Charlie said quietly, reaching up to shake his hand. His grip was firm and his calloused hand, a bit rough though not repulsive, hinted of a hard worker like his grandfather. "It's nice to meet you."

"Same here." His voice was husky and deep.

"A man of few words," Matthew supplied, pushing his chair back and standing up. He turned and gave Paul a huge bear hug and slapped him on the back. "Nice to see you, boy! I thought you'd be here yesterday."

"Couldn't, had to be in Woodford Hall for that meeting, and they're not going for the bid, Granddad—we might be stuck with those horses after all."

"You lowered the bid?"

"As low as I could. If I'd gone any lower, we would have lost a bundle."

Matthew slapped him on the back again. "Well, we'll think of something, boy, we always do."

"You mean *you* always do."

Charlie caught the smallest hint of a smile Paul gave his granddad, and it seemingly changed his entire facial expression. The lines around his mouth softened and the piercing look in his dark, expressive eyes disappeared, revealing an extremely handsome younger version of Matthew, and Charlie suddenly felt her heart do a little two-step.

Great. If you drool any more, you won't need milk in your tea. She quickly took a gulp to hide her obvious pleasure.

"Well, if I'm going to get that shed repaired, I'd better get started."

"Now, wait a minute, you and I were both going to repair that shed, remember? The old boy still has a few good years left, you know." He looked over at Charlie and winked and she smiled and winked back.

"There's plenty to do, Granddad. You just stay and visit with Charlie here. I would if I were you." He turned to leave and then looked back over his shoulder. "Nice meeting you, Charlie. I hope I run into you again sometime."

Charlie nodded, feeling her heart do that little two-step thing again. "It was great—it was won—it was real nice meeting you too, Paul." She stammered, and when he was gone, she turned to Matthew with a wry look on her face. "Well, wasn't that special? I should have just latched onto his ankles and drooled on his boots! 'Oh, it was so wonderful and splendid and oh-my-god-rock-my-world-fantastic meeting you, Paul!'" She exaggerated, rolling her eyes. "Could I have *been* more obvious?" She always could tell Matthew anything.

"He's a ladies' man, that's for sure. Nice-looking boy, isn't he?" Matthew winked and Charlie blushed.

"I really hadn't noticed."

Matthew opened his mouth to comment but quickly closed it again. Some things were better left unsaid. "So, princess, what brings you all the way over here to see old Matt? I know you didn't come just to visit!"

"Why, Matthew, I did, too! I haven't seen you in so long that I decided it was about time, and—"

"And you don't make a very good liar, Charlie, in more ways than one!" he said knowingly. "So why don't you get down to things and tell me what's on your mind?"

Charlie grinned guiltily. "Well, I guess I do have something on my mind." She hesitated for a moment and then decided to just come out with it, completely forgetting that Matthew knew nothing about her encounter with the mayor. "Well, after Mayor Braxton threatened me the other day, I—"

"Threatened you?" Matthew thundered, interrupting. "What do you mean 'threatened' you?"

"Oh! Wait a minute, maybe I'd better start from the beginning before you really blow your top." Charlie then proceeded to give Matthew the condensed version of how she wanted to bring Christmas back to Braxton, ending with her dreamy-eyed look about how much she wished the pond and the old Kissing Bridge could be reopened again. "I know it sounds ridiculous to want something so badly, especially when it's in such bad shape, but can't you just imagine horses pulling carriages over that bridge? I've seen pictures from years ago, and it looks positively romantic. I mean, I realize that the parasols and long dresses are completely out of the question, I guess." She grinned sheepishly, realizing she must sound incredibly immature. "But I love that covered bridge, Matthew, and I honestly believe it could be the highlight of the entire campaign. And since it does cross over the spillway and connect to Main Street, the first thing people would see is the street lit up and a huge tree decorated in the middle of the square. It would look like a step back in time, and I think it would be a terrific way to make the people fall in love with Braxton all over again."

Matthew smiled warmly, loving her all the more for her enthusiasm and old-fashioned way of thinking in a world he considered too modern for its own good. Her nostalgic way of thinking was such a refreshing change for one so young. "Well, as true as that might be, Charlie, and not wanting to burst your bubble, I don't think it's possible to fix that old covered beauty, she's been through a lot down through the years. Besides, according to John Braxton, it would take far too much money to renovate her."

That's when Charlie spoke up and told him how she had already gone to the mayor for help and met with his adamant refusal to lift even one finger to get things going, and when she was finished, Matthew leaned back in his chair and stroked his jaw.

"Well, that certainly sounds like John," he said quietly. "And there probably are things that contribute to his reluctance to help, Charlie. He's a hard man to convince of anything."

"But he has to realize how much revenue he could bring to Braxton if he showed a little effort to try and help make this work. It would provide work for so many people, as well as getting them involved in Braxton again. Of course, Pete only adds to the problem by agreeing with him. He nearly took my head off when he found out that I'd gone to the mayor in the first place. What is the matter with everyone? Doesn't anyone care about Christmas anymore?"

"I'm sure they do in their own way, darlin'. It's just that things have changed so much over the years that most people aren't so eager to let loose of a dime because they work so darn hard to get it."

"But I'm not really asking them to give much. They could offer their services instead of money, like doing construction work or whatever, and if the mayor would help out just a little monetarily, we—"

"You can forget that, darlin'," Matthew said, propping his feet up on the chair next to him. "I've seen things that man has done to people that would curl your hair. He won't even allow a kid's center to be built when he knows it would help keep them off the streets. No sir, not old John, he won't part with one red cent."

"Well, you just have to look around to know that he certainly doesn't use any of the town's money to make improvements. Have you seen the gazebo? It was so beautiful, and now it's practically falling apart. There has to be more than enough to help pay for it to be repaired, as well as some of our projects, and well, I'll just go to the Finance Committee if I have to."

Matthew suddenly looked solemn and leaned forward in his chair. "Now, there's where you're gonna get your feet more than just a little wet, darlin'. Like I said, don't think for one minute that he didn't mean that threat he gave you. Trust me, he meant every word of it."

"But, Matthew, you don't understand. He did a complete turnaround and went from a lion to a lamb and practically handed me the keys to this town."

"Well, what'd you do, threaten him first?" His endearing smile lit up the room.

"Well, now that you mention it—" Charlie looked guilty as sin, and Matthew's face grew solemn.

"What do you mean 'sort of'? What the heck did you say to him, darlin'?"

Charlie sensed impending doom. "Well, I guess I sort of told him that I thought he was hiding something."

Matthew slowly pulled his feet from the chair and stood up, shoving his hands deep down into his pockets. "You did, huh?" He strolled to the back door where he just stood there staring out the window. He didn't speak for several long minutes, and Charlie didn't know what to make of his reaction.

"I goofed, huh?" She ventured cautiously, "And I would say, by the look on your face that it was a pretty big goof."

He didn't turn around, and when he spoke, his tone was quiet. "You have to watch yourself with John Braxton, he can make life hell for you if you give him a reason." He paused for only a second. "Does he have a reason, Charlie? Do you suspect him of something?"

"Well, I may be way off the mark, but he seemed almost too angry about my wanting to start a Christmas tradition in Braxton. And forget about the fact that I even mentioned his family, he practically charged over his desk and grabbed my throat. I've never seen anyone so angry, not even Pete."

Matthew finally moved away from the door and returned to the table and sat down again. "He is very tight-lipped about his family, he doesn't like to talk about them at all."

"I think it does have something to do with his family, although I'm not sure why. I do know that his granddaughter Christina is exactly like him, right down to his mannerisms, it's really weird! I don't know, Matthew, call it a feeling, but something just doesn't seem right somehow."

Matthew reached out and covered Charlie's hand with his wrinkled, weathered one. "It might be better if you didn't pursue this, Charlie."

"What do you mean, why in the world not? Christmas can be such a happy time, and I just want to share some of that happiness—what is so wrong with that? Everyone is being so stubborn about this, and I would love to know why."

"Sometimes you just have to let sleeping dogs lie, Charlie."

"What aren't you telling me, Matthew? You know something, I can feel it." Charlie watched as Matthew's expression became vague and distant, and it was then that she knew she'd lost him; he'd closed up. Still, she sat back in her chair with an odd look of satisfaction on her face. "You don't have to say another word, Matthew Torrance—it's what you *didn't* say that just convinced me that I'm right. He is hiding something, and I intend to find out what it is, with or without your help, no offense."

"None taken, darlin'—just be careful is all I'm saying."

"Oh, for Pete's sake, Matthew, I—"

"Yes, for *his* sake, as well." Matthew warned. "He's another one you have to watch."

Charlie looked stunned. "What do you mean by that? You aren't telling me that Pete is involved in something? I can't believe it, even about Pete."

"No, what I mean is that if he gets wind of what you're planning—and it's probably a doozey—he'll have your hide."

Charlie laughed. "Well, you're probably right on the money about that, but what he doesn't know won't hurt him. I'll be fine, Matthew, really." She stood up and walked over to his chair and stood behind it, sliding her arms around his neck and kissing his head. "You are a treasure, Matthew Torrance, do you know that?" He reached up and patted her arm, and she closed her eyes and hugged him tighter. "Don't worry about me so much. I'll be fine, and I promise, I'll let you know what happens." She leaned over and kissed his cheek, said goodbye, and was gone, leaving him alone with his thoughts.

"You're leaving?" Charlie heard a voice call out just as she got to the driveway, and she turned to see Paul casually leaning against a tree, watching her.

"Yes," she answered shyly. "I don't like to wear out my welcome."

"You could never wear out your welcome," he said. "With Granddad, I mean. He loves you, you know."

"Yes, I know," Charlie said warmly. "I love him too. He's a wonderful man, but I suppose you already know how terrific he is."

"I do," he said simply, staring as though he was trying to burn a hole right through her, and Charlie blushed at the intenseness of his eyes.

"Do you always stare like that?" she asked, feeling a bit uncomfortable.

"Like what?"

"Like you're doing right now." She snapped, knowing he was well aware of what he was doing. "That's not very polite, you know."

"Sorry. I happen to like what I see."

Charlie blushed again. "Well, you certainly are blunt, I'll say that."

"That's the way I am. I'm not going to pretend that I don't find you extremely attractive."

"Discretion is the better part of valor, Mr. Torrance," she murmured, not caring much for his attitude. "And I don't like being stared at like I'm tonight's dessert." She turned her back on him and purposefully walked away, but not before she heard his rude snicker. She considered turning around and telling him exactly what he could do with his snicker, but she thought better of it and simply walked away, grumbling to herself. "Well, it's easy to see you're nothing like your grandfather." But he'd heard her every word, and she missed the smile fade from his face.

"Looks like you made an enemy, boy," Matthew said quietly, leaning against the column of the porch.

"A bit stuck-up, isn't she?" Paul asked his eyes still on Charlie.

"There's not a stuck-up bone in that girl's body, she just doesn't care much for arrogance, and you sure showed her enough of that. I can't believe my daughter didn't teach you better manners."

"I speak my mind, Granddad, you know that."

Matthew frowned. "Well, in that case, you should learn that some things are better left unsaid. She's a sweet girl, Paul and you'd best watch how you act around her."

"Say, what is it with you two, anyway?" Paul asked seconds later, but fortunately, Matthew had gone back inside. He wouldn't have liked Paul's insinuation one bit—no matter how innocently it was meant.

CHAPTER IV

———— ❋ ————

Going to work almost seemed a pleasure for Charlie the next several weeks. The sun was shining; the flowers were beginning to bloom—a sure sign that spring was definitely on its way. The fact that the girls were buzzing with new ideas as well as revising old ones merely added to her feeling that all was right with her world despite her run-in with the arrogant Paul Torrance. Or because of it she wasn't quite sure which. The only thing she knew for certain was that she couldn't get him off her mind.

Jean had crocheted a bushel of craft items, and even Helen seemed more animated, allowing them to look at the sailboats and wagons she'd constructed, while Mary decided that crocheting angels were to be the project of the hour. She made dozens of them—some flying, some praying, and some even sleeping. Their office had become a safe haven for each of them to come to and add a bit of crafting along with their work, and they seemed content with their accomplishments.

Charlie was also thinking about the Sunday school children. They had been working hard on their play, and though there were a few fights about who would be who, for the most part, they were becoming quite serious about their share in Charlie's plan to bring back Christmas. The best part was the fact that Christina Braxton had obviously chosen not to tell her family about their little project because no one had come around to tell them that they couldn't do it. Of course, the fact that she was in the running to play Mary might have had a little something to do with her silence, but Charlie was only guessing.

She was walking rather proudly one particular Sunday during those weeks and the children had been wonderful. Though some of them had slipped and told their parents, to Charlie's surprise, some were now offering to help with her campaign, and it seemed like she just might get her lifelong wish of a holiday festival. For the first time in a long time, she was feeling good about everyone's efforts—up until the moment anyway.

"Hey! How about an apple for the teacher?" Charlie heard a familiar voice behind her, and she rolled her eyes knowingly.

"Oh, it's you." She tried to sound disinterested, although she couldn't control the sudden excitement she felt hearing his voice. "Shouldn't you be fixing your granddad's shed or pulling the wings off butterflies or something?" She didn't look back at him but continued walking.

"I'm not cruel, just arrogant, remember?" He teased. "And the shed's finished, want to come and see it?"

"No, thank you." She still refused to look in his direction. "I'll take your word for it."

"Granddad misses you," he said now, getting her attention, and Charlie immediately turned around, and he noticed her expressive green eyes widen with concern.

"He's all right, isn't he? I mean nothing is wrong?"

"He's fine, Charlie, you know Granddad. You can't keep a man like him down." He smiled, and Charlie felt her heartbeat go into overtime.

Does he look different today, or is it just his smile that makes him look even more—oh, I don't know—sexy maybe? She wondered. "He certainly is energetic for a man his age," she said instead, finding it amazing just how much he and Matthew did resemble one another. It was uncanny really. "Do you see him often? I don't remember you being there when I visited the last time. Well, not this past time, but—"

That's the way to ignore him, Charlie, keep talking.

"That was over a year ago, if I recall," he said knowingly, and Charlie blinked.

He recalls? she mused, not remembering his being at his granddad's at the same time she'd been there.

"I don't get to see him as often as I would like." They fell into step together. "My work keeps me away a lot."

"Do you travel all over?"

"I usually stay fairly local and that's why I bought a place outside of Braxton, but lately, I've been going out of town, sometimes several weeks at a time. That's why my visits to Granddad's are so few and far between. I think you see him more than I do."

"Wouldn't it be easier just to share a house with him? Then you could see him all the time."

"Move in? With Granddad? Not a chance."

"Well, why not? Seems to me you could save on expenses and help out around the place at the same time."

"Uh, I don't think so. We're too much alike, we'd be arguing all the time. You live at home, are you going to tell me you don't argue with your family?"

"Sometimes," she admitted. "Mostly it's with my stepfather, Pete. My mother and I get along really well. I've been thinking about getting my own house for quite a while now and I'm pretty close to buying a little Cape Cod near the end of town. I really like it, but it needs some work. It's not that I mind getting my hands dirty, and I think I would kind of like a little fixer-upper, but I guess I've been pretty bush and haven't had time to give it much thought lately."

"Granddad mentioned something about it quite a while back and said if you did buy it, he'd help you get it in shape."

"I know, he told me. He is such a sweetheart," she said, suddenly aware that they had actually been talking and she didn't feel irritated with him anymore. "I've loved him since I was a little girl and used to sneak over to his house. My mother would tell me not to go to see him because it was too far for me to walk alone, but when I thought she wasn't watching, I'd run like crazy until I was out of sight—as if she wouldn't notice I was gone." She grinned sheepishly. "I used to get into so much trouble doing that, but I couldn't help it—I guess I sort of adopted him as my grandfather since I never knew mine—he passed away long before I was born." Her grin faded. "I haven't seen much of him lately though. I've been pretty busy with work and the Christmas thing and all."

"Christmas thing?" Paul looked confused.

"Oh, Matthew didn't tell you? I'm trying to start a traditional Bring Back Christmas campaign, which has made me the proverbial thorn in the mayor's side, I might add. He probably wishes I'd move to Outer Mongolia or Siberia—or at the very least to somewhere he isn't." She glanced at Paul, catching his look of utter confusion, and she grinned. "Never mind, it's a long story."

"I'm not going anywhere, I have all day."

They stopped at the diner, and after a while—two hours and several cups of coffee later, to be exact—Charlie finished her story and looked over at Paul expectantly. "So what do you think?"

"Personally, I think it's a fantastic idea." He handed the hostess the bill and money and told her to keep the change.

"You do?" Charlie asked as they exited the café and began strolling along the sidewalk.

"I always did think Braxton could use a shot in the arm to get it on the map."

"You did?"

"Sure. I don't know why someone didn't do something like this a long time ago."

"You don't?"

Paul stopped walking to look down at her. "Well, why do you sound so shocked?"

"Well, no one else seemed to think it was such a great idea in the beginning." She resumed walking. "Everyone I talked to, with the exception of my mother and the girls I work with, had something negative to say about it. Some of them have changed their minds, but it took a lot to get them going in the right direction. I don't understand people, what's not to like about Christmas?"

"Well, not everyone is a hopeless romantic, Charlie. Most people worry about money or the lack of it. No one seems to have the time to care about the way it used to be."

He thinks I'm a hopeless romantic?

"You just have younger ideas than they do, that's all. Most of the people in Braxton get old before their time, but not you, I think you'll always have a young-ness about you."

Charlie looked surprised. No one had ever said anything like that to her before—at least no one who mattered anyway—and the warmth spread through her body like melting butter. If nothing else, Matthew's grandson certainly had his charm. Although she suspected that he was probably just saying it to make up for the way he'd acted when he first met her, it sure sounded nice.

"What makes you think I'm a hopeless romantic?" she asked softly, not at all fishing for a compliment, just very flattered.

"It's not hard to miss, it's written all over your face." He smiled, but the smile faded slightly when he couldn't take his eyes off her. She was a beauty all right, stunning actually with soft green eyes and incredible lashes. "A very pretty face, I might add," he said quietly, and embarrassed, Charlie looked away.

"What, are you going to tell me that no one has ever told you that before?"

"Not that I care to recall." She didn't appreciate his insinuation. Did she seem that shallow?

"I find that hard to believe."

She stopped walking and looked up at him. "Well, what's so strange about that? The way a person looks has nothing to do with the way she is, or at least it shouldn't. Beauty's only skin deep, you know — it's what's on the *inside* that counts." She was making an obvious point, but he wasn't getting it.

"Have you looked in a mirror lately?"

"Look. Just stop, okay?" She disliked talking about herself, and this was getting downright embarrassing, but Paul suddenly stopped in the middle of the sidewalk and stared down at her.

"What?" she asked, irritated.

"You honestly don't know, do you?"

"Know what?" She was completely and wonderfully innocent.

"How beautiful you are."

She didn't say anything and just turned and walked away from him, and for the life of him, he couldn't understand why. Most of the women he knew were well aware of their beauty and their charm—and the fact that they had the ability to lure a man into giving them his shoes in the dead of winter—but obviously, this woman wasn't capable of any type of conceit. In fact, she wasn't like any woman he'd ever known before—both beautiful and humble, but real at the same time. He caught up with her and grasped her arm, turning her around to face him.

"Listen, this isn't a line, and I never say things that I don't mean—I told you as much at Granddad's place. I meant what I said."

She tried humor to put him off. "Oh, really? Well, how do you know I'm not some spoiled brat who stomps her feet and turns into a witch if she doesn't get her own way? See?

You don't know me at all, so how can you possibly say that?"

"I have twenty-twenty vision!" He joked before becoming serious again. "I don't need glasses to see your beauty—and that you obviously care more about people than you do about yourself." He grinned then. "Of course the fact that my grandfather thinks you're an angel doesn't hurt."

"Actually he's the angel," Charlie said, flustered by his forwardness. She turned around and began walking, and again, they fell into step together. "He's the sweetest man I've ever known and he always has time to listen—even though I haven't always taken the time to talk to him; but I intend to change that. I didn't realize just how much I've missed him until now."

"The feeling is mutual, you're all he seems to talk about. I think you're good for granddad—he needs someone to look in on him once in a while."

Charlie gave him a sideways glance. "Okay, I give, who are you and what have you done with Paul Torrance?"

Paul chuckled. "What do you mean?"

"Well, you aren't exactly the same person that I met at your granddad's—you weren't nearly as nice."

"Wasn't I? Well, I apologize. I was probably just in a foul mood."

"No, I don't think that's it." Charlie looked thoughtful. "Your granddad didn't say anything to you, did he?"

"About what?"

"Oh, nothing." She decided that some things were better left unsaid. Besides, there was no sense in spoiling a perfectly good day.

They strolled on in silence for a few minutes before Charlie spoke up again. "If you don't mind my asking, what did you mean when you told your granddad that you lowered the bid on some horses? I don't mean to be nosey, but what is it that you do again exactly?"

"I'm a consultant for a construction company, but I work with Granddad on the side, buying and selling stock."

"Stock—as in Wall Street?"

Paul grinned. "No, I mean as in horses and cattle on his ranch."

Charlie's mouth dropped open in shock. "Matthew owns a ranch? Huh! He's been holding out on me. Either that, or I don't know him as well as I thought I did."

"He doesn't talk about it much. I sort of take care of the details for him so he doesn't have to."

"I don't understand. If he doesn't live on it and he doesn't like to work it, why does he keep it?"

"My grandmother loved that ranch. Granddad bought it for her as a wedding gift when they were married and she swore she would never leave—even when my mother left for Vermont where she'd been offered a good job. They lived there for years until my grandmother got sick, and Granddad suggested that they rent a house in Vermont where my mother could help look after her while she recuperated. My grandmother agreed, but only if they could move back as soon as she was well enough, and six or seven months later, they did. Unfortunately, she died a short time later. After the funeral, he came back here and bought the house they'd been renting. He moved in and hasn't been back since."

"That's so sad. I never knew."

"Like I said, he doesn't talk about it much."

They walked awhile in silence and were nearing the gazebo in the middle of the town square. Many of Braxton's citizens gathered there after church, one of the rare times the townspeople got together. It was an odd sight, since the citizens always seemed so close-mouthed and private, and the strangeness of it never ceased to amaze Charlie.

"So where is Matthew's ranch?" she asked, stepping inside.

"Wyoming," he said joining her. Charlie stopped and turned around.

"Wyoming? But that's clear across the country! Wouldn't it be a lot easier if he just sold it? How can he take care of it from here?"

"Like I said, I take care of things for him."

"Well, now I really don't understand. He should just sell it! Wouldn't that make it a lot easier for everyone? I mean, Wyoming, that's practically a day away and if he never goes there, what's the point of—"

"It's the only thing he has left of Grandmother," he interrupted kindly. "I think Granddad believes that if he gets rid of it, it would be like burying her all over again. It's a part of her that he just doesn't want to give up."

"Oh," she said thoughtfully. "I can't imagine a love that strong." She looked up at Paul and felt something click between them, but the feeling was so fleeting she thought she imagined it. "That tells me a lot about how much he loved her."

Paul handed her his handkerchief. "See what I mean by a hopeless romantic?"

Charlie sniffled in answer, and Paul smiled.

"You know, I think Granddad found a real treasure when he met you. Of course, he always was a good judge of character."

"We do have a special bond, he and I." She blushed prettily. "And you already know how I feel about him."

"I think you're the granddaughter he never had. He and Grandmother always wanted lots of kids, but they only had my mother, and now that she's gone, he just has me. And you, of course," he added, and Charlie smiled shyly.

"You can be sweet when you want to be, do you know that?"

Paul shrugged. "I'm not sure I would say that, exactly. Sometimes saying how you feel can work against you, but that's the way I am, good or bad. I never say things I don't mean."

She hesitated for just a moment, then asked, "What made you act the way you did at your granddad's? You crossed the border on rude, you know."

"I thought you were stuck-up."

"Stuck-up? Why in the world would you think that I was stuck-up? Did I act stuck-up?"

"You didn't say much."

"Well, that's a lot different than being stuck-up. I guess I didn't know how to take you or what to say."

"Do you always have trouble talking to people?"

Only to you, she thought. "No, not really."

"But you had trouble talking to me?" It was more a statement than a question, and Charlie sensed the possibility that he'd read her mind.

"Well, sort of, I guess."

"Why?"

"Because I didn't, I couldn't, well, I don't know, I just did, that's all." She was so flustered by this time, she didn't know what to say. Of course, she could always tell him the truth—just jump right in there with both feet and tell him he was the sexiest thing she'd ever seen on two legs, and that she was having a hard time getting past his intense eyes. "Could we please talk about something else?"

He looked at her curiously. "I don't make you nervous, do I, Charlie?"

"Nervous? Don't be ridiculous, of course, you don't make me nervous! What makes you think I'm nervous?"

"Well, the fact that you've managed to make my handkerchief look like a wrung-out, overused dinner napkin sort of gave me the idea."

Charlie's face flamed red. "Oh. Well I, you—"

He took a step closer. "And you're stuttering."

Charlie took a step backward but came up against the railing of the gazebo and could go no further. "I'm not s-stuttering. You just, you make me nervous."

"How can you say that when I haven't done anything?"

"Well, for one thing, you're standing awfully close." *Way too close.* She thought with nowhere to run.

"I want to kiss you, Charlie." There wasn't a trace of a smile on his face. "Does that make you uncomfortable?"

"Yes, as a matter of fact—"

"Well, get ready because I am going to kiss you."

"I really don't—"

"I think you do," he said softly, coming dangerously close to her lips, and Charlie swallowed again.

"Listen, Paul, I—"

"I've wanted to kiss you since the first day I met you."

"You have?" She watched his lips, mesmerized, as he moved closer.

"Yes, I have."

"But we barely know each other—"

"How well do you have to know someone to kiss them, Charlie?"

Charlie felt his breath flutter across her eyes, and they involuntarily closed on their own. Then he kissed her—a warm, sensual kiss that started a tiny fire deep down inside of her looking for something to catch onto and ignite, but when Paul felt her arms creep up around his neck and pull him closer, he was shocked at his own reaction. The kiss was meant to throw Charlie a bit off balance, but Paul wasn't prepared for the emotional turmoil he felt. While he tried to brush off the feeling of being out of control for the first time in his life, Charlie watched his eyes darken in intensity when he backed away. "You're right, I shouldn't have done that. I'm sorry, Charlie."

Sorry? Her mind yelled frantically. *Say anything, but don't say you're sorry!* She suddenly remembered what he'd said about never saying anything he didn't mean, and she stiffened in his arms.

"I told you not to kiss me!" She angrily twisted away from him, and Paul grabbed her by the arm.

"Wait, Charlie! I didn't mean it the way—"

"No problem, I understand perfectly!" she said, pulling herself out of his arms, not understanding at all. "You did exactly what you wanted to do, and I didn't measure up, and now you're sorry you did it. What's to understand? You don't have to make excuses, Paul, it's no big deal." She wasn't having a bit of trouble stuttering now. "Don't you have to be somewhere? I know I do!" Her long auburn hair shimmered in the sunlight when she turned, swept her head around, and sprinted down the steps and walked briskly down the sidewalk.

The next morning, she didn't say much more than "hello" to the girls, and it continued that way for the rest of the week. It was rare for Charlie, and Jean couldn't take it any longer and finally spoke up.

"Charlie, is something wrong?"

Charlie's eyes grew misty at Jean's sympathetic tone. "Nothing that a good stiff drink wouldn't cure."

"Is there anything I can do, honey?"

"No, but thanks for asking. It's just something I'll have to work out on my own."

"But you've been miserable for days. I hate to see you like this."

"Don't worry, it'll pass."

Jean patted her shoulder. "Well, if you need to talk—" She didn't finish, but simply walked back to her desk.

The day seemed to drag on and on, and at ten minutes to four, Charlie managed to slip out of the office unnoticed and head home.

She was thinking about the picnic, which was just three months away, and how excited everyone was anticipating a good time, and still, she couldn't seem to pull herself out of her dark mood.

"Charlie, telephone." Her mother called in to her from the kitchen later that evening, but when Charlie didn't respond within a moment of two, her mother appeared at the living room doorway. "Didn't you hear me? What is wrong with you lately?" She held the receiver out to her daughter. "The phone is for you."

"I heard you." She said, still not moving, and her mother cupped her hand over the mouthpiece and took a few steps in front of her.

"You had better snap out of this mood you're in, Charlie."

"You don't understand, Mom," she said flatly. "I just don't care."

Her mother was angry. "Look. I don't know what the problem is, but if you give up on this project now, you'll lose everything, not to mention the respect of everyone who has come to believe in you, and then you can forget ever getting anyone to help you again."

"It has nothing to do with that, Mother."

"Well, whatever is bothering you, you had better deal with it. You made a commitment to the people of this town, and it's up to you to follow through with it, now take this call, it's Eleanor Loganberry." She held out the receiver, and Charlie reluctantly took it.

"Hello, Miss Loganberry, how nice of you to call," she said dispassionately, fully expecting her to say she was backing out. "Please don't feel bad about the barbeque. I'm sure you did everything you could to—"

"Why, whatever do you mean, my dear? Everything is fine, just fine! I was merely calling to inquire about the number of persons who will be attending the festivities. I must call the caterers and give them a count, you see."

At the sound of Eleanor's positive attitude, Charlie came to the realization that if nothing else came of her Bring Back Christmas campaign, everyone could at least have a good time at the barbeque. She could explain her failure to bring everything together later, in a letter, after she was settled in Outer Mongolia.

Fortunately, her near mistake went completely over Eleanor's head, however, and she half-smiled her relief. "Oh, that. Well, as near as I can tell, there will be over three hundred people." A prickle of guilt ran up her spine, and she suddenly felt compelled to apologize for the large number.

"Apologize? Oh, my dear, I expected much more than that. Do you suppose I should order enough for seven or eight hundred people? I am sure that there will be many more who just have not responded as yet."

"Well, I don't know, Miss Loganberry, that certainly is a lot of food, not to mention a lot of money to—"

"Nonsense, child! Money is no object, and one must eat to survive, and I am quite sure many of the citizens of Braxton could do with a good meal. Heaven knows John Braxton does not contribute to their survival. I will plan on seven hundred then, with plenty to spare."

"That's really very kind of you, Miss Loganberry." Charlie was suddenly ashamed of her willingness to just give up when the going got a little rough, and it took this woman's enthusiasm to show her. "I can't thank you enough, and I'm sure everyone will have plenty to eat at the picnic."

"Wonderful, it's settled then. Well, I must be off. I have much to do and July 4 will be here before we know it. Ta-ta, Charlotte."

"Goodbye, Miss Loganberry, and thank you again."

"Nonsense!" The older woman sniffed, refusing to take any credit at all. "It will be a welcome respite for us all. I am quite excited about it," she said, although you wouldn't have guessed it by her reserved, well-cultured tone. "Take care, Charlotte, and I will phone you soon."

DeeDee entered the room just as Charlie was hanging up the phone. "Well?" her mother said expectantly, obviously irritated with her only daughter.

"Everything's great. The Loganberrys really are wonderful people, aren't they?" Not waiting for an answer, she turned and walked away, missing the look of shock on her mother's face at her daughter's sudden change of attitude. She decided not to share her sudden but short-lived feeling of doom, knowing that Paul Torrance could never be a part of her life or her heart. After all, she got along without him before she met him and she could certainly get along without him now. And as far as her project was concerned, she decided to cross each bridge as she came to it. And the end result was that she returned to work refreshed on Tuesday.

Although the three women were extraordinarily busy for the better part of the day, there was a lull during the afternoon with all the lawyers out of the office, and they were able to relax and talk about the picnic.

"Everything seems to be going well, don't you think?" Jean inquired. "I've finished all my crocheting, and there are only a few more squares to finish on the quilt we'll be raffling off. How are things going with everyone else?"

"Well, I heard from Miss Loganberry last night and she's really excited about the picnic. Do you know she's ordering enough food for seven hundred people? We'll have food coming out of our ears."

"Oh, I don't know about that, Charlie," Jean countered. "There are a lot more people coming than we first thought. Besides, you know how my husband and kids can eat."

Mary and Charlie burst out laughing, while Helen merely looked bored with the whole thing. "Well, I don't know about you, but I'm sick and tired of hearing about this picnic, let alone the craft show. If I look at another piece of wood, it'll be too soon! I must have made a million of those sailboats and stupid little carts, my hands look like they belong to my great-grandmother."

"Oh, quit complaining, Helen." Mary scolded. "It's for a good cause and don't tell me you didn't enjoy every minute making those little sailboats and carts because I don't believe it."

"Humph!" Helen scoffed, ignoring Mary's comment and sauntering back to her desk, but she didn't deny it.

Charlie rechecked her list. "Well, Caroline Webber offered to man the refreshment stand, complete with her famous hot chocolate, I might add." Then to Jean's odd look, "I know, I know, it's summertime, but the kids will love it. And let's see, Jack Morgan who owns the hardware store is handling the sack races, he ordered twenty-five potato sacks to make sure we have enough, and Bill Johnson is not only lending us his little popcorn stand, he's going to run it for us too, so you don't have to worry about finding someone else to do it, Mary. Oh, and by the way—" Charlie looked up from her notepad. "Guess who offered to run the Moon Walk machine? The Daywoods, do you believe it? I go door to door begging for volunteers and she tells me they can't possibly be a part of things, but then she calls and tells Mom they'll be happy to help. Of course, I'm ecstatic that they changed their minds, and if they're going to do anything, the Moon Walk is the best choice. They do have five kids with one on the way. What a great way to keep track of all of them, huh?"

"I think a lot of people have had a change of heart, Charlie," Jean said. "Even Jake Somersby, you remember him, he runs that little carnival in Westchester? Well, he offered to haul his Kiddie Train all the way over here, free of charge. It's amazing how people are changing their thinking."

"Well, I have it on very good authority that about a dozen teenage girls said they would babysit the smaller kids for nothing so the parents could have some fun, isn't that great?"

"Oh, do tell how you got *that* information, Miss Sticks-her-nose-in-everyone-else's-business?" Helen asked crudely.

Mary put her hands on her hips and looked over at Helen triumphantly. "I asked them to do it, that's how, Mrs. Smart Mouth, what do you have to say about that?"

"Humph!" Helen sneered but said nothing more.

"Ha! Your bark is *so* not worse than your bite."

Helen childishly stuck out her tongue, but Charlie quickly changed the subject before all hell broke loose. "Mr. Glenshaw has offered to raffle off some of his stained glass potteries and decorative windows, plus selling fifty-fifty tickets. That should bring in a good share of money, not to mention the fact that someone gets half of it."

"Well, I'm proud to say that my sixteen-year-old Jeremy offered to handle the basketball shoot booth." Jean's already large bosom puffed up. "And I didn't even have to ask him, he volunteered."

"Well, good for Jeremy, he's always been terrific at sports," Charlie said, and then she checked the list one last time. She sighed and placed the clipboard on her lap, looking thoughtful. "You know, we owe an awful lot to the Loganberrys. Do you realize that they're handling the picnic entirely on their own? The money part of it, anyway, they're having people come in to set up everything. They even offered Joan of Arc for free pony rides for the kids, as well as supplying the pig for the roast—and that's *in addition* to offering their tennis courts, volleyball courts, and their two horseshoe pits for anyone interested in playing. We have to do something really nice for them after this is all over, agreed?"

"Agreed," Mary and Jean said, and then the three of them all looked over at Helen, who said nothing.

"What?" she asked sharply, acting innocent.

"Do you agree?" they all demanded in unison.

"Yeah, yeah, whatever." She quipped, quickly burying her head in her ledger, and then a few seconds later, her semi-muffled voice came back, unexpectedly. "They happen to have their own petting zoo about a yard away from the main house, too." She glanced over and caught Mary's gaping mouth. "Well, don't look so surprised, Mary—you aren't the only one who asks questions and finds things out, you know. I also have it on good authority that their landscaper offered to ride the kids all over the place on his tractorwell, actually in a wagon hooked to his tractor—they're called hay rides, in case you didn't know." She buried her head in her books once again, and Mary smiled knowingly but wisely said nothing. She liked Helen a lot even though she teased her to distraction, but she also knew that Helen liked her, too, she just didn't show it at all.

"Well, Theodore Loganberry is not only our entertainment, he's our projectionist and offered to show movies in his barn for the older kids after his concert," Charlie added.

"Well, that'll be a first—he doesn't even like kids." Helen scoffed, back to her old, grumpy self.

"He does too," Mary defended.

"And how do you know that, Mary?" Helen challenged, and Mary clicked her tongue.

"I just know, that's all."

"That's what I thought, you don't know diddly."

"I do, too," Mary bantered. "Listen, Helen, just because he never married and doesn't have any kids—"

"Precisely my point." Helen stood up and took a bow, then gave the thumbs-up sign. "Yes! The older and more experienced woman wins yet again." To which, Mary literally growled in irritation.

"All right, girls." Charlie laughed warningly. "Call a truce, will you?"

Helen stuck her tongue out at Mary once again, and Mary simply stuck her nose up in the Air, dismissing her.

Charlie went down the list for the girls. "Now, I'll be handling the egg toss and the treasure hunt, and Jean, you'll be handling the craft booth, right?"

"Right." Jean agreed. "Might as well sell 'em as make 'em."

"Okay, and, Helen, you'll take care of your wood craft booth."

"I can't wait."

"And, Mary, you'll be—"

"Ooh, Charlie, how about a kissing booth? I'd love to handle the kissing booth. Wouldn't that be a great idea, guys?"

"No, Mary, it would not be a great idea," Charlie said without a moment's hesitation as Paul's image immediately popped into her mind. "Absolutely no kissing booth."

"Well, why in the world not?" She was absolutely sulky. "Other fairs have them, why can't we?"

"Shame on you, Mary, you're engaged to Tom, for heaven's sake. Why in the world would you want to kiss someone else?" Jean asked, shocked.

"Well—" Mary hedged. "It doesn't mean anything, it's just for fun."

"Well, well, well! It seems that Little Miss Innocent isn't so innocent after all, eh?" Helen interjected sarcastically. "Whatsa matter, Mary, not satisfied with Tom's kisses? Wanna play the field a little, do ya?"

"Be quiet, Helen, no one asked your opinion."

"Yeah, well I'm givin' it. It's about time you showed the real you—that shy little Mary Poppins routine was really getting on my nerves—no one is that innocent. Yessiree, this sure puts things in a whole new light for me."

"Helen, so help me—" Mary countered, but Charlie stopped her where she stood.

"All right, that's enough out of both of you. The kissing booth is out, and I don't want to hear another word about it. Mary, you're on the Christmas ornaments booth with your angels, and that's *all* you're on. And that just leaves the wood chopping contest for Mr. Weatherby," Charlie concluded, slamming her notebook shut. She took a deep breath and let it out. "Well, I'd say we're all set. Good job, ladies, you should give yourselves a big hand, this barbeque picnic is going to rock!"

Mary and Jean began to clap, and Helen let out a dispirited "Yipee."

The girls even decided to go door to door again in the hope of perhaps getting some of the citizens to reconsider their original decision not to be involved and did manage to get a few yeses this time. Charlie also spent the next two Sundays with the children at Sunday school, deciding which pictures of the three wise men they would use for the manger, planning their party, and even singing Christmas carols to stay in practice.

Then, the Mother's Day raffle finally arrived, and all plans for the barbeque were temporarily put on hold. It looked as though the entire community had turned out to see who would win the beautiful, brand-new, thirty-two-inch television set Zeke had offered for a prize, but since his pizza shop wasn't very big, the huge crowd overflowed out the door, onto the sidewalk, and into the street. Two-thousand tickets had been pre-sold—most of them at three tickets for two-fifty, excluding some stragglers who would purchase them at the event, and they already had an estimate of the profits. But with so many people turning out, Charlie was fairly certain that they not only hoped to hear their number called, they wanted to hear the total money collected for the campaign too.

"Okay, everybody, check your tickets because here we go!" Zeke called out through the megaphone while spinning the huge barrel filled with raffle tickets. "Can we have one of the little people come up and draw the lucky ticket?" He was referring to the children in the group, and dozens of little hands began frantically waving their hands in the air. "Well, the first hand I saw go up was little Jimmy Gibbons. Big Jim, as you know, runs Gibbons Jewelers just two doors down. Come on up here, Jimmy, we have a lot of anxious people waiting!"

Jimmy fought his way to the entrance of the pizza shop, then he turned around and grinned, showing two empty spaces where his front teeth had been, and the crowd laughed out loud.

"Better watch out, Jim!" someone yelled from the crowd. "Someone might knock out your other teeth if you don't pull their number."

"Yeah," someone else yelled. "And you don't have many in there to lose."

The crowd roared, and the mischievous little six-year old stuck out his tongue playfully.

Zeke then opened the door and lifted Jimmy up to reach into the barrel. He shuffled the tickets around and around before finally pulling one out and holding it up in the air.

"I got one, I got one!" he shouted. "Read it, Mr. Zeke, read it. Maybe it's my daddy's."

The crowd laughed again but grew silent as Zeke held up the ticket and squinted, trying to read it. "Let's see, the winner is lucky ticket number four, five, seven, two, four—" He hesitated before reading the last number, and the crowd began to boo and heckle him to "read it already."

"Three!" he said finally, and a cheer went up from the crowd as he began to read the name. "The lucky winner is—"

"Me!" Someone shouted from the middle of the crowd. "That's my number."

As the noise died down, Zeke was finally able to speak. "As I was saying, the winner of the television set is none other than Me. And for those of you who don't know who Me is, it's our own school maintenance man, Ted Carpenter. Congratulations, Ted, it couldn't have happened to a nicer guy."

Everyone in the community knew Ted and the fact that he lost nearly everything he owned in a devastating fire that had swept through his trailer home the year before. He'd had most of his furniture, clothing, and necessities replaced through the Red Cross, the Salvation Army, and many of the townspeople—everything but his most prized possession, his television set. At the time, he was asked what else he needed, he'd left out the fact that it too had been destroyed, considering it an unnecessary expense, although in reality it was the only thing he seemed to enjoy. Everyone was happy for him and not in the least bit disappointed that their ticket wasn't called, and they cheered his good fortune.

After the chaos finally died down, Zeke made another announcement. "And now, I'm proud to tell you that through all your efforts, at final count, we've managed to collect one thousand two hundred and fifty dollars toward Charlie's Bring Back Christmas campaign! Charlie, come on up here and say a few words to these fine citizens!"

Charlie slowly made her way up to the front of the cheering crowd, embarrassed at being the center of attention and not at all willing to take the credit. "First of all, I would like to clarify that the Bring Back Christmas campaign is not just mine, it belongs to every citizen in Braxton, and I am so proud of all of you for showing your support and giving so much to make this happen."

The crowd once again cheered, and it was several minutes before the clamor subsided and she was able to continue. "I'm excited to report that with the total of all profits from this raffle and the car

wash, we have one heck of a start on making our project work."
Then, over the crowd's noisy whoops and hollers of joy, she yelled,
"And with Miss Jenny's fourth grade dance recital scheduled on
Flag Day, the barbeque on the Fourth of July, and the craft show
being held in August, we may not be able to have everything we
need, but we can definitely have a wonderful Christmas in Braxton
this year, thank you, everyone!"

While the cheers subsided and the crowd began to dissipate,
Charlie went to stand with her mother.

"Do you see how perseverance pays off, dear?" she asked, hugging
her daughter. "You're really working hard to make this dream of
yours a success, and I am so proud of you, Charlie."

"Well, I have a lot of help. I couldn't have done this alone, that's
for sure, and I really have you to thank for giving me that extra
boost." She kissed her on the cheek and handed her a gift. "Happy
Mother's Day, Mom."

"What's this?" DeeDee asked, taking the small package from
her daughter.

"Well, it is Mother's Day, did you think I forgot?"

"Well, you have been busy," her mother remarked, tearing open
the package. "I guess I didn't really expect anything."

"I just hope you like it."

DeeDee quickly ripped the paper from the small box, and her
breath caught in her throat when she lifted the lid. Inside the box,
nestled in the fluff of cotton, was a beautiful gold heart with two
little diamond chips on either side of the curves of the heart, and
there was a crack carved down the middle. On one side of the crack
written in beautiful calligraphy was the name Pete, and on the
other side was the name DeeDee.

"Charlie, it's the heart Pete gave me on our wedding day, but
this was lost years ago. Wherever did you—"

"I have a confession to make, Mom," she said quietly. "Do you
remember that old shoe box where I kept my secrets? They were all
the things I didn't want anyone to see."

"Yes, I remember—you kept things like your dad's old Air Force wings, little trinkets you received for your birthdays, and even some lucky stones and seashells if I remember correctly. I'd completely forgotten about that box—I haven't seen it for years."

"Yes, but what you didn't know was that I also put things in there that you gave me, like the necklace you bought me with my birthstone, things I hid in there whenever I got upset with you and wouldn't wear it, and the reason you never saw the box is because I hid it under a loose floorboard in my closet. I'd forgotten all about the box too until maybe a month ago when I was looking for something and accidentally hit the loose board and remembered that's where I used to hide my little box. So when I pulled it out and looked inside, I found the heart."

"All these years I thought I'd misplaced it." There was sadness in her voice that nearly broke Charlie's heart as she watched her finger the pendent lovingly, and when she looked at Charlie, there were tears in her eyes. "I don't understand—how did it get there?"

"I didn't have any idea how it got there either at first, but then I remembered the day I took it and hid it in the box. At the time, I was pretty mad at you for marrying Pete. You were with him a lot, and I felt like you didn't care if I was around or not, so I guess I thought if I took it and hid it in the box, you couldn't wear it—just like I hid the necklace you gave me and never wore it."

DeeDee looked lovingly at her daughter. "I never dreamed you felt that strongly about me marrying Pete. I mean I knew you were upset, but I guess I thought it was just a phase and you would get over it. Or maybe I didn't see it then because I was too wrapped up in my own happiness to think about yours. I'm sorry, Charlie."

"You cared about how I felt, Mom, you told me all the time, but I was just acting like a spoiled brat and didn't want to share you with anyone, I guess. It was in pretty bad shape when I found it though—I guess I was pretty rough with it because it had a lot of little scratches on it and one of the diamonds was missing. So I took it to Gibbon's Jewelers and had them clean it up and buff out the scratches and had him replace the diamond." She touched the pendent carefully. "You know, for the longest time, I couldn't figure out why there was a crack down the middle of the heart. I was so young that I probably thought I did it somehow which was all the more reason to keep it hidden, I guess, but Jim explained that Pete actually had it made that way. He knew how broken-hearted you were when Dad died, and when he asked you to marry him, he purposely had that heart made with a crack—a mended crack—to show you that he loved you enough to want to put your heart back together again. So when I found the heart, I realized how much it meant to you and Mother's Day seemed like the perfect day to give it back."

"Thank you, Charlie. You have no idea what this means to me." She touched her daughter's face gently. "But you have to know that I would never have married Pete if I'd realized how much it bothered you."

"I know that, but I probably would have thought that about anyone you were dated. Look, the fact that Pete and I don't see eye to eye doesn't change how you feel about each other. We'll probably always have our problems, but you love him and that's all that matters. I'm just sorry it took me so long to realize it."

Charlie learned a lot about herself on Mother's Day as well as about her mother and stepfather. DeeDee was a smart woman, and she would never have married Pete if she thought he wasn't right for her, although she might have put her happiness on hold if she had known her daughter was so unhappy, so in some ways, omission of the truth was a good thing. And even though Charlie knew that they would more than likely continue to have problems, she could live with it knowing how happy he made her mother.

The Mother's Day raffle seemed to really kick things into gear, and the townspeople seemed more interested than ever in Charlie's campaign. They began holding private garage sales and offering the proceeds to the campaign, and many of them even solicited for money by going door to door for the cause as well as doing anything they could think of to raise money during the next month to keep the project moving. The older children even got into the act by collecting bottles for refunds, mowing lawns, and babysitting and deposited their proceeds into the Bring Back Christmas account at the bank.

In the meantime, the girls at the office continued making even more crafts while Charlie worked relentlessly with the smaller children in an effort to keep them focused on the play in the midst of all the chaos. And when cries of "But I wanna play Mary!" "No, I want to play Mary!" And "I don't wanna play a dum-ole sheep!" became too frequent, Charlie finally decided that in fairness to everyone so no one would get slighted, she would do it the democratic way—pull the names from a hat.

In addition to all the bedlam of the play, the day of the dance recital with Jenny's Little Butterflies troupe came and went with only one or two mishaps: two little girls colliding with one another, and one other little tyke not able to perform because she had the jitters and "frowed up" and had to go home. Everything considered, it was an exciting day for the fourth grade class, and they made a whopping four hundred dollars on the recital, not bad at all for a dreary, rain-soaked day that produced soggy butterfly wings, wet and drooping antennae, and children too tired and cross from flitting around the stage to behave like little ladies.

In the interim, more and more people were becoming involved and offering whatever they could in the way of donations, new craft ideas, and bake-offs to try and raise money for their affair. Days turned into weeks, and before they knew it, the day of the barbeque had arrived.

Because of the influx of cars and people jamming the makeshift parking lot set up on one of the Loganberry's many acres, it was close to one o'clock before the girls met at the entrance while they had agreed to meet at twelve, and Charlie was nervous.

"Everything will be fine, Charlie." Jean reassured her when they finally made it through the crowd and walked under the high arch spanning the entryway onto the property. "Just look at the people, everyone in town must be here, including all their friends and relatives."

But Charlie barely noticed the people; she was too distracted by the sign, "Loganberry Dairy Farm," which now had an addition beneath it which read, 'Welcome to the Annual Bring Back Christmas Festival'. It was the lovely little word *annual* that brought instant tears to Charlie's eyes as well as renewing her initial excitement to bring Christmas back to Braxton. After all, if Eleanor Loganberry had confidence enough to believe that Charlie's plan would become a successful yearly event, why shouldn't she?

"You really did it, Charlie." Mary's eyes sparkled. "And do the Loganberrys know how to throw a barbeque or what? Look at all the food stands, there are dozens of them! And look over there!" She pointed to the immense barbeque pit situated in the middle of the lawn to the right of the driveway. "They're roasting a whole pig— I've never seen a pig so big!" She was as animated as the children, whose squeals of delight could be heard echoing throughout the estate grounds.

As they walked up the long driveway, they couldn't help marveling at the exquisite salmon-hued cobblestone pavers, each one expertly placed with extraordinary precision and looking brand-new as though they'd just been laid. And bordering the extravagant driveway on either side were sunflowers seemingly the size of small trees, with booths situated neatly between them. Mary was right; there were dozens of them and even more along the inner perimeter of the circular drive at the base of the rounded pink marble staircase leading up to the elegant entrance of the stately mansion.

"This driveway must have cost them a fortune." Mary was awestruck, but Helen wasn't the least bit impressed.

"They can afford it," she said sarcastically.

"It is beautiful, isn't it?" Charlie had only admiration for the Loganberry's love of beauty and their ability to blend it in with nature.

"I've only seen things like this in magazines." Jean was captivated. "It's like it belongs in the middle of a storybook forest, it's so breathtaking."

Well, it's a damn waste of good money if you ask me!" Helen added, and Jean batted her lightly on the arm.

"Could you at least *try* to understand their reasons, Helen? The Loganberrys are sponsoring this festival out of the pure goodness of their hearts, not to gloat about their good fortune. Not to mention the fact that without their help, we wouldn't have a chance of this plan working."

"Yeah, well, I think they're just showing off. I can think of good and practical ways to spend my money is all I'm saying."

"Yes, well, it's not your money, now is it?" Jean shot back, and with that, Helen was put in her place.

The thrill of actually seeing the much talked about eighteen-room English Tudor mansion made it feel like a step back in time for Charlie. From the intricate black ornamental iron railings that bordered the rounded marble steps to the elaborate stained glass double doors of the entrance—it was, quite simply, a magnificent work of art.

Upon reaching the circular drive at the entrance, the girls opted to follow the cobblestone path as it wound around the side of the mansion and out into the back courtyard, continuing on toward the carriage house. And of course as was appropriate and in the true spirit of the fundraiser, Christmas carols played softly in the background.

As the girls strolled from booth to booth while waiting for their shifts to begin, they couldn't help remarking about how beautiful and original each craft was. The talent of each contributor was remarkable. Their incredible works of art ranging from wood carvings to pot holders, lace angels to jewelry, and hand-sewn quilts to Christmas wreaths, including those made by the girls, would have impressed the most scrupulous dealer. Each lovely craft was in a category all its own.

"You know, Helen, you really outdid yourself with those little red wagons, they look great—really professional," Mary remarked, forgetting their fight, and Helen just grunted her thanks or a facsimile thereof.

"It's just something I do is all—nothing special."

"How can you say that? Just look at the detail on them, they certainly are special. You know you don't give yourself enough credit, Helen. I *know* my worth—without sounding conceited of course—but you don't even see the talent you have and maybe that's your problem. I've noticed for a long time now that you just don't—"

"Okay, okay! So they're good, quit trying to butter me up, Forsythe."

"I am not trying to butter you up, I am just saying that you should be proud of the—"

"Okay, I'm proud, you happy now? Geez, knock it off, will ya?"

"Girls, give it a rest," Jean said tiredly. "Can't you both just try and get along for once?

Your constant bickering is giving me a headache, and I would like to enjoy myself today."

"Well, geez, who bit your nose?" Helen's tone was caustic. "You sure are touchy these days, Jean."

Jean stared at Helen for a few seconds and opened her mouth to say something and then thought better about it. She just rolled her eyes and shook her head, knowing it just wasn't worth it. Though she loved her like a sister, most times, Helen had no clue how annoying she could be.

A short time later, after playing the penny pitch and winning a whopping two dollars and seventy-five cents, Mary stopped dead in her tracks and sniffed the air, causing Helen to run smack into her.

"What the heck—" Helen said, annoyed. "Why don't you watch what you're doing?"

"Oooh, can't you smell that?" Mary ignored her, taking in another deep breath. "It's heavenly!" The succulent aromas of home-made pies, funnel cakes, barbequed pork, and freshly baked bread intermingled, wafting past their eager noses, and they hurried over to the food booths.

While the other girls continued their stroll from booth to booth examining all the different crafts and merchandise for sale, Charlie stayed behind munching on a piece of funnel cake. A few minutes later, she felt a gentle tug on her shirt and looked down to see little Amanda Daywood smiling up at her.

"Hello, Miss Faraday."

"Well, hello, Amanda! How are you?"

"Good," the little girl answered. "I just winned a teddy bear, see?" She proudly held it out at arm's length. "I winned it at the fish pond."

"You mean you won it at the fish pond."

"That's what I said, I winned it at the fish pond."

Charlie glanced around. "Where is your family, Amanda? You aren't here all alone, are you?"

"No, a'course not, my mommy's right over there—" She pointed to the Moon Walk. "I got a little sick in my tummy, and she told me I shouldn't go back inside for a while."

"Oh, I see," Charlie said solemnly.

"Wanna ride the train with me?" she asked out of the blue, and Charlie smiled down at her.

"Well, it's very nice of you to ask, Amanda, but I'm afraid I'm a little too big to ride the train."

"Oh, you're not so big, lotsa mommies ride the train." She looked toward the Moon Walk ride. "'Cept my mommy, she's too big." She looked up at Charlie somberly. "She has a baby in her tummy."

"Yes, I know, and I'll bet you're excited, aren't you? Just think, pretty soon, you'll have a little baby brother or sister."

"I want a baby sister, I already have a baby brother. Acshally, I have three brothers. They fight a lot." She sighed, sounding older than her five years. She pulled a piece of cotton candy from a huge cloud of pink fluff and popped it into her mouth. "Do you have any brothers?"

"No, I'm afraid not. I'm the only one in my family."

"Oh." She popped another tuft of the sticky stuff into her mouth, and Charlie cringed, envisioning her bouncing off the walls later that night from sugar overload. "The doctor says Mommy can't keep havin' babies 'cause she'll get sick, an' Daddy says we have anuff already an' we don't have money for anymore. He just got laid off work." She looked up at Charlie. "What does laid off work mean, Miss Faraday?"

Charlie couldn't help feeling sorry for the little girl, but she was extremely uncomfortable hearing about the family's problems. She was just glad that they decided to join in the festivities—at least they didn't have to spend much money for a good time.

She was about to suggest that Amanda go and check in with her mother and let her know she was all right, when she heard Mrs. Daywood's worried voice call out her daughter's name. When she spied her standing with Charlie, she hurried over to her side and, with much effort, knelt down and gently grasped her daughter by the arms.

"Amanda, honey, you know you aren't supposed to wander off. I've been worried sick!" She fiercely hugged the little girl for several long seconds, but when she tried to stand, she had a difficult time of it, and Charlie reached out a helping hand. She gratefully took hold of it and managed to stand up.

"I'm so sorry, Mrs. Daywood. If I had known you were looking for Amanda—"

"No, please don't apologize, Charlie. This isn't the first time she's done this. I'm just so grateful that she wasn't, well, that she was with you." She finished and then looked sternly down at her daughter. "You know better than to wander off without telling me or Daddy, don't you, Amanda?"

"Yes, Mommy," the little girl said meekly. "But I wasn't too far, I was just here."

"Yes, but I didn't know you were here, and you know you are never, ever to go off by yourself. Mommy and Daddy have told you that time and time again, haven't we?"

"Yes, Mommy," she said quietly. "I'm sorry."

"I'll tell you what, Amanda—" Charlie grabbed the little girl's hand after seeing a tear slide down her cheek. "If it's okay with your mommy, maybe we can take that ride on the train together."

"Oh, please, Mommy, can I go on the train ride, *please?* I won't never go away by myself again, I won't, never! Please, please can I go?"

Charlie looked at Mrs. Daywood expectantly, and though the woman hesitated for a moment, she smiled slightly and nodded.

"You can go, but don't let go of her Miss Faraday's hand for any reason, do you understand?"

"Oh, yes, Mommy!" She gripped Charlie's hand tightly. "I won't let go, I promise."

"Here, let me hold that until you come back." She took the cotton candy from her daughter and reached into her oversized handbag and came out with a packet of wet baby cloths. She popped one out of the container and handed it to Amanda. "Here, wipe your hands. I'm sure Miss Faraday doesn't want that sticky mess all over her nice clothes." She took one out for herself and wiped a bit of the stickiness from her own hands. "Your father bought this for you, didn't he?" she asked, shaking her head and half-smiling at Charlie. "Men! You would think they would know better, wouldn't you? She'll be up all night if she eats this entire thing."

"Can we go now, Mommy?" Amanda asked impatiently. "The train will be leaving soon."

"If you wouldn't mind bringing her back to the Moon Walk, Charlie, I would really appreciate it. Someone is coming to take over so that I can at least get something substantial into their stomachs before they fill up on junk, and they should be there by the time you get back."

"Sure. Since I do have to come back and set up for the Egg Toss and then get the straw spread out and the gifts hidden for the Treasure Hunt, bringing her back here won't be a problem. Oh! And don't forget to bring your children to the Hunt, okay? I'm sure they'll have a great time—we have a lot of really nice things for them to find." She looked down at the little girl and wiggled her hand slightly. "Well, if we're going to make the train, we'd better get going, what do you think? I just heard the whistle blow." She looked back at Mrs. Daywood. "She'll be fine. We'll be back shortly."

"Bye, Mommy!" Amanda said, tugging on Charlie's hand. "We'll see you shortly." She called over her shoulder, mimicking Charlie and then, "Hurry, Miss Faraday, we don't wanna to miss the train!"

Fifteen minutes later, with Amanda returned safely to her family, Charlie finished setting up for the Egg Toss and people started lining up.

"Okay, here are the rules of the game," she announced a few minutes later. "If you haven't chosen a partner yet, please do find one and form two lines on either side of me about five feet apart. Cameron, the young man standing beside me, will then hand an egg to each of you in the row next to me and at my signal, you'll toss it to your partner on the opposite side. If you catch it and it doesn't break, you'll still be in the game. I sure hope no one wore their good clothes today because eggs sure are messy when they break. Now, do you all understand the directions so far?"

"Man! This is too easy!" one young boy shouted.

"Yeah, I can win this with my eyes closed!" another one yelled.

"Okay, all you smarty pants, here's the hard part, after all of the eggs have been tossed to the other side, everyone is to take two giant steps backward, and no cheating, I'll be watching. Then everyone will toss their egg back to their partner, and the same rules apply: if you catch the egg and it's not broken, you'll still be in the game, but if the egg breaks, you'll not only be eliminated, you'll be covered in egg yolk."

Among cries of "Ew, gross!" and "Oh, yuck!" and "Aw man, that's jive!" Charlie shouted, "This will continue until there's only one couple left with their egg intact, and they'll be the winners. If everyone ends up with a broken egg, the couple who lasted the longest gets a consolation prize. Now, everybody, get ready! Get set! Go!"

The first toss was a success, as was the second and third, but with the fourth, splats were heard one after the other from both lines as eggs hit faces, heads, chests—anywhere they found a target. When the lines were moved back still farther, it was down to only two couples—a man and his wife and a brother and sister. Charlie yelled, "Go!" and the husband fired an egg at his wife, hitting her dead center in the middle of her glasses, and while everyone watched her chase him clear across the lawn, tossing one egg after another at him, the two siblings handed their unbroken eggs to Charlie and happily walked away with their prizes.

Soon afterward, Charlie made the announcement that all the children should gather in the middle of the huge courtyard in the back of the mansion to get ready for the big Treasure Hunt, and children of all ages and sizes ran full-tilt onto the back lawn and stood anxiously waiting in line.

"Okay!" Charlie yelled into the megaphone. "I want all parents of one to three year olds to bring your children over to stand beside me. All four to six year olds are to stand next to Miss Loganberry under the green umbrella, and all children from seven to ten will stand with Mr. Loganberry under the yellow umbrella." She looked around to see that all children were grouped and made a final announcement that if anyone noticed a child not already in a group, would they please show them the way into the courtyard. "All right, everyone, each group will have ten minutes to look for prizes. Parents, please stay behind the yellow caution tape. For those children who have difficulty finding a prize or holding on to to it, the younger teenagers will be sent in to help. Now, at the sound of the cap gun, the first group will start, so let's all be quiet so we can hear the signal." She began the count down from five seconds, and when she reached one, the gun went off and all the tiny people were seen running helter-skelter toward the bed of straw and diving into it. Soon afterward, all you could see were little heads bobbing up and down everywhere as they searched for treasures.

"Okay, just five more minutes before the gun goes off and your turn is over. Then, you'll have to hurry to your parents so the next group can have their turn, okay?" she announced, and the other two groups began cheering them on. Five minutes later, the gun went off, and each child stood up one by one, holding prizes. Charlie looked around, making certain that no one left without at least one prize in their possession; although she had no idea what kinds of prizes were hidden as their most generous hostess, Eleanor Loganberry, provided all of the bounty. However, she was truly amazed to later learn that not only were there toys, there were also certificates for shoes, clothing, and food hidden among the treasures. And when the stock was depleted before everyone could discover a prize, Eleanor simply had her little elves scurry in and replenish them; she too, claiming that no child would walk away empty-handed. For older children eleven to fifteen, they could win prizes by sinking baskets at the basketball shoot, and by the end of the games, every child in attendance gleefully walked away with at least two cherished prizes.

The remainder of the afternoon went by much too fast, but Charlie was happy to see that whether the people were manning booths, playing one of the many games that had been set up, browsing through the craft booths looking for that special something, or simply lazing in the fresh air and sunshine for a change, it didn't seem to matter. It was obvious that they were enjoying themselves, especially later on that evening when Theodore Loganberry put on a fabulous two-hour concert. Everyone, including the children, seemed mesmerized by his ability to play everything from classical and jazz to pop and rock. He truly was a magnificent pianist, and by the looks on everyone's faces he'd made a smash hit.

As far as she could tell, the picnic was a huge success, and everything was going far better than she could ever have hoped. That is until the sun went down. And though it wasn't a sudden chill in the air that settled over her like a wet blanket, something completely changed her attitude.

"Why didn't someone set up a kissing booth?" a voice behind her asked, and Charlie swung around to see Paul Torrance clad in a sky-blue polo shirt and jeans standing behind right behind her, looking wonderful as usual.

"That's quite a loaded question coming from you, don't you think?" Charlie asked, remembering his last kiss.

"Every fair I've ever been to had a kissing booth, why don't you?"

"Because one never knows who they are going to have to kiss, and in order to prevent the humiliation of possible rejection, we voted against it." She didn't miss a beat, but Paul didn't flinch.

"Was that your idea?" he countered, and Charlie's eyes narrowed.

"Now, why would you think that?" she asked, avoiding his original question. "And what possible difference could that make to you?"

"Then you *were* the one to veto the vote."

"There were others involved in the decision."

"Uh huh, but you were the deciding factor."

"No, not exactly."

He cocked his head to one side suspiciously and wagged his finger at her. "Oh, what tangled webs we weave when first we practice to deceive."

"You should know." She turned away from him and started toward the courtyard. "Excuse me, I have things to do."

"Such as?"

"Such as cleaning up the egg yolks and straw all over the courtyard lawn if you must know."

"It's already done."

"Oh, really?"

"Yes, really. Anything else?" His intensely watchful eyes were beginning to make her nervous, but she refused to let it sway her. She was still mad, and she was going to stay mad.

"Well, you just have to look around to see that there is still a lot that has to be done to get the estate back the way it was."

"You know they have a maintenance crew to do all that. I have it on good authority that they don't need your help."

"Whose good authority?"

"Mine."

"Oh really? Since when?"

"Since a few minutes ago when I spoke to Theodore Loganberry."

"Well, fine then. I still have to gather my things together and get ready to leave."

"It's only seven forty-five, isn't it kind of early?"

"I'm very tired." Her petulance sounded out of character.

"You were raring to go to get this place cleaned up a few minutes ago."

"That's different."

"How so?"

"Because I planned to help, and—"

"And now it's done. Next?"

"I, we, that is, the girls and I—"

"You're stuttering."

"I am not stuttering."

He leaned closer. "Ride the Ferris wheel with me."

Charlie backed away. "No."

"Come on, ride the Ferris wheel with me, Charlie." He tempted, his voice deep and persuasive. "Just one ride."

"No. I don't like Ferris wheels." There was no way she was getting on that ride with him, not with the seats in such close proximity.

"Then take a walk with me around the grounds. The moon is out."

Now that was totally out of the question, she thought. "I don't think so."

"Then let me walk you to your car."

"I didn't drive, I walked." *Damn! Bad move, Charlie—now he's going to ask to walk you home.*

"Then let me walk you home."

Didn't I tell you? "No, I don't think so. I'm supposed to meet the girls soon, and I don't want them to think—"

"Come on give me a break, here, Charlie. I'm trying to be nice."

Charlie stopped and turned around to face him. "You're *trying* to be nice? Well, do yourself and me a big fat favor, don't bother!"

"You know what I mean, it came out wrong."

"No, it came out right because according to you, you never say anything you don't mean, remember?"

"Can I tell you something?"

"I'd rather you didn't."

"Look, when I kissed you that day—"

"I don't want to hear this." She held her ears and spun around to leave, but he grabbed her arm and swung her back around and grabbed her other arm.

"Oh no, you don't, you're not doing that to me a second time, oh hell! Come here!" He pulled her to him and kissed her hard, not a punishing kiss, but a too-sexy kiss, a kiss to top all kisses, a kiss meant only for the night, behind closed doors. And right when she started to pull away her bruised lips, he wrapped his arms around her and the kiss changed and became softer, gentler and wonderfully long and luxurious, a kiss that made her toes curl, her head spin, and even dulled the sound of the fireworks going off in the background—except that there were no fireworks going off in the background.

And then after what seemed an eternity, he pulled back slightly, still holding her in his arms. "*That* is what I wanted to do to you that day I kissed you and the reason I apologized. It had nothing to do with you not measuring up but everything to do with how I felt."

Stunned, her resentment spent, Charlie couldn't speak. It was moments later when she felt Paul's arms tighten around her that she fully understood the impact of his words.

"Now do you understand why I said what I did?" he asked quietly.

"Well, couldn't you have just told me?"

"First of all, you took off and didn't give me a chance to tell you anything. Secondly, what was I supposed to tell you, Charlie? That I didn't want to kiss you because I wanted to take you right there in the gazebo? Or that I had everything all figured out in my life but then you came along and those plans went to hell?"

She so wanted to sound nonchalant, but her nerves were standing on end and her knees felt like mushy Jell-O. Besides, after what he'd just said she could barely stand up straight let alone think straight. "I didn't realize—"

"There's a lot you don't realize, Charlie," he said as he cupped her face in his hands tenderly. "Like how your eyes turn to dark emerald when you're mad as hell at me but get pale and almost transparent when you're happy to see me. They tell me things you can't."

She couldn't deny it, her betraying eyes wouldn't let her. Worse still, her heart betrayed her too because she knew without any doubt that she loved him. It was too soon. He was little more than a stranger to her. Yet she knew the minute she laid eyes on him that she wanted to be with him for the rest of her life, but was that enough for him? Just like wanting her whole old-fashioned Bring Back Christmas wish with all the peace and joy and happiness, she wanted the whole "walk down the aisle, happily ever after" fairy tale, but did he just want to divide and conquer and move on?

"Hey, Charlie!" Mary came from behind one of the refreshment booths. "Are you coming or what?"

Charlie looked up at Paul, and he nodded. "Go ahead, they're waiting for you."

"Yes, but—"

"Go!" he said, giving her a playful push. "I'll be around."

An odd look crossed Charlie's face as she walked toward Mary. He'll be around? He practically set her world on fire just a few minutes before, and all he could say was he'll be around? That's exactly what she was afraid of. Once she gave him her heart, what would he do with it?

"Come on, Charlie, we don't have all night—we were supposed to pick up Jeremy at the entrance a half hour ago," Mary yelled, and a confused Charlie quickly turned and walked toward her friend.

It was close to eleven when Charlie got home and she found her mother sitting at the kitchen table reading a book. "You're still up? I would have thought you'd be in bed by now." She opened the refrigerator and took out a bottle of milk and held up the carton. "Milk?" she asked, and without looking up from her book, her mother shook her head.

"No, thanks."

Charlie grabbed a glass out of the cupboard, poured herself a glass, and put the carton back on the shelf and closed the door. She took a large swallow of milk and sat down. "The Treasure Hunt and

Egg Toss were great. The kids loved them. There was egg yolk all over the place." She took another sip of milk. "How'd the Bakery Booth go? I was going to stop back for some croissants, but I got a little tied up with the girls and didn't make it. Then it was so crowded, we could barely get out of there. The Loganberrys put on a really great picnic, don't you think? Is that book a good one?"

DeeDee finally put the book face down on the table. "I'm glad to hear that the kids liked the games, the bakery went pretty well, it wouldn't have done you any good to stop by anyway because the croissants were all gone in half an hour, the picnic was fabulous, and the book is a good one, yes."

"Oh." She took another sip of milk. "Where's Pete?"

"He went to bed early. Charlie, do you have something on your—"

"Mom, can I ask you something?"

DeeDee smiled indulgently. "You can ask me anything, Charlie, you know that."

"When you first met Dad, how long was it before you knew you loved him?"

"The first time I saw him." DeeDee smiled and answered without hesitation.

"Really?"

"Really. He came into the hospital where I was volunteering and waited for his buddy to get sewn up."

"And?"

"And that was it. I knew then that I was going to marry him."

"Did he feel the same way?"

"I think so. But we played cat and mouse for a while."

"You mean you let him chase you?"

"No, I mean I chased him until I let him catch me." Her mother smiled a beautiful smile then, remembering. "I don't mean to give you the impression that I was a tease, I just mean that I believed he loved me, but I had to make sure he was ready. So I didn't tell him I loved him until he figured out that he loved me. It's a toss-up as to who told who first." She looked at her daughter and caught the unguarded look in her eyes and suddenly understood the reason for her questions. "Oh, Charlie," she whispered softly, reaching over and covering her daughter's hand, and Charlie looked over at her, surprised.

"What? Why are you looking at me like that?"

"It is Paul we're talking about, isn't it?" she asked, and Charlie just looked at her. "You're in love with him," she said simply, and Charlie's eyes glistened with unshed tears. She set her glass on the table and began tracing its rim. "You're not sure he feels the same way and you're afraid to take a chance?" It was more of a statement than a question, but Charlie nodded.

"Both, I guess."

"Oh, honey, I'm so sorry. Is there anything I can do?"

"I don't think anyone can do anything. This is just something I have to work out for myself, I guess."

"Is it really all that hard to figure out, Charlie, or are you afraid to try?"

"I'm not sure, maybe. It's just that I feel, I don't know, different with Paul. I mean, I've dated guys I liked a lot and maybe even loved some of them, but I'm just afraid that—"

"There are no guarantees in life, Charlie, sometimes you just have to take a chance. If it doesn't work out, you may have a broken heart for a while, but at least you tried. But one thing is for sure, you'll never know unless you do. I was crazy about your dad and he felt the same way about me, but we played the game of trying to figure each other so long that we lost precious time we could have been together, and that's all I thought about when he died. So don't play the game, Charlie. It's a game you could lose."

CHAPTER V

Sunday morning blended into the afternoon as Charlie, the girls, and several volunteers counted the money from the festival, but she'd been doing a lot of thinking at the same time—too much thinking.

Charlie understood exactly what her mother was trying to tell her and it made sense. She could take her chances and come right out and tell Paul she loved him, and if he loved her back, it would be like landing on soft grass. Then again, if he told her he didn't love her—

Charlie suddenly realized she'd lost track of her count for the fourth time and decided she'd better leave her love life to the fates for the time being. As it was, they didn't finish counting until shortly before dinnertime, leaving Charlie no choice but to balance the combined profits and expenses from the monies they made so far. And though she had to fight to keep focused on the money and not her heart, she actually had a total to give them Monday morning, but not until long after midnight.

"We had approximately three hundred and eighty-three families, including friends and relatives, although I'm sure there were far more than that." She began at coffee break. "And according to my calculations, at five dollars per family, plus all the money from the crafts, the paintings, the candles, and all the other items that were bought—and this is excluding what we made on the raffle, the dance recital, or the craft show coming up—" She hit the total button. "We made five thousand, five hundred, and eighty dollars. And I'm sure when we add everything in that we've made so far, we're going to be able to pull this off."

"It's a drop in the bucket." Helen sneered, and Jean immediately berated her.

"Aw, come on, Helen, quit trying to put a damper on things. That's a lot of money."

"It's chickenfeed," she argued, glaring at the older woman. "That won't cover half or even a quarter of the things Miss Money-bags Charlie has plans for." She stood up and joined the others. "What is wrong with you people? Don't you understand that it's going to take money—a lot of money—just to string lights along one lousy city block? And forget about the covered bridge fairy tale—you couldn't fix that thing if you had a magic lamp! And even if you did have the money to do it, which you don't, it could take years! Look, don't you get it? You couldn't raise enough money for this thing in three years, let alone a couple-a months, and you're never going to have enough people to volunteer! You're beating a dead horse and you don't even know it!"

"Well, I'm sure we'll have more volunteers after what happened at the Festival," Charlie explained, but Helen shot her down again.

"To do what, manufacture money? Okay, so maybe you can buy enough lights to make Main Street look all pretty and sparkly and maybe you can buy a gigoonda tree for the middle of the square and decorate it with pretty little baubles and even find enough volunteers to put it up and hang the lights on it. Heck! You might even be able to afford cute little hats for your carol-singing goon squad to keep their little headies warm if you really pinch your pennies. And then maybe, just maybe, you'll even reopen the pond—providing you kill the mayor because that's the only way you'll get him to agree. And then, if you still plan on getting that bridge in shape, which is the dumbest thing I've ever heard because it cannot be done, you'll have to manufacture the money because that's the only way you'll get it. You can have all the volunteers you want, but if you don't have miracle in your pocket, volunteers are *all* you've got. Do yourself a favor: take the money, buy a Merry Christmas wreath, hang it around Braxton's neck, and that's about all you'll get for your trouble. It's a pipe dream, and it's never gonna happen."

"Now that's where you're wrong, missy!" came a voice from the doorway, and Charlie, knowing full well who that voice belonged to, immediately swung her head around to see Matthew Torrance standing in the doorway.

"Matthew!"

"In the flesh, darlin'!"

"What in the world are you doing here?" Happy to see him, she crossed the room to give him a hug.

"Well, I sort of heard through the grapevine that you're down on your luck and think you can't have your Christmas after all."

Charlie wondered how he could have known that, when they were just talking about it, but she felt too deflated to try and figure it out. "Well, I thought we could, but Helen brought up some good points about not having enough money. It is going to take an awful lot to get this to work, and I'm afraid I have to agree with her that it just might not happen—at least not this year."

"Or next year or the year after." Helen snapped.

"Well, I have it on good authority that it *can* happen—and this year too," Matthew said casually, and Charlie's eyes widened.

"You do? Whose authority?"

"Mine, of course!"

"Matthew, what's this all about?"

"Oh, just a little something I have up my sleeve." He winked at Mary, and she blushed.

"Matthew Torrance, you have that look in your eyes! What are you up to?"

"You just wait and see, little darlin', you'll know soon enough! Well, I have a lot to do, so I'd better be moseying along." He turned to walk toward the door, but Charlie caught the sleeve of his shirt and forced him back around.

"Wait a minute, Matthew, how did you know about our money situation?"

"I have my methods," he said evasively, and Charlie shook her head.

"I don't think so. The three of us never talked about it until just this morning—try again."

"Well, I didn't actually hear about this morning's discussion, but I heard something about it the money situation a little while back."

"From whom?" Charlie insisted.

"Oh, let's just say a little birdie told me." He winked at the girls, not meaning a thing, but Charlie misunderstood it to mean that one of them may have been the mouthy bird, and she looked at each one of them individually.

Jean shrugged her shoulders, looking surprised; Mary shook her head looking like the wide-eyed innocent she was; but when Helen said nothing and tried to slip back into her seat unnoticed, Charlie walked toward her desk her gaze unwavering.

"What?" She shook her head and went back to her work.

"Helen, did you say something to Matthew about our money situation?"

She didn't look up from her desk. "How would I tell him? I don't even know the man."

"Well, how did he find out?"

"How the heck should I know?"

"He looked at you." Charlie stated, and that certainly got Helen's attention.

"So, he looked at me, big deal. I'm not *that* bad to look at. Besides, he looked at Mary and Jean too, why don't you ask them?'

"I mean he looked at you," Charlie emphasized. "You know, like you were the 'little birdie who chirped' perhaps?"

"Look. I have never seen nor have I ever spoken to this man. How can you stand there and accuse me like that?" She looked around Charlie at Matthew. "Have we ever met, Gramps?"

"Hey! Watch that Gramps stuff!" He pretended to be insulted, then, "And the answer to your question is no, we have never met." He glanced at Charlie's look of doubt and crossed his heart. "I swear!"

Charlie frowned at Helen. "Then why do you look guilty?"

Helen stood up in a huff. "Now look, Charlie, the only one I ever told about us was Willy, okay? Just Willy and no one else."

"I thought we were keeping this among ourselves." Charlie's frown deepened.

"Willy Grouse?" Matthew piped up, and Helen looked surprised.

"You know my Willy?"

"*Your* Willy? You mean you're actually married to that tightrope walker?"

"I am—do you know my Willy?" She came out from behind her desk, fully interested now.

"Well, I'll be—you're Sweet Pea!"

Helen stopped dead in her tracks while all three girls slowly turned their heads in her direction.

"Sweet Pea?" they all echoed at the same time, their mouths hanging open, and Helen's face turned the most brilliant shade of red they had ever seen.

"Sweet Pea?" Mary bit the insides of her cheeks to keep from grinning. "Willy calls you Sweet Pea?" She looked at the others, her eyes dancing mischievously. "Willy calls Helen Sweet Pea."

Charlie and Jean had to look away, but Mary started to giggle. Soon the laughter was bubbling up inside her and she tried to hold back as long as she could, but she suddenly burst into fits. "Oh, I can't stand it!" She was laughing so hard she had to hold her stomach, and before long, the others were laughing right along with her. "Oh, Helen," she began, trying to catch her breath. "I can think of a dozen nicknames for you, but Sweet Pea sure as heck isn't one of them!" Several guffaws erupted until Mary was laughing uncontrollably and the others couldn't help but join in again. It was as hilarious as it was contagious, but there wasn't a hint of a smile on Helen's face.

"Well, what's so funny, Mary? Are you jealous?"

Her question was Mary's undoing, and she let out another loud guffaw, followed by waves of laughter. "Oh, yeah, that's it!" she said, between fits. "I'm just so upset that I don't have a, a swell name like Sweet Pea!"

Charlie looked sharply at Mary and tried to compose herself, but it was no use; by now Mary was laughing so hard, she was snorting.

Jean had been biting her lip to keep from laughing, but nearly passed out when she heard Mary snort and she let out a rude guffaw of her own. She really hadn't meant to laugh—she'd been trying so hard not to—but Mary's snort had done it. She tried coughing as a cover up, but it was too late—Helen had heard it all.

"Well, it's certainly nice to know who your friends are!" Helen glared at Matthew. "No thanks to you, Gramps!" she said viciously, then turned on her heel and stormed back to her desk in a huff. Meanwhile, Mary doubled over, too overcome with convulsive laughter to even try to control herself and Matthew looked at Charlie a bit shamefaced.

"Well, how was I to know she was Sweet Pea?"

"How *do* you know Willy, Matthew?" Charlie wiped the tears from her eyes while Mary hobbled back to her desk, her entire body in spasm.

"Oh, shut up, Mary!" Helen snapped. "You are so juvenile!"

Mary managed to compose herself and even look indignant for a moment, but it was short-lived. "Well, fine then, be that way, Sweet Pea!" She suddenly burst into another fit of laugher that sounded oddly like a hyena with the hiccoughs. She was laughing so hard, she actually had to leave the room, but they could still hear her halfway down the hall.

"I guess I caused quite a stir." Matthew ran a hand through his graying hair, looking uncomfortable.

"It'll pass," Charlie said, walking toward Matthew again. "It always does. So how do you know Willy?"

"He did a couple of renovating jobs for me, is all," he said, stealing a look at Helen, who was still red in the face while trying to look busy. "Uh, sorry about the slip-up, Helen. I didn't realize that—"

"Don't mention it!" Helen snapped, not lifting her eyes from her desk. "Ever!"

Matthew looked back at Charlie and shrugged his shoulders. "Well, I really have a lot to do, so I'll be seeing you, Charlie, real soon!" He gave her a quick hug and couldn't open the door and get out of there fast enough.

"You're not going to tell me, are you, Matthew?" she asked, as he stepped outside.

"You'll find out soon enough, you take care now, you hear?" He closed the door softly behind him.

"Well, what do you suppose he meant by that?" she murmured to no one in particular, but Helen picked up her cue.

"He's an old man who talks too much, that's what! I wouldn't believe a word he said!"

"Oh, you're just pee-oed 'cause he let the cat out of the bag, Sweet Pea." Mary grinned comically as she entered the room.

"You'd better have your running shoes on, you little backstabber!" Helen's tone was venomous as she jumped up and sprinted around her desk. "Because when I get a hold of you—"

"Girls, girls!" Jean scolded, coming between them. "We'll have none of that." She held them both at arm's length. "Helen, you have got to do something about that temper of yours, and, Mary, you've had your fun, now let it go."

Helen continued to glare at Mary, and Mary stuck out her tongue, which only spurred Helen on. "Ooh, when I get my hands on you—" She tried to push Jean out of the way, but Jean held her ground.

"I'm a lot stronger that you think, Helen," she warned. "Now, back off!"

Helen looked startled and actually backed away. Jean had never shown force of any kind since they'd known her, but they soon found out that she was a definite force to be reckoned with.

"You seem to forget that I have seven kids, and I'm always breaking up fights, now get back to your corners."

Mary slowly backed up to her desk while Helen returned to hers without another word, though they both had eyes fixed on one another. It wasn't until they were in their seats that Jean figured it was safe and then she turned around, rolled her eyes at a surprised Charlie, and returned to her own desk.

"They're worse than my kids," she mumbled, then secretly smiled, feeling very pleased with herself.

Several days went by since Helen and Mary's little tirade, not to mention Matthew's surprise visit. The picnic was over and the money counted, and Charlie still didn't know whether or not they should go ahead with their plans.

"I don't know, maybe Helen is right," she told her mother after dinner one evening. "I'm not sure we'll be able to raise enough money if we waited two years." She blew out a stream of air. "Everything seems to be working against us. The stores don't carry the supplies we need—even Jean is fed up, and she's the positive one of the group. I honestly don't know what to do."

"Have your craft show and whatever else you have planned and cross the bridges as they come," her mother said nonchalantly, and Charlie frowned.

"How is that going to help our money situation?"

"You did make quite a bit so far, Charlie, and you still have more events coming up. You may not be able to do everything you want to do, but it can still be a wonderful Christmas celebration for Braxton, and everyone will appreciate the effort you've put forth."

"Mom, have you heard anything I've said? This thing is going to fall apart, and you're talking about still having the Christmas celebration like it's a walk in the park! I had to go and make such a big deal out of this Bring Back Christmas thing that now everyone's counting on me and I might have to tell them that it isn't going to happen."

"Why?"

Charlie looked stunned. "Why? What kind of question is that? You know what's going on, and—"

"Yes, I do, and I know how much this means to you, but why not take things one step at a time instead of looking at the big picture? You aren't going to lose anything by having this celebration, no matter how big or small it turns out to be. You can still get the tree you want for the square and you have more than enough money to do a lot of the other things you've planned, so you can't give up now. You still have the raffles and the craft show and all the other things you've set up, so you'll make more money, you can worry about the rest later. Just do what you can with what you have, that's all."

"But if I can't raise all that we need, I'll be taking what money we do get out of everyone's pockets and they'll get nothing in return! The point of the picnic and all the other things we planned is to eventually work toward making this a yearly tradition—not just for one year—and if I can't produce it this year, I sure as heck can't do it next year or the year after, then it's all for nothing."

"Then tell them that."

"Tell them what? Tell them that they're donating money and volunteering their time and energy with the chance that nothing will come of it? No way! They'll crucify me!"

Even though she wasn't a drinker, Charlie was closer to buying and polishing off a bottle of Tequila than she cared to admit. She drank wine once—one glass—and got sicker than she'd ever been in her life, but at this point, she was willing to make the sacrifice.

The following morning, Charlie managed to convince herself that her mother was right and decided to postpone her self-pitying bender. She knew in her heart that she couldn't quit her project after coming this far, but before making any decisions, she decided to run things by the girls and see how they felt—with the exception of Helen—she had her own ideas about where she stood. When they got around to the subject of the pond, each offered suggestions about possibly talking to people who might be able to offer information as to why it had been shut down for so many years.

Jean suggested going to see Carl Freeman, the editor of the Braxton News, and Mary mentioned talking to the editors of neighboring communities and researching their local library's past newspapers for possible clues.

Although there was quite a bit of opposition from Helen concerning Charlie's suspicions about the mayor, the girls all agreed to do what they could to find answers and promised they wouldn't quit until they found them.

Although Miss Tucker suggested that Charlie look through some of the old dailies that provided information about the town as a whole which included bits and pieces about the covered bridge, the old firehouse and the pond as well, she didn't really learn much at all except that the pond was a natural artesian well and had been used for ice skating in the winter and a swimming hole in the summer back in the eighteen hundreds and up through the seventies. And while it had mentioned that it had been closed for a time when the interest appeared to wane and had been opened again to skaters quite awhile before Charlie was born, from there on, there were merely little chit-chat pieces about skating parties and bonfires in the fire pit where they roasted marshmallows and wieners or simply kept warm on those frigid December nights. They were merely bits of fluff information—nothing to indicate any problems.

But three days later in the midst of their search, Charlie received an anonymous letter in the mail. The envelope had no return address and had been sent from two counties away and simply stated, the letter strongly advised that it would be in her best interests to forego plans to reopen the pond for ice skating, suggesting that it would be a waste of time and effort and might become a possible danger to the community. It also stated that some of the townspeople were afraid that no good could come of it and that bad things could happen if all concerned parties didn't rethink their decision. It was signed, "A concerned citizen," and without thinking twice, Charlie immediately suspected John Braxton.

"Do you believe this?" She shook the letter at her mother. "He had the audacity to send me a letter warning me not to reopen the pond."

"Calm down, Charlie, who sent you a letter?"

"John Braxton, that's who."

"He did what?" her mother asked, reaching for the letter. "Let me see that."

She read the short note and looked at her daughter skeptically. "There is no signature on this letter, Charlie."

"Well, of course, there's no signature. He wouldn't be stupid enough to sign his name, but there's not a doubt in my mind that he wrote it."

"Charlie, you don't know that for certain."

"Well, who else would threaten me again? Come on, Mom, you have to know it was him."

"I don't know anything of the kind, Charlie, and neither do you. You simply cannot accuse someone without proof."

"You're damn right you can't," Pete suddenly spoke up from the doorway. "You've been causing trouble for the mayor ever since you started this Christmas campaign, and now you're accusing him of writing you a threatening letter? Well, this is going to stop right now. I'm fed up with you making John a laughing stock of this town and making me look like a fool. And in case you didn't know it, my job is in jeopardy because of it, and I'll be damned if I'll let it go any further. I'm tired of having to make excuses for you."

"No one asked you to make excuses for me." Charlie shouted back. "I can't help it you work for a crook, and that's just what he is, a lying, sneaking crook!"

"Prove it!" Pete challenged. "You show me proof to back up all your accusations, and I'll be the first one to help get him thrown out of office."

"I don't need proof, I know the way John Braxton thinks." She countered. "I haven't spoken to anyone but the girls at work about this, yet *someone* found out about it. How do you explain that, Pete? I know he was the one who sent this letter—it's just another devious plot of his to try and ruin everything we've worked so hard for. I'm sorry if he's threatening to fire you, but doesn't that tell you something? God, Pete, are you blind? If he doesn't have anything to hide, why is he so against such a simple thing as a Christmas celebration and reopening the pond? He's been hearing about these things somehow, and if it isn't coming from you, where is it coming from?"

Pete was outraged. "So now you're accusing me of collaborating with him? What is wrong with you, Charlie, have you lost your mind altogether?"

"No, but if it wasn't you and I didn't know better, I'd swear he had people watching my every move."

"You have been watching too many movies." He snorted. "No one in their right mind would believe he'd stoop to something so stupid—"

"You can insult me all you want, Pete, but I'm telling you he's not going to get away with it. I intend to go down to his office and confront him!"

"Like hell you are!" He warned, taking a step toward her. "You'd damn well better think twice before you go off on some kind of vendetta." He snatched the letter from DeeDee's hand and quickly scanned it. "Besides the fact that this letter doesn't have a signature on it, I wouldn't be so quick to put the blame on John Braxton if I were you. You above anyone else should know better after working in a law office for seven years that he could sue you for slander or at the very least, defamation of character. You're treading in water way over your head, Charlie. And for your information, the mayor isn't the only one who isn't so happy about that pond opening up again. Trust me on that one." He tossed the letter on the table and stalked away, leaving a shocked Charlie to think about what he'd just said.

"What did he mean by that? Have others been complaining?"

"Charlie, you'd better back away from this. I've never seen him so angry."

"I'm sorry, Mom, but I can't do that. There's something going on, and I want to know what it is." A strange look crossed DeeDee's face for just a moment, but Charlie caught it. "Mom, do you know something you aren't telling me?"

"No, well not exactly. Besides, it's probably just a rumor and nothing to worry about. I would be more worried about Pete if I were you."

"Mom, I know you. You wouldn't have said there was nothing to worry about if there wasn't something to worry about."

DeeDee sighed. "Well, I guess you might as well hear it from me than from someone else. When I was at the beauty shop a week or so ago, it seems my hairdresser overheard a conversation between two very reliable sources that something bad could happen."

"What reliable sources? What could happen?"

"It was a friend of John Braxton's daughter and another woman, I don't know who she was, but as I said, it's probably just a rumor."

"But that proves Braxton was behind it—"

"Charlie, there are more important things to worry about right now."

Charlie didn't respond to her mother's warning, but if others heard the rumor, they just might agree that it was a bad idea. After all, many of the people of Braxton had children and she was sure that even the slightest hint that anything could go wrong could send panic throughout the entire town. And though she was sure now that the mayor had something to do with it, she said nothing more to her mother. She had already stoked the fire by accusing him of sending her the letter and infuriating Pete, and this would only succeed in putting a match to it. However, she still intended to approach the mayor about it one way or another, and less than a week later, she got her chance—when he paid her a visit at her office.

"Well, good morning, Mayor Braxton!" Charlie heard Mary exclaim, although Charlie didn't so much as afford him a glance. "Do you need a lawyer?" Mary asked, giggling at her poor attempt at a joke.

"No, I do not need a lawyer." His clipped tone brought a frown to Mary's normally smiling face. "Furthermore, you can rest assure, Ms. Forsythe, that if I did need a lawyer, I would certainly not come to this establishment. I merely wish to speak to—ah! Just the person I came to see!" he said, walking toward Charlie's desk. "I would like to have a word with you alone, Miss Faraday."

"Anything you have to say can be said in front of my coworkers, Mayor Braxton. I have nothing to hide from them," she said, not looking up.

"Well, be that as it may, Miss Faraday, I would like a word with you *alone*, please."

"And as I said, anything that you might have to say can be said—"

"*Now*, Miss Faraday!" he snarled, and a surprised Charlie instantly raised her head.

"Ladies, if you please?" He smiled at them, sweeping his arm out toward the door, though his smile failed to reach his cold gray eyes. "You have my permission to take a break, fifteen minutes should give you a lift, don't you think? And don't worry about punching your time clock, this break is on me." He offered. "And should you have a problem explaining your additional break with pay to Mr. Smithton, just tell him to see me." He chuckled as the girls angrily filed out of the office before he focused on Charlie once again. "You see, Ms. Faraday, everyone must answer to me eventually."

"Is that so?" she asked, casually going back to the papers she had been working on. "It must be nice to have that kind of power."

"Oh, it is, it is," he said smugly, seating himself in the chair next to Charlie's desk. He brushed at nonexistent lint on the arm of his immaculate five-hundred-dollar suit jacket.

"Just what is it that you want, Mayor?" Charlie looked up from her work once again, her tone matching the disinterest on her face. "I'm very busy."

"Word has it that you want to refurbish the skating pond for your Christmas quest after I told you it was not possible," he said, coming right to the point. "Is that correct?"

"That is correct," she enunciated deliberately.

"I thought as much." He leaned back in the chair and casually clasped his hands behind his head. "You do realize Ms. Faraday that you must go through me to obtain permission for that or any other endeavor?"

Charlie kept her eyes on him but said nothing.

"No comment? Well, no matter, let me make it easy for you. The answer is still no. You see in the first place, we simply cannot afford the exorbitant cost of insurance—God forbid anyone should get hurt on the ice. In the second place, we do not have the additional funds to pay the salaries of emergency crews or inspectors that would be needed on a daily basis, and in the third place, the cost to maintain the pond would simply be far more trouble than its worth. But more importantly, Ms. Faraday, and to be quite frank—" he said smoothly. "No one is interested in a plan to reopen the pond now or any time in the future."

"Well, you are entitled to your own opinion, of course," Charlie offered.

"And my opinion is the only one that counts because I have the final say on any and all projects concerning my community." His tone was disturbingly matter of fact, and though Charlie could feel her blood pressure rise slightly, she remained cool and collected.

"It happens to be my community as well, Mayor Braxton, and I am sure that if I would speak with the head of the Planning and Economic Development Committee, John Dickson, I believe is his name." She name-dropped a bit pompously. "I'm sure he would have something to say about this."

"Do not attempt to threaten me, Ms. Faraday, you are entirely out of your league."

"Threaten you? How in the world did you ever get the idea that I was trying to threaten you? Of course, if there is another reason why you are dead-set against putting Braxton into the limelight, I would be very interested to hear it."

"Don't be ridiculous," he said indignantly. "Contrary to what you might believe, Ms. Faraday, I am not against improvements for my town, but to put it in simple terms that you may understand the only prerequisite is that they must meet the criteria of priority and importance—and my approval," he added.

"And the pond is not on that list."

"Exactly! I'm certainly glad we understand one another."

"Oh, I understand, all right," Charlie conceded. "Just like I understand why you sent me the letter."

"Letter? I am afraid you are mistaken, Ms. Faraday. I never sent you a letter." The slight flush that appeared on his face told her he was lying.

"Of course you did, Mayor Braxton. It was the letter you sent suggesting that I reconsider my idea of opening the pond. Ring any bells for you?"

"I am sorry to disappoint you, but I really have no idea what you are talking about."

"Oh, I think you do. Why else would you have come here about the very thing contained in that letter?"

"You really are trying my patience, Ms. Faraday." He stood up and the cold smile reappeared. "Although I must say that I agree with his or her opinion to forget the idea completely, I am afraid that you have confused me with someone else. If I have something to say to you, you can rest assured that I will say it to your face as I have done today and not in a letter. I do hope you enjoy the rest of your day, Ms. Faraday."

Charlie didn't believe him for one minute. She knew he would stoop to any level to get what he wanted and what he wanted—as Helen had so eloquently put it—was her heart on a platter. What she didn't know was why, and while he had succeeded in raising her suspicions to the point of digging deep to find the answers, for now she would concentrate on the pond—with or without his consent.

After researching the archives at the library, Charlie learned that the pond had been used for years by ice skaters in the past until it was suddenly closed to the public. And though there was no reason given for its demise, Charlie could only come to the conclusion that the townspeople grew weary of the sport perhaps due to the busyness of their lives or the daily maintenance it demanded or simply because the mayor demanded its closure for whatever reason. She learned little else except for technical facts indicating that the pond's size and its necessary depth of eight or nine inches needed to freeze solidly enough to support skaters was more than sufficient. The fact that it would never grow stagnant due to it being a natural artesian well was a good thing, but the overgrowth surrounding the pond was in particularly bad shape. She realized that it would take a good bit of work to make it more attractive and decided to ask some of the older teenagers for help.

Although some of the young men balked at the idea of dealing with the cesspool, as they referred to it, claiming that ice skating was for sissies, they reluctantly agreed to help. However, Charlie didn't set anything in motion until she had a chance to talk with Braxton's resident ice fisherman, Clay Dugan, several days later.

"You want to do what?" He looked at Charlie as though she'd lost her mind.

"I want to get the pond in shape for ice skating again," she said simply. "It's been some time since anyone skated on that pond, Mr. Dugan, but I think it could be a great way to get our Bring Back Christmas campaign in gear, don't you think?"

Clay frowned. "That's a mighty big undertaking, little girl. Are you sure you want to go to all that trouble?"

"Well, I want to try," she said, suddenly anticipating a logical reason why she shouldn't go on with her plans. "Although I realize there is no way we can never go back to exactly the way things were in the past, I would like to include some of the things they used to do like having skaters on the pond again for example, things that go hand-in-hand with an old-fashioned Christmas. I know that may sound impractical to you, but everything has become so commercialized that the kids don't even know what a real Christmas is about anymore. All they think about is hanging out at the mall or just sitting around doing nothing and I'd really like to change that if I can."

But like Matthew, the older gentleman seemed to understand her logic. He too missed the old way of doing things and hearing it come from one so young gave him hope. "Well, if you're sure this is what you want, I'll certainly do my best to help you. I was stationed in northern Canada for four years, and believe me, I know all about ice. Come on, let's go down and have a look."

It took them only a short time to walk to pond, and with little effort at all, he scaled the four-foot chain-link fence that the mayor insisted be constructed to keep out trespassers and took a short survey of the area.

"Well, I'm no expert in this field," he said, coming back and standing beside Charlie. "But it actually doesn't look too worse for wear. Granted, it does need some work, but as far as I can see, it looks as though it can be done easily enough."

"Well, what about the freeze-over in the winter? I've done a little research and I know it's at least eight to ten feet deep and that's sufficient enough to hold skaters, but how many skaters? I really do want this to work, Mr. Dugan, but not at any risk to anyone."

"Well, there aren't any clear-cut rules, but I can tell you that new clear hard ice is strong enough at eight or twelve feet to drive a small car or pickup across it. If memory serves and there haven't been any drastic changes, the pond is about two hundred or so feet long and close to a hundred feet wide so you wouldn't have a problem with it freezing up good and solid, but if the temperature drops fast, it makes the ice sheet brittle and that means it wouldn't be safe enough to walk on for at least twenty-four hours or so until the temperature rises a bit." He wagged his finger warningly. "But your main concern, little lady, is that if the temperature stays above freezing for twenty-four hours, the ice starts to lose its strength, and when that happens, you've got to stay clear of that ice. My advice to you when you do get this project moving is to have a professional crew check the pond's conditions each day. It wouldn't be a bad idea to have an emergency crew on hand either and maybe some of our firefighters could help you out there."

They started back, and when they reached his small bait and tackle shop, he stopped and looked at Charlie long and hard. "You have to know that your biggest problem is clearing all this with John Braxton, Charlie, and he's not so easy to convince."

It was then that she decided to explain everything: the mayor's total disregard for her plan, the letter, his unexpected visit, and when she heard her own words out loud, her face took on a strangely troubled look. "You know now that I think about it, I shouldn't even be bothering you with this. The mayor and I aren't on such good terms, not that we've ever been, but according to him, I don't have a snowball's chance of making this thing happen because he'll never give his permission to use that pond, especially to me, not in this lifetime anyway." She sighed heavily. "It seems to me the closer I get to actually trying to make things work out, the more hopeless it becomes."

"Well now, don't go getting yourself all upset and chucking the whole idea, we'll think of something." He pulled off his ball cap and scratched his head, then seconds later, slapped the hat against his leg and jammed it back on his head. "Now, why didn't I think of this sooner?" he said, walking ahead. "You just come with me, young lady!"

"Think of what—where are we going?"

"We're going to go and have a little talk with John Dickson, that's what."

"You know him?" Charlie asked, running a few steps to catch up.

"Oh, old John and I go back a long way, Charlie. As a matter of fact, we were both stationed in Canada for a short time, and I got to know him pretty well." His long strides were making it difficult for her to keep up. "But that was long before he became such a big shot in the community." They reached his truck, and he held the door for her and then sprinted around to the driver's side and slid in. "John and I still manage to get together for a fishing trip or two every now and then and talk about the old days. He's a good friend, and if anyone can help us, he can—or at least he might be able to tell us who to talk to."

Several minutes later, they were seated in John Dickson's office and Clay introduced him to Charlie. "She'd like to ask you a few questions, John, if you don't mind."

"Sure. What is it you need to know, Charlie?"

"Well, for one thing, is there a committee who decides which projects are accepted in order to improve the community?"

"That all depends, what kinds of projects are you talking about?"

"Well, let's just say for the sake of argument, that someone has an idea to turn an old building into a civic center or perhaps a local children's museum. That would be an improvement to the community as well as a place for parents to take their children for learning or even a pleasure experience, correct? But let's suppose that a person *or persons* in the community rejected the idea for one reason or another. Who would have the final say in whether or not the project would be accepted or rejected?"

JUDY BABILON

"Well, I believe your question would have to be answered in two parts, Charlie. First of all, the mayor usually decides which projects are accepted, along with the municipality. However, if there are enough votes from the citizens to promote any kind of plan that promises to strengthen a community's involvement or participation, they can and often do supercede the mayor's veto and allow the project."

"Well, that's good news. I was under the impression that—"

"But I must also tell you," he interrupted. "That it takes a great number of those votes, including that of the Finance Committee *and* Municipal Council, and they must all be in total agreement with the project."

Charlie's heart sank when she heard that news. She knew that even if she did manage to get the needed votes to reopen the pond from the citizens of Braxton and the council, she would never get the approval of at least one member of the Finance Committee, a member who not only agreed with the mayor that the whole Bring Back Christmas campaign was ridiculous and an absolute waste of money, but who also considered Charlie crazy enough to think that the townspeople would go along with it. And that person was none other than her stepfather. But she would soon learn that that was just the tip of the iceberg.

"May I ask just what it is that you would like to see established in Braxton, Charlie?" he asked kindly, and Charlie grimaced, expecting resistance.

"Well, I want to bring Christmas back the way it used to be, Mr. Dickson, and one of my biggest hopes is that the pond could be used for ice skating again. That pond hasn't been used for years, and I really would like to make it part of Braxton's culture again, as well as making it one of the focal points of our campaign. I'm sure I could convince everyone that it really is a great idea if I was just given a chance."

"Oh, I see, the pond," he said perceptively. "And you have obviously approached the mayor regarding this and he refused, which is the reason why you've come to me."

She searched for something to say to make it sound less scheming, but nothing came. "Yes, I guess it is, but I really didn't intend for it to sound so devious."

"You didn't do anything of the kind, Charlie. It's just that I work in close proximity with the mayor dealing with him on practically a daily basis and I know firsthand how difficult he can be if not downright ornery about certain subjects. Unfortunately, the pond is one of them, has been for years."

That particular problem was really beginning to get on Charlie's last nerve, especially the part about the mayor being so against it. There was something about his reaction that just didn't sit well with her. "Can you tell me why?"

"That I can't tell you, I'm afraid. It's just a major bone of contention with him for some reason." He thought for a moment. "If I remember correctly—now this is going back a number of years, you understand—someone else brought up the subject of the pond. I believe it was a man who was just passing through on a business trip and happened to notice the high fence surrounding the pond, and innocently enough, he went to the mayor to inquire about it and hearing that it was used for nothing at all, merely suggested that it might possibly be turned into a skating/swimming pond as a way to raise money for the community just as his own hometown did. He even mentioned someone who would be happy to explain how to go about it in detail and that he would be more than happy to contact him and John nearly blew a gasket. He flat out refused to even listen to the man let alone consider his idea, and I understand, they got into a hell of an argument over it and John practically threw him out of Braxton."

"Really?" Charlie mused. "That was rather bizarre, wasn't it?"

"It seems so, but I suppose he had his reasons."

"Yes, I'm sure he did." Charlie said, the wheels inside her head spinning crazily. The mayor's actions were showing a definite pattern, and Charlie didn't like the direction her thoughts were taking her.

"Well, if there isn't anything else I can help you with, I don't mean to rush you, but I do have a meeting in—" he glanced at his watch. "Five minutes to be exact."

Clay and Charlie stood up at the same time, and Clay held his hand out to shake his. "No problem, John, didn't mean to keep you back, but we thank you for your time."

"You didn't keep me back at all, Clay, you know you're always welcome here. I just have to gather some papers together and be across town for the ribbon-cutting ceremony for the new school library that starts next week." He turned his attention to Charlie. "You see, young lady? There are some things that take precedence over others, I'm afraid, but don't give up on that project of yours. I think it's a damn good idea, and I'll do my best to talk to the council and the others." He grinned knowingly. "I'm afraid that's all I can do at this point, and even in that, I can't promise anything you understand. But Clay can let me know if there is anything else I can help you with." He reached for Charlie's hand then and took it into both of his. "It was certainly a pleasure meeting you, Charlie, any friend of Clay's is a friend of mine, especially one who is interested in improving our little town. Now, if you both will excuse me, I have to leave ten minutes ago if I'm going to make it on time, so if you don't mind, my secretary will show you out."

In the meantime, while Charlie had been trying to get answers to her questions, Matthew Torrance was busy trying to find answers as well—for Charlie actually—concerning the covered bridge. He knew how much she wanted it to be a part of her Bring Back Christmas campaign, and he was determined to do whatever he had to do to make that happen.

CHAPTER VI

———— ✳ ————

*A*n historic landmark, the Kissing Bridge, built in 1870, had been beautiful in its day, with its diamond-shaped portal windows, steep-sloping roof, and interior and exterior walls painted crimson red and trimmed in white. For years, the beautiful covered bridge stood proudly in the middle of Kissing Lane atop the spillway, the water beneath it frozen in time with thick crystal icicles hanging from its deck in the dead of winter and cool, sparkling clear water rushing below it while wildflowers and tiger grass caressed its walls in the heat of summer.

Truly an extraordinary piece of artwork that was quite renowned for its historic as well as sentimental value, it had at one time easily supported both pedestrian and light vehicular traffic such as farm wagons and horse-drawn carriages and was treasured by communities all over Vermont. But even after two small renovations were done to improve it, the mayor, having no idea of its worth, demanded that the eyesore be torn down due to its age, appearance, and deteriorating structure. However, the town council and the Committee for the Preservation of Covered Bridges refused its demise, and in an effort to preserve it, suggested that the mayor borrow money from the state or perhaps obtain a grant from the Jefford's Funds to rebuild or at least refurbish the beautiful work of art, but Braxton refused. Instead, he took it upon himself to hire several inspection companies—companies who all claimed that it was structurally unsound—and succeeded in having the bridge closed indefinitely. The fact that the bridge was merely a quarter of a mile from the interstate and a much closer access to Braxton and that closing it would require an addition four or five miles further down the main highway plus an additional four miles to reach Main Street didn't faze him either. But now after all these years, Matthew had an idea that just might resurrect the beloved bridge back to life again, and there were people he knew would help in any way they could.

Matthew Torrance's word meant something. He was quite well-known and respected in Braxton, not to mention most communities in the surrounding areas and pretty much in and around the state of Vermont. Many people in various positions of authority valued his opinions, which were not only based on his knowledge but his compassion which was legendary. However, neither Charlie nor the mayor nor anyone else knew that he had not only gone to the Department of Transportation and the National Society for the Preservation of Covered Bridges, but to the Board and the Council in Braxton as well, with his request. He even went as far as contacting Jim McGuire, the best Preservation Specialist in Vermont, asking him to evaluate the fourteen-and-a-half foot wide, thirty-eight foot long bridge, and in less than a week, Jim revealed his findings to his friend.

"He lied, Matt, plain and simple. First of all, there is no need for the main support beams or stone abutments to be replaced as his so-called specialists claimed, and the cost wouldn't be anywhere near the one hundred thousand dollars he argued with the council about. If my estimate is correct, and it usually is, we'll need to replace the two queen posts and the two damaged floor beams, remove the deteriorated deck, temporarily replacing it with scaffolding planks which will lessen the cost, build scaffolding in order to remove the roof sheathing, rotted roofers, rafters, and sills. We'll cover the roof with canvas so we can continue to work underneath if the weather doesn't pose too much of a problem. It won't do us much good in high winds or blowing rain, but it can help provide some protection. Then we replace the rotting materials, install a new galvanized metal roof which will hold up a lot longer than the original roof and require a lot less need to replace it every ten years, and if you give the okay, we'll replace the portal windows on either side, add a new coat of paint and that's about it."

"Okay, give me the bottom line, Jim."

"The entire job shouldn't take more than two or three months, depending on where we have to get the materials, how soon we get them, and the weather, and the cost for labor, materials, wages, insurance, and the like, shouldn't exceed twenty-eight thousand dollars, give or take a thousand." He looked Matt straight in the eye as though this kind of money was an everyday occurrence, and Matthew responded in kind.

"It sounds like a plan, when can we get it started?"

"It might take two weeks, it might take three to get the materials delivered, and if the weather cooperates, we can get started in as little as three weeks." At that precise moment, both men were hit with a few drops of rain, and they both looked up.

"Like I said, if the weather cooperates—"

"Unfortunately, we don't have control over that." Matthew laughed, shaking his friend's hand. "Order the materials you need, and I'll have a check for you in a week. You did a fine job, Jim, and I can't thank you enough."

The total amount for the job was just a number to Matthew, and he was more than satisfied when Jim told him that the supplier could have the materials delivered and the project underway in several weeks. But it was John's mention that the job could easily be completed in two or three months—in plenty of time for Charlie's Christmas—that clinched the deal. Charlie would have her dream after all. But before he told her, there was something else he had to do first.

"You can't do this." John Braxton's voice thundered behind the closed door of his office the next morning. "I won't allow it."

"You don't have a thing to say about it." Matthew fired back.

"Like hell I don't. That bridge was declared unsafe, and I will not have you endangering the lives of the citizens in my town by—"

"Too late, Braxton—everything's been approved. Besides, you don't give a damn about the people of Braxton, all you care about is your precious ego because your decision was overruled. Face it, it's out of your hands, *mayor.*"

"The hell it is. This has to go before the board and approved by the council." Frustrated and overwrought, he screamed like a maniac. "You won't get away with this, Torrance, I'll go to the governor if I have to."

"Be my guest," Matthew said, heading toward the door. "And be sure to tell him thanks again—it was great seeing him," he said, slamming the door behind him, and by the time he paid Charlie a surprise visit later that evening, the rain was coming down steadily.

"Matthew, what a treat, come in."

"Who is it, Charlie?" DeeDee asked coming into the room, and then smiled broadly, seeing Matthew standing in the doorway. "Well, Matthew Torrance, what a wonderful surprise." She gave him a huge hug and kissed him on the cheek. "Come in out of the rain." She took his coat and hung it on the rack. "What in the world brings you out on such a dismal evening?" She motioned for him to sit down, and Charlie sat down beside him on the sofa while DeeDee remained standing.

"Well, I have a bit of news for Charlie," he said, stretching his long legs out in front of him.

"Oh, well, I'll just leave you two alone then, I do have some things in the kit—"

"No, DeeDee, stay. You'll want to hear this too."

"Hear what? Does this have anything to do with Paul? Is he all right?"

Matthew grinned knowingly. "No, little darlin', it's not Paul, although he does send his very best." He winked at her and Charlie blushed.

"I didn't mean—well, I was just—" She cleared her throat. "So why are you here? Is everything okay with you?"

"Everything's fine. I just wanted to stop by personally and tell you the news. You see, I've been checking on a few things, talking to a few people trying to find some answers about your bridge."

"You have?" Charlie held her breath. "Matthew, that's wonderful! What did you find out?"

"Well, there are problems. I'm not going to lie to you. According to the experts I've spoken to at the Department of Transportation, among others, the main requirement for a covered bridge when it's renovated is that it be upgraded to hold more weight than it was originally designed for and that normally means a whole new floor system which can run into some pretty high costs. Then if you have to replace abutments or trusses—" Matthew stopped in midsentence, catching the look of utter confusion on Charlie's face, and he laughed. "Let me put it in terms you can understand, little darlin'. The Preservation Committee won't make any major changes that would destroy a bridge's credibility as an historic bridge like this one. They do insist that it be kept in its original state or as close as possible and its original state is pretty bad, so there's a lot to be done to get her back in shape."

Charlie looked at him from under long lashes. "I'm ashamed to say this, but I didn't give much thought to their point of view. I mean, I know they want to renovate the bridge to preserve it and that's wonderful, I think they should all be preserved, they're part of what makes Vermont so special—to me anyway—but I just want to use the bridge because I think it sounds so romantic. How bad is that?"

Matthew laughed out loud, sounding oddly like Paul. "Look, darlin'. I know that and you know that, but they don't know have to know that—they're very protective of their covered bridges."

"I can't believe you went to all this trouble, but I know you did it for me and I love you dearly for trying."

"Well, according to Jim McGuire, and he's the best bridge specialist around, the entire decking would have to be replaced along with the two support beams underneath. They wouldn't need to do anything so complicated as piers and trusses because they would temporarily replace the decking with scaffolding planks, which would be strong enough to carry people and maybe a tractor and wagon or so, but nothing extremely heavy, otherwise the cost would be exorbitant. The bottom line is, they like your idea, Charlie, but they insist on renovating the bridge as close to the original as possible." As he watched her expression grow despondent, he thought he'd better tell her the rest of it. "And while there's more technical jargon than you could possibly comprehend, that's the bottom line. I know how badly you wanted this to be part of your Bring Back Christmas campaign, Charlie, but they're simply going keep it as close to the original as they can while strengthening it enough for what you want so they'll get their get their preserved bridge, and you'll get your romantic Kissing Bridge that'll carry your horse and buggies right into town."

"What?" Charlie shouted the realization of what he'd said just sinking in. "They're actually going to—" She was speechless for a moment, not to mention dangerously close to tears. "I can't believe it, they're actually going to fix the bridge? It's really going to happen?"

"You can tell ole Sweet Pea you got your wish after all, little darlin', and here's the best part, with God's speed and a little luck, we should have the bridge finished by mid to late October."

"By October? That'll be in plenty of time for Christmas." He stood up then, as though to leave, and Charlie jumped up and threw her arms around Matthew's neck. "I can't believe it, Matthew, you are the dearest man in the entire world, do you know that?"

"Well, I couldn't let my favorite girl down, could I? Now, there are a few things needing done before the actual renovation begins, but I promise to keep you posted."

DeeDee stood up then and took both his hands in hers. "This is a wonderful thing you're doing, Matthew. Thank you so much."

"You're welcome, DeeDee—you have a pretty persuasive daughter there."

"Yes, I know." She draped her arm around Charlie's shoulders. "She's pretty strong-willed, my girl."

"Well, she comes by that honest," he said, and DeeDee blew a kiss in his direction. A few more amenities were exchanged about seeing each other more often, and then Matthew was on his way.

"Do you believe this?" Charlie said, tears glistening in her eyes. "And if it hadn't been for you, I might have given up on this whole project. Now look how far we've come? You and Matthew believed in me when no one else did, so I really have the both of you to thank for this." She gave her mother a quick hug and then quietly slipped upstairs.

"So you're in this thing with her all the way no matter how I feel about it?" Pete asked quietly, and DeeDee suddenly turned to see him standing in the doorway.

"Why didn't you come in when Matthew was here?" she asked, sitting back down in the chair and casually picking up a magazine. "You always do that."

"Always do what?"

"Lurk in the shadows listening when you could have joined the conversation."

"I wasn't lurking." He snapped. "I just didn't have anything to say—anything that would have made a damn bit of difference, anyway." He turned and walked back into the dining room.

DeeDee thought about going after him but changed her mind. If he didn't care enough about trying to understand his stepdaughter and her wish to make Christmas special again or about his own wife's feelings, then he could try to find his own way back into her heart.

At work the next morning, Charlie could barely contain herself and went on and on about Matthew this and Matthew that and what this was going to mean to the people of Braxton and how wonderful Christmas was going to be this year.

"Can you believe it?" Mary exclaimed. "After all these years, we're going to have the Kissing Bridge back, isn't it great? It'll be so romantic. And it's even more exciting for you, Charlie, you absolutely love that bridge."

"It sure will be a welcome change from all those kids blasting the speakers out of their radios, I can tell you," Jean added. "It's no wonder the bridge was collapsing."

They all laughed and even Helen seemed less grumpy. Well, at least she didn't have anything smart to say anyway.

"Let's keep it quiet until Matthew tells me everything is set to go and then we'll make the announcement. I have a feeling everyone will have the same reaction we do—everyone but the mayor, that is. I mean I'm sure he's not going to take this sitting down, but he'd better not cause any trouble."

"I doubt that he will." Jean reassured. "Matthew knows what he's doing, and he wouldn't let anything like that happen."

"Yeah, well, while you guys are all skippy, happy, jumpy, wait until he does hear about it. I'm telling you, it ain't over 'til the fat lady sings, and mark my words, you'll hear her loud and clear!" Helen spouted, but no one cared. Nothing could dampen their spirits now. Besides, she waited five whole minutes before saying anything, and that was a record for her.

The first half of the day flew by with Charlie getting completely caught up with the pile of letters sitting on her desk needing typing and decided to skip lunch and take a walk down by the pond.

In Charlie's mind, after accepting the fact that the bridge would never be a part of their Christmas campaign and then getting the surprise of her life when Matthew proved her wrong, she now felt more optimistic about the pond.

As she walked along the edge of the fence, she was pleasantly surprised to see that one side closest to her had been completely cleared of weeds, bushes, and broken bottles along with other bits of trash littering the inside of the fence.

She was proud of the way they had taken her seriously and had done such a great job, but she was a little worried that they'd probably gone ahead and done it without seeking permission from the mayor, another obstacle she was sure she would have to deal with. On the other hand, what could he possibly say about it? *Hey, you boys there! Don't ever let me catch you cleaning up around that pond again!* She heard it play in her mind and giggled out loud. Well, if the use of the pond was out of the question, it would at least look nice even behind the unattractive four-foot fence. Besides, she had her covered bridge now and she was feeling pretty content with herself.

It was an awesome day, cloudless sky of crayon-perfect blue, sunlight glowing like a huge heat lamp out over the valley warming her body as she lay back in the soft grass. The birds were singing their sweet songs while the seductive aroma of roses wafted about her like sweet perfume. It felt like a little bit of heaven, and all she needed was soft music and an easy voice singing in the background to make her world perfect.

"Hey! Shouldn't you be at work?" Paul's voice suddenly cut through her thoughts like a scraping needle on a record, and Charlie started, wondering if she had imagined it. But when she shaded the sun from her eyes, he was standing there as plain as day.

"What in the world are you doing here, or do you just enjoy sneaking up on people?" she asked for lack of something better to say. He did have a habit of showing up when she least expected it, not to mention causing her heart to go into overtime just hearing his voice. And the fact that she'd been thinking about him didn't help.

"No, not usually, only when someone's thinking about me," he said uncannily. He sat down beside her and leaned back on his elbows. "Were you thinking about me, Charlie?" he asked looking down at the pond, and Charlie glanced over at him looking surprised.

"No."

"Do you have to be that honest?"

"Would you rather I lied?"

"That would have been nice."

Charlie laughed. "Okay." She lay back on the grass beside him, putting her arms behind her head. "I was thinking about you."

"You were?"

"No, of course not, you wanted me to lie, remember?"

"You're killing me here, Charlie."

She laughed again. "I like it here, it's so peaceful."

"Do you come here often?" It was a simple enough question, but to Charlie it sounded like the proverbial pick-up line and she immediately leaned up on her arms and looked over at him.

"You're kidding, right?"

"You know I didn't mean it to come out that way."

"I'm sure you didn't, you just have this magic way with words." She giggled as she lay back against the grass again, but he sat up and leaned over her.

"You're bordering on rude, you know."

"Aw, did I hurt your feelings?" She grinned up at him. "Poor baby, now you know how it feels."

"I already apologized for that." He watched her eyes until the smile left her face and was replaced with a lovely shade of pink.

"I, you, you're making me nervous."

"You're stuttering again." His voice was deep. "I seem to have a knack for that, don't I?"

"No, I—" She stopped in midsentence, her heart beating like a war drum. "You just make me uncomfortable, staring at me like that."

"Have you noticed that you never seem to have a problem stuttering unless I'm extremely close to you? Although I have to say you didn't seem nervous at all at the picnic." He leaned down and lightly brushed his lips against hers. It was a nice feeling, and she didn't want him to stop, but they were lying in the grass in the middle of a hillside outside her office in broad daylight after all. She struggled to sit up. "I, we'd better go. Someone might see us here."

Paul moved closer, ready to kiss her. "So what if they do?"

"People talk, you know, and it would be us they would be talking about."

Paul's eyes held hers steadily. "Is there an 'us,' Charlie?"

Her breath caught in her throat. She wanted there to be, but she wasn't sure she was ready to tell him that or if he was ready to hear it.

"There are no guarantees, Charlie." He seemingly reading her mind again. "But I'm willing to take the chance."

She watched his eyes grown more intense, as they always did when he was being totally honest, something she'd just that moment figured out. "You are?" she asked, and he carefully slipped his arm under her back and pulled her close

"Yes, I am, are you?"

She bit her lower lip. "Well, I think my mind says I am."

"And what does your heart say?"

She put her hand to her chest. "I don't know, but it's beating pretty fast right now." Paul hesitated for a second, then laid his hand on top of hers. "I can feel it, does that mean you're happy to see me?"

"Maybe." She searched his eyes for a clue that he was happy to see her, just before she asked. "Are you happy to see me?"

"Always." He kissed the tip of her nose, then stood up and held his hands out to her and she grabbed hold of them and let him raise her to her feet. "Maybe you'll tell me the next time I see you. I have to be getting back. Granddad will be wondering what happened to me." They walked hand-in-hand up the hill toward Charlie's office. "Oh, by the way, I heard about your victory with the bridge—congratulations."

"Matthew told you, then." She looked over at him. "I don't know how he did it, Paul, but I've never been so happy. I don't know how I'll ever repay him."

"He wants you to be happy, Charlie, he doesn't expect you to do anything, and he would be insulted if you tried. He did what he did because he loves you, that shouldn't be so hard to figure out."

Charlie could have sworn she heard a trace of something in his voice just before he turned and walked toward his car in the parking lot. Anger, maybe? But that was silly, there was no reason for him to be angry. Or had she missed something?"

"See you around, Charlie."

"Hey." She called out before going back into her office. "How did you know I was here anyway?"

"A little birdie told me." He called over his shoulder as he backhandedly waved good-bye as an odd look crossed Charlie's face. She remembered hearing that phrase somewhere before, but for the life of her, she couldn't remember where.

The rest of the day seemed to breeze by, and after the girls discussed a few incidentals about the bridge, Helen again brought up the fact that Charlie was building herself up for a letdown.

"I wouldn't get my hopes up too high, kid, even if they do manage to get everything together, they probably won't finish it in time."

"They'll finish it, Helen." Jean sounded aggravated. "Have a little faith, will you?"

"I'm just sayin'."

"Well, if there's one thing I know for certain." Charlie insisted. "It's that Matthew follows through with whatever he starts, and it doesn't really matter what anyone else thinks. I have complete faith in him and I know the bridge will be done in time. As a matter of fact, I'm so sure of it, that I called the Graystone Hotel in Burlington yesterday."

"What's your point?" Helen could sometimes be downright rude, but Charlie rarely paid any attention to her moods.

"Well, it just so happens that they own horse-drawn carriages which they provide for their patrons at the hotel. They're hay rides to and from the lake in the summer, and sleigh rides all over the grounds in the winter. And since they're remodeling the hotel to look exactly like the Greystone did nearly a century ago, they've closed down for repairs and remodeling until next year. So I asked if we could rent them from December 12 to January 1. What do you say to that?"

"Good luck is all I have to say, but go ahead, make a fool of yourself. First of all, when you tell them what you want them for and how much you *don't* have to pay them, they'll laugh in your face. And even if there is a snowball's chance they let you rent them, when the time comes that this thing falls apart and you don't have any need for horses and buggies, you'll be crying the blues."

"I have them on hold with a refundable deposit, out of my own money, by the way, so don't you worry about that."

"*I'm* not worried, *you* should be worried."

Just then, Mary stood up and walked to the middle of the office where she stood with her hands on her hips looking madder than anyone had ever seen her. "Listen here, Helen, I've had about all I can take of your crappy doomsday attitude! I'm not kidding— stop trying to make everyone as sour as you are! If you don't like Christmas, keep it to yourself! If you don't like participating in anything and don't want to do anything from here on in, then don't! And if you don't care about making Braxton a great place to live, then move! Just do us all a favor and don't invite us to your pity parties, we don't like the bull-crap you serve!" That said, Mary turned around and walked back to her desk, threw open the huge index book she had been using, and buried her head in it.

"What did I say?" Helen looked around innocently, but no one said a word; the office was as quiet as a morgue. "Fine then, be that way, but you mark my words—"

Mary instantly looked up, giving Helen a warning glare, and she immediately shut up and buried her own head in a book. "Geez! You say one little thing—"

Nothing more was said until quitting time, and even then there were only quiet goodbyes from Charlie and Jean as they hurried out the door, leaving Mary and Helen alone to fight their own battle.

"Hey!" Helen shouted across the room, not able to keep quiet any longer. "What's up with you anyway?"

"Don't start with me, Helen, I'm not in the mood!"

"Oh, really? Well, I'm not in a very good mood myself, no thanks to you! What the heck's your problem?"

"Don't ask the question if you don't want the answer."

"Yeah? Well, I'm askin'!"

Mary closed her eyes and took a deep breath, and then looked over at Helen. "Okay, since you really want to know. You have been a royal pain in the neck since Charlie first suggested the Bring

Back Christmas campaign, and to tell the truth *you* are one of the biggest reasons we're all doing this!"

"Me? What do you mean me?"

"It's people like you, who 'bah humbug' every good thing about Christmas! You hate the lights, you hate the Christmas carols, you hate buying gifts, you hate the whole idea of

Christmas! Just like everyone else was in this town, you're too preoccupied with your own problems to even try to help make this work! Everybody is going through hard times, not just you. All of us are trying to make the best of things even though we all have bills and jobs that don't pay enough to meet them every month, but you act like you're the only one in the world who has problems. What you need to do is to stop feeling sorry for yourself and quit your belly-aching for a change!"

"You don't say?"

"Yes, I do say! Get off your high horse and start acting human, why don't you?" She slammed the book shut and stood up. "And furthermore—"

"Never mind!" Helen interrupted, holding up her hand to silence her. "I get the point, okay? Now you'd better get out of here before I really get mad and throw something at you!"

"What's the matter, Helen, did I hit a sore spot? Well, that's just too bad! Charlie has bent over backward, as have the rest of us, to make you a part of the Bring Back Christmas campaign, and if you can't see that we care enough about you to include you and want your input, maybe you'd better stay out of it and stay out of our way! It's not anyone's fault that your idea for Helen's Little Workshop on the Corner fell through, so quit blaming everybody! Willie offered to build your shop in the front of your house, but that wasn't good enough for you, so you only have yourself to blame! Sweet Pea my Aunt Fanny! I don't know how he stayed with you this long—there's nothing sweet about you!" She turned on her heel then and stalked out of the office, leaving a red-faced Helen to sit and stew alone.

Things quieted down at the office after that, with a sullen Helen not speaking to a self-righteous Mary, and Jean and Charlie counting the hours until quitting time. They knew the rift between the two girls would pass, but how long it would take was another story, so they simply decided to wait it out by working together on different ways to add to the success of the campaign.

In the meantime, while Paul was out of town for the next week, Charlie helped Miss Hathaway and Mrs. Dunn, the music teachers at Braxton Middle School, begin the process of training the children and any adults who might be interested in participating as background singers in the play of Joseph and Mary's journey to Bethlehem. In addition, when they asked for volunteers to learn the songs for caroling, they were surprised and more than pleased to see that many of the younger adults seemed eager to participate. No one was turned down of course, no matter how flat their voice, and they had more than enough volunteers to relieve a group who might need a break. It appeared that a lot of people in Braxton were having a change of heart. Neighbors were greeting neighbors for the first time in a very long time, and a rather warm pleasantness seemed to be settling over the little town, although admittedly, there were some who just would not change their ways, namely the mayor.

He stopped any and all progress on the pond despite the Council and John Dickson's efforts to sway his decision, flat-out refusing to acknowledge John's proof from the neighboring county of Hectorville that it worked to help raise money for a badly needed youth center. He had evidently turned a deaf ear to all of them.

"I have made my stand, and I will not deviate from it," he announced at the monthly Council meeting, a meeting in which Charlie was in attendance.

"But what's so wrong with making money for our community, Mayor?' John asked. "We've been trying to find ways to meet the budget, and this fits the bill. Granted, it wouldn't bring in a great deal of money, but it is a way of getting our children off the streets and into their own backyards again. The fact that the pond could be used as a swimming pool in the summer and a small ice-skating rink in the winter is a great idea, and the best part about it is the fact that we don't have to spend much money to improve on it. With a little clean-up and a small crew of maintenance men, the upkeep would be minimal, and—"

"The answer is no." He resounded, pounding his fist on the table for the third time. "I will not be forced into putting my money into a project that will never work and would only be a constant reminder of, of past failures."

Charlie stood up then. "With all due respect, Mayor Braxton—" She called out from the back of the meeting hall. "It's not your money, it's the town's money, and what past failures are you referring to?" She'd heard enough of his excuses and wanted some answers. "Just what is it that about that pond that you're so afraid of?"

Suddenly without warning, John Braxton stood up, slammed the gavel down, and announced, "This meeting is adjourned!"

Without another word, he turned on his heel and walked out of the hall, leaving everyone in shock with most of them getting up and leaving the hall right behind him grumbling to one another about his strange behavior.

John Dickson looked as though he could have chewed nails and spit them out. "Well, what the hell was that all about?" He demanded after all of them had gone—all of them but Charlie, but no one seemed to notice, not even Pete.

"I have no idea, but something's stuck in his craw," Chuck Chamberlain, head of the Council spoke up. "And this isn't the only thing he's vetoed something without a majority vote. Just last month, he wouldn't listen to anything regarding the sewage treatment plant even though he knows damn well Carter City was responsible for the leak in our system. He refused to address the issue, and now the taxpayers are now stuck paying for the mistake and he won't do a damn thing about it. What's going on, John?"

"I don't know, but I'd sure as hell like to find out. He's been moody and quick-tempered since this whole Christmas subject came up. Personally, I think it's the best thing that could happen to Braxton, but he blows his top at the mere mention of it. Hell. He doesn't even talk to his own family. Something isn't right, and it hasn't been for a long time. Maybe this job is getting to be too much for him. He is fifty-nine—not that that's old; hell, I'm sixty-two! He's just too damn bull-headed to listen to anything anyone has to say."

"Now hold on a minute," Pete interjected. "The mayor's health hasn't been all that good, and maybe that's more of a problem than we think. In all fairness, we have to give him his due, he's done a lot for our community."

Charlie groaned inwardly, thinking Pete just might kiss the mayor's feet if it meant keeping his job. Little by little, she was losing respect for her stepfather's misplaced admiration for a man who needed to be investigated rather than praised, and John seemed to speak her thoughts.

"Like what, Pete? He hasn't lifted one finger to help Braxton— besides the fact that he's impossible to work with, irrational in his decisions, and refuses to listen to reason! I think he's deceived you into thinking he's someone he's not. Your complaints are unfounded, my man, and I think you'd do well to re-examine your conscience!"

"You're not seeing the whole picture," Pete said hotly. "You people don't seem to understand that the man is trying to run an entire community, obviously without help from his own townspeople." He glared back at Charlie momentarily, obviously aware of her presence and picking her out as a major thorn in the mayor's side. "We did help to vote him in, after all."

"Yes, an obvious mistake that I regret we all have to live with. You'd better get your priorities straight, Pete, you've obviously lost your ability to see the forest for the trees somewhere along the way!"

The discussion became a bit more heated, but Charlie managed to slip out the side entrance just before it broke up, avoiding a confrontation with Pete who seemed to be heading in her direction. Fortunately, John stopped him for a word before he could reach her, waylaying the inevitable—for the time being, anyway.

As Charlie walked to her car, she couldn't help thinking that the meeting might have been a complete failure if it hadn't been for John and Chuck, who agreed that something had to be done and soon. Although she'd begun to lose hope that anything could move the community to do something about the imprudent mayor, she now had faith that the truth of his bizarre actions would stir up enough doubt in the town as a whole to do something about it.

She had just reached her car when someone tapped her on the shoulder, and fully expecting to find Pete standing there behind her, she swiftly turned around ready for a fight, but was shocked to see a stranger standing there.

A thin ghost of a man with a rather haunted look about his eyes, Charlie guessed him to be about thirty years old. He didn't seem threatening or intimidating and there was something about him that touched her heart.

"I don't know John Braxton very well, but I have heard stories about him."

"Yes?" Charlie was a little confused.

"You must be careful of him. He is not who you think he is."

"What do you mean? Who are you?" she asked gently.

"I'll be able to answer all your questions about him, including ones that may surface regarding his integrity, but now isn't the time," he said nothing more and left as mysteriously as he appeared. But it didn't stop the hair on the back of Charlie's neck from standing straight up on end.

Along with her already heightened suspicions about John Braxton, the appearance of the mystery man sent Charlie's mind into a tailspin, not to mention her nerves, and she suddenly found herself questioning everything, including her unexplainable fights with the mayor concerning just about everything, her arguments with Pete, her indecisions about Paul and the fact that she hadn't heard from him at all just to name a few, caused her to second-guess herself and wonder why she started this campaign in the first place. Instead of feeling good about it, she began to consider, not for the first time, that she might have made a mistake and that maybe Pete and Helen were right—maybe she was living in a fantasy world thinking she could pull this off. After all, things had been going against her since the beginning and maybe she was just ignoring signs that it just wasn't meant to be. And if that wasn't bad enough, the fact that Matthew said he would keep her posted on the bridge's progress but hadn't called yet didn't do a whole lot to make her feel better.

She thought about calling him when she got home, but he'd been doing so much lately that she didn't want to bother him and made up her mind to wait until she heard from him. But a week later, her nerves got the best of her, and she picked up the phone to call him when she heard his voice on the other end even before his phone even rang.

"Matthew? I was just trying to call you!"

"Well, how's that for mental telepathy? Getting a little anxious were you, little darlin'?"

"Well, I was just—"

"It's okay, Charlie, I understand," he said kindly. "I was kind of feeling the same way myself, but the good news is the materials arrived just as Jim promised they would, to the day, as a matter of fact."

"Oh, Matthew, that is good news! I guess I was getting a little nervous."

"Well, you can stop worrying, everything is going to be fine. Jim will be watching over the crew to make sure things go right as far as the actual restoration goes, so there are no worries there—he's the best in the business. I'll let you know once things have started, but you're free to check on the progress anytime you feel like it, Charlie, it is your project, after all."

"Actually, it's everyone's project, Matthew, but without your help—" Her voice caught in her throat. "I just wish there was some way I could pay you back for all you've done. You've been wonderful."

"You already have paid me back, little darlin' in more ways than you know."

"Yes, but without you—"

"Without me, you would have figured something out on your own eventually. I'm just glad I was able to help. It means more to me than you know to see you happy, Charlie."

Neither of them said anything for a second or two, and then he cleared his throat and went on. "Well, I've got an important appointment to keep, so I'll talk to you soon, and stop worrying, everything's going to turn out just fine."

Charlie heard the click of being disconnected and slowly hung up the receiver. Matthew really was the sweetest man she'd ever known, and she knew he was going to all this trouble because it meant so much to her. He not only felt like the grandfather she never had, he acted like it as well, and it was at that moment that she understood what he meant when he told her that her happiness meant so much to him. In his own way, Matthew was telling her that she was the granddaughter he never had. And now, unbelievably and against insurmountable odds, she would have her covered bridge—and in plenty of time for the Bring Back Christmas campaign.

However, much later that night, an unexpected rainstorm came through, and her hopes were dimmed when the downpour continued for three days straight. By Saturday, it had slowed down to a trickle, but obviously, the work on the scaffolding for the deck had been delayed, and Larry called Matthew and asked him to meet him at the site.

"The wood is protected by tarps, but everything else is a muddy mess, as you can see," Larry commented as they stood gazing down at the gully under the bridge. "Normally, it takes my men one or two days to build the scaffolding, but this storm has thrown them off schedule, and they can't do a thing until the entire area dries up. The ground has to be completely solid under the bridge for a structure like we need, and there's no way it would hold in this—it would sink into the mud and collapse for sure. Even though it's only a ten foot drop, we'd not only lose the false work, but my men could get hurt bad falling into those rocks. With any luck, the rain will stop and we can start again on Wednesday, Thursday latest if this dries out enough, but I can't guarantee anything." He shook his head. "I'm sorry, Matt, but that's the best I can do."

"That's not a problem, Larry. A few days one way or another isn't going to make that much of a difference, and even if it did,

I wouldn't expect you to risk your life or anyone else's for that matter—nothing is that important." He shook Larry's hand and told him to keep him posted, deciding then that it was best not to tell Charlie about the unforeseen delay. The work would start soon enough, and there was no use giving her anything else to worry about. Unfortunately, the weather had other ideas, and the rain continued off and on, delaying work nearly a week longer than expected, and to say that it put a damper on everyone's spirits was an understatement. However, that was only a prelude of what was to come.

Charlie knew they did have the craft show to look forward to however, and while Saturday was a dismal rainy day to have to carry your wares into the school cafeteria, the turnout was unbelievable.

There were more tables sold than was originally expected, and by eight a.m., the cafeteria was overflowing with hordes of people selling as well as buying beautifully made crafts, domestic as well as exotic foods from every nationality, and more hand-made Christmas items than Charlie had seen in her lifetime.

While the girls each set up their tables fairly close to one another, Charlie walked around, jotting down numbers of tables, and each type of craft they had on exhibition, and even bought one of the Miss Creighton's paintings entitled "Park Carousel."

"That's one of my favorites," she remarked when Charlie took it to the end of the table to pay for it. "Now I see where you get your idea for an old-fashioned Christmas, Charlotte." She said, never having called her anything but Charlotte since grade school when she had sternly informed her mother that young ladies should have ladies' names, and young gentlemen should have gentleman's names. "It certainly was a different way of life back then, wouldn't you say so? It was a gentler, more eloquent time, if you will." She stroked the painting wistfully. "How I too long for those days long since past." She suddenly looked at Charlie a little indignantly. "Not that I remember that era, mind you, that was before my time of course."

She quickly took the money Charlie held out to her and put it in a metal box and then carefully wrapped the painting, put it in a bag, and held it out to her. "Here you are. I do hope you take great care with it," she said staunchly, back to her old nature again. "One should take great care of their possessions as I have always done. Good day, Charlotte."

"Goodbye, Miss Creighton, and thank you. I'll take excellent care of it," Charlie said, trying not to grin. Miss Creighton was the most proper person she had ever known in her life, and she wouldn't have offended her for the world. The fact that she'd tried to hide her age didn't surprise her at all either. She'd been doing it for as long as Charlie could remember.

It was close to two in the afternoon when she made another trip around the cafeteria and noticed that more and more tables were looking emptier, which told her the sales must not be going well. When she stopped by her mother's table, she noticed her folding the tablecloth and gathering her money box and purse together. "You're leaving, are you that tired already?"

"Nope," her mother said, folding up the table. "I'm finished, I've sold everything."

"You have? Good for you! I told you your candles and placemats would sell fast. I guess you sold all your cookies too, huh?"

"Every last one, so you're out of luck!"

"Oh well, I didn't really want any, I was just asking." She lied, and her mother handed her a small container.

"Except for these, I kept them back for you. Well, I've got to go. I need to stop at the store on my way home, I'll see you later." She walked toward the exit, and just then, Mary came up behind Charlie and put her chin on her shoulder.

"Ummm! Chocolate chip cookies!" She smacked her lips, and Charlie turned around amazed.

"Now how do you know they're chocolate chip? They're in a container."

"Oh, I love chocolate chip cookies, I can smell them a mile away!"

"How do you stay so thin?" She grumbled, handing Mary the container. "Here, take 'em—you need them more than I do!"

Mary greedily snatched the cookie tin out of Charlie's hand before she could change her mind. "So horsp efjthng cmng?" she asked after stuffing a cookie into her mouth.

"You mean 'how is everything coming'?" Charlie asked, laughing.

"Umph hum." Mary garbled, swallowing the last morsel. "Uh huh," she said a little more clearly, and Charlie laughed again.

"Well, it looks like things are going really well. Mom sold all her crafts and all her cookies, including the ones she kept for me that I just gave to you!" She teased. "And most of the tables look kind of bare, like our contributors sold everything. This should prove very interesting when the money is counted."

"I sure hope so." Mary agreed. "Everybody worked so hard!"

Mary sold every angel she made and was just waiting for the other girls. They'd agreed to meet at the entrance at four when the craft show was over to help Jean and Helen carry anything they might have left over, but to their joy, no one had a thing to carry out.

"We sure made a killing today!" Jean said, sighing. "I'm tired!"

"You're tired?" Helen sniped. "I've been on my feet all day and—" She instantly shut up when Mary frowned and took a step toward her. "But it was sure worth it, wasn't it Jean?" she said, giving her a half-smile instead, and all three girls walked out the door together laughing.

When they reached their cars, Charlie told them they were off the hook for counting money because Miss Creighton and ten or so volunteers offered to do it that night and the next day if necessary, and hearing that, the girls raced to their cars to try and get out of there before traffic got too congested and they were stuck there for another hour or more.

Sunday morning, the principal called her to report that they had collected an amazing three thousand dollars due to everyone's hard work and participation, and for the first time since Charlie knew her, she sounded positively giddy, along with calling her by her nickname, which was miracle enough within itself.

"My goodness, Charlie, I never expected to make this much money. I shall tell the school board that we must hold these craft shows more often. We need so many improvements for our school, and this would be a wonderful way to ease the burden on our budget. Well, good luck, Charlie, I hope we managed to lessen your burden too. I will see you soon, I'm sure. Take care."

Charlie was ecstatic. So many people were involved in the campaign now doing more than their part, and she was becoming more and more confident that this could actually become a tradition. Something wonderful was happening to Braxton just as she'd always hoped. People were changing; she was changing, and the best part was there didn't seem to be the feeling of hopelessness and misery that had become a way of life for so many. And word was spreading fast to other communities to get on the bandwagon and try to bring the same kind of closeness to their own communities.

As far as the work on the bridge, it took more than a week before the mud dried up but amazingly, once the laborers began working again on Monday (Monday, August 18), the scaffolding was up and secure in less than two days, and when Matthew stopped by with Charlie (Tuesday, August 20), they already started on the decking with Larry telling them there was a chance they'd finish the deck sooner than they thought. But again, the weather had other ideas, and another storm hit the following Friday around six in the evening, this time, a much stronger one with fierce lightning and ear-shattering thunder.

Charlie had been at the church since just after dinnertime, helping Emma and Sally teach the children their lines for the play as well as practicing the Christmas carols when they heard a second rumble of thunder and the lightning light up the sky like it was the middle of the day.

While the interior lights of the church flickered, they didn't go out, but the three women immediately went in search of flashlights and candles in case they lost electricity altogether. The children were supposed to practice until seven, and it was well after six when the thunder rumbled deafeningly and they heard a loud crack as the lightning lit up the sky for the second time. While the women contemplated calling parents to pick up their frightened children a bit early, they suddenly heard the screaming of sirens and rushed to the window to see three fire trucks racing down Main Street toward the northern part of town.

Charlie instantly felt a sinking feeling in the pit of her stomach, although she had no idea why, but after telling the women to go ahead and call the parents and then go home after the children had been picked up, she immediately rushed to her car and followed the trucks. The closer she got, the more flames she saw shooting skyward, and she instinctively knew before she rounded the bend near the end of Main Street, that the bridge was on fire.

The fire trucks were already there and had the first hose attached and huge sprays of water were shooting out onto the flames when Charlie pulled up. As she watched the flames grow higher, seemingly engulfing the entire bridge, a second hose was attached just as a truck pulled up behind her with a Blazer right on its heels, and within seconds, both Matthew and Paul were standing beside her car.

Paul jerked open the door. "What the hell do you think you're doing, coming here like this, are you crazy?" he demanded, and Matthew grasped his arm.

"I'll handle this, boy," Matthew yelled above the noise. "You go and try to find out what you can."

Without only a second's hesitation, Paul tore off down over the little knoll to the bridge, slipping twice and nearly losing his balance in the wet grass, while several voices were heard shouting out orders above the roar of the raging fire.

"Keep the water stream on the south end!" one voice yelled from the creek bed to the men inside the bridge.

"We need more water on the south end of the deck, soak the deck!" another shouted, and while he focused his spray on the underside of the deck, the men inside focused their spray on the topside.

Firemen could be seen running from one side of the bridge to the other as they tried to prevent the north wall from burning while trying to maintain control of the hoses, the writhing snakes nearly yanked out of their grip from the water pressure, when someone yelled out, "Get out of the way down there—it's gonna go!"

Charlie clapped her hands over her mouth in horror as an agonizing groan emanated from the weakened bridge, and the men ran helter-skelter out from under it in all directions just as the cracking, splintering wood of the south wall ripped away from the structure, and as if in slow motion, it came crashing down onto the rocks below with a deafening roar. Two firemen, one standing safely on the grassy area to the side of the bridge and one on the road at the entrance, continued to spray steady streams of water onto the burning structure, and as the flames slowly died down, a white cloud billowed upward, polluting the air with deadly choking smoke and debris. Then all was silent.

It was difficult to see exactly what condition the bridge was in due to the darkness, and they would obviously have to wait until morning to check out the damage, but what they could see silhouetted against the dark sky was the roof and one wall, half the deck, and support beams and columns ,the south wall was completely gone.

"Is everyone okay?" someone yelled out.

"Steve's down!" another yelled back, and then, "Wait, hold up!" Several seconds passed by. "No broken bones, he's good, he's good!"

Without warning, the emotions Charlie had been holding inside suddenly swept over her as she stared at the beautiful bridge in ruin, her thoughts running in every direction—her insistence that the bridge be a part of her Christmas campaign, her selfishness for wanting it because she wanted it and not entirely for the betterment of Braxton, and the lengths Matthew had gone to, to get the bridge done in time—things she'd tried to ignore suddenly over-whelming her. And while trying to hold back the tears as she stared out at the charred mess in front of her, praying she would awaken from this horrible dream, someone reached down and pulled her out of the car and cradled her in his arms.

"We'll fix it, Charlie," he soothed, holding her tightly against him and kissing her hair. "I promise you, we'll fix it."

Tears streamed down Charlie's face as she stared out at the surreal sight of what had once been a beautiful covered bridge but was now a mere skeleton of its counterpart—a half-bridge to nowhere.

"Everything we all worked so hard for—the work, the time, the money—gone."

"I know, baby, I know, but we'll make it right, we'll make it through this."

And suddenly, in the middle of everything running through her mind, the only thing she could think about was that Paul called her baby.

Did she imagine it? No, of course she didn't, she'd heard it as plain as day. It was an absurd thought given the circumstances— outrageous actually, and the thought that she might be in shock or had maybe gone temporarily insane clouded her thinking even more. She wanted to tell him then that she loved him and that she could make it through this or anything that came her way if he loved her. And she was just about to tell him that when Matthew came up beside them.

"Are you okay, little darlin'?"

"I'm, I just—" She sighed, thinking fate had taken away her chance. "I just need to go home."

"You're not driving anywhere, I'll take you home." Paul was emphatic, but his command made her furious, and her voice of reason was nonexistent.

"I'm just upset, I'm not dying and I'm perfectly able to drive! Matthew? Would you please call me the minute you hear the extent of, when you hear any news?"

He promised he would, but before she could leave and Matthew could tell Paul to follow her, the fire marshal approached Matthew.

"I have to tell you, Matt, there is no way in hell lightning caused this fire." Sam Wainwright's voice was barely audible above the din of men shouting orders and all the chaos going on as he talked to the three men and Charlie had to strain to hear him.

"What are you saying, Sam?" Matt asked suspiciously.

He looked around, making sure they were alone. "This is absolutely to stay between us, you understand. At first, I figured it was lightning, but I know for sure it wasn't."

"Are you saying that someone had a hand in this?" John was appalled to think that someone would attempt to destroy such a thing of beauty. "Is there any chance you could be wrong?"

Sam looked like he'd rather not answer. "I hate to say anything before the investigation, but I smelled gasoline as soon as we started hosing it down."

"Gasoline?" Matthew was enraged. "What the hell do you mean gasoline?"

"I mean someone deliberately set this fire, Matt, and they knew exactly what they were doing. The old deck planks were soaked with it. That fire was hot, and that's why the one end went up so fast. Gas soaks into the grain of the wood, and that smoke was heavy and black, and it makes sense, gasoline is usually the accelerant of choice," he said sarcastically. "Besides, it looks like there might have been two fires set: one on the old side, and one on the side under construction. The new timbers were treated and prevented from catching fire, but there's a scorch mark where they tried. At this point, all we know for sure is that the south wall will have to be replaced, it's completely gone, and as far as the north wall's concerned, it'll have to be inspected to see if it needs replaced. And there are the columns and support beams—" He shook his head. "There's just no way of knowing how badly they're damaged, your buddy Jim and the fire inspectors will have to be consulted on that. The fire was burning pretty good when we got here, but if another fire was started where that scorch mark is, that'd be proof right there that someone's responsible for this, the rain stopped, but the wind was blowing, and I don't think anything could have dropped down or blown from another location, although it's not impossible. But these are all things the inspectors will have to find out, they're trained for that. As far as the damage goes, there's no way of telling how bad it is, and we won't know anything for sure until they finish their inspection. That's the reason we can't say anything or do any clean-up until we get the official report, so for now this stays strictly between us."

John looked worried. "We'll have to get a bulldozer in here somehow to move some of those rocks and a truck to haul all this waste." His distraught tone clearly reflected the feelings of everyone. "And like Sam said, after they're through with their inspection and depending on the degree of damage we're dealing with it could take weeks to estimate the cost." John's outlook was not optimistic.

"Well, at least the fire didn't get to the new timbers, thank the Lord they were out of the way, but there's a lot of replacing to be done," Sam offered.

"I'll take care of that," Matthew said harshly. "I just need to find out who the hell did this."

"Now, don't go getting any crazy ideas, Matt," Sheriff Conley warned, coming up on the tail end of the conversation. "The last thing we need is a vigilante traipsing all over Braxton. Just let us handle things."

"Sure, Bill, whatever you say." Matthew conceded much too calmly. He turned to see Charlie suddenly take off down the road. "Paul, you'd better go and make sure Charlie stays put and doesn't get any hair-brained ideas about going on a witch hunt. If I know my girl, she'll be on John Braxton's doorstep. I'll talk to you later."

"Where are you going? You're not going to go and do something hair-brained, are you? You heard what the sheriff said—"

"You let me worry about the sheriff. There's something I have to do."

"Look. You're not in the best frame of mind right now, Granddad. Maybe I should go with you, and—"

"If I need your help, I'll let you know—just see to Charlie, boy."

With a rage in his eyes that Paul had seen only once before, Matthew strode to his truck and, within minutes, was gone. Shortly after, Paul went after Charlie, but the street had become congested with rubber-neckers and people standing around trying to see what was going on that he couldn't see Matthew, let alone any sign of Charlie; neither of them were nowhere in sight.

After trying a few side streets without any success, Paul decided to ride past her house on the chance that she'd gone home, and he was relieved to see her car parked in the driveway. He thought about checking in on her to make sure she was all right, but he reconsidered now that he knew she was safe at home. He only wished he could say the same about his granddad.

When the headstrong Scotsman set his mind on something, there was little you could do to change it, and at the moment, anger had taken over his sound judgment and Paul wasn't sure what he was capable of. There was only one other time he could remember his granddad angry enough to cause Paul to keep his distance, and that was the day his wife passed away.

Shortly after Cherry, the pet name Matthew had given his wife of forty-plus years, had become ill with a heart condition, Matthew suggested they go back to Vermont where she could be with family while she recuperated, but she refused to leave their home. Matthew had pleaded with her for weeks until she finally gave in, but only with his promise that they would return to the ranch when she was well again, reminding him that it was their home and that is where she wanted them to live out the rest of their lives together, and Matthew agreed.

After six months and much therapy, the doctor reluctantly gave his permission for Cherry to return home, but only with the understanding that she would take it nice and slow and promise to return to him within three months for a check-up. But with her own Scottish heritage and stubborn streak matching that of her husband, she fought the doctor and his demands, complaining that she didn't like to fly and that the expense was far too much, but with his threat of banning the idea altogether, she finally agreed.

While Paul was very young at the time and not aware of what was going on, Matthew thought it might be a good idea to take him back to the ranch, claiming that the precocious little six-year-old would be good company for his grandmother and could perhaps even stay with them through Easter while he took care of the some of the work needing done on the ranch. And though Matthew and Cherry's only daughter had planned to go back with them for a short vacation, their decision to return couldn't have been a worse time of year. Since her recent promotion to head tax consultant for a large corporation took up much of her time and wouldn't allow her the luxury of a vacation—along with the necessity of having to leave Paul with a sitter most of the time—it was reason enough to let him go.

While Susie promised to make the trip later in the year, she still felt badly about not having the time to spend with her energetic son, but Paul had been ecstatic about taking time off school and staying with his grandparents, and the three of them returned to the Circle C on March 12, Cherry's birthday.

After only a week, Cherry had actually begun to look healthier and had even ventured out for short walks with Paul to the mailbox and back. It appeared that Matthew's decision to bring their grandson along was the best decision he could have made and he was elated with her progress. Cherry had even remarked about how good she felt and said she had even been sleeping better—the clean, unpolluted air just what the doctor ordered. She was happier than she had been in a very long time, while Matthew was ecstatic to have his wife back. However, though seemingly cruel at times, destiny would not be ignored, and just three weeks later, Cherry died quietly in her sleep.

At her request, she was buried in the cemetery next to the little church at the top of the hill just off their property line so she could "look out over the ranch as well as look after Matthew" as she'd put it. But after the funeral, Matthew went into a rage, blaming himself for taking her back home too soon, and was inconsolable for days. Then, without explanation, he packed up little Paul's clothes along with his own, and leaving everything else behind, they returned to Vermont. He never went back.

Several years later, when Paul's mother passed away from complications of pneumonia, he went to live with Matthew where he stayed until he graduated from college and got a job as a consultant with a construction company. Since his mother never married, Matthew became the Father Paul never knew, and he idolized him, and a year later when Matthew asked if he would take care of the Circle C, he'd agreed and had been doing it ever since.

Paul's thoughts were running a little wild by the time he pulled into the driveway leading to his granddad's place. While they both were now aware that someone had had a hand in the fire, there was no actual proof yet. And John Braxton was admittedly their first choice of a suspect. Paul could only hope that his granddad hadn't gone off on some sort of vendetta which could prove fatal if it turned out they were wrong, and his heart sank as he approached the house and Matthew's truck was nowhere in sight. He immediately threw his Blazer into reverse and turned around to leave when Matthew suddenly pulled up behind him.

"What the hell are you doing here, boy?" he yelled, climbing out of the truck and slamming the door shut. "I told you to watch—"

"She's fine. Granddad, I saw her car in her driveway. She didn't go anywhere unlike you, where were you?"

"Isn't this a little backward, boy? I thought I was the parent and was supposed to ask those kinds of questions." Matthew didn't crack a smile, but Paul inherently knew he wasn't as angry as he sounded.

"You were pretty teed off you know, and I just assumed—"

"Yes, and I still am but never assume anything, boy, you should know that by now, and I didn't go and knock anyone's block off if that's what you're getting at, although the thought had crossed my mind. Damn John Braxton! I know he's behind this somehow, but he hasn't been out at all—at least his Cadillac hasn't—the hood wasn't even warm."

"So you did go to his place?"

"I had to be sure, the man is like stale air hovering all around you. You know he's there, but you can't see him." He started toward the house, sensing Paul following behind. "Go home, boy, I'm not going anywhere tonight. I'm too tired I need some sleep. I'll talk to you tomorrow."

Back at the site, the sheriff ordered several men—armed men—to station themselves at certain points around the bridge site throughout the night to make certain that no one, including camera-happy reporters, disturbed the area until the fire investigators were on the scene at first light the next morning.

"When did you get the call, Chief Wainwright? And exactly what time did you arrive at the scene?" The examiner flipped his notebook open as his team of investigators searched for clues around the perimeter of the bridge as well as what was left of the deck.

"I'd say it was close to seven when the call came in, and we arrived at the scene no more than ten minutes later."

"Who made the call?"

"Several calls came in, along with a Mrs. Lakewood, she lives a few blocks east of the bridge on Sycamore Street. She claims she saw a huge flash of lightning along with a loud crack and ran to her window to see if anything had been hit, and that's when she noticed flames shooting up in the air in the area of the bridge and called 911. When we arrived on the scene, black smoke was billowing upward and I smelled gasoline the minute we hit the bridge area. It's my opinion that the fire was deliberately set, Inspector."

"We'll check it out. Thanks, Chief, we'll take it from here."

By early afternoon, news of the fire had already spread to several neighboring communities, and after hearing that it could possibly take weeks to clean up the mess, about thirty or so men offered their help. Since they'd heard about Charlie's Bring Back Christmas campaign through the grapevine and had liked the idea, hoping to one day bring something as unique as an old-fashioned Christmas to their own town, but they'd also heard about her struggle with Braxton's own mayor, and that made them even more determined to help. They asked Montgomery County's sheriff to contact Sheriff Conley to find out what they could about the situation and to offer whatever help they could, and before long, the news that they were coming spread through Braxton like wildfire. Unfortunately, they could do nothing until the investigation was completed, but with Matthew pulling a few strings and asking that the Arson Squad make it a priority so the clean-up could be done and the added restorations could begin, they promised to do what they could.

In the meantime, Charlie had been talking with her mother over the conversation she'd overheard between Matthew and Sam Wainwright.

"Are you sure that's what he said, Charlie?" her mother questioned. "Maybe you were so upset, you only thought you heard what you did."

"I was upset, Mom, there's no denying that, but I know what I heard. They found traces of gasoline, and that spells arson in anyone's language."

"But why, Charlie? What possible reason would he—" She immediately corrected her mistake. "Why reason would *anyone* have to want to destroy the bridge?"

"Maybe it was a warning. Or maybe he thinks that by destroying the bridge, everyone will lose interest and forget about the campaign and he'll have his town back, I don't know." She was more than a little frustrated. "Look, Mom, I know Pete thinks I'm out of my mind for accusing Mayor Braxton of hiding something, and maybe he's right. But you didn't see the look on his face or hear him threaten me. Something's not right here, and with or without Pete's or anyone else's help, I'm going to find out what's going on before anything else happens."

"I want you to stop this now, Charlie. That suspicious nature of yours is going to get you into a whole lot of trouble, and if you are right, you could be in danger. If you won't do it for your own sake, then do it for mine. I'm worried about you, and if what you say is true, this isn't just some empty threat. Maybe you should tell the sheriff."

"Don't worry, I'm not going to do anything until I know something for sure and having someone behind me to back me up, but you know the mayor was against this Christmas campaign from the beginning, and when I started it without his approval, that made him madder than hell for one reason and you know it. He gave an order and I didn't follow it, but he sure changed his tune when I told him that I'd go public and tell everybody he threatened me to stop! Butter would have melted in his mouth, he changed his mind so fast! And you and I both know that's not the way he works. He doesn't care what anyone thinks. He wants things his way, and he doesn't care what he has to do to get it, you told me that yourself. And then all of sudden, he changes his mind and tells me I just need to ask and he'll help me? It sounds pretty fishy to me, Mom. And then, when I get that letter—I know, I know!" She held up her hand when her mother opened her mouth to say something. "I don't know for sure if he was actually the one who sent it, but come on, Mom, right after I get it, he stops by my office and wants to talk about the very thing that was in the letter? He told me straight out that there was no way I could use that pond, and he nearly had a stroke when the council agreed that it was a good idea and he storms out of the meeting! Now, a fire destroys the bridge, and there's no way they can have it done in time, even if we had the money to do it." She shook her head in disbelief. "It's not just for me anymore, Mom, it's for everyone who worked so hard to keep this going, and now what? Does someone have to get hurt or worse before he's stopped? I'm sorry, Mom, but there's a lot more here than anyone realizes, and I'm going to find out what it is he's up to before something else happens, and maybe Carl will have some answers for me."

At the same time, Matthew had been on top of things, talking to Jim McGuire about possible solutions to refurbish parts of the bridge that were destroyed in addition to what was needed in the beginning, but Jim could offer little if any hope until he was able to evaluate the damage himself. The entire area had been roped off as a possible crime scene due to Sam Wainwright's statement that there was more than just the possibility that arson was the cause, and while the investigation of the bridge fire was already underway and no one was permitted anywhere near the site while the fire inspectors and Arson Squad sifted through what was left of the bridge looking for clues.

CHAPTER VII

--------- ✖ ---------

*H*enry Williamson, the mayor's assistant, walked into Braxton's office and tossed a newspaper on his desk. "I think you'd better read this, but you're not going to like it."

"What the hell is it, Hank?" John sniped. "I'm busy!"

"Well, it seems Carl has gotten into the act now and decided to run a story in the paper about that campaign, including the 'suspicious' bridge fire."

"What? Give me that damn paper!" He snatched it from the desk and began reading out loud.

By Carl Freeman: Braxton, VT Aug. 25, 1998

Mysterious Fire Nearly Destroys Famous Covered Bridge.

One of Braxton's historic landmarks, the old covered bridge, or the Kissing Bridge as it was named many years ago, was nearly destroyed by a fire last night during an electrical storm. While fire fighters worked for several hours to put out the fire and succeeded in preventing it from spreading to the new timbers to be used for the deck as well as the picnic area on the opposite side of the bridge, half the deck and the north wall were destroyed. The half already under construction was spared since it had been treated with a retardant; although the roof and south wall

were charred. It's unknown whether or not they will have to be replaced, but work on the famous bridge has been postponed indefinitely due to the extensive damage,

When asked if lightning had contributed to the bridge's near-demise, Fire Marshal Sam Wainwright said he wasn't certain of anything at this point and refused comment pending a full investigation. However, several complaints were heard by bystanders who claim they smelled the distinct odor of gasoline, and in this editor's opinion, that may very well indicate that lightning may not have been the cause.

Disappointed at the setback of the restoration progress, one of Braxton's loyal citizens, Charlie Faraday was hoping to give our little town the gift of an old-fashioned Christmas this year, complete with use of the bridge as well as possibly opening the pond once again, as an ice skating rink. While the mayor has refused to allow the use of the pond, for this or any other endeavor, perhaps he will have a change of heart by permitting it to be reopened again. With prayers and a lot of luck, the devastating fire of the Kissing Bridge hasn't put an end to what may be just what Braxton needs to put it back on the map, and this could still be a valiant effort to make Christmas a special time this year, and not only does this editor happen to believe in miracles, he's more than willing to get on the bandwagon to help make that dream a reality. Call me a hopeless romantic if you will, but I'm man enough to say I wouldn't mind taking a carriage ride over the Kissing Bridge with my best girl or maybe blending my old voice with those of the carolers or even taking a spin or two around the ice with my grandchildren. So if you don't have anything better to do, come out and lend a hand to get the bridge back in shape or offer your services in any way you can to help get this celebration back on track. If all goes well, as we hope it will, all are invited to join in the festivities this

coming holiday season as we Bring Back Christmas to Braxton!

This is Carl Freeman on this beautiful day in August, wishing you and yours a very Merry Christmas!

"Get Pete Faraday in here now!" He slammed the newspaper down on his desk and stood up suddenly, sending his chair slamming against the wall. He was staring out the window with his hands clasped behind his back when Paul walked into his office.

"Henry told me you wanted to see me, John."

"Read the newspaper this morning, Pete?"

"No, I haven't had a chance, I've—"

"Read it."

"Can it wait? I'm late for my meeting with—"

"I said read it!"

Pete snatched the paper from his desk. "The news in the mideast—"

"Not that, you idiot, read the headline!"

Pete took a deep breath. He despised when the mayor took out his personal frustrations on anyone in his path, but like most of his employees, he refrained from telling him what he thought about his attitude lately and what he could do with his newspaper. Instead, he tersely began to read but stopped short when he came to the third paragraph.

The mayor spun around. "I said read it, damn it!"

"I read it!" Pete's teeth were clenched tight. "What about it?"

"I warned you!" He bellowed. "I warned you to stop that bitch of a daughter of yours from going through with this Christmas circus of hers, and now look what she's done! I told her she absolutely could not use that pond, but she went straight to the newspapers with her story, and now the whole town knows about it! I'm holding you personally responsible for this, Faraday, and I'm warning you now—you either tell your stepdaughter her to back off or else!"

"Or else what?" Pete sneered, taking a step around the desk toward him. "I don't like threats, *Mayor*, and I don't like you calling my daughter a bitch, so you are the one who had better back off!" Neither of them spoke for a second or two, and then the realization that Charlie's accusations may have been right on the money about him hit Pete like a freight train. "Well, I'll be damned if Charlie wasn't right!" he said out loud. "And you just dug your own grave, you sorry son-of-a-bitch!" He turned to leave but stopped and turned back. "And just for the record, you can take this job and shove it—I quit!"

Braxton's face puffed up like a blowfish and turned a blotchy red. "You can't quit, I'm firing you!"

The door slammed in the middle of his tirade, but he yelled again. "Fired, do you hear me?" He jammed down the call button on the intercom. "Williamson, get in here now!" And in less than two seconds, Henry walked through the door.

"I want guards set up at the entrances of Kissing Lane and Main Street. If people coming in aren't recognized, don't let them pass through! I don't want any strangers in my town, you hear me?"

"That's crazy, Mayor! You can't stop people from—"

"You'll do as I say, or you'll be out just like Faraday, do you hear me? Now get out of my office!"

Surprisingly, a little more than a week after the fire investigators and Arson Squad had finished their search, the crime lab had examined all the evidence, and when they reached their conclusion, they called Sam and the sheriff to sit in on their final report.

"First of all, we ruled out any possibility of extraneous chemicals used to fight the fire on the bridge because only water was used. We then searched the fire scene from the area of least damage to that of most damage, that is, we searched the perimeter first and moved inward. And as you well know, Chief, that area is the most difficult to secure because it's normally destroyed while the firemen are trampling everywhere, trying to do their job. No offense meant." He added.

"None taken, Mr. Striker. I've been in this business a long time, and I know that most times, evidence is destroyed."

"In any case, we examined the most heavily damaged area where the fire was hottest, and we did manage to find some interesting pieces of evidence. First of all, we found, as you suggested, traces of gasoline leading from Kissing Lane to the bridge. They were scant but were there nonetheless. There were also patterns burned into the deck and holes in many of the old scaffold planks, the ones not treated with a fire retardant. We collected the ends of some of the boards and examined them, and we also examined the beams on the roof and found that the corners were charred and rounded, also indicating an incendiary fire, although the actual fire was started on the deck, the boards were soaked with gasoline. And strangely enough, we did find a lighter or what was left of one when we sifted through the ashes and debris on the deck. So in essence, Chief Wainwright, your statement was right on target: this was the job of an arsonist and had nothing whatsoever to do with a lightning strike. And now, we have to ask why the fire was set and why this particular target. Obviously we know why he or she did it under the cover of night, although it was still relatively light at the time the call came through, so, Sheriff, we'll have to check with everyone we can to find out if anyone saw anything. Secondly, is there anyone you know who might have set this fire? Someone with a grudge or someone who was trying to prevent the bridge from being restored, perhaps? We found no evidence at the scene, whoever was responsible for this covered his tracks very well. There was a partial fingerprint on the lighter, and though it's not much, it is something. We've checked all hardware stores within a fifty-mile radius to see if anyone purchased a gas can or container to carry the gas in but no luck at all with that, and we found nothing to indicate that he purchased anything using a credit card or anything requiring a signature on a receipt or document so this doesn't appear to be the work of a professional so we're at a standstill until we get the results of the fingerprint. Are there any questions?" He looked around the room, and when no one raised a hand or spoke up, he ended the meeting. "I understand that this bridge was in the process of being renovated at the time of the fire and everything is now behind schedule, but since our work is done here, you're can bring in your crews for the overhaul. We'll let you know the results of our findings as soon as we know anything."

Jim McGuire was finally able to do his own inspection and was able to give Matthew the results in just a few days. "The south wall will have to be replaced as will the decking. Unfortunately, though the treated side wasn't burned, there are scorch marks on it, and to be on the safe side, the committee wants the entire deck replaced, for safety reasons, of course."

"Of course, I agree one hundred percent." Matthew conceded. "Do whatever you have to do, this has to be done right."

"Well, in this case, we have no choice, Matthew. The committee wants this bridge preserved exactly to their specifications, so what they say goes. In addition, several of the beams on the roof were charred, and they'll have to be replaced as well. Though they look sturdy enough, once something has been burned enough to change its appearance, you can rest assured the timbers have been weakened, and we can't take any chances that something might happen down the road. Now as far as the roof goes, that would have to be replaced simply for safety reasons, but that was already figured into the original restoration price, so that won't have any effect whatsoever. Oddly enough, the north wall wasn't touched. Most, if not all damage was confined to the south side of the bridge, and with the exception of smoke damage, we're okay there. We'll have to scrub it down, and we may find problems there, and we'll have to rebuild the scaffolding. So in essence, Matthew, the original cost of twenty-eight thousand has now gone up to thirty-five thousand, but since the damage was due to fire and not normal wear on the bridge, we can procure an additional five thousand from the Jeffords Fund, which would bring your total cost to thirty thousand, give or take anything unforeseen. Is that a problem?"

"Not from where I sit, Jim. A few extra thousand isn't going to break me, I assure you. Now if we can order all the timbers and beams and whatever else we need, we can get started in a few weeks, as I understand it. And, since we now have volunteers, we can get this job up and running in no time, what do you think?"

"I think it's a go, Matthew, and you do plan to have watchmen on the job day and night, I'm told."

"That's right, no one will get to that bridge again, I can promise you that."

"It's a done deal, then. I'll get this thing going on my end, and you do what you have to do on yours, and we should be up and running in no time."

Matthew shook his hand. "I can't thank you enough, Jim."

"It's my pleasure, Matthew, I want this as much as you do, if even for different reasons. I'll be in touch in the next few days and let you know how things are progressing. In the meantime, you can get your clean-up crew in here as soon as possible, and we'll put a rush on the materials so we can get this bridge back on track."

The men who volunteered to help showed up at first dawn Friday morning, and the guards on Kissing Lane readily let them pass. Although the guards had been told about the mayor's orders to keep all strangers out, they ignored the orders and let everyone through.

"Let him try to fire us," the sheriff told his deputy. "And I'll have the governor down here so fast, he won't know what hit him. Stopping people from coming into town, has he lost his mind?"

The crew, consisting of about thirty men, some hired on as security guards and some actual construction workers, arrived at site dressed for work. While the security guards had been instructed to guard the site day and night and were stationed at strategic points around the bridge, all of them had been told to keep their eyes open in the event that another incident might take place. Fortunately, nothing happened during the next several days, and they managed to get the scaffolding up faster than anticipated. Matthew called Charlie to tell her the good news, and that it would be no time before the bridge would be under construction.

To say that Charlie was elated was an understatement, but she now had good news to tell them at the PTA meeting, which had been postponed until the following Thursday, because of the fire, but she still had more news for Carl to add to his column. However, there was a more pressing matter at hand concerning her stepfather.

Because she didn't have to go in to the office until ten Tuesday morning due to the lawyers having to be in court by eight, Charlie hoped to sleep in, but as usual, she awakened promptly at six. Instead of going back to sleep for a few hours, she grabbed her robe and shuffled down the stairs to put on the coffee, only to find Pete sitting up on the sofa, asleep. The television was a snowy blur, and she reached for the remote control to shut it off when he stirred and opened his eyes and stared right into hers. It was unnerving to someone who was barely awake.

"Sorry, I'll turn it back on. I thought you were asleep."

"I wasn't asleep, you can leave it off." He grumbled, and Charlie gently set the controller down on the end table and turned toward the kitchen.

"Sit down for a minute, Charlie." Pete ran his hands through his hair in frustration and leaned forward, his face in his hands, his elbows resting his knees. "I'd like to talk to you."

"Well, I was just about to make coffee—"

"That can wait. Please sit down," he said quietly.

Charlie hesitated for a moment and then sat on the edge of the chair. After several moments of uncomfortable silence, she began looking about the living room, chancing a glance once or twice in his direction. Something was wrong, she could feel it.

"I got fired yesterday," he said simply, and Charlie felt like someone just kicked her in the stomach.

"You got fired because of me."

"Your name did come up in conversation, but that's not why I wanted to talk to you."

Charlie waited. For what, she wasn't sure, but she sensed it wasn't good news; anything good between them would be nothing short of a miracle.

Pete took a deep breath and stared down at the carpet. "This isn't easy for me, I want you to know that, but it needs to be said."

Well, here it comes, she thought. *This is where he tells me to move out—preferably to somewhere east of nowhere—anywhere, just as long as it's away from him. Well, so be it. If that's the way—*"

"I owe you an apology, Charlie."

"What?" Charlie looked stupefied, as though someone just told her to jump in front of a moving train.

"You were right about John Braxton."

She wasn't exactly at a loss for words, but nearly. "I am? Well, yes, I am, but what changed your mind?"

"Something's been up with him for quite a while, but I guess I was too wrapped up in my job to see it. Or maybe I didn't want to see it."

Charlie suddenly felt genuinely sorry for Pete. She knew she'd given him a hard time for most of his married life to her mother, and sometimes with good reason, but now this? Even though he'd warned her it could happen, it didn't seem fair. Actually, she hadn't always been exactly fair, and she could see that a little clearer now. "I'm sorry, Pete." She felt utterly helpless, but it was all she could think to say.

"It's not your fault, Charlie. A lot of it isn't your fault—I know that now." He looked at her and almost smiled. "I still think your Christmas whatever-you-call-it is an insane idea, but it does seem to appeal to a lot of people—including John Dickson—and your picnic was handled well."

"You were there?" She thought she must still be dreaming. There was no other explanation because there is no way he would have gone to that picnic or anywhere else she may have been.

"I stopped by for minute."

"I didn't see you."

"I thought it best."

"Yes, I suppose." It was a surreal conversation, like a dream she couldn't wake from, and when he didn't say anything more, she wondered if the conversation was over and she should just get up and leave. Whatever this was, to say she was uncomfortable was an understatement.

"If you're still planning on making that coffee, I could sure use a cup."

Charlie immediately stood up and headed for the kitchen. "Yes, I could use one myself." *Along with a shot of something a lot stronger than cream,* she thought, trying to make sense of everything that had just happened.

"Oh, and by the way—" he added, and Charlie turned back.

Pete hesitated for a moment. "I'm, uh, I'm sorry about your bridge. I know how badly you, I mean I know how hard everyone's been working on it. I hope the damage isn't too bad and it can still be restored."

"Oh, well, thanks," Charlie said, too stunned to say anything else. She didn't know exactly what happened to cause this change in Pete; getting fired was not exactly at the top of everyone's to-do list, but something had changed his tune, and she could only think that he had finally seen John Braxton's true colors. What she didn't know was how fast his colors could turn to black.

The PTA meeting was scheduled to start at six-thirty, but it was closer to seven before Margo Detweiler managed to settle everyone down and call order. "We have quite a few subjects to cover this evening, people, but before we get started, I would like to introduce our guest speaker, Charlie Faraday, who has agreed to bring us up to date on the Bring Back Christmas campaign. Afterward, we'll have a short question-and-answer period, and then proceed with our regular meeting. Charlie, if you're ready?"

Charlie made her way to the podium. "Hello, everyone, I'm sure most of you know who I am, but for those who don't, I'm Charlie Faraday, part of the group who started the Bring Back Christmas Campaign a while back. And for those of you who don't know what we're all about, we're just a few citizens who want to have an old-fashioned Christmas like the ones Braxton used to have years ago, to help bring the life back into our little town. Through your efforts and the efforts of so many people too numerous to count, we've managed to earn quite a bit of money toward making the project a success, and we're hoping, if all goes well, to make it an annual event. So far, we've already had a car wash, a raffle on Mother's Day, and a picnic at the Loganberry's ranch which were all huge successes, and there are still a few projects out there that I'm sure will add to the monies we've already made. Crafts that everyone contributed to the campaign are still coming in daily, and I'm sure we'll have more than enough tables set up for the craft show to be held in the school cafeteria in just a couple weeks.

"As for the children, they've been working very hard on the play, 'A Journey to Bethlehem,' to be put on two days before Christmas, and they're making terrific progress. Actually, I didn't realize we had so many actors in our little town, and they're really good! They've also been working with Miss Hathaway and Mrs. Dunne learning all the Christmas songs, along with many of you adults, and believe me when I tell you that you all have better voices than I do! I've been listening to them practice, and we all should be proud of how well they're doing." After the applause died down, Charlie looked out over the crowd hesitantly.

"And sadly, as you also know, the old covered bridge, many of you know it as the Kissing Bridge, caught fire this past Saturday, and I'm sorry to say that there was some fairly extensive damage." She stopped speaking for a moment when the crowd began to talk among themselves about the disappointing setback. "But—" she continued, holding her hand up to quiet them down. "Even though the bridge now needs more work than the original renovation estimate, a good part of it can still be salvaged and we're hopeful that it can be restored in time for our Christmas celebration. But we need a lot of help to get it back into shape, as well as volunteers for other projects needing attention. So if you're interested, willing, and able, there's a sign-up sheet in the back of the cafeteria if you would like to volunteer your time in a particular area that you might excel in, such as carpentry or painting or even just clean up. Whatever your skill, we'd be more than happy to put you to work! Of course, once we've gotten things back on track, we'll also need volunteers to print up flyers announcing our Bring Back Christmas festival and post them up when it gets closer to Christmas and even to make additional crafts for the show. Just remember that everything you do helps put more money toward the campaign, so if these are things that might appeal to you, please add your name to the list.

"And last but far from the least, there is the subject of possibly turning the pond into a skating rink again. Now, I've heard that there may be those of you who may not be happy with the idea and if that's the case, I would like to run a few ideas past you. I'll explain them as I go, and for those of you who still have concerns or questions, I'll be more than happy to address them one at a time after I've explained them. Now, I'm not going to lie to you, I'm having a problem convincing the mayor that this is a good idea. For some reason he is dead-set against using the pond for an ice-skating arena, and so far, he hasn't budged from his decision to bar it from use in the Christmas campaign. I'm still working on it, but if I can't convince him, then we'll simply do without it."

"Well, I think it's a wonderful idea!" Grace Milford, one of Braxton's older citizens spoke up. "Why, I skated on that pond years ago, and I must say I got to be pretty darn good! Better yet, I enjoyed every minute of it, and it would be a darn shame if the children were denied an opportunity like this just because the mayor doesn't happen to like the idea, John Braxton be damned!"

The crowd clapped and roared with laughter, knowing only too well how Grace spoke her mind, no matter who or what happened to be the subject. "He doesn't own that pond, and no one asked him to go skating on it anyway! He's just an old fuddy-duddy that doesn't know how to have fun, that's what he is!"

"Well, look who's calling who an old fuddy-duddy, Grace, you're older than anyone of us here!" Lyle Hornsby yelled from across the room. "And I for one would like to see you out on that ice today, old lady, you'd break your neck! Then again, now that I think about it—" He stroked his bearded chin. "If you were to wear that real short skating skirt of yours—"

"Now, you just watch your mouth, Lyle Hornsby, you aren't but two years younger than I am, so don't you be calling the kettle black! And short skirt or no short skirt, I could still skate circles around you!"

The crowd broke up with laughter once again, and it took Charlie several minutes to settle them down again. "Well, as much as some of us would like to see the pond open again—" She wiped tears of laughter from her eyes. "As far as I know, the mayor has the final say, so until we know for sure whether or not we can go ahead with our plans, it's kind of on the back burner for now. I will tell you that I talked with Clay Dugan, our resident fisherman, who was stationed in Canada for four years. It seems he knows all there is to know about ice conditions, and without getting into all the details, he said he doesn't see any reason why we couldn't use the pond for an ice skating arena, so his input could definitely help us. He did suggest having a maintenance crew on hand to test the ice daily, as well as using the fire department as an emergency crew, which I thought was a terrific idea, and he's going to get back to me after he's checked a few things out. In the meantime, part of the plan was to build a little hut or some sort of stand where we could serve hot chocolate and coffee and maybe add some benches around the perimeter, you know, a place for skaters to sit and take a break. And as far as providing skates for rental, we've been tossing a few ideas around, but we haven't really ironed out all the details on that yet. In any case, Braxton doesn't have a whole lot to offer in the way of fun and entertainment as incentive for the children, or the adults for that matter, to enjoy or give them a reason to stay, especially the younger ones who might eventually want to raise a family, and I think this would be a great way to get them more involved and interested in Braxton.

"Now, as far as lighting the area around the pond, I'm told it wouldn't cost much to string lights instead of installing expensive street lights. I mean, we do need to see where we're going, and that may be the perfect solution." She looked out over the crowd of people and smiled. "Now just because I happen to think this is a great idea, it doesn't mean that you all must think the same way, and that's okay—I don't want to influence you one way or another—but if you have anything to say, good, bad or otherwise, I would appreciate it if you would bring it up so we can talk about it. So that said, does anyone have any questions?"

More than just a few hands shot up in the air, and Charlie took a deep breath. She guessed she would have opposition; she just hoped there wasn't too much of it.

"I do think it's a great idea, but my main concern is the children's safety," one woman commented.

"Well, as I said, we are in the process of asking the fire department to be our safety net, so to speak. There are many who have volunteered to help out should the occasion arise that the fire fighters are doing what they do best, putting out fires, and the volunteers will be trained in the same manner as the firemen, and the safety of everyone comes first, no matter what."

"Well, it sounds safe enough," Mike Woods, the assistant principal spoke up. "But if that isn't the problem, why is the mayor so against the pond being used again? I skated on it myself many years ago, and we had no problems then, why is he so adamant about its use now?"

"That's a very good question, Mr. Woods, and I wish I could answer it for you. It may just be a personal thing, but no one really knows. Perhaps someone should ask him, but I'm afraid it can't be me, I'm already in enough hot water with him about this entire project!"

"What do you mean you're in hot water?" someone asked.

"Yeah, what's wrong with sharing Christmas with the whole town?" Lyle spoke up. "I think your idea's a great one, and it sure would liven things up a little around here!"

"Well, the mayor claims I'm wasting my time trying to get this town interested in such an old-fashioned fairy tale, not to mention wasting money, that's his biggest complaint."

"Whose money is he talking about?" Grace shouted out again "It's certainly not his, as far as I can see, he hasn't contributed one red cent! And what, may I ask, is so wrong with trying to liven up this place? Like Lyle said, it's been deader than a doornail around here for years! He's just a selfish old Scrooge who needs the Ghost of Christmas to scare the pants off him, that's what he needs." She swore out loud, and everyone burst out laughing again, while someone told her to watch her step, he just might have her run out of town on a rail. But before Grace could comment further, a small voice was heard from the back of the room.

"Well, there are some of us who weren't so interested in Charlie's project in the beginning, Grace," Cecelia Daywood said quietly. "Of course many of us love the idea now, but you have to admit, some of us, a lot of us, were all too involved in our own lives and problems and didn't want to be bothered. I know I was." She looked straight up at Charlie. "I've since changed my mind thanks to you, Charlie, and I'm just sorry that I didn't come forward before I did. If you recall, when you came to ask for help, I was bigger than a house with Helena." She smiled down at the newest member of their family. "And as you could easily see, I was up my ears in kids! Besides, Jim was out of a job and things just weren't going very well. But even with all our problems, Jim was really disappointed that I didn't offer our help, and that got me thinking about all the blessings we did have. Our children were healthy, Jim's unemployment did put food on the table and we were able to pay our bills, and now with little Helena, well, we have so much to be grateful for that we kind of figured it was time we showed some appreciation for all we do have. And that may not have happened if you hadn't started this project and come to our door, Charlie. Oh! And I would like to add that Jim has a wonderful job now, building homes in Southport, and the work will be steady for a long time. So you see, you've helped us in more ways than you know, which is why Jim wants me to sign your volunteer sheet tonight."

"Well, I guess we all were a little short-sighted and selfish with our time," Mike Woods commented. "And I, more so than most, should have seen what you were trying to do to help the children. But as Cecelia said, our small town seems to be turning around a bit thanks to you, Charlie, I know the children's attitudes have certainly changed."

Charlie looked embarrassed but pleased. "Well, I couldn't have done any of this alone. I have an awful lot of good people working with me, and if the truth be known, when the going got tough, I wanted to bail out too. But I know that if we all work together, we can make this Christmas a success! Oh, and just a reminder, if you would like to speak to the fire chief or Clay Dugan, they said they would be more than happy to talk to you concerning any doubts you might have. Now, does anyone else have any more questions?" She looked around, and seeing no more hands in the air, she brought her speech to a close. "In the meantime, we're still hoping to bring the pond into play, and you will more than likely be hearing more about that in the Braxton News. Hopefully, everything will be ready for this Christmas, and if anyone has any suggestions to make that happen, we would love to hear them. Thanks so much for listening, and remember the volunteer sheets posted at the back of the cafeteria."

Charlie had done all she could to persuade the people of Braxton that the Bring Back Christmas campaign could work, and now it was now up to them to step up and do their part if they wanted it to succeed. She stepped down from the podium, elated that she had received such a positive response, but the proof would be seen on the volunteer sheets.

When Charlie left the building, she saw Paul sitting on the concrete wall at the side entrance "Nice speech you gave in there."

"Hello! What are you doing here?"

"Waiting for you." He grinned, sliding down off the wall. "How do you think it went?"

"Pretty well, I think. It seems that a lot of them really want this as much as I do."

"No one wants this as much as you do, Charlie, but I think they're beginning to feel your excitement."

"I hope so. Sometimes I think I'm just doing all this for me."

"Well, aren't you?"

"At first, I was," she admitted. "But then when things finally started to come together and everyone suddenly wanted to get involved, I realized that not everyone is like John Braxton."

"You didn't expect it?"

"Not really. Oh, my car's over here." She motioned toward the corner of the parking lot nearest Main Street, and they started walking toward it. "When I first started planning this campaign, I literally went door to door asking for help, but no one wanted anything to do with it. They acted like they couldn't be bothered or they didn't have the time or whatever other excuses they came up with. I was beginning to think this town really didn't care."

"You've obviously changed your thinking."

"Actually, it was my mother who did that. If it wasn't for her, I would have given up on the whole project a long time ago."

"Your mother's a smart woman."

"Yes she is." Charlie smiled warmly. "She wouldn't let me give up."

"You're a fighter, Charlie, I don't see you giving up on anything."

"Yes, but that tends to get me in trouble, a lot."

"You fight for what you believe in, there's nothing wrong with that."

Charlie stopped and cocked her head to one side and looked up at him. "Hmmm. I think I'm beginning to like this side of you."

"You do, huh?" he asked, suddenly wrapping his arms around her. "Does that mean I might have a chance after all?"

Charlie's shy smile seemed to light up her eyes. "I never said you didn't have a chance."

"You couldn't prove it by your actions."

"Well, you were so busy being arrogant, maybe you didn't see it." She teased.

"Is that what I was, arrogant?"

"Well, what would you call it when someone walks away from you, making you feel like you're just along for the ride?"

He tightened his grip around her waist and pulled her closer. "You want the truth?"

"Of course."

"You scared me, Charlie."

She leaned back and stared up at him. "*I* scared *you?*"

"You scared the hell out of me, if you want the truth. I wasn't prepared when you walked into my life."

Charlie hesitated only a second. "Well, I wasn't exactly ready to have my world turned upside down either."

He watched her eyes shimmer under the glow of the street light. She had no idea how incredible they were or that they told him things she would never dream of telling him, at least not out loud. "Is that what I did, Charlie?"

"I'm afraid so," she said softly, running her hands up his chest and wrapping her arms around his neck.

"Uh, you do realize that you're this close to entering dangerous waters." He warned when she began to play with the hair at the back of his neck.

"Too late, I'm already in over my head," she whispered, standing on tiptoe and kissing one side of his mouth. "I hope you have a lifeline." She kissed the other side of his mouth, and he suddenly pulled her up tight against him and moved his head to claim her lips in a searing kiss. Their mouths met again and again, one long passionate kiss after another, until her senses began to spin out of control, and she was completely unaware of time or place or anything but his mouth on hers. That is, until someone laughingly yelled, "Get a room!" from a passing car, and Charlie immediately pulled out of Paul's arms and tugged her jacket back in place.

"Well, that was a little embarrassing."

He laughed and the sound was pure magic. "Don't worry, it's not like they know us."

"True, but maybe it was a wake-up call."

"Things were heating up a bit." He reached out and tenderly stroked her cheek as she watched his eyes grow more intense. "But that's what you do to me, Charlie. You just have to look at me with those big brown eyes and I'm a goner."

Charlie's heartbeat went into overtime. "I'm not exactly sure what to do with you either," she said softly. "You make me feel like I'm sixteen and going out on my first date, all giddy and excited and shy and scared at the same time," she blurted out without thinking, the wonder clearly evident in her voice.

"That's not a bad thing from where I'm standing."

"No, it's not a bad thing," she said, boldly lifting her head for another kiss. "Dangerous maybe but definitely not bad."

"Are you sure you know what you're doing, Charlie?"

Her face took on a serene look as she smiled up at him and gave him a quick kiss to give her courage. She knew she was taking a chance, but she'd already made up her mind that it was now or never. "You know, I've done some things I'm not exactly proud of, like not spending a lot of time with Matthew and giving Pete a hard time about my mother and going after the mayor with a vengeance because I know he's not who he appears to be. And maybe I'm even expecting the impossible by wanting that bridge in time for Christmas this year, but of all the dumb or careless things I've done—" She bit her bottom lip like she always did when she was nervous. "Falling in love with you wasn't one of them."

Paul's intense eyes grew even more intense if that was possible, and he pulled Charlie up tight against him. "Do you know what you're saying?"

"Yes," she said softly caressing his cheek. "I know exactly what I'm saying, and for the first time, I'm not afraid to say it. I love you so much it scares me, but no matter what happens—whether you accept it and stay or whether you don't want to hear it and leave— that's the way it is and nothing is going to change that."

Paul was lost in her beautiful eyes as he watched them grow misty. "I'm not going anywhere," he said his voice husky with emotion. "Do you know how many times I wished you'd said that?"

She smiled a beautiful smile. "Do you have any idea how many times I've wanted to say it?" she asked, feeling a tear slide down her cheek.

"What took you so long?" His voice had dropped about ten octaves, and Charlie thought her heart would beat right out of her chest.

"I was waiting for you to be sure."

"Sweetheart, I was sure the minute I walked into Granddad's kitchen!"

"You were?" She wiped at another tear that slid down her cheek. "Well, why in the world didn't you tell me before this?"

"I wanted you to be sure."

"I was sure the first time we met at Matthew's too, and so was he."

"You told him?"

Her grin was full of mischief. "I didn't have to, apparently it was written all over my face."

"He warned me, you know."

"He warned you? Why?"

"He knows me, Charlie. He knew I was a love 'em and leave 'em kind of guy, and my own granddad warned me not to hurt you."

"He always did watch out for me, so you'd better watch how you treat me, I could get you into a lot of trouble with your granddad!"

"You mean like the night the bridge caught fire? He wouldn't let me near you after I yelled at you for showing up." He gave her a light kiss on the corner of her mouth. "Maybe it's a good thing he isn't your grandfather, he would have spoiled you to the point where no guy would have been good enough for you because they couldn't measure up to him."

"That's because he loves me," she said playfully, and Paul held her even tighter.

"I never thought I could feel this way about any woman, Charlie. I planned on playing the field until I was too old to chase them."

Charlie giggled, and a playfully angry look crossed his face. "Are you laughing at my declaration of love, woman?"

"No," she said dreamily, tracing her finger over his mouth. "It's just that it reminded me of something funny my mother told me when you said you planned on playing the field until you were too old to chase women."

"Oh yeah, what's that?"

"She said she chased my dad until she let him catch her."

"Is that what you did, Charlie? Did you chase me until I caught you?" he asked, his tone growing husky again, and she smiled up at him lovingly.

"You didn't have to catch me. Paul. You already had me, you just didn't know it."

"You're damn lucky we're in the middle of this parking lot, woman." He groaned, covering her mouth with his in an explosive kiss that rocked his world and tilted hers on its side. When their kiss finally ended and he pulled away and saw the passion in her eyes, he sensed it was time to put on the breaks. He was on fire for her, and it wouldn't take much to get it blazing to the point of no return, so he gently put her away from him. "I want you to get into your car and go home, Charlie," Paul said quietly, and a look of surprise crossed her face.

"Oh, and we were just beginning to have a good time too," she said her eyes wide with innocence as she reached out to caress his chest.

Paul took her hand and placed firmly back at her side. "I said I want you to go home, Charlie."

"But I'm not ready to go home yet." She pouted, reaching out to touch his chest again, and he took a step backward.

"Charlie," he said warningly, his voice stern.

"I don't want to go home, and you can't make me," she said mischievously, and he suddenly grabbed her to him and then leaned her against her car.

"But I *need* you to go home, *now*." He grated, suggestively pushing up against her, and Charlie swallowed hard, getting his obvious hint.

"You know, I was just thinking," she said breathlessly, wriggling until she slid out from under him and reached for the door handle, "that maybe I should, you know, go home now." She opened the driver's side door and slid into the seat, then closed the door quickly and opened the window a crack.

"Uh huh, I thought you might be thinking that." His intense, knowing eyes held her wide-eyed deer-caught-in-the-dark stare. "You take care now, you hear?"

"Right!" She gulped nervously, fumbling to get her key into the ignition after realizing she'd underestimated his passion as well as her own. She'd come close to setting a fire she wasn't sure she could put out or wanted to. So she did the safer thing. "Good night, Paul."

"Good night, Charlie, and do sleep well."

CHAPTER VIII

———✳———

*C*harlie barely got to sleep when her alarm went off, and she angrily knocked it to the floor. "You, I can do without!" she said, flipping over and pulling the covers over her head. Ten minutes later and nearly asleep, she heard a knock.

"Charlie, you up?" her mother called through the closed door.

"I am now," she mumbled, pulling the covers tighter over her head. "No!" she answered sharply. "I'm still sleeping!"

"Matthew's on the phone, Charlie, and he sounds upset."

Charlie instantly ripped the covers away, jumped out of bed, and yanked her door open.

"What is it, what's wrong? Is it Paul? What's happened?"

"I don't know, dear, he didn't say. He just asked for you."

Charlie grabbed her robe and flew past her mother and down the stairs, trying to put on her robe while trying to disentangle the belt from the arm and not trip on the hem. She finally gave up, flinging it to the floor, and was out of breath when she picked up the receiver. "Matthew? What is it, is it Paul?"

"No, it's not Paul, darlin', he's standing right here with me. It's Carl Freeman."

"Carl? What's wrong? Did something happen to him?"

"No, he's fine except for a few minor burns on his hands and face, but his barn burned to the ground last night."

"Oh my god, that's awful!" she said, sitting down heavily in the phone chair. "How did it happen?"

"They're not sure. Everything was fine at ten o'clock last night, but he was awakened by the smell of smoke around three this morning and ran out to see his barn in flames."

"Is everyone else all right, Lila and the grandchildren?"

"Yes, everyone's fine. The grandkids went home day before yesterday, so it was just him and Lila there and the barn's far enough away from the house not to cause a problem. Luckily, the only two horses he has left were out in the corral. They must have jumped the fence and took off, Carl's out rounding them up now."

"Oh, Matthew, he lost everything?"

"There are only ashes left, darlin'. Luckily, he only stored old equipment in there, along with his grain and feed of course and some boxes of old newspapers he stored in the loft."

Charlie was sick at the news. She'd spoken with Carl just days before when he called her at the office with another idea for a story on the campaign. She was so excited that he was willing to help spread the news, but she'd been even more impressed that he thought it important enough to run his story by her before it went to print. He'd also told her he needed to see her as soon as possible and that they needed to meet at the diner instead of at her office. He hadn't explained why, and though she'd found his request a bit odd at the time, she agreed, but it was that last thought that sent a chill up Charlie's spine and she sat stock-straight in her chair.

She hadn't told anyone she'd spoken to Carl, not even the girls. It had been so hectic that day with the lawyers coming back from court at four o'clock and the girls rushing out the door at the same time that she hadn't had the chance to tell them. And it was then that it hit her. There was only one way anyone could have known that Carl had called her that day and why, someone had been following her or perhaps even Carl.

"Charlie, are you still there?" Matthew asked for the third time, snapping Charlie out of her stupor.

"I'm here. "I was just thinking about Carl, that's all." She hedged.

"Well, don't worry, darlin', he's fine. I only told you because he had a message for you."

"Oh? What kind of message?"

"He said he still needs to meet with you, but something came up and he needs to change the story before he runs it. He said not to bother calling him, just meet him where you'd planned on Sunday at ten o'clock."

When she didn't respond right away, he asked, "Did you get that, darlin'?"

Unaware that she'd been clutching the phone like a lifeline, she eased her grip, but it didn't stop her heart from thumping like war drums. She took a deep breath and let it out slowly before answering. "Yes, I got it, Matthew," she said quietly. "I understand completely, thanks for calling."

"That's okay, little darlin', I'll talk to you again when—"

Charlie slowly hung up the receiver before he could finish, her mind wandering. She realized she should have told Matthew and reassured herself that she would, but at the moment, her thoughts were focused on the one person she now suspected even more than ever to be responsible for all the strange accidents that seemed to be happening one after the other. She'd suspected that John Braxton was behind everything—the only thing she didn't know was why, and she hoped Carl had some of the answers.

She dressed quickly and arrived at work just in time, and while she informed the girls about Carl's barn, she left out the part about her suspicions which were only speculations at best. Besides, she was really in no mood to hear any of Helen's brilliant pearls of wisdom concerning her wild imagination running away with her. Helen was like Doubting Thomas—if she didn't see proof positive right in front of her eyes, she'd argue the fact that it didn't exist until she was blue in the face, and right now, that was that last thing Charlie needed. She was worried about Carl and almost felt guilty because she'd agreed to let him run the piece in the newspaper. After reading the article which included a comment about the bridge as well as the possibility of the mayor rethinking his refusal to let her use the pond in her Bring Back Christmas campaign, she suspected that it might have been the reason behind Carl's barn being burned down. While she expected the mayor to be a bit upset by the fact that something negative had been said about him, she never dreamed it would make him angry enough to do something as incredibly heinous as burning down Carl's barn. Surely, he knew there was a chance that someone could easily have been hurt or worse, but it was that very thought that had caused her suspicions about him in the first place. While she'd suspected for a long time that there was more to him that met the eye, she considered that it was merely due to her innate dislike of the man and not from anything concrete. But now, however, she suspected that her first impression may well have been right on target: there was something unscrupulously evil about the man.

All the same, after working with lawyers for so many years, she had learned that nothing lawful could be done on mere conjecture; you needed fail-safe proof of someone's guilt before you could accuse them of anything. And that is exactly what she planned to do.

Charlie didn't sleep well again, which seemed to be the norm lately, and she was still staring up at the ceiling at six o'clock the next morning. While she planned to go back to the library in the hope that she might find a clue she may have missed concerning the pond, she still had several hours before the library opened, and after putting on the coffee, she took a shower and washed and dried her hair while waiting for it to brew.

She thought of calling Matthew for advice, when it suddenly dawned on her that she hadn't heard from him in quite a while. Although he'd told her he would let her know when the work began on the bridge, for some reason, she hadn't heard a thing from him— or from Paul for that matter. It was strange for Matthew because he was always prompt and rarely forgot anything that important, but not wanting to bother him, she decided to do as he suggested and go see for herself how work was progressing. She had no idea how far they'd gotten in the past few weeks, but she warned herself not to expect much. So many things had happened to delay the project that she was afraid to get her hopes up even a little. On the other hand, seeing any progress was better than not knowing anything.

When she arrived, she was shocked to see how far they'd come in such a short time. From her vantage point on Kissing Lane near the entrance of the bridge, she could see that the entire deck had been laid, and they already had three quarters of the south wall completed. By the looks of it, it would be no time before they had the beams and roof replaced, which only left the portal windows and a brand-new coat of paint. And with all the men stationed at strategic points around the perimeter, it was a safe bet that no one would try to sabotage it again. Although it was an eerie sight to see the men armed with rifles, after the recent problems, it was rather reassuring, and Charlie left the site convinced that it would surely be done in time for the Christmas celebration since they were so far ahead. And that of course gave her the opportunity to focus on the answers to some disturbing questions.

It was only seven forty-five when she arrived at the library, but Miss Tucker saw her peeking in the window and let her in early, and with Miss Tucker's help, it only took her a short time to find issues about the Braxton family dating all the way back to John's great-great-grandfather's long run as mayor. Though it wasn't an extremely valuable piece of information within itself, when combined with some very interesting or perhaps disturbing facts, whichever way one chose to look at it, it did shed some light on some issues that may have had an influence on John's character.

One of the few things that did bear mentioning was the fact that John Braxton's great-great-grandfather for whom he was named had discovered the town of Braxton. At that time, when someone was sworn in as mayor, he remained in that seat until he died or stepped down, but either way it was passed down to the son. That was the way it was back then: each generation passing on the title down through the generations until it changed in the early nineteen hundreds.

In her search, Charlie also came across a brief article concerning one of the prior Braxton men who occasionally had bouts with his health and often spent several weeks to a month in a sanitarium. Although the illness was not named, she knew from history class back in grade school that a sanitarium in those days usually suggested tuberculosis or consumption, as they called the lung disease back then and of course insanity. However, if his hospitalization was due to anyone of those, she had to wonder why he would have been hospitalized for only a month or so and then released, but apparently, it hadn't been important enough to mention. And while Charlie thought it odd that the information was so vague, she realized that in those days, things were kept in the family and not for public viewing which could bring on disgrace, so in a way it made sense. However, something told her that the mayor's recent track record for outbursts of temper and strange behavior had nothing to do with tuberculosis, consumption, or even the common cold as she recalled true stories of centuries past when those with mental problems were kept behind locked doors away from everyone and in some cases were sent to institutions for their out of control behavior. That could possibly explain why those records, if they did in fact exist, may have been expunged from public view; mental illness was just not talked about in those days. But one interesting fact was clear and could possibly help to explain the mayor's unusual and often bizarre behavior: there was history of mental illness in the Braxton family.

As she flipped through page after page after page of rather trivial information concerning the family tree as a whole, she skipped ahead several generations and began scanning more recent articles from the flapper era, on up through the nineteen sixties. And while things had changed drastically from one decade to another, the Braxton family continued to make history although the stories seemed to become even less informative, unless one considered a piece about John Braxton receiving medals for being a champion swimmer interesting. The only thing remotely fascinating about it was the fact that the son, John Braxton Jr. was the exact opposite of his father: he was deathly afraid of water. But while on a community picnic one summer day when the son was quite young, John Sr. had laughingly thrown him into the pond in the hope that his son would get over his fear and perhaps become even more famous than his champion father but had nearly drowned before the senior Braxton realized he was not destined to follow in his footsteps and was going under for the third time and dove in to save him.

Charlie shuddered, thinking that was a horrible lesson to learn and in front of everyone at the picnic. No wonder the man had problems. Still, by the time she reached the seventies and eighties, she'd come to the sad conclusion that despite some minor scandals, mishaps, and arguments between the family here and there, for the most part, they were a rather average albeit wealthy family who had a sincere love and respect for family and tradition and of course for their favorite holiday, Christmas, but that seemed to be the extent of it.

She'd just about given up when something caught her eye, and she backtracked through the pages and began searching through them again one by one, thinking she'd missed a page, and found that she'd been right—the pages she'd been reading went from fifty-seven to sixty. She retraced her steps again to make sure they weren't just stuck together but in rechecking, found that the two pages were definitely missing. She took the book up to the front desk and showed Miss Tucker what she'd found and asked if there was any way to find out what was on those pages.

"We did convert them to microfilm some time ago, and the pages should be there. I can't understand what happened to them, but if you do find them within the microfilm archives and would like copies, it will cost around three dollars. Would you like to have them?"

Charlie said she would and paid for the copies, and when she received them back, she laid the pages out on the table and read:

TRAGEDY STRIKES BRAXTON COMMUNITY

A five year-old boy was found drowned in Braxton Pond near the spillway yesterday just a block and a half from his home.

Boyd Caldwell was playing with a friend about 5:30 p.m. in the backyard of his home on Main Street while his parents were nearby in the kitchen, Braxton police reported.

When Ron and Melissa Caldwell looked out to check on their son five minutes later, both boys were gone. Mrs. Caldwell, believing that they wandered off, went looking for the little boys with the help of neighbors but became frantic after Boyd's friend arrived at his own home two doors away and told his parents that his friend was in the pond.

The family immediately dialed 911 and ran to the pond.

Assistant Police Chief Ron Dietz, living close by, was the first one on the scene and saw a ball floating in the middle of the pond and, upon wading out to retrieve it, found Boyd in several feet of water. Dietz said he had no pulse and he was not breathing and carried him to the edge of the pond where he administered CPR and began mouth-to-mouth resuscitation until firefighters arrived with the rescue truck.

When the crews arrived, they attempted to revive him, but the little boy was pronounced dead on the scene.

"The child was in cardiac arrest," said Raymond Smith, Braxton Paramedics spokesman. "They did all they could, but he had been under the water too long and they weren't able to revive him. It was just too late," added Smith.

A close neighbor told police that she often saw the two boys playing ball in the backyard. "Boyd never left that yard. His parents watched him constantly—he didn't even play out in the front, he was always where they could keep a close eye on him."

Boyd's little friend, whose parents do not wish his name revealed, told the chief of police that someone was there at the time young Boyd drowned, but he could only say that it was a man and that he went out in the water but came back without the boy and drove away in a black car.

Authorities did a thorough search of the area, and while footprints had been noted, most had been destroyed in the attempt to bring little Boyd out of the water and no clear imprint could be attained for analysis. A further investigation is pending and no suspects have been found.

Mayor John Braxton Sr. stated, "This is tragic, and my heart goes out to Mr. and Mrs. Caldwell in their loss. While their grief is overwhelmingly felt by all of us here in Braxton, our prayers and support are with their entire family."

The mayor's son, John Braxton Jr., had this to say: "I have tried numerous times to persuade my father and the council to have that pond filled in and have been unsuccessful. Not only was the pond an accident waiting to happen, it's an eyesore and a haven for geese that use it for a resting place while leaving their droppings for the town to clean up after. Maybe now, something will be done about it."

While funeral announcements have not yet been released, there is speculation that the family may not wish to have little Boyd's funeral here in Braxton, but that has not yet been confirmed. Boyd's parents, understandably, could not be reached for comment.

We at the Braxton News send our deepest condolences to the Caldwell family in their loss.

Joe Messing: Braxton Vt. 15July1978

Charlie was stunned. She had never heard that story, not even in passing. The fact that she was only four years old at the time most likely had something to do with it, but because they were so close in age, the tragic story touched her heart.

She glanced down at the picture of both John Sr. and John Jr. shaking Assistant Chief Dietz's hand for his valiant effort to save little Boyd, and though the resemblance between father and son was uncanny, that's where the likeness stopped. There was nothing sinister about the elder man's eyes, but she definitely saw something evil in the younger one's, and that difference made her shudder as it had the day she'd spoken to him in his office. Though she'd battled with him in the past over needed improvements for the town, it was usually at a meeting and never up close and personal, but there was no doubt that she could plainly see cruelty in those eyes now.

She flipped to the next page where she saw father and son obviously in the middle of an argument. The two were face to face—the elder Braxton seemingly shaking his finger at the younger man whose fist was clenched and obviously ready to strike while the caption read, "Father and Son Duke It Out!"

She read on to learn that John Braxton Jr. had made his decision to run for mayor, although his father had previously been quoted as saying that his son was not ready for the responsibility. However, when John Sr. died a year later and the younger John began his fight to take his place; it was at that moment that Charlie understood his demand that she keep his family out of the way he ran things. It was the same reason she'd suspected him from the beginning: he had no conscience about whose feet he stepped on to get what he wanted, including that of his own father, and it was clear that he didn't like anyone going against him.

Still, two questions plagued her. First, how did he manage to be voted in as mayor while his father, who was obviously loved and respected by the townspeople, made it clear to everyone that his son wasn't ready?

Charlie could only guess that although John Braxton most likely had some mental problems perhaps no one was aware of, people noticed something radical about his sometimes strange behavior. And though his father never suspected that his only son hated for what he did at the pond that day as well as allowing the townspeople in on the fact that he considered his son too irresponsible to become mayor, but after conning the people into believing that he had the same scruples as his father, they had voted him into office. After that, it was more than likely a matter of paying off the right people to get him reelected year after year.

The second and more important question of the two was why he felt the need to remove these particular pages. Due to rather heated past encounters with the mayor, Charlie's first instinct was that he was responsible for removing them, but she had to be realistic. If it had been him, what possible reason did he have?

Spurred on by this new information, Charlie stuffed the articles into her purse, gathered up her things, and left the library, her suspicions on high alert. As she drove home, her mind flashed back to the council meeting when he'd become infuriated and stormed out after his mention of the pond project not working and being a reminder of past failures. Although Charlie could understand how a public statement from your own father regarding your inadequacies could be interpreted as a failure, for the life of her, she couldn't figure out how a little boy drowning in a pond could be connected, and if it wasn't, why was that article removed as well?

While trying to figure out anything John Braxton did was like trying to put a puzzle together without all the pieces, Charlie needed no distractions, and after arriving home and going straight to her room, she laid on her bed going over what she'd learned her mind inevitably strayed back to the same questions: What did all this have to do with him? More importantly, what was it about those articles that had caused him to remove them from legal public records?

And then there was the stranger who stopped her in the parking lot. How did he fit into all this? While he said he could answer her questions, how could he possibly have known *what* questions? Of course, he could have been at the meeting, but that still didn't explain anything—there were a lot of people at that meeting who had no idea why the mayor had become upset enough to leave. Something didn't fit. And then it hit her. The man had said he could answer all her questions including ones about his integrity, and though Charlie didn't catch it at the time, in thinking back, she remembered asking only one question really and that had to do with the pond: so what had he meant? Did he know something about the pond or was there even more about the mayor that she didn't know?

Charlie suddenly had that sick feeling in the pit of her stomach again. The man obviously knew something. Unfortunately, she had never seen him again and had no idea who he was or how to reach him, so there was really only one thing to do and that was to confront the mayor. She would simply show him the articles. If he has no reaction, she'd lean toward the possibility that she was wrong and that someone else removed the pages for whatever reason. If he does react as she suspects he will however, she'll be more inclined to believe she was right and that he was the one responsible for their disappearance. But that still left the question "why"?

Charlie re-thought her theories, considering that her suspicions were nothing more than an overactive imagination and that she was trying too hard to find some connection between the mayor and the articles. If she was way off the mark, she would look like a fool trying to convince anyone that he was anything more than an overzealous mayor trying to prove his father wrong, and that actually made more sense than trying to find needle in a haystack when there was no haystack. She weighed her options and considered that she had little to lose but much to gain by her possible exposure of a man who had perhaps been lying about many things from the beginning. He'd threatened her to give up on the pond idea for some reason, and she made up her mind to confront him. Better to be safe than sorry, and the sooner she exposed him, the better.

Although the chance of finding him in his office on a Sunday was slim, Charlie decided to try since his office was close, but when she arrived at his office, she found she'd been right—his Cadillac was not parked in its usual place out front and was nowhere in sight. However, on her way home as she neared the end of North Main Street, she caught sight of the vehicle parked in front of the diner—in a handicapped zone no less—which of course enabled him to keep a close eye on his precious car so that no one vandalized it, that fact alone hinting that the townspeople weren't exactly fond of their mayor.

Although she'd considered waiting until Monday when she could simply go to his office, she decided her original idea was better. Because she planned to show him the articles, talking to him in a public place might cause him to think twice before making a scene. Besides, she wanted witnesses—plenty of witnesses—just in case.

When she entered the diner, she immediately spied him sitting alone and walked back toward his seat.

"Good morning, Mayor Braxton!" she said, loud enough for those around him to hear, and the man, obviously not at all pleased to see her, quietly stated that he was having breakfast *if she didn't mind.*

"Oh, thank you, that's very kind of you to offer, but I've had my breakfast." She slid into the booth seat opposite him and saw the waitress walking toward them. "Hi, June, just coffee for me, thanks." She called out, and several people looked up curiously.

"So how are you this lovely morning, mayor? I see you're out and about early, been to church already, have you?"

The mayor smiled though his icy glare belied his pretense of warmth. "No, I'm afraid I haven't been to church, Miss Faraday, and you?"

"No," she said sheepishly. "I'm afraid I've missed the service again." The waitress brought her coffee, set it down, and left.

"What, no practice this morning?" he asked astutely. "I would have thought you wouldn't miss a single chance of meeting with the Sunday school children. Christmas is not very far off you know, and you certainly do want them to be ready."

"True, true! But I must say, they are all doing well, especially little Christina. She has quite a voice, your granddaughter. Does she get that particular talent from you? She is quite the little speaker and already has many of your admirable qualities." She took a sip of coffee and looked at him over the rim.

The mayor smiled and leaned forward, but his forced tone of voice and steely gray eyes in no way matched his demeanor. "I have no idea why you are carrying on this façade, but I do not have time to listen to your inane drivel, Miss Faraday," he said, placing his napkin on his plate. "I have more important things to do." He grabbed the bill and stood up. "Please don't worry yourself about your bill, Miss Faraday," he said loudly. "I would be more than happy to pay for your coffee."

"Oh, do have another cup on me, Mayor, I have something to show you." She reached into her purse and brought out the copied articles. "See?" She waved them at him, and he merely ignored her, tossed a dollar on the table ,and turned to leave.

"It's a picture of you and your father," she said deliberately, and while he turned back around to look, he didn't sit. "Oh, and here's another one as well." She laid them both out on the table, and he glanced at them and immediately sat back down.

"Wherever did you get those articles?" His attempt at nonchalance fell short when his already pale complexion turned two shades lighter.

"Well, actually I had to have them copied from microfilm at the library. Would you believe that someone actually tore those pages out of the archives? I can't imagine what could possess someone to deliberately remove them, but—"

"And why pray tell, were you researching these particular articles?"

"Well, actually I'm still hoping to find some information about why you won't permit the pond to be used in the campaign," she admitted. "And since it was originally closed to the public around that particular time, I thought perhaps I might find out the reason why." She picked up one of the articles. "Although I can understand why you might have removed the article displaying an argument between you and your father, it can't make you feel good to know that he didn't believe in you enough to support your desire to be mayor. And that poor little boy, what was his name?" She picked up the other article. "Oh yes, Boyd Caldwell, the little boy who drowned in that pond. How awful for you, not to mention his poor parents. I do wish you'd just told me that in the beginning. I wouldn't have dreamed of including the pond in the Christmas campaign had I known."

"Well then." He began his eyes cautioning and lacking any warmth whatsoever. "I take it you are now convinced there is ample enough reason to keep it closed then?"

"Well, I have to admit that now that I've read this article, I couldn't possibly use it." She lied. "I realize now that this little boy's accident could be the reason why I received that letter we spoke about. It's certainly easier to understand their fear after seeing this article."

"Yes. Indeed it is." He took the handkerchief out of his breast pocket and dabbed at his forehead. "I am grateful to you for coming to me with your decision to forego use of the pond under these circumstances." He ground out, and Charlie felt a prickle of apprehension run up her spine. She had never seen him so angry although he did very well concealing it. But then no one else could see his face.

"Yes, I'm sure you are, but I can't help wondering why the articles were removed in the first place. It seems as though someone didn't want them found. I mean, I do realize that this happened a long time ago. The family most likely isn't even around anymore, it happened so long ago, but I'm ashamed to say that I may have opened an old wound by mentioning the use of the pond for the Bring Back Christmas campaign, and now I feel that I owe it to the family to make amends."

"My dear Miss Faraday, I am quite sure that is not necessary. I am also sure they have most likely not heard of your campaign." He could barely say the word without gritting his teeth. "And even if they had, your decision to forego incorporating the pond into your activities will quell any foreboding they may have had."

Charlie looked over at him and smiled sweetly. "Well, of course you're right." She conceded. "Removing those pages from public record was probably nothing more than malicious mischief or perhaps merely a coincidence, and here I am looking to make more out of it than it really is. I'm probably wasting my time researching clues that don't exist—sort of chasing ghosts as it were."

"Precisely." He agreed. "Although your concern for the family is admirable, I'm sure it is perhaps guilt gone astray and your worry has been for naught."

"That's probably true." She agreed and then paused just long enough. "Then again, if there is more to this than meets the eye, I do owe it to them to find out. I mean either way, I won't have lost anything but time, but I'll feel so much better knowing I tried, wouldn't you agree?" She slid out of the booth. "Well, I do have to be running along myself, Mayor, but thank you so much for the coffee and the conversation. It has been extremely enlightening. Have a nice day."

Just before she walked out the door, she glanced back to see him still sitting in the booth where she'd left him. Though her heart was beating a mile a minute and a million butterflies were doing a frenzied dance in her stomach, by the look on his face, he'd walked right into her trap and had taken the bait. She wasn't sure exactly what she expected, but if she was right about him, she knew it wouldn't be long before she found out.

In the meantime, she did stop by the church to see how the children were doing. They had been working so hard on their manger scene and practicing their songs that Emma and Sally decided it might be a good idea if they spent a few extra Sundays getting a bit more practice in and this was one of those Sundays.

"So how is everything going?" she asked the children. "Miss Hathaway and Mrs. Dunne say you're all doing great."

"We are!" some of them shouted, producing their projects for Charlie's inspection. She knew that the two women had been helping them along by outlining everything and all they had to do was fill it in, but they were doing a wonderful job and everything was beginning to look a little more like Christmas. "And how is the singing and the play coming along? Does everyone know their lines?"

They all screamed a resounding yes! And Charlie congratulated them one by one and added, "This is going to be the best play Braxton has ever seen! I'm very proud of all of you, keep up the good work." She stayed awhile longer ,suggesting several ways to improve on the play and the manger, and before she left, she told the women to feel free to contact her if they needed additional help.

Charley was still ten minutes early for her meeting with Carl when she arrived a second time at the diner. After looking around for several seconds and not seeing him, thinking he'd possibly forgotten about the meeting, she finally caught sight of him seated in a booth in the far corner of the diner with his back to the door; she'd almost missed him.

She walked back and slid into the seat across from him and was startled by his appearance. He looked as if he hadn't slept for days with dark circles under his eyes and his face drawn and haggard.

"Carl, you look awful, what happened?"

The waitress came with a coffee pot, looked at Charlie rather oddly but said nothing as she filled the cup Charlie held up to her. She then dropped a few small creamers on the table, looked as though she might say something but changed her mind and sauntered away.

"I haven't been sleeping very well."

"Obviously." She absentmindedly opened the creamers and poured them into her coffee while watching Carl. "What's wrong?"

"I sent Lila to her mother's for a few days."

"Oh, because of the fire, I was really sorry to hear about that, Carl. Matthew called—"

"No, it wasn't because of the fire, Charlie—not directly anyway."

Charlie frowned, not understanding. "Okay."

"Listen, I've been thinking that maybe it's not such a good idea that I involve you in this after all."

"What do you mean? I'm already involved. Besides you can't ask me to meet you and then not tell me why, you sounded so mysterious. What's going on?"

"Well, it's just that something isn't right about this whole thing."

"You mean about the fire or the story or what?"

"Both." He looked over at her strangely, and once again, the hair on the back of her neck stood on end.

"Both? What do you mean both? What could the story possibly have to do with—oh my god!" she said, and then quickly lowered her voice. "You think your barn burning down has something to do with the story you wrote in the paper?" She searched her mind for a few seconds and then looked directly at him, the recognition all over her face. "Of course, it has to do with your article, doesn't it? You did mention the pond." She leaned toward him and began talking low. "Do you know that he actually came to my office and warned me in no uncertain terms that I couldn't reopen that pond? And on top of that, he nearly went berserk at the council meeting when I asked why he was so against it."

"Are you serious?"

"I'm dead serious. Right after I asked what it was about the pond that he was so afraid of, he adjourned that meeting so fast, no one knew what hit them and he stormed out of the hall like a crazy person. I never would have believed it if I hadn't seen it with my own eyes."

"Well, that doesn't surprise me, and it certainly explains things a little more clearly."

"Explains what things, Carl, what's going on? This whole thing keeps getting more and more bizarre. First he threatens me not to have the Christmas campaign, then he tells me I can't reopen the pond, and then I get a letter—"

"A letter, what kind of letter? Who sent it?"

"Well, I don't know exactly who sent it, it was signed 'A concerned citizen,' but I have my suspicions. Anyway, to make a long story short, it said that it wasn't a good idea to reopen the pond, that if I did it could be bad for the community and someone might get hurt. Then to top things off, he actually walked into my office a few days later telling me that he'd heard that I still wanted to use the pond in the campaign and came right out and told me it was never going to happen. He said he didn't write the letter, but why would he come to see me about the very things mentioned in it if he isn't the one who wrote it? It seems too coincidental to me."

"I got one too."

"What do you mean, you got a letter too?"

"Shh! Keep your voice down! If someone's listening—" He looked around as though he was expected someone to be doing just that. "That's why I sent Lila to her mother's for a few days. I didn't want her involved."

"Involved? What do you mean involved, in what?"

"When I was cleaning up the mess in the barn, I found a note—well, half of it anyway—and I managed to make out 'You've been warned to keep' and that's it that's all I could make out of it, the rest of it was burned off."

Charlie sat back against the booth. "And then the bridge is destroyed." She looked pensive. "I don't like this, something strange is going on around here."

"There's something else. I had boxes of old newspapers stored in the loft of the barn which were also destroyed."

"I do remember Matthew telling me something about that and I was going to ask you about them, were they important?"

"Well, at the time we were renovating the newspaper office, we had nowhere to store a lot of the newspapers from years back and I suggested keeping them at my place temporarily. It was no big deal except when Lila complained that we had too much around the house as it was and I ended up storing them up in the loft. I didn't know when we would be able to get things organized again, so I put them in black garbage bags and kept them out of the light so they wouldn't fade. Although we started to record them on microfilm, when the renovation started, we had to put it on hold. I don't know if they got them all entered or not."

"You don't think, wait a minute, did he know about the newspapers?"

"I'm sure he did, he knows everything that goes on in this town and he was consulted on the renovation. I'm not really convinced that the newspapers had anything to do with the fire. It would make more sense that he was trying to warn me to back off too, and that the pond is the real issue here. You don't happen to have that letter with you?"

Charlie fished around in her purse. "I brought it with me in case you wanted to see it." She handed it to him, and he scanned it.

"It's the same printing, Charlie, right down to the crooked 't' crossed in the middle. It seems both the letter and my note were written by the same person."

"Maybe we should tell the sheriff, Carl, there's no telling what he might do now that—"

"We can't do that. We don't know for sure who wrote the note or the letter, and we have to have some kind of proof before we tell the sheriff anything."

"You're right, you're right, but what do we do in the meantime? If it is him, there's no telling what he might do next."

"Have you told anyone else about the letter?"

"Just my mother and Pete, and I really don't think they'll say anything to anyone, Pete especially. He went into a rage when I told him I suspected the mayor of sending the letter. And there's something else, Carl. The mayor knew things he couldn't possibly have known, things I only said to you from my office, and—"

"Why do you think I asked you to meet me here, Charlie? Look, it's probably just a coincidence, but for the time being, just keep things to yourself until you hear from me. I have an idea that might just bring things to a head." He got up to leave. "Stay put for a while so it doesn't look so obvious that we were meeting unless someone knows it already."

"What are you going to do?"

"You'll find out soon enough, but for right now, the less you know, the better. Just remember, not a word to anyone about our meeting or anything else. I'll call you as soon as I know something."

"Listen, Carl," she began, but he was already walking up the aisle to the counter where he paid his bill and left.

To say the least, Charlie had a lot on her mind after her meeting with Carl, especially since he'd been so mysterious and wary of everyone around them, but she forced herself to put it out of her mind and wait for him to contact her before she assumed anything. She just hoped he wouldn't do anything crazy and make more trouble for himself. Whoever was responsible for the accidents proved he was ruthless enough to use whatever means necessary to get what he wanted and it was obvious that hurting whoever got in his way was not a problem—Carl's barn was proof of that. But now that Braxton knew that she knew about the missing articles, it could prove even more dangerous, especially if he was the one who disposed of the originals, although at this point, Lord only knew why.

Charlie suddenly felt the need to get away from everything and everyone. So many things had happened that lacked answers—at least viable ones that made sense anyway. Although it didn't take a psychology major to realize John Braxton had problems and that some may have turned a blind eye because of a misplaced sense of loyalty, Charlie was fairly certain that if she was right, in his mind, they weren't problems he needed answers to, they were problems he needed to eliminate, and the frightening part was how far he would go to eliminate them. And with that thought, she decided to make a visit to Pine Cone Bluff, the only place she knew to go when she was looking for answers to impossible questions.

The bluff, merely a wide pull-off close to the top of Pine Cone Hill, was not only a place where she could be alone to sort things out without distractions, it was also a great place to forget your problems and become a part of nature without all the rigors of a time-clock, demands and a sense of urgency to get things done before one's life-span ended. Up here, it was slow and easy and time stood still if only for a little while.

Only ten minutes from town, the four-mile long road up to the bluff was like entering another world untouched by man.

Surrounded on both sides by deep woods and a steep incline on the right, the winding road required an even slower speed when an occasional deer or chattering squirrel or chipmunk darted across your path. And while it took a short time to reach the top, the drive was peaceful and blissfully quiet with none of the distractions or problems everyday life offered, and lately, Charlie had had too many of both. What added to the calm serenity was the fact that there didn't seem to be anyone else on the road, spare a car or two back down toward the bottom of the hill. The solitude was comforting, and comfort was just what she needed.

It was a beautiful afternoon, still warm enough to have the windows down and Charlie breathed in the musky earthen smell of the woods all around her. Although the leaves hadn't yet turned, she knew it wouldn't be long before they would change, and it was the time of year she enjoyed the ride most.

Just before she reached the top of the hill, she came to the bluff and pulled off to the side and shut off the motor. When she got out of the car, she immediately searched for her favorite sitting rock and found it hidden under much overgrowth, the realization that it had been a lot longer than she thought since she'd been there. She'd missed those times when she could sit and think about absolutely nothing for as long as it took to clear her mind, just unwind and enjoy the serene quiet and beauty without having to think one solitary thought. Unfortunately her mind was as unsettled as the wind and everything that had happened since she began the Bring Back Christmas campaign seemed to swirl around in her head, and instead of relaxing, her mind was again a whirlwind of unanswered questions and suspicion.

While nothing ever seemed to go as smoothly as people imagined it in their minds, far too many things had been happening lately for them to be called coincidences. The fire on Kissing Bridge, Carl's barn burning to the ground, Pete getting fired, and now the missing newspaper articles all seemed to add up to one ugly word: conspiracy.

Someone was trying very hard to ruin everything she and so many people had worked so hard for and she couldn't help thinking that John Braxton was behind it all, and now that she had set the stage by confronting him with the newspaper articles, she was expecting a bomb to drop—she just didn't know where or when or on whom. So far, by the grace of God, no one had been hurt, but she was afraid that it was only a matter of time before he made a careless mistake and someone did get hurt or worse.

Charlie didn't know how long she sat there thinking, but she was even more frustrated and knew less than she did before she came. There was one thing she knew for sure, however, and that was while most of her trips to the bluff helped to her clear her mind and often provided solutions to her problems, this trip succeeded only in giving her a nasty headache.

Disgusted, she stood up, snatching the jacket she'd been sitting on, and dusted off her jeans. *Well, whatever happens, happens,* she thought, slinging her jacket over her shoulder as she walked to her car. *Destiny sometimes has a way of surprising us when we least expect it, and I'll just have to deal with things as they come.* She stopped for a second and gazed all around her and then looked up at the sun filtering through the tall trees. Actually, the trip wasn't a total loss; she did manage to get away from the rat race if only for a little while anyway, and despite her headache, she felt strangely peaceful and calm.

After carefully turning her car around and starting down the hill, a bee suddenly flew in the window and landed on her arm, and she immediately jammed on the brakes and stuck her arm out the window, frantically trying to shake off the pesky insect before it stung her. She was horribly allergic to the bee's poisonous sting and hadn't even thought to bring the kit she was supposed to carry with her all the time, mistakenly believing they'd all found a place to hide until next year. Fortunately, it flew off a second later, and she quickly rolled up the window. That's all she needed to make her day: a migraine, her arm swollen up to her armpit, and her throat closed up tighter than a bank vault.

You need to relax, Charlie, she told herself. *Just clear your mind and don't think about anything.* But she'd only driven a short distance when her thoughts inevitably drifted back to the mayor, and it was then that she made up her mind that she would tell the sheriff everything she knew. Although it wasn't much, it was something, and with a little subtle persuasion, she was sure she could convince him to at least investigate her argument that he was deranged.

Well, maybe not deranged, she thought, half-smiling, conjuring up a picture of him with his hair sticking straight up and a demonic grin on his face. *Maybe disturbed is a better word.*

In any case, if he was the one responsible, she now realized that she alone could do nothing to stop him. However, if others were made aware of his seemingly darker side, she just might convince them to back up her opinions and see things the way she did. She sighed contentedly, thinking that maybe something good had come out of this little trip after all and slipped the car into second gear as Pete had taught her. When she was about a quarter of the way down the hill, the incline grew steeper, and she lightly pressed the brake to slow down. She continued to do it intermittently to avoid burning up the brakes as Pete had drummed into her head a thousand times, but as she wound around one bend and started into another and pressed the brake, her foot suddenly went to the floor. She tried pumping them again and again, but she felt no resistance, nothing—and it was then she realized she had no brakes.

Charlie tried not to panic as the car gained momentum, now taking the curves at a horrific speed as she struggled to maintain control, and twice, she just missed slamming into the guardrail as she tried to keep the swerving vehicle on the road. When the driver's side tires suddenly slid in the gravel, Charlie jerked the wheel back, sending her to the opposite guardrail where the car bounced off it and the steering wheel was ripped from her hands. As she tried to grab the wheel, the car began to fishtail, the tires screeching, and the smell of rubber burning as it slid sideways across the pavement where it slammed into the driver's side guardrail, flipped over it sideways going airborne for several seconds. While Charlie's bloodcurdling scream heard by no one, echoed through the woods, the car flipped again before hitting the embankment with a sickening thud and slid on its roof, the horrendous scraping of metal on stone reverberating through the woods like a machine gun before it slammed against a tree in a dead stop sending out sound waves like a cannon going off. And then there was silence.

Unbeknown to anyone that the horrible accident had happened, Matthew had just called Charlie at home with good news and her mother answered.

"I'm sorry, Matthew, but I haven't seen Charlie since this morning."

"Well, I know she had a meeting with Carl, would you know where that was by any chance?"

"No, I'm sorry I don't, but if the meeting was early, I doubt that it lasted this long, it's already twelve-thirty. Did you check the bridge site? Maybe she went there, I know she's been dying to see it."

Matthew laughed. "I know what you mean, and if she was anywhere, it would be there, but I was just left the site, that's the reason I wanted to talk to her. The guys did say she'd been there Saturday morning, but they haven't seen her since. But it's good news so not to worry. I can talk to her tomorrow. Would you mind telling her I called? It just might make her day."

"I sure will. Take care, Matthew."

Pete noticed a strange look on DeeDee's face when she hung up. "Is something wrong?"

"I'm not sure," she said quietly, then a second later, she brushed it off. "It's probably nothing. Just a mother thing, I guess."

"What's 'just a mother thing,' something I wouldn't understand, I suppose?"

"Well, no, nothing like that. It's just—" she paused for a minute, arousing Pete's curiosity.

"Uh oh, when you get that look on your face, Deanna, I know something's up, even though you're usually wrong. What's the matter?"

"Well, I'm not sure exactly. Charlie had a meeting this morning with Carl Freeman—you know, the editor of the paper—but that was earlier and I haven't seen or heard from her since. And now with Matthew calling, I just have this feeling—"

"Don't do this, Dee. You're always telling me she's not a kid anymore, so what's the big deal? She doesn't tell you everything she does or everywhere she goes, she's twenty-five, remember?" He shook his head and went back to his paper. "Quit worrying so much. She probably had something to do and just didn't say anything about it."

DeeDee thought about that for a second. "I guess you're right, it's just that she usually calls."

"You're worrying for nothing, Deanna." Pete placated. "She's a big girl. She can take care of herself."

"Yes, well just the same, I'm going to call Carl and see if he knows anything." She looked up his number and dialed.

"She's going to be madder than hell with you checking up on her and you know it."

"Well, she'll just have to get over—hello, Carl? This is DeeDee Faraday, and—I'm fine, thanks. How are you both doing? We were so sorry to hear about your barn, is there anything we can do to help?" She listened for a few moments and then smiled. "Yes, I know, Charlie told me—be sure to tell her I said hello." She looked over at Pete. "Yes, I'll tell him, thanks. Listen, Carl, I know you had a meeting with Charlie this morning, but I was just wondering if she mentioned any plans she might have had or where she might be going—" She paused again, and then sighed. "Oh, I see. Uh huh. No, no, nothing's wrong, it's just that I haven't heard from her since she left, but I'm just a natural worrier, I'm sure she'll show up. Yes, I'll tell her. Thanks anyway, Carl." She hung up and still had a strange look on her face. "He said he left the diner before she did, and she didn't say anything about any plans or going anywhere, so I'm sure she'll be home soon."

"She's probably practicing with those kids or something, and while you're moping around worrying about he,r she'll come waltzing in here and you'll feel like a damn fool for worrying so much," Pete said it, but he didn't believe it. He lied when he said DeeDee was usually wrong when she had those anxious feelings.

On the contrary, nine times out of ten, her feelings were right on the money, but there was no way in hell he was telling her that.

By two-thirty, DeeDee was pacing. "Something's wrong, Pete, I can feel it. I called Jean and Helen and they said they haven't seen her since Friday, and Mary's out shopping with her mother. I'm going to the diner and see if I can find out anything."

Pete put the crossword puzzle he'd been working on aside. "I'll go with you," he said without an argument, and DeeDee knew right away that he was as concerned as she was. Pete rarely agreed to anything without some sort of complaint and that alone worried her.

"Oh sure, she was here," June said, chomping on her gum as she bussed a table. "She and Carl were sitting right back there in that booth. They were here for about forty-five minutes or so I guess, and then Carl left and Charlie left about ten minutes later. As a matter of fact, now that I think about it, I've seen her more in the past few days than I've seen her in a month—she was just in here with the mayor."

"The mayor?" Pete shouted as they headed toward the car. "What the hell was she doing with the mayor?"

"I don't know, Pete, but I don't like this, I don't like this at all."

When they turned onto their street and caught sight of the sheriff's car parked in front of their house, DeeDee grabbed Pete's arm. "Oh my god, something's happened to Charlie!" The fear in her eyes grabbed at Pete's already pounding heart.

"Take it easy," he said, putting his arm around her. "Let's not jump to any conclusions."

They got out of the car and walked toward the sheriff who met them halfway. "Pete, DeeDee." Sheriff Conley greeted them. He looked as if he'd been out on a bender, and this was the last place he wanted to be.

"Bill." Pete said, shaking his hand. "What's going on?"

"It's Charlie, she was in an accident and is in the hospital," he said straight out, and DeeDee's legs sagged under her, but Pete caught her before she fell. "She's going to be okay, Dee, she's a little busted up, and right now, she's unconscious, but the doc says she's going to be all right. I'm just sorrier than hell to have to bring news like this folks." He cleared his throat.

DeeDee was shaking so badly her knees were knocking, and Pete tried to persuade her to sit down on the brick wall alongside the driveway, but she violently shook her head. "No! I want to see her." She managed.

Pete nodded at the sheriff, and he grabbed DeeDee's other arm. "Come on, we'll take the squad car."

Fifteen minutes later, they were walking down the second floor corridor of St. John's Hospital toward Charlie's room, when Bill whispered to Pete that things looked worse than they were, but maybe he should prepare DeeDee.

"Uh, listen, honey," Pete began. "She's pretty banged up, like Bill said, so don't expect, you know, don't be surprised when you see her."

"I know, Pete," she said, understanding. "I know how accident vic—" She bit her lip. "I know what to expect."

"Well, it's just, it's got to be different with your own," he said gently, and DeeDee patted his arm.

"I know what you're trying to do, Pete, and I love you for it, but I'll, I'm sure I'll feel better once I see her no matter—" She took a deep breath. "No matter what she looks like. Oh! Someone should call Matthew and Paul. They'll want to know."

"I've already done that, honey, they're on their way."

"And the girls at the office—" she rushed to say, and Pete nodded.

"I called Jean and told her to call the others," he reassured her, and DeeDee looked up at him and tried to smile.

"What would I do without you?"

"Let's hope we never find out." He kissed her forehead, not smiling. "Now, let's go in and see our daughter." He grabbed her hand tight, and they walked into the room together.

DeeDee's eyes immediately filled with tears as she looked at her daughter lying motionless in the bed, looking paler than she'd had ever seen her. There were tubes connected to hanging bags full of solutions, one dripping down into an intravenous needle inserted into the back of Charlie's hand and one inserted into her arm. Wires came out of machines that were attached to her head while electrodes on her chest measured her heartbeat and oxygen tubes in her nose helped her to breathe. It seemed that tubes were intermingled with wires, and they were all going in every possible direction. It was frightening, and DeeDee instantly understood Pete's comment about it being different with your own, and just as he grabbed a chair and slid it close to the bed for DeeDee to sit down, the doctor walked in.

"Hello, I'm Doctor Ward, your daughter's attending physician."

"It's nice to meet you, doctor. I'm Charlie's mother, Deanna, and this is my husband, Pete."

He shook Pete's hand and then DeeDee's. "It's good to meet you both. Now, I must tell you that she looks much worse than she is, so don't let all the paraphernalia scare you. We're monitoring her very closely and taking every precaution, so don't pay attention to all the beeps and clicking noises, they simply tell us what we need to know. However, I don't want to make light of the situation. Your daughter has been through a lot, but fortunately, she has youth on her side, an older person would never have survived an accident like she did, and to be brutally frank, she's lucky to be alive. I don't know how much the sheriff told you if anything, but from what I understand, her car was completely demolished in the crash. And while she does have a concussion and is unconscious, she is not in a comatose state, and there is every indication that she'll come out of it without any problems. She does have a few cracked ribs and a broken wrist and she will be sore, but I can assure you that with rest and a little care, your daughter should be just fine. I am going to insist that she stay in the hospital for a few days however, just to make certain everything is as it should be, and barring anything unforeseen, she'll be able to go home. Now, do you either of you have any questions?"

"I think you've explained everything, Doctor, and although I do realize you can't know for sure, do you think she'll know us when she wakes up?" DeeDee asked, and the doctor looked around DeeDee to her daughter and nodded in her direction.

"Why don't you ask her yourself?"

DeeDee spun around then and saw the faint hint of a smile on Charlie's face.

"Hi, Mom," she whispered, raising her good hand in an attempt to wave, and DeeDee immediately went to the bed.

"Charlie, thank God," she said, gently taking hold of her daughter's outstretched hand blinking back the tears. "I want to give you a hug even though I know you don't like the fuss, but and I'm afraid I'll hurt you, not to mention disconnecting some of these wires," she said warily.

"I know, Mom, it's all right, don't worry about it."

"Charlie, what on earth happened?"

"I'm not exactly sure." She managed. "I'm still kind of groggy."

"That's the pain medication, young lady," the doctor said, reaching down to take her pulse. "And you'll be feeling like that for a few days I'm afraid. You have a couple fractured ribs and a broken wrist that are going to give you hell for a while." He gently patted her hand and smiled. "In the meantime, just take it easy and don't expect too much, you have some healing to do." He turned and held his hand out. "It was nice meeting you both, Mr. and Mrs. Faraday. If you have any questions, let the nurse know and she'll notify me. Now if you'll excuse me, I have another patient to look in on so I'll let you get to your visit but only for a short time. Your daughter needs her rest."

Pete pushed the chair close to the head of Charlie's bed and had DeeDee sit down.

"You gave us quite a scare," Pete said. "I can't tell you how glad your mom and I are that you're all right." He kissed her forehead, and Charlie felt tears sting her eyes when Pete pulled away. It was the first time in years he'd shown affection of any kind toward her, and it touched her heart. He told DeeDee he would be right back and then he stepped out in the hall, giving them needed time together, as well as giving him time to talk to Bill.

"What the hell happened, Bill?" Pete asked, but before Bill could answer, Matthew and Paul came walking down the hall toward them.

"Bill." Matthew shook the sheriff's hand and then Pete's. "Thanks for calling me, Pete, I appreciate it. This is my grandson, Paul, this is Pete, Charlie's stepdad."

Pete reached out to shake his hand. "I hear Charlie talking about you quite a bit, but of course, she'd have my head in a sling if she knew I told you that."

Paul tried to smile and Pete couldn't help but notice his face was drawn and haggard as if he hadn't slept in a week, and if he didn't know Paul's intentions toward his stepdaughter before, he knew now.

"She's going to be all right, isn't she?"

"The doctor was just in and he says she needs to heal, she does have a concussion, a few broken ribs, and a broken wrist, but he said she'll pull out of this just fine."

"Do you have any idea how this happened, Bill?" Matthew asked, and the sheriff motioned for them to move down the hall a bit.

"I was starting to tell Pete that from what we can tell, Charlie apparently lost control of her car. At first, we figured she swerved to miss a deer or something, but we don't know for sure. How in hell she managed to keep the car on the road as long as she did is anyone's guess, but by the looks of the skid marks, she must have hit the guard rail on the passenger's side, fishtailed across the road and hit the guard rail on the driver's side, then flipped over the guard rail. We figure she was airborne because there aren't any marks at all until farther down the embankment where you can see a deep indention where she hit and then slid about a hundred feet before slamming to a stop against a tree. She's damn lucky to be alive. I can tell you that because that's what saved her from going all the way to the bottom of the cliff. Personally speaking, I don't believe she swerved to miss a deer because there were no marks matching that kind of a skid, and if she had hit one, we'd have found fur, blood, something, and there was nothing. I don't believe she was driving too fast either, not by choice, anyway."

"What the hell do you mean by that?" Matthew asked, the muscle in his jaw twitching.

"Just what the hell you think it means, Matt, someone cut the front brake line. It wasn't hard to spot since the car was upside down, there was brake fluid all over the frame."

"So this was no accident, somebody tried to kill Charlie," Paul said, and Bill nodded.

"I'm afraid so, son, and they damn near succeeded."

"Son of a—" Matthew began, but Pete stopped him.

"Now hold on, Matthew, maybe the brake line was cut when she went over the guardrail."

The look on Matthew's face told him otherwise, but Pete tried to keep him calm. "Look, I know it's a stretch, but—"

"Too much of a stretch, Pete." Bill broke in. "From what we can tell, she hit that guardrail full on the driver's side, flipped over it, and then flipped again before the car landed on the roof and slid into the tree. That's why it's caved in so much more than the passenger's side, but the underside was clear at all times, it never hit a thing. Besides, we found a small puddle of brake fluid up near the bluff. It probably leaked out when she turned around or something, and if she did have any left, she lost it the first time or two she braked coming down the hill. But there's something else, something none of us can explain, besides the fact that nobody knows who called or where the call came from, although I don't know why that should be a surprise—nothing about any of this makes any damn sense. Anyway, when we found Charlie, she was lying in a grassy area about a hundred feet or so from the car just like she was put there. She wasn't thrown through the windshield because it was still intact if you can believe that, and both doors were caved in so bad there was no way anyone could have opened them and gotten her out of there."

"Well, how the hell did she get out?" Pete asked. "This is ridiculous, there has to be another explanation."

"Well, maybe you can tell me, Pete, because I don't have one damn clue. Even if she could get either door open, she was upside down, remember? All her weight would have been pushed against the seat belt, and there's no way in hell she could have unlocked it in that position. Besides, she couldn't have been in any condition to pull herself out of there, think to shut the door, and walk a hundred feet and lay down in the grass, it's humanly impossible. But that's exactly how we found her."

"There's the possibility that someone actually saw the accident happen and helped her and then called to report it," Pete insisted, but the sheriff blew off that theory as well.

"Pete, there were no footprints anywhere near the car and the ground was pretty soggy down there—it usually is in wooded areas, especially after a rain—but there were deer prints all over the place."

"Well, how the hell *did* she get there?" Matthew asked.

"Maybe we can get something out of Charlie because I sure as hell can't figure it out."

Pete asked the doctor if it would be all right to question her about the accident and he gave his permission, cautioning them not to excite her and not to stay long, and that's when Paul spoke up.

"I'd like to see Charlie for a few minutes before you go in if you don't mind."

Pete lightly clapped him on the shoulder. "I don't see that as a problem under the circumstances, just let me go in and talk to my wife."

He disappeared into the room, and he and DeeDee came out a minute later. She immediately gave Matthew a tearful hug, reassuring him that Charlie was going to be all right and thanked them for coming. "She's has been asking to see you both," she told them, and then she smiled up at Paul. "She was calling your name in her sleep," she said softly and then she grabbed his hand and squeezed it. "But don't tell her I told you."

"You have my word," Paul said gruffly, trying to smile. "Thanks." He went into the room while Pete and DeeDee went for coffee, and the two older men talked outside the door.

"Someone wanted Charlie dead, Matt," Bill said bluntly. "But my question is why? I know she had some resistance from quite a few people about that Christmas thing, but that's hardly a motive for murder. I'm sorry, but there's only one reason someone would deliberately cut the brake line of a car and I can't think of one good reason to hurt that girl unless it's somehow connected to all the other *accidents* that have been happening around here." He started pacing. "I really need a cigarette."

"I thought you quit years ago," Matthew said.

"I did, but right about now, I'm thinking about starting up again."

In the meantime, Paul was still standing near the door of Charlie's room. Her eyes were closed, and it was a good thing because he had a hard time getting past all the apparatus she was hooked up to and the strange pain he felt around his heart was all too clear on his face. He took a deep breath and let it out slow before walking over to the head of the bed and got down on his haunches. He gently grasped Charlie's good arm and leaned close to her face. "Jesus, Charlie, what happened?" He asked not really expecting an answer. "What in the hell did you do that someone would want to—" He closed his eyes as the realization of what almost happened to her actually sunk in, and he pressed his forehead against hers. "I don't know what the hell I would have done if I'd lost you, Charlie."

"You mean it took this for you to realize you can't live without me?" she asked softly, and Paul looked up surprised to see her awake.

She looked into his eyes, and even in her weakened state, she saw the fear and uncertainty and the hope. It was a heady combination especially from a man who was always so sure of himself, and she slowly reached up and touched his cheek. He hadn't shaved and looked like he hadn't slept in a week. It was endearing in a strange sort of way, and Charlie felt a need to reassure him. "You look worse than I feel." Her eyes blinked slowly, and she talked like she was slightly tipsy. "But you don't have to worry, I'm fine. The doctor said so."

"I'm not worried."

"Then why do you look worried?" She blinked slowly again.

"Because I know you, and I know this happened because you were impulsive and reckless trying to play master detective and I'm mad as hell about it." He didn't sound mad.

"I didn't plan on having an accident," she said sleepily, closing her eyes.

"No, but you probably helped cause it with all your nebbing around."

"Wow," she said flatly. "I'm happy to see you too." She opened her eyes then, looking confused. "Nebbing around?"

"I know you had a meeting with Carl, Charlie."

She frowned, trying to concentrate. "You do?"

"And I know what it was about."

"You do?" She was still frowning. "What?"

He looked at her strangely. "How much pain medication are you on, anyway?"

"Oh, lots!" she said dreamily, closing her eyes again.

"I thought so, you probably won't remember one word of this conversation."

She opened her eyes again, the glazed look clearing for just a moment. "I heard every word you said," she said quietly, her eyes staying on his.

He considered what she said to be just talk, suspecting that her medicine was beginning to kick in, but before she went completely under, he wanted to ask about the accident. "Hold on, baby, for just a few more minutes." He quickly stood up and went to the door, quietly motioning Bill and his granddad in, and they stood close to the bed on the opposite side where she couldn't see them.

"Charlie?" Paul knelt by the bed again. "Are you still awake?"

"Um hum," she murmured before opening her eyes again. "Oh, hello, Paul honey," she said, slurring her words a bit, and Paul frowned up at Bill when he heard a snicker.

"Where's Matthew, is he here?" she asked, her eyes opening wider.

"Right here, little darlin'." Matthew answered, coming to the edge of her bed and kneeling down beside it. He carefully took her good hand, and her fingers automatically curled around it as she slowly turned her head to look at him.

"Hello," she said her voice wavering a bit, and Matthew leaned down to kiss her cheek. "I didn't think, I didn't see you." A tear slid down her cheek, and Matthew wiped it away, his own eyes stinging.

"Wild horse couldn't have kept me away, darlin', you know that."

She smiled a weak smile. "Yes." Another tear slipped out of the corner of her eye and slid down her cheek. "I know."

"Okay, Charlie, I know it's hard, baby, but try and concentrate." Paul urged gently. "Can you do that?"

"I'll try for you." She grinned dreamily, and again a little snicker was heard.

Charlie was quiet for a moment and then, "I was at the bluff." She paused, thinking.

"Can you remember what happened, Charlie?"

"There was a bee, I tried to get it—" Her eyes blinked slowly but then they suddenly flashed wide open and her face grew chalk white. "I tried to stop—" Her fingers gripped Matthew's hand tighter, and she began breathing heavily. "I was upside down, screaming, I don't, I was—" Her eyes filled and the tears spilled down her cheeks. "I had no brakes." She looked straight into Paul's eyes. "I tried. I tried to stop—" She was still breathing heavily but her voice had dropped so low he could barely hear her.

"I know, sweetheart, I know," he said, fighting back his own demons. "But you're safe now, you're here with me."

"But then the man came." She closed her eyes, and Paul looked across at the three men.

"What did she say?" Bill asked, and Paul shook his head.

"I think she must be delirious."

"Why, what'd she say?" He insisted, and Paul looked at his granddad and then back to Bill.

"She said a man came."

"A man, what man?" Bill whispered fiercely. "There wasn't anyone there, no footprints, nothing. That doesn't make any sense at all—ask her again."

"Charlie? Charlie, are you awake?" Paul asked, but Charlie didn't respond, and just then, the nurse told them they would have to leave.

"She's exhausted and she needs rest. I'm sorry, but you'll have to come back tomorrow."

"Well, maybe we could come back a little later—" the sheriff began, and the nurse's eyes narrowed slightly.

"Tomorrow."

Paul leaned down and whispered, "I love you, Charlie." And kissed her lightly on the lips and Matthew followed suit, kissing her forehead.

"Sleep safe, little darlin'."

While they all filed out of the room, DeeDee and Pete came back from having coffee. "Did you find out anything?" DeeDee asked.

"Not much, but we'll try another time," Matthew said. "She's been through a lot, she needs to sleep." He kissed DeeDee's cheek, then shook Pete's hand. "I'll keep you posted."

Paul and Bill said their goodbyes, and just as DeeDee and Pete were about to go back into the room, she held back. "What did Matthew mean he'd keep you posted, keep you posted about what?"

"Damned if I know," he said, urging her toward the room. "He was probably just talking about where to take the car, I guess." He couldn't be nonchalant if his life depended on it, but DeeDee was like a mule who wouldn't be led.

"Peter Faraday, you make a terrible liar," she accused, brushing off his hand and looking straight up into his eyes, but he still took a stab at being blasé.

"He didn't really mean anything, Dee, he was just—"

"No stories, Pete, I want the truth."

He sighed, stuffed his hands into his pockets, and walked to the window and gazed out.

"You do realize that what you're not saying is making me more nervous than if you just came out and told me?"

He sighed and turned to walk toward her. "I just don't want you going all crazy and—"

"What am I, a child? Just tell me for the love of Mike!"

"Okay, this was no accident, Dee. Charlie's brake line was cut."

"What?"

"The sheriff and his men found brake fluid up near the bluff, and it was all over the underside of the car."

"You all right, boy?" Matthew asked turning off Main and heading north on Sedgewick Avenue.

"I'm fine." Paul was sullen, thinking, and that worried Matthew. "Do you know where the bluff is?"

Matthew kept his eyes on the road. He knew where the conversation was heading, and he really didn't want to go to either place. "I've been there a time or two."

"I want to go up there."

"Now look, boy—"

"You can either take me, or I'll find it myself—your choice."

Matthew sighed, knowing it was no use trying to talk him out of it. His grandson was just like him when it came down to it; when he made up his mind, there was no changing it. Besides, they'd both been on the same wavelength since they left the hospital, and he immediately swung the truck around in the middle of the busy avenue and headed south toward Pine Cone Hill.

As they neared the top, Paul saw the guardrail before they reached it and Matthew heard the swift intake of his breath. It was smashed and bent inward into the shape of a wide V where Charlie's car hit before it flipped over it; and though he couldn't see anything from his vantage point on the road, the thought of what Charlie must have gone through while it was happening cut through his heart just as sure as someone sliced it open with a knife.

Matthew went up ahead to the bluff where he pulled in off the road, and they just sat there for a few minutes. "It's not going to be a pretty sight, boy, so be prepared."

"I know that," Paul said quietly. He reached for the door handle and Matthew grabbed his wrist. "Just remember that she's safe and sound back at the hospital."

Without a word, Paul opened the door and started down the hill toward the accident site, quite a ways down from the bluff. It was a bit of a walk, and it gave them both too much time to think, but no matter the advice given by his granddad, there was no way he was prepared for what he saw.

When they reached the site, just seeing the car upside down was enough to take the wind out of anyone's sails, but that was far from the worst part.

While the police had already been there and had taken their pictures and checked everything out, the caution tape was still up, and since Matthew had already talked to Bill at the hospital, he was given the okay to check things out once the forensic team was gone from the scene. The tow truck hadn't been there yet, but they knew it wouldn't be long before it would arrive and haul the mangled Avenger up out of there.

"We've just about through here if you want to wait," one of the investigators told Matt, and he and Paul stayed up on the road until they were finished, and after they'd gone, Matthew and Paul climbed over the guardrail and carefully made their way down slope, seeing the long skid mark leading to the car.

As Bill had said it was still fairly damp and they slid several times in the mud, but they finally reached the car and managed to make it around to the driver's side door. It was practically embedded into the tree it had hit so hard, and the door was caved in so far, it was a miracle Charlie wasn't killed on impact and Paul closed his eyes for a several seconds.

"I don't know how she survived this," he said out loud, though talking more to himself. "Somebody sure as hell must have been watching over her."

Matthew said nothing, too overwhelmed by the shock of actually seeing the condition of car. As they continued to feel their way around to the other side, they noticed that the windshield was still intact, and while the passenger's side was smashed in, it wasn't nearly as bad as the driver's side. The left headlight was gone but the right one was still there as was the side-view mirror, but it was obvious the car was totaled.

When they'd seen enough and started back up the hill, Paul noticed the grassy area where they'd found Charlie. Though much of it was trampled down, he could still see part of an impression where she had been laying. It was surreal, as if he was not there physically but watching through a clouded window. He turned away then and started back up the embankment staying to the right of the skid mark and walking through the underbrush. When he reached the guardrail and climbed back over, Matthew was already on his way up the hill toward the truck, but before Paul got to it, he noticed that the oil Bill mentioned was no longer a puddle but had run downward, leaving a path of rainbow-colored liquid on the pavement where it disappeared into the tall weeds beyond the guardrail.

Matthew immediately started the engine and turned around when Paul reached the truck and got in. As they headed down the hill, it was several minutes before either of them said anything.

"I know this was tough on you too, Granddad, but I had to see for myself."

"No explanation necessary," Matthew said quietly, and without another word spoken between them, Matthew drove Paul home, dropped him off, and left, his next stop, Carl Freeman's place.

"Jesus, Matt, I hadn't heard. She's going to be all right, isn't she?"

"The doc says so and we don't have any reason to believe otherwise. She's still pretty out of it right now with all the medication, but he says she'll be fine with some rest and quiet. It's still damn hard to believe she came out of this with only a concussion, a couple broken ribs, and a broken wrist. By the looks of her car—" He stopped himself, not wanting to go there again, and got right to the reason he'd come. "I'm here because I need your help, Carl."

"Anything I can do just ask. She's a sweet girl, Matt, I like her a lot. She has a lot of spunk."

"Yeah, maybe too much for her own good. Listen, I need to know what went on at that meeting you two had. I need to know if it had anything to do with this."

"I'm not sure I follow."

"This was no accident, Carl. Charlie didn't just lose her brakes, someone deliberately cut her brake line."

"Holy hell."

"That's why I need to know. Did she give you any impression that she knew something or that she suspected someone of setting fire to the bridge, anything at all?"

Carl leaned the shovel he'd been using against a tree. "Maybe you'd better come inside."

Once inside, he offered Matthew a beer, which he immediately opened. He took a large swallow and Carl did the same. "Some time back, Charlie and I were talking about her Christmas campaign and I mentioned running a story about it in the paper to try and get more people involved. She liked the idea, and after I wrote it and ran it by her, she agreed that it was just the thing they needed to help get this campaign moving, but before I got the chance to run it, she called and told me to hold off a bit. She only said that she was having doubts about the campaign because of a problem with Braxton or something and she didn't want to jump the gun. I didn't question it because it didn't seem like that big a deal, I just told her to give me the okay when she was ready. Personally, I thought she was doing a fine thing, Matt, and I still do. It's about time somebody did something to get this town on its feet again."

"She's the reason I took on the bridge in the first place," Matthew said. "She was determined to do whatever she could to make it part of her plan, but when I started checking into things, I knew there was no way she could have raised that kind of money, not in that short amount of time. And I knew there was no use talking to Braxton, he's the one who had the bridge closed in the first place, so I went over his head. Then when I told him the bridge was going to be renovated and opened to the public again, he wasn't happy about it. I thought his main gripe was about her wanting to reopen the pond."

"Apparently, it was because he made a little visit to her office about it."

The nerve in Matthew's jaw flexed. "He did what?" The more he learned, the more irate he became. It was clear that Braxton had some sort of personal vendetta against Charlie for some reason and he wanted to know why.

"Charlie told me she thought it was all about the pond too but—"

"What the hell is it with that pond? That's been a problem since she first started this campaign."

"Well, like I was saying, Charlie and I had several conversations on the phone about the articl,e and when it seemed like a lot of the people were finally becoming involved, she finally agreed to let me run it, but—"

"That's when you added the part about the fire being suspicious." He finished for him. "I remember thinking it may not have been such a good idea to mention that."

"Right, because a few days later, my barn was burned down."

"So you think there was a connection?"

"What else could it be, Matt? Why else would they burn down my barn? But when I told Charlie, she didn't agree, she was convinced that it was because I mentioned the pond— wait a second." He opened a drawer from his filing cabinet and produced a sheet of paper. "Here's the article right here, and I quote, 'Perhaps now the mayor will have a change of heart by allowing the pond to be reopened again.' Charlie was convinced it was the pond, especially after she got a letter in the mail. It was unsigned but basically told her the same thing Braxton told her: that she should forget about the pond and that something bad could happen if she didn't."

"That sounds like a threat."

"Charlie was convinced that the letter came from Braxton because it was shortly after that that he showed up at her office, and there's no way I believe it was just a coincidence. The worst part is that I found a note when I was cleaning up the barn—part of one actually, the rest of it was burned—but I was able to make out 'you have been warned to keep' and that kind of tipped me off right there my barn was no accident, but what confirmed it for me was when I compared my note to Charlie's letter and found that the writing matched, that and the fact that he knew things he had no way of knowing, things that only we talked about that never left that office. That's why we met at the diner."

"What the hell, are you implying that Braxton actually bugged your office?"

"No, I'm saying that I think he bugged Charlie's office or maybe he had someone following her. People are in and out of that office every day, anyone could have overheard her conversations. Neither one of us actually came out and said it, but the inference was there. How else do you explain him knowing we talked about the pond?"

Matthew was livid. He somehow suspected that Braxton was responsible for Charlie's accident, and this only reinforced his theory. Now he just had to find a way to prove it.

The next morning, Jean, Helen, and Mary were just leaving, and DeeDee was sitting next to the bed when Paul walked into Charlie's room. The girls were just saying their goodbyes to Charlie, said a quick hello to Paul, and had started out the door when DeeDee told them to wait.

"I think I'll just walk out with the girls and then grab a cup of coffee, Charlie. Can I get you anything?"

"I would like some orange juice if you wouldn't mind."

"Sure. I'll be back in a bit. Hello, Paul, it's nice to see you."

"Hello, Mrs. Faraday, I hope you aren't leaving on my account."

DeeDee smiled. "Not at all. I really would like a cup of coffee." She joined the girls, and Paul took the chair she'd been sitting in beside the bed and turned it around backward and sat down.

"You look better this morning, you're obviously feeling better."

"I don't have a headache and I'm not so foggy," she said, smiling. "I was pretty out of it yesterday I hear."

"Just a bit." He grinned. "But nobody noticed."

"Liar," she said, wincing when she tried to sit up a little.

"Do you need anything, can I move your pillow up a bit?"

"Yes, if you wouldn't mind, I need to sit up just a little. I've been in this position too long."

Paul stood up and gently pulled her pillow out from under her head, fluffed it a little, and tucked it behind her again. "Better?"

"Much! Thank you."

He stood there for a few minutes undecided about whether or not to kiss her hello, but looked at all she was hooked up to and thought better of it and sat back down.

"I have to admit, I don't remember a whole lot, bits and pieces here and there, but that's about it."

"You were in pretty bad shape." His expression was solemn.

Charlie's eyes met his. "I heard one of the nurses talking about my car earlier this morning. I guess it doesn't look much like a car anymore."

Paul didn't know what to say to that, but he felt that strange pain around his heart again. He only hoped she didn't ask him any questions; he wasn't sure he was ready to answer them. Unfortunately, he had little choice.

"What exactly did happen, Paul?"

"Listen, Charlie, you really don't want to talk about this right—"

"Yes, I do," she said firmly. "Everyone else is walking around on egg shells, but I want to know."

He took a deep breath and exhaled. "I just don't think I should be the one—"

"You and Matthew are the only ones who will tell me the truth. My mother keeps changing the subject, and Pete keeps saying I shouldn't be thinking about it and should just try to put it out of my mind. I know they're trying to help, but they can't protect me forever. I need to know, Paul. Besides, maybe if you tell me something, it'll jar my memory."

"Do you remember anything at all?"

"I do remember some things, but it's all still a little hazy. Every now and then, something jumps into my mind, but then it disappears again." She looked at him strangely. "And some of the things I do remember, I'm afraid no one would believe."

"Like what?"

"Well—" She hesitated, not knowing if she should tell him or not, but she took a chance, hoping he would understand. "Like how I ended up in the grass away from the car."

"You mean you remember how you got there?" He didn't want to sound too eager, but if she could at least give them some sort of clue, it might help solve some unanswered questions.

"Yes. But before I tell you anything, I want to know what happened."

Just then, there was a knock on the door, and Matthew peeked around it. "You up to some company, little darlin'?" he asked and Charlie smiled.

"Matthew! Of course I'm up to company, come in."

He walked over to the bed and kissed her on the cheek. "You look great, how are you feeling?"

"Much better now that both of you are here. I'm so glad to see you."

"That goes triple for me, little darlin'!" He grabbed the extra chair and turned it around backward and sat down, and Charlie grinned, noticing they even had some of the same mannerisms. "At least I can understand what you're saying this morning."

She turned toward Paul. "See? People did notice how out of it I was." She teased, and Paul just shook his head.

"So, Matthew—" Charlie began, her expression growing serious. "I told Paul that I want to know what happened, and I know neither one of you will lie to me," she said straight out, and Matthew and Paul looked over at each another. "I'm a big girl I can handle it, trust me."

They both shrugged their shoulders and asked the same question at the same time. "What do you want to know?"

"Why did I lose my brakes?"

"Someone cut your brake line, Charlie," Paul said outright, and Charlie closed her eyes for a second before opening them again.

"I thought so," she said softly. "I just had my car inspected a month and a half ago and my brakes weren't even worn, but I had to ask, I had to be sure."

"Do you remember anything about the accident at all, little darlin'?"

She looked at Paul and then back at Matthew. "I remember starting down the hill, but when the bee flew in my window—"

"The bee!" both men exclaimed, understanding.

"Anyway," Charlie began again, looking curiously at each of them. "I slammed on the brakes and stopped while I tried to get him off my arm and then I started down the hill again. I'd only gone about half a block maybe, and when I tried to use the brakes around a sharp bend, I realized I didn't have any. The car was gaining more and more speed until it was almost impossible to keep it on the road. I guess I hit the guardrail and I think I slid across the road and hit the guardrail on the other side and I remember screaming, but then all I remember is opening my eyes and being upside down. Then the man came and—"

"You saw a man? Are you sure?"

"I'm positive, Matthew. He was a tall man, very tall."

Matthew looked over at Paul. "Then there was someone there."

"Yes." She looked straight into his eyes. "He opened my car door, and he must have been shining a really bright flashlight in my face and I couldn't see anything. Well, I don't actually think the man who took me out of the car was the one holding the flashlight, it must have been someone else, but I didn't really see anyone else—oh I don't know, Matthew, I'm not sure who was there but the man reached in and unfastened my seat belt and lifted me out of the car and carried me over and laid me on the soft grass over to the side. He said I would be safe there and not to be afraid that help would arrive soon. Then he disappeared."

"But it was light out, little darlin', why would they use flashlights?"

"I don't know. All I do know is that the light was so intense that I couldn't look at it."

"Maybe he's the one who called it in, Granddad," Paul said. "He probably didn't want to hurt her by moving her any more than he had to and went for help."

"I don't think so, boy."

"Well, what else could have happened?"

The door opened just then and DeeDee walked in. "Well hello, Matthew. I didn't know you were here too." She gave him a hug, and Paul immediately stood up. "Oh, don't bother about me, Paul, I'm fine." She handed Charlie the orange juice. "Great news, the doctor said you could come home tomorrow, providing you take it easy that is." She cautioned. "He'll come in and explain it all to you this afternoon."

"Well, we're going to get out of here and let you visit with your daughter, DeeDee." Matthew stood up. "We've probably worn her out with our talking." He looked at Charlie and winked. "Oh, by the way, I forgot to tell you the good news! You already know the deck is done and they have the south wall finished but they didn't have to replace the north wall after all, it just needs cleaning up a bit, and with a little elbow grease and a new coat of paint, it'll be good as new. Then all they have to do is put the new roof on and we're good to go. It should take less than a month the way they're going if the weather cooperates."

Oh, Matthew, you're kidding?" She was so excited she tried to sit up, but a pain shot through her head, and she immediately laid back against the pillow again. "I can't wait to see it."

"Well, it'll be a while before they're done, but there will be plenty of time for you to come and check it out. In the meantime, you just take it easy." He leaned down and kissed her on the forehead. "Take care, little darlin', I'll be seeing you soon, you too, Paul. I'll call you later tonight about that deal we were talking about. Dee, can I talk to you for a minute?"

"Sure. Be right back, Charlies" she said, leaving Paul and Charlie alone while they went out into the hall.

Paul walked over to the bed and sat down next to her. "I've got to get going myself, Charlie, but I am glad to see you're feeling better. You had us pretty scared yesterday."

She looked deep into his eyes. "Paul, do you think I'm crazy?"

Paul grinned. "No more than usual, why?"

"Do you think I could have just imagined that I saw that man there?"

"I think you believe what you think you saw."

"Then you do think I imagined it?"

"No, that's not what I said. Look. They did find you in the grass away from the car and there's no way you could have gotten there yourself, someone obviously helped you. Now, get that worried look off your face, we'll figure it out."

"I hope so, but even if we do find out someone did help me, there's still the fact that someone tried to—" She bit her lip, and Paul reached out and gently took her in his arms.

"I know, Charlie. We'll find out who did this, I promise you that." He kissed her lightly and laid her back on the pillow.

"Would you answer a question truthfully?"

"Yes."

"Does anyone besides me think that John Braxton had something to do with my accident? Just tell me the truth, tell me what you think."

Paul watched her eyes steadily. "Truthfully, I don't know. Hypothetically, yes, but that's doesn't go any further than you and I, and I don't want you getting all crazy when you get out of here trying to find out, do you hear me? I happen to like you in one piece, and I want you to promise me you won't go snooping around playing detective or going anywhere near Braxton. We'll take care of this."

"You're really sweet, do you know that?"

"Yeah, I know, I'm a real prince, now promise me."

"I promise." She crossed her fingers under the covers, and he kissed her again then got up and walked to the door. "No more plotting or even thinking about this, get your rest, woman." He ordered opening the door. "I'll see you tomorrow." Just before the door closed shut, it opened again and he peered around it. "And you can uncross your fingers now, that only works when you're a kid." The door closed with a thud, and he was gone before she could say anything, and a few minutes later, DeeDee walked back into the room.

"So how did it go?" she asked, and Charlie gave her a sideways look.

"And they talk about me being a hopeless romantic."

"What do you mean? I merely asked how it went, that's all." She smoothed out the covers on the bed and hung Charlie's robe in the closet, pretending to be busy.

"It went just fine, Mom," she said, shaking her head, smiling.

DeeDee turned around and smiled at her daughter. "I like him a lot, Charlie."

"I know you do." She made an effort to sit up, and DeeDee gave her a hand before finally sitting down on the bed.

"He really cares about you."

"You're not going to let this go, are you?"

"Well, you can't miss it, it's written all over his face."

"Oh, you think so?"

"Yes, I do."

Charlie looked doubtful. "What if it's just because of the accident? What if it's because of all the drama of what happened and—"

DeeDee looked questioningly at her daughter. "Do you really believe that, Charlie?"

Charlie sighed. "I'm not sure what to believe."

"You have to have more faith in yourself to believe he's the one."

"What do you mean?"

"I mean that you have to trust your heart to give you the answer, you can't second-guess yourself when it comes to love. He genuinely loves you, Charlie, and this accident scared the daylights out of him. Matthew and I were just talking about that."

"Oh what, you two are playing matchmaker now?" she teased.

"I don't have to play matchmaker. Paul's in love with you, but that's strictly my, well, actually both mine and Matthew's opinion actually. Look, Charlie. I will tell you that Matthew has never seen Paul this way before with any woman, and that's *all* I'm going to say."

"Well, he's not the same man I met at Matthew's house, that's for sure. He was arrogant and cocky, and I wasn't impressed by him at all."

"Oh, really?"

"Why? What did Matthew say to you?"

"Nothing," she said smoothly. "Nothing at all."

"Oh, by the way, Pete said to say hello." She suddenly changed the subject, and Charlie let it go but only because she had wondered where Pete had been; he hadn't been in to see her much at all. Not that she'd given it much thought, she just wondered.

"Oh. Well, tell him I said hello back."

"Actually he planned to come in, but he has an interview today."

"That's fine, I'm sure he's been busy." She avoided her mother's eyes. "People do have their priorities like you said." She didn't know why she suddenly felt offended by his absence. Most times, she looked forward to it.

"Yes, he has been busy actually," her mother said uncertainly, not exactly sure what to make of her daughter's indifference. But she was a smart woman and knew better than to ask. Although she was painfully aware of Pete and Charlie's normal fingernails-scraping-on-the-blackboard relationship she thought she'd sensed a change lately. "He was offered a position with Matthew as a matter of fact."

"That's good, doing what?"

"The same thing he was doing for the mayor, he'll be on Matthew's finance committee."

"That's great, Mom, it really is." Charlie leaned back against the pillow and closed her eyes. It really was great news, and she was glad that Pete had found another job so fast especially working for Matthew, but she couldn't help thinking he could have at least taken a few minutes to stop by and see if she was still alive. But then again, why should he bother? She probably wouldn't have taken the time to go and see him if the tables had been turned, would she?

She sighed, tired of her mind playing ping-pong with her heart and not at all under- standing why Pete was taking up so much of her thoughts, and now she felt a headache coming on.

"You know I'm feeling kind of miserable right now, Mom, and though I love having you here, I'm not very good company when I get like this—"

"I understand, honey, believe me and it's okay." She quickly gathered up her things. "It's probably a combination of the medication and people coming in and out and you not getting your proper rest. I'll come back later when you're feeling better or maybe I'll just wait until you're ready to leave tomorrow, well, why don't I just call and see how you feel and we'll go from there, okay? In the meantime, just relax and get some rest. I love you."

"I love you too, Mom, and thanks for understanding."

Charlie did feel better finally being left alone. She had a lot on her mind and hadn't been able to think straight since she'd first come into the hospital, although she'd been doped up too much of the time to care. And maybe that was a good thing because now she was thinking too much. She was happy to see that Pete had finally come to his senses and realized Braxton was a man not to be trusted, and after everything that happened, she was sure he now had his own suspicions. Still, it must have been hard on him after working for the man and trusting him for so many years. And that thought alone gave Charlie the idea that it might be a good time to pick Pete's brain. It was possible he may have noticed things about Braxton down through the years, things that might have indicated a pattern to his strange behavior that Pete never thought to question. Then again, maybe she was just shooting at ducks in a barrel trying to find out if there actually was a problem with him. After all, there was the outside chance that she was way off course on this one and that he had nothing whatsoever to do with her accident or the bridge or anything else for that matter. Of course, there was also the chance that she'd hit her head a little harder than she thought, and the logical half of her brain was lying somewhere in the mud on Pine Cone Hill.

CHAPTER IX

———— ❊ ————

The next morning after the flurry of activity to get Charlie's things together and transported home from the hospital in Paul's car, Charlie lay on the sofa, looking a bit tired.

"Maybe you came home sooner than you should have, you do look pale," Paul remarked, sitting on the sofa beside her.

"The doctor said I could go home, and I'm sure he knows what's best for me, Paul." Charlie soothed. "But it's sweet of you to worry about me."

"Can I straighten your pillow for you? Are you thirsty, can I get you something to drink?"

"No. I'm fine, please don't fuss. I get enough of that from Nurse DeeDee, thank you very much. Now tell me again why you had to go out of your way to bring me home?"

"I didn't go out of my way, I wanted to do it. And for the second time, Pete was having another meeting with Granddad and needed his car, and your mother's was in for a tune-up."

"Oh, that's right, sorry, I forgot. It is great that Matthew offered him that job. I'm a little surprised, but I am glad for Pete. He's actually very good at what he does, even though he sometimes takes things to the extreme with the finances."

"They're both stubborn as hell which means they'll probably go at one another's throats occasionally, but Granddad knows people and he hasn't hired the wrong man yet. And speaking of hiring, I might be looking for another job myself if I don't get back to mine. You'll be all right?"

"I'll be fine. If I need anything, you'll be the first to know." She snapped and then looked at him apologetically. "I'm sorry. That didn't come out exactly right. I didn't mean it to sound—I only meant that—oh never mind." She finished lamely, burying her face in the pillow.

"I know what you meant, Charlie." He grinned, pulling the cover up tighter under her arms, and she turned back to look at him. "I don't know why I do that. I'm always saying the wrong things to you, aren't I?"

"Not always," he said, smiling tolerantly. "Just get some rest, Charlie, I'll talk to you later." He leaned down and kissed her lightly. "And stay out of trouble."

The next couple of days were trial and error for Charlie. She could go upstairs, but she had to be careful because there were still times when she would feel lightheaded or unstable. To make matters worse, the doctor had also told her she couldn't go to work for at least a week. Although she couldn't do much with only the use of her left hand, she claimed she could at least answer the phones, but the lawyers had told her not to come back until her wrist was healed and the girls agreed, saying they would cover for her. Worst of all, she wasn't allowed to drive and though that didn't make a whole lot of difference since she no longer had a car, having to depend on others to chauffeur her around didn't help her independence or her attitude.

By the second week, she was beginning to get a little snappy as well as stir-crazy, but her inabilities severed her last nerve when she stopped in to see how the children were progressing on the play and their other projects and she couldn't do a simple thing like help them paint.

"I can't take much more of this," Charlie complained as her mother drove her home.

"Just hang on, Charlie, the doctor said your cast could probably come off in another two weeks."

"Two weeks? I'll go nuts before then! I feel like an invalid and I can't even help the kids with their projects. My wrist feels fine, I should just tell him to take it off now."

"You're lucky you don't have to keep it on for six weeks, now stop acting like a two-year-old and deal with it. If you take it off now, you could do more injury than good and you know it. Besides you should be grateful that's all you have to worry about, you could have been killed in that accident, Charlotte, in case you've forgotten."

Charlie swallowed hard, feeling guilty. She hadn't been thinking about what her mother or anyone else had gone through, especially after learning that her car flipped twice and practically embedded itself into a tree with her in it, and here she was complaining about a little broken wrist. And by the looks of her car, which she had insisted on seeing after her first week home, Charlie knew she had survived only by the grace of God. Even now, she could still see the image of car, the driver's side caved so far inward, it was a miracle she wasn't crushed to death. She still had dreams about it.

"You're right, Mom. I'm sorry for upsetting you. As terrible as it sounds, I guess I wasn't thinking about what everybody else was going through."

Charlie did a lot of thinking that night and remembering. And while things had been coming back to her slowly, she was still having a problem trying to figure out who helped her and what had happened to him. She purposely held back saying anything about his disappearance because in essence that's exactly what he did—one minute he was there and the next minute he was gone, that fast. She'd considered the possibility that she might have been hallucinating but quickly brushed the thought aside, the pain she felt was no hallucination. Still, there were unanswered questions she was hesitant to even ask herself, like how in the world he managed to get her door open. It was so smashed in, the metal so grotesquely twisted and mangled, that it was humanly impossible to get it open. The men at the garage said that the jaws of life couldn't even budge it; they had to use blowtorches to cut through. But no matter how hard she tried she couldn't make sense of all that had happened. The only thing that did make sense was that losing her brakes was no accident, which meant that someone intended her to die in that wreck, and she would have bet her life that that someone was John Braxton.

When Matthew stopped by the next day, Charlie was in a better frame of mind, but she wasn't prepared for his questions or his anger.

"I want to talk to you, Charlotte, and I want you to be straight with me."

Charlie's hand froze in the middle of pouring him a cup of coffee, and she stared over at him as the hot liquid continued to pour into the cup, over the brim and slosh onto the saucer. Finally aware of what was happening, she quickly set the coffeepot down and began blotting at the spilled coffee with the tea towel. She had never heard Matthew use her given name in all the years she'd known him and that alone told her he was madder than hell at her.

"Sit down." He ordered, and she immediately sat like an obedient child.

"Matthew?" she said, finally finding her voice. "What's wrong?"

"Why didn't you tell me about your meeting with Carl?"

Charlie's eyes opened in a deer-caught-in-the-headlights stare, a dozen excuses swirling around in her mind. "Well, I, I was going to. I just—"

"Just what, didn't get around to it? Didn't think it important enough? Or was it because you knew I wouldn't approve of what you were up to?"

"I wasn't up to anything." She swallowed. "I mean I just—" She'd never seen Matthew this angry before, at least not with her and she couldn't think.

"I talked to Carl and he told me everything or at least I think he told me everything. You didn't happen to leave anything out, did you?"

Her stomach tightened up and her mouth was as dry as a cotton ball. "Well, I—"

"If there's anything else, you'd better tell me now because if I find out later that you haven't told me everything—"

"I just, I only wanted to give him something to think about."

"Give who something to think about, Carl? Why would you want to—?"

"Not Carl," she said quietly.

His hands clasped together, Matthew slowly leaned forward in his chair, his eyes darker than she'd ever seen them. "Well, if it wasn't Carl, who was it?"

Charlie mumbled something incoherent and Matthew leaned closer, cocking his head to one side. "What did you just say?"

She took a deep breath and closed her eyes for a second and then opened them again. "The mayor," she said finally, and she watched his knuckles turn white.

"You wanted to give the mayor something to think about?" he asked as though mulling over her words. "And what exactly was it that you gave him to think about, Charlie?" Matthew asked a few seconds later, his tone steady and controlled or at least it sounded that way, and Charlie took a deep breath trying to sort out her thoughts.

"I told him I found some articles in the old newspapers at the library and that I was just—I'd been looking for something about the pond, something that might explain why he was so against using it and—" She lost her breath and swallowed. "While I was looking through them, I noticed that two pages missing. I wondered if they might have been important somehow so I made copies from the files on microfilm, and—" she swallowed again. "I showed them to him to the mayor."

"What kinds of articles?" Although Matthew appeared to have calmed down a bit, he was now sitting on the edge of the seat, as though trying to restrain himself.

"One of them was an article with a picture of the mayor and his father and the other one was about a little boy who had drowned in the pond about twenty years ago."

"And of course, through your brilliant powers of deduction, you naturally thought he was the one who took them out of the record book because they concerned him?" It was more a statement than a question and full of sarcasm, and Charlie raised her chin, her answer bordering on arrogant.

"Yes. Apparently, he wanted to run for mayor, but his father didn't think he was ready and the article was mainly about the ongoing argument they'd been having about it. But when his father died about a year later, John was still determined to get into the race and somehow got voted in. Naturally, that made me wonder how he managed to do that when the people knew his own father didn't think he was ready."

"Naturally." Again more sarcasm and Charlie's eyes narrowed. She didn't like where this was going and she could feel more tension building between them. "Anyway, I can only guess that either enough time passed by, and people forgot about their differences or that John somehow managed to get the town to vote him in."

"And that's where you came in with your little detective's license and decided you would find out." He stared at her through cold gray eyes. "What about the other article?" The disgust in his tone made Charlie's eyes smart, but she'd be damned if she'd let her emotions stop her now.

"It was about a little boy who drowned in the pond. His name was Boyd something, I can't remember his last name, but I had to wonder if there was any connection between his refusal to let me use the pond and, well, the little boy drowning. So I showed him the articles, hoping that if he did have something to do with it or knew anything about it—"

"He would make another move." He finished for her, and she nodded.

"Yes. And that it might somehow connect him to the bridge fire and Carl's barn and—"

"And you were planning to do this all by yourself, why?"

"No, not really, I planned to tell you and the sheriff—"

"But you didn't."

"Yes, but I was going to tell you just as soon as Carl—"

"Carl is just as much to blame as you are. He withheld evidence from the sheriff just like you did with the letter you received in the mail."

"I didn't. I—" She felt her reserve slipping and the dam was ready to burst. Pete and Mom knew about the letter. There was just no proof and—"

"The writing in both the letter you got and the note warning Carl to back off matched, Charlie, and that's enough evidence to get the sheriff involved and start an investigation, but that wasn't good enough. You figured you had all the answers and would just put the puzzle together yourself, but when it came right down to it, you almost took them to the grave with you." He was this close to losing control. "Let me have the letter."

"I, I don't have it. I left it with Carl."

"Sonofa—" He immediately stood up towering over her. "He never mentioned having the letter, which means he intends to go to Braxton with it. Dammit, Charlie, why didn't you come to one of us? What made you think you think you could handle this on your own?" He looked like he could explode at any second, but it wasn't his rage at her that upset her most; it was the last statement he made before he left in a huff. "I sure hope Paul knows what the hell he's getting into."

Against her better judgment, Charlie called Carl to let him know Matthew was on his way, but she didn't call to warn him—she called to tell him to stay and wait—that they'd both done enough to hinder chances of proving John Braxton's part in anything. Worst of all, she'd hurt Matthew by not telling him all she knew and she didn't know if anything would be right between them again. Although she hadn't actually lied to him, she was guilty of the sin of omission and in this case, it had almost cost her life—and perhaps her best friend. Worst of all, he thought Paul was making a mistake getting involved with someone who didn't know enough to come in out of the rain.

Two weeks to the day, Charlie had her cast removed, and with the exception of a rather withered hand, her wrist was completely healed. The doctor also told her not to go to work for one more week. He didn't want her jumping right into using her injured wrist, telling her that he wanted her to use the rubber ball and exercise her hand and wrist first and get it into better shape. Although she was glad to be off work for another week and thought she would be swinging-from-the-tree-tops happy for the extended vacation, she was miserable. She hadn't heard from either Matthew or Paul and she was beginning to think they'd both given her the brush-off. Her spirits were about as low as they could get, and though DeeDee had offered her the use of her car, Charlie dragged her feet until her mother convinced her to go out and have a look at the bridge site to cheer her up.

"It just doesn't seem to matter much anymore, Mom. Matthew hasn't made an attempt to call and neither has Paul."

DeeDee sat down at the kitchen table across from her daughter. "You just have to give Matthew time, Charlie. That accident was the most, well, he suffered just as much as we did and you know how he feels about you. And then to find out you lied to him—"

Charlie stopped squeezing the ball and stared at her mother. "I didn't lie to him, Mother. I intended to tell him everything from the beginning, but things started snowballing and then the accidents started happening, there just didn't seem to be any time. It certainly wasn't my intention to hurt him or anyone else for that matter."

"I know that, Charlie, and I'm sure he knows it too, but like I said, you just have to give him a little time."

"What about Paul? You see? I was right, I should never have let him know how I felt. It may have worked for you and Dad, but obviously, it was the worst thing I could have done. He's just not ready for a relationship."

"How can you possibly feel that way? I'm sorry, but I saw how devastated he was at the hospital. His feelings were real, and no one will ever convince me otherwise, that isn't something you can hide no matter how hard you try. You're just depressed and that usually happens after something as traumatic as—" She put her hands up in defeat when Charlie's eyes narrowed. "Okay, okay, no more lectures. Why don't you take that ride out to the site? I'm sure you'll feel better once you do. Besides if you don't face your fears, Charlie, you can't get over them."

"What are you talking about? I'm not afraid of anything."

"Yes, you are." She gently laid her hand on top of her daughters. "You're afraid you'll run into Matthew out there, and you won't know what to say to him. That's why you haven't called him, isn't it?"

"You know something?" She ignored her mother's question and tossed the ball into the fruit basket on the table. "Maybe I will go out and see the bridge and check out what they've done. Besides, if they aren't able to have it finished in time, I'd like to know now so I can at least let everyone else know not to count on it."

"Sure," her mother said, handing her the keys. "It's better to find out now than to be sorry later."

Charlie looked dubious. "I know there's a double meaning hidden in there somewhere, Mother, no matter how innocent you look."

"Nonsense, I just think you'll feel much better if you do." DeeDee soothed. "Go and see the bridge that is."

Charlie's eyebrow went up skeptically. "Um hum, I'm sure that's what you meant."

Actually, it felt good to get behind the wheel again, although she did have a moment's hesitation about driving a car so soon after the accident, but surprisingly, it was as though nothing had ever happened; she had no qualms at all, and for that, she was grateful.

As soon as she reached the bridge and got out of the car, Charlie's mouth dropped open in amazement at how much they'd accomplished in such a short amount of time. The south wall was finished, and it looked like they were getting ready to put the new roof on just as Matthew had said.

"So how does she look?" Jim McGuire asked, coming up behind her.

"Oh, Jim, it looks wonderful. The portal windows really add something special."

"I think so," he said proudly. "But of course, I'm a sucker for a pretty covered bridge."

Charlie burst out laughing. "Love of your life, huh?"

"You bet. After all the trouble we've had, I wasn't sure we'd get her up and ready in time for your Christmas celebration, but it looks like we just might pull it off. We're ahead of schedule right now, and if the weather cooperates, we should have her done in no time." He glanced at her wrist and saw the marks where the cast had been. "I was really sorry to hear about your accident, Charlie. How is everything, are you feeling all right?"

"Yes, I'm doing really well, Jim, thanks, it's sweet of you to ask." She waved her wrist gently. "See? No more cast, thank goodness. I was going a little stir-crazy, not to mention the itching—that about drove me crazy."

"I sure am glad to see you're doing so well. I know Matthew was out of it for a while worrying about you. Well, I've got to get back, some of the guys misplaced the boxes of screws and eyebolts and half of the cans of paint, and I want to be there to kick the butt of the ones who hid them. You take care of yourself, Charlie, I'll see you again soon."

Charlie stood there for several minutes after Jim left letting his words about Matthew's state of mind after her accident sink in. She knew how she would have reacted if it had been him in an accident he could have avoided, and she was beginning to understand why he'd come down on her so hard. She'd never lied to him before about anything, and her only fear was that he couldn't forgive her.

"Miss Faraday?" Deep in thought, Charlie didn't hear the man at first, and when he spoke her name again, she nearly jumped out of her skin.

"I'm sorry I didn't mean to startle you."

She had her hand on her chest. "That's okay. I, I just didn't hear you come up behind me." She stared at him for a second or two before recognition set in. "You're the man at the Council meeting."

"Yes, and I must apologize for my strange behavior. I wasn't able to talk to you then but—" He gently touched her arm. "Are you able to walk while we talk?"

Charlie held back a bit unsure of the man, but as before, he seemed harmless enough—almost timid really—and it was broad daylight with workers everywhere. "Well, I guess it would be all right but not too far."

"Perhaps over here under this tree will do. Believe me, Miss Faraday, I mean you no harm, but I do feel I have to talk with you before anything else happens."

"What do you mean?" she asked, the hair again tingling at the back of her neck, and she stopped to look at him. "Who are you, and why have you been following me?"

"At the moment, my identity is not important, however, I need you to listen carefully. I have reason to believe John Braxton is quite dangerous and that he will stop at nothing to prevent you from learning the truth about him."

"What do you mean the truth—what truth?"

"I believe you may be getting too close and that he will try to stop you again."

"Are you telling me that he was the one responsible for my accident?"

"I can't say for certain of course, but there are many things you don't know. You must be very cautious. Please don't approach him as you did at the diner."

"The diner, you were there?"

"Admittedly, I have been following you for quite some time, very early on when I came back after learning that you wanted to include the use of the pond in your Christmas campaign. Contrary to what you see before you, I am a private investigator."

"You are?" She didn't mean to sound so surprised, but the image of a skinny weakling on the beach being pushed around by a muscular lifeguard came to mind.

"I realize looks can be quite deceiving, but I assure you I am who I say I am." He didn't sound at all indignant. "Often, the obvious is overlooked because it is so obvious."

Charlie turned her head to one side guardedly. "Are you investigating me?"

"No, but you became a part of my investigation when news of your desire to use the pond as an ice skating arena first surfaced. You see I heard about your disagreement with Mayor Braxton and I desperately wanted to speak to you about it."

"Why, do you know something about the pond? I've been trying to find out what I could about it, especially the reason why it was closed, but I haven't been able to find a thing."

"And you won't, at least not through the resources you have been searching. There will be nothing written that will give you any answers."

"But I don't understand, how do you know—"

"As I said, I do need to speak to you, but I cannot take the chance that we may be seen together. I'm not afraid for myself, you understand, but I am afraid for your safety, especially now since he did not hesitate to try and prevent you from finding out the truth about something that happened many years ago."

Charlie suddenly felt her skin crawl, and she shuddered involuntarily. "Oh my god, my suspicions aren't unfounded," she said more to herself than to him.

"Miss Faraday, I'm not sure what you know or what you think you know, but we must meet again, at a later time when I can be assured that you're not in danger. For now, I must go, but I will be contacting you again very soon. Just take great care, he has eyes everywhere." He turned and walked toward the tall pines beyond Kissing Lane.

"Wait, you can't leave now." She called out, but again, he disappeared as mysteriously as he'd appeared into the protection of the tall brush bordering the pines.

Charlie stood there undecided as to whether she should tell someone about the stranger or keep it to herself until she could learn more about him. Of course in truth, there wasn't much to tell. The man could be who he says he is or just some nutcase pretending to be someone he's not, but without a name, she couldn't even prove he existed, let alone prove he knew anything about the mayor because he hadn't really told her anything. She'd already sent up a red flag about her sense of what was real and what wasn't after talking about a man who supposedly helped her after her accident before he disappeared into thin air, and if there was any question at all about her state of mind and they decided to keep a close eye on her, she would never be able to meet with the stranger again. And while she knew that withholding anything else from Matthew would put her in a worse situation with him, at this point, she had nothing to tell and no idea how to get out of the mess she'd gotten herself into.

It was close to six before Charlie got home and found a note taped to the refrigerator saying that her mother and Pete had gone to a double feature and wouldn't be back until late but that dinner was in the fridge.

Forty-five minutes later, her dinner heated and consumed, Charlie decided to try her hand at a little painting and pulled out the stand-up placard of Joseph to be used in the play as well as the box of paints and brushes. She tried a few strokes over what she'd already painted to see how well she could manipulate the brush and discovered that with slow easy strokes she had no difficulty at all with her wrist. She had been working for a while and had just begun to put the finishing touches on Joseph's coat when the telephone rang and she grabbed the phone on the end table next to her. "Hello?" she said but she received no answer. "Hello?" she said again, and when no one answered, she hung up the receiver. The phone immediately rang again, and once again after hearing no response, she hung up. When it rang again several minutes later, she grabbed the entire phone and set it down on the floor beside her. "Hello?" she answered. "Is anyone there? Hello?" Still hearing nothing and now agitated, she slammed down the receiver, but she'd no sooner gone back to her work when it rang again and she grabbed it before it rang twice. "Hello!" She could swear she heard breathing on the phone and instantly thought of a prank caller. "Look! If you don't stop calling this number, I'm going to report you to the phone company. They have ways of finding out who makes these kinds of calls, you know." She slammed down the receiver hard. "Juvenile delinquents." She muttered, taking the phone off the hook. She sighed contentedly and picked up her paintbrush again.

Twenty minutes later, the doorbell rang, and her head dropped in total frustration. "What is going on?" She jumped up and went to the door ready to pounce on the person she was sure was responsible for playing childish games, but when she turned on the porch light and yanked the door open, no one was there. "All right, you can come out now. I know you've been playing telephone tag all night so you might as well show yourself, otherwise, I'm calling the cops." She looked from one side of the porch to the other and out across the yard to the street and saw nothing, but when goose bumps suddenly appeared and the hair on her arms stood on end, she had the weirdest feeling she was being watched and quickly backed up into the house and shut the door and locked it. Then remembering the back door, she dashed to the kitchen and locked it. Her chest felt tight hurt and blood was pounding in her temples as she cocked her head to one side and listened but heard nothing. However, after managing to scare herself silly, she ran around closing all the drapes.

Charlie had never been afraid to be alone at night in her life, but the voiceless phone calls and the doorbell ringing with no one there unnerved her. She didn't like the feeling one bit, and while she contemplated calling someone, the doorbell rang again, making up her mind for her, and she sprinted for the phone and grabbed the receiver. She heard nothing and panicked for a second thinking it was dead until she realized it was still off the hook and she pushed the disconnect button on and off until she finally heard a dial tone. Able to breathe finally, she pushed the buttons for Paul's number, discovered she'd hit the wrong ones, and tried again—hit the wrong ones still again and nearly hit high panic until she finally heard ringing on the other end. "Please be home, please be home," she whispered, but after six rings, she was getting desperate. "Answer the phone, Paul, please answer the phone." She pleaded and nearly had a coronary until she finally heard his voice.

Barely giving him a chance to answer, she began babbling about the anonymous phone calls, but that she wasn't really afraid until someone rang her doorbell but no one was there and she'd never been afraid to be alone before, but now she felt like she was being watched, but when she didn't see anyone, she didn't know what to do so she called him and on and on until he stopped her.

"Slow down, Charlie, you're not making any sense."

"Paul, please, I hate to ask you to drive over here, but I think someone's trying to get in the house or scare me half to death."

"Did you call the police?"

"No." She moaned, thinking she must be the dumbest person she knew. "I didn't think of that I just thought of you and—"

"Lock all the doors and close the curtains—"

"I did that, just please hurry, Paul. I think I just heard something on the porch."

"Hang up and call the police right now. I'll—"

Just then, the phone went dead, cutting off Paul's voice, and Charlie froze where she stood. "Paul?" she whispered frantically into the phone. "Paul, are you there?" Seconds later, she heard rather than saw the doorknob turning back and forth, and she dropped the receiver and turned out the light on the phone table, then ran to the kitchen to turn out that light before sprinting back to the living room and over to the corner where it was darkest. She crouched down her eyes glued to the door and window on the opposite side of the room. As her eyes slowly grew accustomed to the dark, the porch light gave off enough light to allow Charlie to see a shadow pass by the window and her hands flew to her mouth, stifling the scream that came from deep down inside her and caught in her throat. When the doorbell rang, she nearly jumped out of her skin and every muscle in her body tightened while adrenaline surged like wildfire though her veins and the blood pounded in her ears. But when she heard a raspy voice call out, "Come out, come out, wherever you are" in a hideous sing-song voice, her skin crawled and her heart like someone reached inside her and squeezed it. She didn't know how long she stayed hunched down in the corner with her hands pressed over her ears, but it seemed like forever and actually took her a few minutes to realize someone had been yelling her name.

"Charlie, it's Paul, open the damn door."

Relief flowed over her as she struggled to stand on legs that were now jelly and threatened to buckle under her as she made her way to the door in the dark. Her fingers fumbled with the deadlock until she finally managed to turn it, and when she opened the door, she practically fell into Paul's arms.

"Whoa," he said, catching her and half-carrying her to the sofa. "Are you all right?" he asked, trying to get her to look at him, but she kept her face burrowed in his chest.

"Just don't let go, just don't let go." She clung to him like a life raft, and he held her close until her body stopped quaking. "I've never been so scared in my life. I thought it was just kids, but when the doorbell rang and I looked outside, I didn't see anything. I felt like somebody was watching me and then I heard that voice and—"

"Wait a minute, you heard a voice? What voice?"

"It was horrible. It was a man's voice, but it sounded raspy and hideous and he just kept saying 'come out, come out, wherever you are,' and I was talking to you on the phone one minute and the next minute you were gone and I didn't know what to do and—"

"It's okay, Charlie, it's okay." He soothed. "I called the sheriff, he should be here—" Someone knocked on the door, and Charlie panicked.

"Don't open the door, please don't open the door."

"Paul? It's Bill Conley. Paul, are you in there?" The sheriff called out, and while Paul tried to get Charlie to let go so he could open the door, she wouldn't let loose of her death grip on him and he ended up taking her to the door with him. When he opened it and the sheriff took one look at Charlie, he lost his cool. "What's going on, what the hell happened to her?" he demanded, and Paul quickly explained what he knew.

"Did you see anyone, Charlie?" Bill asked and she nodded.

"I, I saw a shadow, a man, he was saying some hideous thing—"
She cringed at the thought of it, and Paul led her over to the sofa
where she sat on the edge, gripping the arm for dear life.

"Jesus, he must have scared the wits out of her."

"Then there was someone out there? Because when I got here, I
looked all around the house, but I didn't see a thing."

"Well, whoever it was is gone now, but someone was here all
right. The phone lines been cut, I checked on the way in. My men
are outside looking around now."

Charlie looked up then, her eyes wide, her face white. "Bur why?
Who—"

"We don't know, honey, but we're checking it out. Don't worry,
nobody can get to you now." Bill motioned for Paul to walk to the
door with him. "You planning to stay around awhile?"

He nodded. "I'll be here until Pete and DeeDee get back."

"Good. I'll leave one of my men to keep an eye out tonight,
although I doubt he'll be back. Whoever it was, he did exactly
what he intended to do, scare the wits out of her for some damn
reason. Believe me, if they'd wanted in here bad enough, they'd have
broken a window. Maybe it was just some kids playing a prank, but
it stopped being a joke when they cut the phone line. In any case,
I think we've seen the last of him for tonight anyway." He looked
over at Charlie and shook his head. "He sure did a number on her."
Then, "I'll need a statement from both of you down at the station,
Paul, but it can wait until tomorrow. She's in no shape to talk right
now anyway, so bring her in around ten or so."

"Thanks, Sheriff, we'll be there," Paul said, sitting next to
Charlie.

"You're in good hands now, honey, and I've got a man outside so
you're safe."

Charlie nodded. "Thank you," she said meekly, and the sheriff
shook his head again.

"Damn shame after all she's been through. Well, if anything else
comes up, Jim will be out there, so don't worry. I'll see you at the
station tomorrow."

After the sheriff left, Paul sat down beside Charlie, and she immediately curled up next to him. He tried to shift her into a more comfortable position as she was sitting crooked while crouched up against him, but she wouldn't budge, and he finally pulled her onto his lap and she snuggled up against him, and they stayed that way until he felt the tension slowly ebb out of her body.

"Better?" he asked quite a while later, and she nodded, snuggling closer.

"I don't know what I would have done if you hadn't come."

"Well, I'm here now, so you don't have to worry."

She leaned back slightly and looked up at him. "You must think I'm an awful coward. Being home alone never bothered me before, but I just, I don't know what happened."

"Someone did a real good job of scaring you that's what happened. There's no shame in that."

"But why would someone do that? Who would—?"

"I don't know, Charlie. Maybe we'll find something out tomorrow when we go see the sheriff tomorrow. He might be able to tell us something then."

"I don't know what I would have done if you hadn't come." He watched her eyes go from misty green to dark jade when she lifted her head and kissed him lightly. She kissed him again and again feeling herself being swept away, forgetting what happened and becoming completely lost in the moment until the reality of what she was doing caught up with her and they both backed away.

"Things could really get out of hand here, Charlie," Paul said gruffly. "And it's way too easy to get caught up in the drama." He brushed her hair away from her face. "When it happens, I want it to happen because we both want it, not out of desperation or—"

Charlie put her finger to his lips and smiled. "I know," she said softly. "I feel it too."

Paul stood up then grabbing her hands and pulling her up with him. He held her face gently in his hands and kissed her lightly. "Do you know what I think?" he whispered, and she could only shake her head. "I think it might be a real good idea if you made some coffee right about now," he said, turning her around and gently pushed her toward the kitchen. "I could sure use a cup."

She hesitated, and he nudged her again. "*Now* would be a good time, Charlie." And with a wistful smile on her face, she went to make the coffee.

When DeeDee and Paul returned a short time later, Paul and Charlie were seated at the kitchen nook, and by that time Charlie was calm enough to explain what happened without all the fear and hysteria and after assuring them that the sheriff had come out and left an officer on guard for the night, Pete and DeeDee said their good nights and went up to bed.

"I'm going to leave now Charlie. It's getting late and I think you've had enough excitement for one night."

"Do you think he'll come back?"

"I doubt it. Whoever it was has to know the sheriff was here. Besides, he left one of his men standing guard outside. I so agree with him that someone wanted to put a damn good scare into you, and maybe when we talk to him tomorrow, he'll be able to tell us something more. In the meantime get some sleep, I don't think anyone's going to bother you anymore tonight." He walked to the front door and opened it, gave the thumbs up sign to the officer, and then turned around to say good night one last time, and Charlie looked up at him with a shy half-smile.

"Thanks again for coming over. I know I must have seemed like an idiot not calling the sheriff instead of asking you to come all the way over here to rescue me."

"Well, what kind of prince would I be if I didn't save my damsel in distress? Besides, knowing you thought of calling me instead of the sheriff does an awful lot for my already big ego." He smiled and reached out to pull Charlie close, wrapping his arms around her, but his smile faded as he searched the gold-flecked green of her eyes, something in them stirring an unfamiliar reaction deep in his soul. He was dazzled by her and fascinated by the hold she seemed to have on him, yet he had no idea that his mere presence did things to her that she couldn't explain like zapping every ounce of strength from her body each time he looked at her and her legs were made of Jell-O for all the good they did to hold her upright. It seemed her normal ability to maintain control seemed nonexistent whenever he was anywhere near her, but he was the one to speak what they both were feeling. "I don't know what you're doing to me, Charlie, but you have me going in twenty different directions at the same time."

"It must be contagious," she said shyly. "I'm just glad Mom and Pete didn't decide to stay for the triple feature."

Paul kissed her lightly, not trusting himself to do any more than that after seeing the un-guarded look of passion in her eyes. "Good night, Charlie." He turned and walked out the door relieved that she hadn't called him back, and he heard the door close behind him. He wasn't sure how long this newfound chivalry toward protecting her virtue would last—he was only human after all.

The trip to the police department the next morning didn't reveal much, but Bill took Charlie's statement and said he would be sending a car out periodically to check on things and make sure nothing else was going on. He told her that if anything came up or she noticed anything out of the ordinary, she was to call him anytime day or night. In the meantime, he said not to worry and that he would keep in touch.

Several weeks went by since she'd heard from Matthew and though she did occasionally stop to check out the bridge, the near-completion of it didn't seemed to hold as much pleasure for her. She'd felt as thought she'd lost her best friend, and after finally given up hope of hearing from him anytime soon, she went so far as to write Matthew a letter, saying that she would pay him back every cent he'd spent on the bridge although she never received an answer.

Charlie had no idea what she was doing. Lately she'd just been going through the motions of trying to stay busy and keep up the front of being happy, but it wasn't working. Even when the manager of Greystone called her at work to tell her they had an extra horse and carriage and that they were going to loan to her at no extra charge, it didn't seem to make a difference. As a matter of fact, she'd nearly canceled the whole deal but reconsidered knowing that even though she had little interest now there were so many others who were thrilled about the idea and she didn't want to disappoint them.

After spending the next couple weeks not seeing or hearing from him, she resigned herself to the fact that he no longer wanted to be a part of her life. But she was angry too, angry that he could think she would purposely withhold information merely to solve a case, but more than that, she was hurt that he couldn't believe that he didn't believe in her anymore. Though it may have appeared that she was trying to hide something from him, her thoughts were that if he knew her as well as he claimed, he would never have doubted her explanation that she needed proof of Braxton's involvement before she told him anything. She hated having to keep things from him them, but mostly she hated not seeing him. They had known one another too long to let something like this ruin their relationship. It was at that moment that she decided to take another look at the house she'd considering buying and drove over to Maple Street to take one final look before making up her mind. It was a big step, and because she'd made enough mistakes with her life already, she certainly didn't need another one.

As Charlie gazed at the newly sand-blasted red brick walls, wraparound porch, green shutters, and beautifully landscaped yard, she caught herself wondering if perhaps it might be a better idea to just move away from Braxton and start fresh somewhere else. There were a lot of memories in this town—some good and some not so good—and she wasn't so sure she wanted to stay. Although she'd always dreamed of getting married and raising a family here, she now knew firsthand that dreams don't always come true and sometimes you didn't get what you wanted.

"Good evening, Miss Faraday." A familiar voice said behind her, and she swung around to see the stranger she'd met before. She was happy to see that he wasn't a figment of her imagination and really did exist; she'd begun to wonder about so many things that had happened that couldn't be explained and the fact that she hadn't seen him in quite awhile either hadn't helped reassure her.

"I do apologize for taking so long to get back to you, but do you think we might talk inside? Do you have a key?"

"Well, yes, I do actually, but—"

"I would prefer not to be seen with you as I have mentioned before and being out here in the open leaves us exposed to wandering eyes."

Charlie felt she knew enough to know he wasn't there to do her any harm, and she took out the key as they walked up onto the porch. She unlocked the door and they both went inside, and Charlie left the door open for the benefit of possible nosy neighbors. She didn't want to make a bad impression before she even had a chance to move in. She found two good-sized orange boxes and offering him one they both sat down.

"I realize that I have been quite secretive during out last two meetings, and I believe the time has come when I feel I at least owe you an explanation as to my identity as well as sharing information with you, therefore, I will get right to the point. My name is Simon Cartwright, and I once lived in Braxton years ago although we moved from here when I was quite young. I still manage to keep in touch with relatives who live close by however, and it is through them that I learned of your upcoming Christmas celebration. You see my aunt often sends news of Braxton, and in addition to the flyer she recently sent, she also sends the daily newspaper, and it was through reading of the possible reopening of the pond that I became interested. That and the covered bridge fire as well as the editor's barn being burned down shortly after his article appeared. I felt the need to come back although my mother was not happy with my decision."

Charlie nodded, easily understanding his interest in news about the town he grew up in. Her mother often revisited Fletcher, a small rural town not far from Braxton where she spent much of her young life growing up. She said it rekindled past memories and helped her remember fun-filled, carefree days of her childhood when things became challenging or stressful in her adult world. But Charlie was more than a little curious about his mother not wanting him to come back.

"Your mother didn't like Braxton, I take it?" she asked, not wishing to pry but merely to satisfy an innate curiosity.

"Oh no, on the contrary, she liked it very much. That is until Boyd Caldwell drowned. It was very soon afterward that we moved away."

Charlie felt a chill run the entire length of her spine, and for a second, she felt like the wind had been knocked out of her. "You knew of his accident?" she asked, not wishing to sound brutal.

"Oh yes, I knew him. You see, I am the boy who was not identified in the newspapers, Boyd was my best friend."

"You, you were the little boy who had been with him when he—" She couldn't believe it; it was as if by divine intervention that she was to meet him, especially after only recently learning of the little boy's drowning. "Mr. Cartwright, I'm so sorry. I can't imagine the horror you must have gone through."

"I do still have dreams about it admittedly, but since it did happen many years ago, I had managed to block it from my memory until recently."

Charlie suddenly felt like she'd found Pandora's Box and opened it without any regard whatsoever to the consequences. "And I awakened that memory. I can't tell you how sorry I am for stirring up such a horrid nightmare. If I had had any idea—"

"No, no, please don't blame yourself. Although I had stored it in the recesses of my mind, there was never a day when I wasn't reminded of it in some way. Perhaps in a dream or even an innocent remark made it was somehow brought to my attention once again. I had even thought of seeking therapy to perhaps help me to deal with it, but I'm afraid I never followed through. However, when I learned that someone wanted to reopen the pond, I somehow knew that I was meant to come back and possibly put an end to the dreams, perhaps put them to rest finally. I'm not sure what I hoped to learn, but in the process of my search, I did stumble upon some things that I am fairly certain might help you in your own search for answers. But perhaps I should tell you what I do remember about that day in the hope that it might help in some way." He had a pained look on his face, and Charlie felt rather than knew his heart must be aching. It wasn't a good memory by any means, but obviously, it was one that needed tended to.

"As it stated in the paper, we were playing ball in Boyd's backyard for quite a long time." He began, "In short, we had become bored with our little game and began kicking the ball quite hard until it ended up outside the yard into the front and eventually into the street. And while we knew we weren't permitted out of the yard, you know how children can be when they get caught up in what they're doing. In any case, we kicked it again and again and found ourselves running further and further to get it until we were quite close to the pond, which was only a block or two away if memory serves. As I remember, the ball rolled down a little grade and came to rest at the edge of the pond. And as there was a man standing there, Boyd asked him to give us the ball, but he yelled at us and told us to get away from there. I stayed behind, but of course, Boyd ventured closer and the man became quite upset and yelled at him again to get away, but Boyd was determined to retrieve his ball, however, just as he was close enough to reach it the man kicked it into the pond." He gazed straight ahead as though remembering. "Boyd went in after it, and I remember laughing when he slipped and went under because I knew he would be in even more trouble when he got home for getting wet. He appeared to be splashing around, and it seemed he was merely acting the fool until he went under a second time."

The man's voice grew weak as she watched his eyes grow misty staring out at the picture he must have had in his mind for all those years, and her heart hurt for the pain he couldn't have known then as a young child, but that he was feeling at that very moment.

"I watched him go under again and then the man did go out toward him, but then about halfway, he turned around and came back and just stood at the edge watching. However, when Boyd didn't come up again, I saw him turn and walk to his car and drive away, leaving Boyd there in the water." He seemed to come out of his trance and looked straight at Charlie as if the reality of it just surfaced. "I don't know if he ever saw me or just forgot I was there, but I ran home then and told my parents what happened. I didn't know what else to do. I didn't know how to swim, but even if I did, I don't know how I could have helped him at such a young age." He breathed deeply and reached for his handkerchief to wipe his forehead. "I had managed to put all of this out of my mind back then as an act of self-preservation, I suppose, and it was not until much later, and quite by accident that I learned that my parents did not wish my name mentioned in the newspapers because of the publicity as well as to keep me from being traumatized by the media." He sighed again. "It was quite difficult, Mother, as she had been very close to Boyd's family, and though she did keep in touch for several years, the letters simply stopped coming. It was Mother's claim that Mrs. Caldwell had never recovered from Boyd's death and had slipped from reality. I do believe they moved as well, but of course, I can't be sure. As I said, I was quite young at the time, and I could say no more than the man had just left Boyd there and drove off. While I imagine they did search for the vehicle, they had no license number or description with which to trace it. I found out later through my aunt that it was considered an accident and was closed to further investigation." He sighed heavily. "And though I have tried to put it out of my mind, I have never forgotten Boyd and have always felt somehow responsible for what happened to him. And then when you found that those articles were missing, I sensed rather than felt that something wasn't quite right."

"You were at the diner, you saw the articles?"

"I didn't see them of course. I merely overheard you and the editor talking about them."

"Mr. Cartwright, not to change the subject, but the last time we met, you said something about John Braxton being a dangerous man and that I was getting too close to the truth. I asked you then if you thought he was responsible for my accident and you said you didn't know for certain but that there were many things I didn't know. What exactly did you mean by that?"

"Unfortunately, what I was referring to has nothing to do with the pond incident, but there are things I have discovered about the mayor that I believe are important. As I told you before, I am a private investigator, and while in search of my own answers, I inadvertently became aware of certain rather strange activities involving the mayor."

Charlie frowned. "What kinds of strange activities?"

"A case in point," he said, flipping through the pages of his notebook. "On the night of the covered bridge fire, the mayor was working in his office which I found a bit peculiar for that time of the evening, but what stirred my suspicions most was the fact that when the fire trucks went past his office, he never acknowledged them."

Charlie looked puzzled. "I'm sorry?"

"Miss Faraday," he said patiently. "If you were the mayor of a small town such as Braxton and you first heard the fire alarm and immediately following you heard the screaming sirens of fire trucks racing through the street directly in front of your office, wouldn't you at least—"

"Take a look and see what the commotion was all about?" She finally got it. "Yes, I suppose I would."

"He did not," Simon interjected. "As a matter of fact, he did not even attempt to look out the window directly in front of him. I know this because I was watching him at the time and had a very clear view from my vantage point in the parking lot of the neighboring savings and loan. He never made a move out of his chair nor did he call out on the telephone or receive any calls. Less than an hour later, he got up from his chair, put on his suit jacket, shut off the light, and left his office. He did not speak to anyone, he did not drive in the direction of the fire, he simply went straight to his home because I followed him there. But the very next day, I saw him walk into his office with a man in a business suit. Although I didn't think much about it at the time because many people go in and out of his office every day, when the man came out a short time later and walked two blocks before getting into a black sedan parked at the curb, I became suspicious, wondering why he parked so far from the mayor's office."

Charlie thought his suspicion a bit inane. "Well, perhaps there had been no parking spaces close by."

"There were many open spaces in front of the mayor's office as well as along the street, Miss Faraday, which is why I had to ask myself what reason he would have had to park that far away." He caught Charlie's vacant look and realized she didn't understand his reasoning. "I can see that doesn't make much sense to you, but of course, my downfall is that I rather suspect everyone until I find a reason not to." He flipped through the pages again. "You see, after you spoke to the mayor at the diner I saw the same businessman enter his office yet again, but oddly enough, he went through the back entrance, and through my field glasses, they appeared to be in a very deep discussion. After several moments, the mayor handed the man an envelope and he left the office again using the rear entrance. I managed to get pictures, but I have yet to get them developed, however I am hopeful that they will tell us more about this transaction as well as perhaps what this man looks like. In any case, the very next day when you met Mr. Freeman at the diner, I saw the man walk past the diner toward the south end of town, and approximately ten minutes later, he came past the diner again walking north. Of course, it made no sense at all to me, and I became even more suspicious. In any case, after Mr. Freeman left, I stayed in the diner as you did, and when you left several minutes later and drove out of town, I drove in the direction the man had taken toward my hotel, and that is when I saw the same man park his car just outside the Main Street Bar and Grill and go inside. I waited approximately one half hour, and when it appeared that he was not coming out any time soon, I simply left and went back to my hotel. Shortly afterward, I learned of your accident and suspected that it was more than just a coincidence. Now while this may sound ludicrous to you, ponder this question if you will. What if he somehow knew of your meeting with Mr. Freeman and perhaps did something to your car while you were inside the diner with him? It wouldn't have been difficult at all to get to—you did park your car on the side of the diner toward the back of the parking lot. You see, I can't help thinking it strange that your car seemed to be working just fine before you met the editor, but soon afterward, you lost your brakes and were almost killed on that treacherous hill. Can you see where I am going with this, Miss Faraday?"

"Yes," she said pensively. "And as strange as it sounds, it does make sense because I had no problems with my car at all. As a matter of fact, I'd just had it inspected a week or two before and everything was fine." She looked at him curiously. "So you suspect that this man is working with the mayor, that perhaps the mayor hired him to cause my accident?"

He smiled then for the first time since she'd met him. "I am a private detective, Miss Faraday, and because we are trained to look for the obvious along with the not so obvious most times, we are suspicious of anyone and anything out of the ordinary. You see, when I first saw his reaction at the council meeting, it was bizarre to say the least. That was my first clue that something was not right, and of course, the fact that the pond was the main concern interested me very much for obvious reasons, and it just seemed a good place to start. And as far as your car is concerned, yes, I believe he may have done something to your car to cause the accident."

"There is something else," Charlie said. "Did you happen to hear us talking about a letter or note?"

"No, I can't say I recall. Of course, a family came into the diner a bit before Mr. Freeman left and they were seated in the booth behind me. There were several children, and they were making quite a commotion. It was difficult to hear anything you said after that."

"Oh yes, the Daywood family, I saw them come in, but I didn't pay much attention to them. They are quite a little troupe when they're together," she said, smiling. "In any case, I had mentioned to Carl that I received an anonymous letter in the mail from a concerned citizen who said it would be a bad idea to reopen the pond claiming that no good would come of it and bad things could happen. It didn't have a return address and had been sent from a different county, but I naturally suspected John Braxton after what happened at the council meeting along with several other things. If you had heard our conversation, you would have known that I came out and asked him about it. He denied it, of course, but he got pretty upset when I accused him of writing the letter. And then when Carl told me he received a threatening note the day his barn burned down, we compared the writing, and as it turned out, they matched."

"So you're saying the same person who wrote you the letter burned Mr. Freeman's barn down?"

"Yes, the 't's in both the letter and the note were crooked and crossed through the middle. That's how we knew it was from the same person."

"Ahh! It seems you are a bit of a sleuth as well, Miss Faraday." He smiled, but the smile quickly left his face. "You do know what this means, don't you?" He looked very serious and Charlie somehow knew what his next words would be.

"Whoever is responsible for writing those letters may also responsible for your near-fatal accident as well as the covered bridge fire and Mr. Freeman's barn being burned down. And whoever is responsible for these heinous acts most likely suspects that you both know something, but they cannot be sure what or how much you know or if you have gone to the authorities. Therefore, I suspect that these accidents have merely been warnings. Although in your case, Miss Faraday, I believe that your particular accident was to be one you did not walk away from." He caught the look of fear on Charlie's face and hurried on. "However, you did indeed survive which we are thankful for, but you must understand that you are in extreme danger, and that if all this is true, nothing will prevent them from making another attempt on your life."

Charlie thought hard about that. "We definitely have to go to the sheriff with all this, but I also think we need to find out for certain that the person who wrote the letter is also the person who wrote the note. If they match, we'll more than likely find out they're also responsible for my accident and the fires, but we have to find something we can compare the writing to and that means somehow getting into John Braxton's office."

"Exactly but we must make absolutely certain of our findings before we can reveal any of this to the authorities you understand. Your life may well depend on it." His tone was sharp and held a note of warning.

"You're very sweet to worry about me, Mr. Cartwright, but I'll be fine although I do understand and I won't say a word until I hear from you."

The man smiled uneasily. "Please call me Simon, and I do apologize for my unusual display of temper. I am not in the habit of losing control, but I often tend to overreact when I care what happens to someone I've grown fond of. Although I don't mean that in the sense that, well, what I mean to say is—"

"I know what you mean." Charlie grinned at his rather endearing awkwardness. "I don't have a big brother to watch over me, but if I did, I would certainly want him to be as caring as you are."

"Well, that is very kind of you to say, Miss Faraday. I just did not want you to come away with the wrong conclusion. I have nothing but the deepest respect for you."

Charlie believed him. She had a knack for reading people and the sincere look in his eyes was unmistakable. "Why haven't you married, Simon? I would think some lucky girl would have scooped you up by now especially knowing the exciting line of work you're in," Charlie said easily, and Simon actually blushed.

"Well, I'm not exactly what one would consider the romanticized version of a private investigator as you can plainly see, but I do care about people and do my utmost to help them. I just have had no time to become acquainted with anyone, my job takes up most of my time, but perhaps I will marry someday."

"Well, whoever she turns out to be, I hope she realizes what a treasure she has."

"Yes, well—" He looked embarrassed as he stood up and brushed at the back of his suit pants. "I should be getting along now, I have something I must attend to and I have taken up much of your time as it is. I do have an idea in mind, but in the meantime, do not say a word of this to anyone and I will contact you as soon as I have developed my next plan of action."

Charlie stood up with him. "I think I'm very lucky to have you around, Simon, but please be very careful. If what we suspect is true, there isn't much he would do to anyone who stands in his way."

"Those are my sentiments exactly. I will say goodbye for now, Miss Faraday, but I will be speaking with you very soon. And you might wait for just a while after I am gone, there is no use calling attention to the fact that we were here together, we must keep you out of harm's way."

Just seeing Simon again made Charlie feel a lot better about her situation—relieved really—and though he didn't exactly look the part, Simon Cartwright appeared to be very good at what he did. She actually felt safer, knowing he was around. However, she didn't feel good about keeping even more information from Matthew and Paul, knowing that it would only make their relationships worse, but how much worse could it get when they weren't even on speaking terms? Besides, that was the least of her worries because at the moment, her mind was on the mayor and how she could get into his office.

"You're out of your mind," Carl said an hour later when Charlie stopped by the newspaper office. He'd ushered her into the copy room where he turned on the printer to make several dozen copies of nothing to muffle their voices. "Either that or you hit your head a lot harder than we thought. You're crazy to think you can break into the mayor's office."

"It's the only way Carl and I need the letter and the note to do it. If we can compare them to another document, we'll know for sure whether or not the mayor's behind all this and we can tell the sheriff everything we know, don't you see?"

"No, what I see is a crazy woman looking to get herself arrested for breaking and entering." Carl stopped pacing back and forth. "Besides I'm not convinced that you should have told this

Cartwright character anything, Charlie. How do you know he's who he says he is, how do you know you can trust him?"

"I told you he was a friend of the little boy who drowned, weren't you listening? Besides, he has honest eyes."

Carl shook his head in disbelief. "Come on, Charlie, honest eyes? I think we'd better do some checking on your Mr. Cartwright. If he is who he says he is, then maybe then we'll talk, if he isn't then we've got even bigger problems. In the meantime, you stay away from Braxton and his office and don't say anything more to your *friend*. We'll talk to Matthew and—"

"No!" She practically yelled at him. "We can't talk to Matthew. I, that is, we aren't on such great terms right now." She finished lamely.

"Listen, Charlie, I'm calling him whether you like it or not. I don't know what's going on, and until I do, I'm not giving you the letter or the note. I'm not taking a chance that something else might happen to you so don't go all crazy on me until I get hold of Matthew."

It was inevitable that Charlie would have to see Matthew again; she'd known it the day he'd stormed out after she told him all she knew, but she hadn't expected it this soon nor did she expect it to be under these new circumstances. Although she had every intention of telling him everything when the time was right, she hadn't really decided when that time would be, especially now that Simon had warned her not to talk to anyone until she heard from him. But she knew also there was no way to talk Carl out of calling Matthew and she had little choice than to see him.

At work the next day, although much of Charlie's depression had lifted and though she was feeling a little better about things, Matthew's anger and silence was never far from her thoughts nor was the new information she'd discovered. For weeks, she'd appeared preoccupied at work as well and the girls had become withdrawn. Though she wanted to let them in on her secret, the chance of them becoming involved and possibly putting their lives in danger had been the reason she detached herself from them in the first place and that reason alone had far exceeded her need to put their relationships right again. But then keeping them in the dark wasn't really fair either; after all, they had never once refused to help her and had worked hard to uncover much of the information Charlie needed. She wouldn't have gotten as far as she did without their help.

While she'd already hurt others she loved as well as herself by not revealing important information, she realized that she'd hurt them for the same reasons. As a result, they had withdrawn to the point of speaking to her only when absolutely necessary, and that's when she made up her mind that losing them as friends wasn't an option.

"How about going for lunch today, girls?"

The three surprised women looked at Charlie and then at each other. "No thanks," Helen said gruffly. "I'm busy."

"I brought a lunch today, Charlie," Jean said, going right back to her work, but Mary was all for it until Helen intervened.

"Ooh, lunch!" Mary cooed. "Where'll we go?"

"You're busy, Mary, remember?" Helen said a little too loudly.

"Oh, yeah, I forgot," she said quietly. "I, uh, I guess I'm busy too, sorry, Charlie." She really did look sorry and made an apologetic face.

"Oh, I see. You're giving me the cold shoulder, huh?" Charlie got the point. "Well, I'm buying, does that help?"

"Nope." Helen didn't even look up from her desk.

"Well, since Henry took the time to pack my lunch—" Jean looked as sorry as Mary and just shrugged her shoulders.

Charlie didn't feel snubbed really; she half-expected them all to refuse, and she scribbled something down on paper and held it up for all of them to see. "Excuse me—" she said loudly and pointed toward the paper.

"Do not read this out loud." Mary read out loud, and Charlie quickly shook her head and put her finger to her lips to shush her and scribbled a second note. "Please don't talk, just go to lunch with me. I have something important to tell you."

"Oh, what's this charades? Gimme a break—" Helen began, and again, Charlie motioned her to be quiet and scribbled again.

"Please don't say anything and meet me outside. I'll explain, I promise!"

Jean quickly got up, motioning for Helen and Mary to do the same. Helen rolled her eyes and scribbled a message of her own down on paper and angrily pushed her chair back and stood up holding the note that read, "This had better be good!"

They all met outside and Helen snapped. "All right what gives? You've been acting weird for weeks, and I for one would like to know what the hell is up with you. Why couldn't you just tell us in the office? What's with all the secrecy?"

"I'm going to tell you something, but you can't say anything until I'm finished because it'll probably make you nuts, Helen, okay?"

"Oh, it's about me again, why do you always single me out?"

"Helen, be quiet and listen for a change." Mary blurted out. "Otherwise, you can just go, okay?" She turned back and watched Charlie intently.

"Well, I don't see why—"

"Shut it, Helen, go on Charlie," Mary said while Helen crossed her arms over her chest and stood tapping her foot.

"Well, first of all, I want to apologize for the way I've been acting lately. I was going through something, and well, I'm working through things and I just wanted you to know that it had nothing to do with you guys. Secondly," she began, thinking she might as well come straight out with it. "I think someone may have planted bugs in the office."

"What?" Helen spewed. "Now I know you're crackers! Bugs? Come on, Charlie, give us a break, this is too much even for you."

"I'm serious. Long story short, there were things said on the phone in the office that no one could have known about otherwise, things that I told only one person but Braxton somehow knew about it."

"The mayor? I should have known you were still on that kick. Get off it, Charlie. Maybe Pete is right maybe you have been watching too many spy movies."

"Okay, prove me wrong, Helen. We'll go back to the office and search, and if we can't find anything, I swear I'll never mention it again."

"Yeah, like that'll really stop you."

"I'll give you a hundred dollars if we don't find anything, and I'll never bring it up again."

"You are nuts!"

"I mean it, Helen, and you know I'm good for it."

"Okay, Miss Moneybags, you're on, and I want that in writing."

"It's a deal." They shook on it, but Jean wasn't convinced.

"Look, Charlie, I know John Braxton is a no-good so-and-so, but do you really think he's capable of something like that? That's a felony, and he is the mayor, after all. If he's caught, he'll go to jail, but how in the world are you going to prove it was him? If what you say is true, anyone could have hidden a bug in that office, do you realize how many people come through there every day?"

"I'm not sure he would have done it himself, Jean, he probably hired someone to do it so he wouldn't get his hands dirty, and if that's true, we just have to find out who did do it and get him to say Braxton put him up to it."

Helen rolled her eyes. "Do you hear yourself? You sound like one of those fake detective magazines—that's the only place you could garbage like that. What, your Super Sleuth Junior Detective kit come in the mail and you want to try it out?" She snorted mockingly.

"Actually, even if he did put bugs in the office, it doesn't really matter, Helen, because if what I believe is true, we won't necessarily need that proof to put him away, there's a lot more they can get him with."

"Then why bother?" Mary asked.

"Because I'll know I was right about him, Mary."

"What other things are you talking about now? Are you sure you're not just hoping you can find something on him? Because whatever you think you know, you'd better have proof before you go around accusing him, Charlie." Helen wouldn't believe her own mother unless she had a signed affidavit.

"I can't really go into all that right now, but trust me, there's a reason for all the weird things that have been going on around here, and I intend to find out what it is."

"Jeez, this is like something out of *True Detective!*" Mary gushed. "And right here in our own little town."

"Yes, but you can't tell anyone about any of this Mary, none of us can say anything until we have absolute proof that he's somehow involved, and right now, it would just be my word against his." *Mine and Simon Cartwright's that is,* Charlie thought. But she couldn't say a word about him or his involvement until he gave her the okay—if even the smallest hint about what she was doing and who was involved got out, Braxton would find some way to cover his tracks and then they'd have nothing. Besides if the townspeople even suspected that he may have had anything at all to do with the fires, Charlie's accident or his possible involvement in little Boyd Caldwell's drowning, she was afraid the entire town would come out in full force and hang him from the nearest tree and they would never learn the truth.

They went back into the office, and Helen was the first one to reach for Charlie's phone and she quickly took the handset apart. Seeing nothing, she shook her head at Charlie. "You lose, Faraday." She held her hand out. "That'll be a hundred bucks, please."

"Wait a minute, Helen, let me see that."

"You're not going to find anything so quit stalling and pay up."

Charlie pointed to the bookcases, flower pots, anywhere there may have been another planted, and though they searched in silence for over an hour, they found nothing and Charlie began to wonder if Helen might be right.

Jean searched the bookcases, sliding her hand all along the edges of the bookshelves as well as in between each individual book, while Helen searched the lamps and window blinds while constantly mumbling about being an idiot for even listening to Charlie's wild story. Mary covered every square inch along the underside of the desks, along the legs, and under the ledges of the desk surface— everywhere she could think of—just as she'd seen them do on the detective programs. She didn't miss a single hiding place but could find nothing and she began looking under everything on the desks—paper weights, pencil holders, letter trays, and even under the desk blotters. But none of them found a thing.

"I told you so." Helen snarled. "There's nothing. Besides, you wouldn't know a bug if it bit you on the a—"

"Be quiet, Helen," Jean told her. "It was worth a try."

"Actually Helen's right, Jean," Charlie conceded. "I have no idea what a 'bug' looks like, but somehow, someone heard things that were said in this office." She was so sure they would find something and was almost disappointed when they didn't. "Well, let's get things cleaned up so we can get out of here on time—it's three-twenty already."

At ten minutes to four, the girls cleared their desks and left the office together. "We'll just keep our eyes and ears open just in case. If someone has been in this office listening, maybe we just didn't notice and we overlooked them." It sounded implausible even to Charlie, but she had nothing else to go on. She decided she would go and see the sheriff anyway even though Simon had told her to keep things to herself until she heard from him. It couldn't hurt to give him a head's up just in case; however since he wasn't in his office, she left a message for him to call her, if she hadn't she would have chickened out and not told him anything.

In the meantime, Charlie had no idea that Carl had arranged for them both to meet at Matthew's house, and by the time she arrived home and managed to unlock the door, the phone was ringing. "Hello?"

"Charlie? It's Carl. I set up a meeting with Matt, and we're going out there now."

"No, I can't, I—"

"It'll be fine, Charlie."

"That's easy for you to say, Carl. You weren't there when he nearly ripped my head off the last time."

"I'll be over to pick you up," Carl said and hung up.

"No, Carl you don't underst—" She heard the hum of being disconnected and she sat down hard on the phone chair. This just made her day. Now not only did she have to tell the sheriff what she'd done, she had to face Matthew too and she was sure he wouldn't be happy to know she'd kept something else from him. She was just glad her mother and Pete weren't home. That would have put the icing on the cake, and she didn't relish having to tell them what she'd gotten herself into. She didn't need another lecture about how irresponsible she'd been about taking things into her own hands and nearly been killed because of it, and there was no doubt that her mother would take Pete's side on this one.

"He needs to know, Charlie," Carl said once they were on their way.

"He knows, Carl. Besides, I tried to tell you I planned to tell the sheriff—"

"We don't have proof enough to go to the sheriff, and we need to know if we have any other options."

"I don't know, Carl, maybe you should do this by yourself. You have no idea how mad he was, and this just might set him off again. Besides, I may not even be welcome, did you think of that?"

"Well, that's just the chance we'll have to take because you know a hell of a lot more than I do. Relax. It'll be fine."

"Oh sure, and then we have to repeat everything all over again to the sheriff." *Including the newsy tidbit concerning Simon Cartwright that even you don't know about,* she thought rolling her eyes and staring out the window.

Charlie was quiet on the drive out. She was nauseated and her head was pounding, and she opened the window for air as her mind wandered back to the day she sent Matthew the letter. She had no idea how she was going to pay him back for the money he'd spent on the bridge, but she sure as heck was going to try. She didn't want anything hanging over her head to remind her of how she'd destroyed their relationship, not to mention his trust in her. She felt awful, knowing he'd done it all for her, and in turn, she'd disappointed him by withholding information and renewed fear set in when they pulled into his driveway.

"I can't go in there, Carl," she said, grabbing his sleeve.

"Yes, you can."

"I'm telling you I really can't go in there, I cannot do it," she repeated just as Matthew stepped out his door onto the porch.

Carl got out and went around to the passenger's side, opened her door, and held out his hand. "I'll be right beside you. It'll be fine, I promise."

Charlie closed her eyes, took a deep breath, and then let it out slowly before reaching up for Carl's hand. "So help me, Carl—"

"You'll be fine, let's go." Once Charlie was out of the car, she held back and Carl literally had to pull her along with him. When they reached the porch, Charlie fully expected Matthew to ask her to leave, although she knew she was being ridiculously childish. But this was a man she'd loved since she was little girl and though he could no more tell her to get out than fly, at the moment, she felt like she was facing a firing squad. She raised her head and their eyes met dead on.

"Come in." Matthew held the screen door open, and Charlie hurried through, still clutching Carl's arm in a death grip. He motioned for them to sit down once they were inside, and Charlie sat on the very edge of the sofa, just in case.

"Can I get you a drink?"

"Nothing for me thanks," Carl said.

"Charlie?"

Sure, how about a shot of tequila? she thought wildly. *Or better yet, make that two!* "No, thank you, I'm good," she said instead, taking a deep breath.

"Bill should be here any minute, he's on his way out."

"What?" Charlie croaked, and both men looked at her strangely.

"Well, apparently you left a message that you needed to talk to him right away, but when he called and your mother said you were on your way here, he called me, and since you were both coming out here anyway, I told him to join us. I'm sure all of us will be interested in what you have to say, and since this seems to be the day for revelations, why not tell everyone all at once? The more, the merrier." If Charlie didn't know better, she would have thought Matthew found this amusing, but the fact that his tone lacked any humor whatsoever told her otherwise.

"And speak of the devil, here he is now. Come on in, Bill, the gang's all here."

Bill walked in and looked around. "Would somebody like to tell me just what the hell is going on?"

"Well, who would like to go first?" Matthew inquired. "Carl? Charlie?"

Charlie didn't like the way Matthew was acting and she was sure they wouldn't be on any friendlier terms after she was through saying what she had to say, but she was hurt, and in a way, she wanted to hurt back "I'll tell them, Carl, although Matthew knows some of this already," she said bluntly. "Don't you, Matthew?"

"Some, but I'm sure there's more." He got Charlie's point, and she thought she saw a flicker of a touché in his nod of compliance; still, her palms were sweating and she licked her dry lips and tried to swallow, realizing revenge wasn't as sweet as she'd hoped. She suddenly had the strongest urge to get up and run, but her legs felt like her mouth after a shot of Novocain and she hesitated not knowing where to begin.

"What the hell have you gotten yourself into, Charlie?" Bill wasn't in a good humor obviously.

Charlie looked directly at Matthew eyes narrowed, realizing he'd already prepared Bill; she just didn't know to what degree. "Well, you know about the problems I've been having problems with the campaign for a lot of reasons, but one of the main ones was the use of the pond which the mayor told me I could not do. Anyway, Carl wrote an article—"

"I'll tell him, Charlie," Carl interjected. "After all, I'm the one who wrote the article. "Well, it's like this, sheriff. I thought Charlie's Bring Back Christmas campaign was a great idea, and I wanted to run a story about it in the paper to help the campaign along, so I mentioned the idea to Charlie. She liked it so I ran it, and while I mostly talked about the campaign, I did mention that maybe the mayor might let her use the pond after all and it was shortly after that that my barn burned down. I wouldn't have thought it was due to anything but my own carelessness until I found part of a burned note with a warning, and that's when I suspected that someone might have set the fire deliberately."

"You knew about this note when I was out at your place after the fire?"

"Yes."

"But you didn't see the significance of telling me about it? That's withholding evidence, Carl, what the hell's wrong with you?"

"Granted, I should have shown it to you—"

"You're darn right you should have, that note was evidence, Carl. What, are you both taking the law into your own hands now?"

"Wait a minute, Sheriff," Charlie interrupted. "Let me explain. I don't know if you're aware of it, but in the beginning, when the mayor told me there was no way I could reopen the pond, that started me wondering why. So I looked through the archives at the library about the Braxton family history, hoping to find something that might give me a clue, and while I found some things about the family—regarding the mayor that is—I discovered two pages missing from the old newspapers. I didn't know what they pertained to, but I thought they had to be important or at least knew they had something significant about him or his family since they were originally in there with all the records. Anyway, when I showed Mrs. Tucker they were missing, she explained that they had begun to convert the old newspapers to microfilm, and if they had recorded them before they came up missing, that's where they'd be. I did find them and she printed them out for me and one of them was an article that had to do with an ongoing argument between John Sr. and John Jr. about whether or not Junior was responsible enough to hold office and their arguments about it, and the second one was about a five-year-old boy who had drowned in the pond. At first, I couldn't figure out what was so important about them that someone would want them removed from the archives, so when I read them, I started to see a connection."

"What kind of connection?"

"Well, you're probably already aware of this, but from what I read, everyone liked his father. He was respected by the people of Braxton because he had a lot of compassion for them and was always ready to fight for their causes. Anyway, when Boyd drowned, he was really grief-stricken by his death, but John Junior seemed more concerned about what an eyesore the pond was rather than the fact the little boy drowned. You see he'd argued with his father numerous times about running for mayor if and when he ever stepped down, but because of his father's comments about his lack of responsibility, he figured the people would side with his father and he'd never be elected. Junior obviously didn't have the same appeal with the people, so I believe he thought that if he destroyed the articles, the townspeople would forget all about the dispute with his father and it would better his chances of becoming mayor."

"But what does all that have to do with using the pond?" Matthew asked.

"Well, that's just it. When I got an anonymous letter from a concerned citizen telling me that reopening the pond was a bad idea and that something bad might happen, that's when I began to think there had to be another reason why he felt he had to dispose of the articles. And when I combined that with the fact that he'd gone a little crazy at the council meeting when I asked why he was so against my using it in the campaign, it raised even more doubt in my mind. Did he destroy the articles because he was hiding something or did he simply destroy them because he felt his father made him look bad? I can't prove it was him, Sheriff, but the fact that he showed up at my office a few days later to tell me he'd heard that I still wanted to use the pond was just a little too coincidental and I think he was lying when he said he didn't send the letter. Don't you see? When Carl and I had a meeting at the diner, Carl said he thought there was something fishy about the fire and that his story might have had something to do with it right, Carl?"

"Right, and when Charlie asked if the old newspapers that I had stored in my attic could have had something to do with my barn being burned down, I told her I thought it had more to do with the pond because no one, including myself, really knew what old newspapers were stored up there."

"Anyway," Charlie continued. "I was really getting suspicious about all the strange things that had been going on, and when Carl told me he thought the pond was the issue too and that maybe the mayor was trying to warn him to back off, that's when I showed him the letter and he compared it to the note he found in his barn. We discovered that the writing was the same, which meant that it was written by the same person, and it was at that point that we talked about telling you, but we didn't have any proof. And there's something else. I told Carl things over the phone in my office that the mayor couldn't possibly have known but he did, and as far as I'm concerned, there's only one way he could have known about them—and you have to know what that would have sounded like if I'd come to you with that kind of information, Sheriff. Carl thought the same thing which is the reason he asked to meet me at the diner instead of my office. And then with all the other things happening like the bridge and Carl's barn burning down—"

"And your accident," the sheriff added as though things were beginning to make sense to him, and for the first time, Charlie felt relieved when he seemed to be considering everything she said as possible.

"Uh, there is something else, Sheriff." Charlie realized it was a risk to tell him about Simon Cartwright, but she knew she had to bring all of it out in the open.

"I can't wait." His eyes narrowed as he folded his arms across his chest. "This just keeps getting better and better."

"Well," she hedged. "A man I've never seen before approached me for the first time back in July. Eventually, he got around to telling me that he was a private investigator and that he used to live in Braxton years ago. He said he knew I was looking for anything I could find out about the pond being closed to the public, and that's when he told me about Boyd Caldwell, a little boy who apparently drowned in the pond twenty years ago."

"I've heard the story," he said matter-of-factly. "What about it?"

"This man's name is Simon Cartwright, and he told me he was best friends with Boyd, that he was the one with him when he drowned. At the time, all he could really tell the police about what happened was that a man had been standing near the pond, and when Boyd asked him for his ball, the man yelled at him to get away from there and for whatever reason kicked his ball into the pond. Boyd went in after it, but apparently, it was deeper than he thought, and since he couldn't swim, he went under. When Simon saw him go under again and he didn't come back up, he said he watched the man wade out to get him, but for some reason, he turned around and came back without him and then got into a black car and drove away. Shortly after that is when Simon's family moved away. From what I can understand, he never really dealt with Boyd's death, but after hearing about the Christmas campaign, he thought if he came back, he might be able to find some answers and hopefully stop the nightmares he'd been having since Boyd drowned."

"How did this Cartwright character know to come to you in the first place?"

"Apparently, he has an aunt living in the next county who apparently sends news about Braxton regularly, and after reading about the campaign and me wanting to reopen the pond, he came to me."

"Why did he wait so long to contact you?"

"I don't know exactly how long he was here before he did contact me, but in the interim and without really trying, he began to discover some things about the mayor that he thought might have something to do with all the accidents that have been happening around here."

"What things?"

"That's just it, he would only give me bits and pieces at first, saying he knew things, but it wasn't the right time to tell me. It wasn't until later on that he mentioned seeing the mayor meet with someone several times in his office, and that it was usually before and sometimes after something happened. At the time, I thought he was talking about my accident or the fires and that's when I asked him if he thought the mayor was responsible for it, but he said he didn't know for sure. He did say that there were a lot of things going on that I didn't know about and that I should be careful of Braxton. I didn't have a clue what he was talking about, but when he told me that Braxton might even try and stop me again, that's when I suspected he had something to do with my accident and possibly the fires. I also found out that Simon had been at the diner at the same time Carl and I had been there because he mentioned the missing articles and that was one of the things we talked about." She hesitated a moment. "I should tell you that Simon came out and asked me if I thought the mayor had anything to do with Boyd's death, and I have to admit I tell him that I thought he might have. That's about the time he told me the mayor might be responsible for he fires and my accident, but because he was concerned for my safety, he was pretty adamant about me not talking to you until we got the proof we needed, which I now realize was stupid."

"Where's Cartwright now?"

"I don't know. He did mention something about staying in a hotel, but I don't know where, he always found me somehow, but I have no idea where he is or how to get a hold of him."

"Or if he is who he says he is," Carl retorted, and Charlie just glared at him.

"Is that it?" The sheriff looked more than a little disturbed.

"I think so."

"And you never told me any of this because?"

"I meant to. I wanted to but I just, well, time just seemed to get away from me, I guess." She could see that it wasn't the answer he was looking for, but it was all she had.

"That sounds vaguely familiar," Matthew interjected sarcastically, and he watched Charlie's eyes narrow again.

"Does anyone else know about any of this?"

"No."

Bill looked at her with a calmness she knew he was definitely not feeling. "Is there anything else I should know about, anything you might have forgotten? Because if I find out you're holding anything else back from me, anything at all, I'll make damn sure you and Carl both spend jail time, you can bet on it. Am I coming through to you loud and clear, Charlie?"

"Yes. But I've told you all I know, Sheriff."

"You should have come to me long before this. I just hope it isn't too late. But don't think for one minute that you're off the hook, young lady. You withheld evidence for one thing, but more importantly, your accident might never have happened if you'd come to me sooner. What the hell were you thinking?"

"I just thought—"

"Where are the letters?" he asked, not waiting for her to answer.

"I have them." Carl pulled them out of his pocket, and the sheriff snatched them out of his hand.

"I'll take those. In the meantime, I'll see what I can find on this Cartwright character. And as far as the Caldwell boy—"

"I can take care of that, Bill." Matthew offered. "I'll find out where they moved and try to talk to them and find out the friend's name. I'll find out if he is who he says he is or if this Cartwright character is an imposter."

"Just don't get in over your head, Matt, and keep me posted. And as for you, Charlie, if you see this Cartwright character again, you let me know."

"I'm really sorry, Sher—"

"Save it," he said, cutting her off. "And so help me if I find out you've gone within fifty feet of John Braxton, I'm warning you, Charlie, I'll throw your butt in jail. You stay the hell away from him, and if he tries to contact you, you call me you got that?"

"Yes, I've got it." She didn't appreciate being treated like a child who got caught with her hand in the cookie jar, but she realized it was no one's fault but her own.

"I'd better get back to the office. I'll be in touch, Matt."

Charlie and Carl also got up to leave.

"I'd like to talk to you, Charlie." Matthew spoke up, and Charlie stopped where she was, and after the sheriff and Carl both left, Matthew asked her to sit down.

"No, thank you," she said, turning around to face him. "What do you want to talk to me about?"

"Why did you send me that letter saying you would pay me back for paying to restore the bridge?"

Charlie blinked, surprised because it wasn't the topic she expected. "Well, it was a lot of money and—"

"It was a gift, Charlie. I didn't expect to be paid back."

"I realize that but knowing how you feel about me, I didn't want to leave any loose ends."

"If you know how I feel about you, you wouldn't be talking about loose ends." He ran his hand through his hair, obviously agitated. "Look, I know I was pretty hard on you when I found out you lied to me but—"

"I didn't lie to you, Matthew. Part of the reason I didn't tell you what was going on, why I didn't tell anyone, was because I didn't really know anything, not for sure anyway. And when I did find out, there was no time. The other part of the reason was because everyone was walking around on eggshells with me after the accident when I mentioned that a man helped me out of the car. I saw the looks on your faces and I know you all thought it was my imagination, and if I had told you then what I thought, all of you would have been watching me every minute because you thought I was hallucinating or something. Then I would never have been able to go and meet that man and find out what he knew."

"So you put your life in danger and were nearly killed because you wanted to prove it was Braxton? If you had just told us—"

"Told you what, Matthew? That I *thought* he was responsible for my accident and the bridge and Carl's barn? How could I tell you or the sheriff or anyone else that I thought it was him without proof? You saw what happened here when I told the sheriff, they're only assumptions on my part. I work for lawyers, Matthew, remember?

Every day I hear of cases thrown out or that someone walked away from being prosecuted because there was no way to prove the allegations made against them. John Braxton is a shrewd man regardless of his mental state. He has money and he has power, and I've seen men like him walk right out of the courtroom with sly little smirks on their faces just like his because they were able to beat the system and I wasn't willing to take that chance."

"You wouldn't take a chance on us to try to help prove he was or wasn't guilty, but you would take a chance with your life, does that make sense to you?"

"I didn't think of it that way," she admitted. "Although I realize now, I underestimated him. I never thought he would go that far. Even though I do suspect him, have suspected him, I don't know for certain that he's involved, and even if he is, I have no idea how far that involvement goes."

"But that's for the police to decide, not you." Matthew looked at her long and hard. "I guess in a way, I underestimated you too, Charlie. I watched you go from little girl to grown woman, but I didn't see that you grew up somewhere along the way and that I'm still trying to protect you."

"You can't protect me forever, Matthew," she said softly, her anger diminishing. "But I would be awfully disappointed if you didn't try." She found the courage to walk over to him and looked up into his knowing eyes. "I realize now that what I did was stupid and careless, and I'm so sorry for putting you through all this. It wasn't my intention to hurt anyone and I'm not trying to make light of what happened, but since we have kind of adopted one another as family, we have to take the bad along with the good, right? That means we won't always agree, but it was my understanding that we would always accept one another no matter what happened."

Matthew gazed at her and shook his head. "You never cease to amaze me, Charlie. If someone's in trouble, you have to help them, if you're in trouble—"

"I don't ask for help, I know."

"No, you just don't give any thought to yourself," he corrected. "And someone has to watch out for you." He put his arms around her and gave her a huge bear hug. "If live to be a hundred, I'll never be more proud of you for staying with your convictions." He backed up far enough to look at her face. "But if you ever do anything like this again, I swear I'll make you wish you were never born." His eyes held an unquestionable look of warning that told her he was more than capable of carrying out his threat, and she knew better than to make a joke out of it.

"I really thought you never wanted to see me again."

"We had an argument, Charlie, I never once thought you believed I'd given up on you."

"Well, you have my word that if I ever get in trouble again, you'll be the first to know." Her broad smile faded a bit, and she looked at him a little strangely. "But there is one thing that I'd like you to clear up for me."

"Now look, Charlie, if it's about the money—"

"No, it has nothing to do with the money. I was just being sulky." She looked up into his eyes, knowing he would never lie to her. "It has to do with a comment you made the day we had the argument just before you left. You said you hoped to hell Paul knew what he was getting into. Did you really mean that?"

"Of course, I meant it," he said without hesitation, and Charlie felt the sting of rejection and her eyes welled up. "But not in the way you obviously took it. What I meant was that loving you wouldn't be easy. You're stubborn and hard-headed, and when you go after something, you sometimes do it with a vengeance and without thinking, and if he planned on spending the rest of his life with you, he'd better get used to it because that will never change."

Charlie understood, but her smile was barely there. "Well, regardless of whether he wanted to spend the rest of his life with me or not, I think he's just as upset with me, so we don't have to worry about that anymore, do we?"

"Well, I wouldn't say that," Paul said, walking in from the other room, and for a brief moment, Charlie couldn't breathe.

"How long have you been standing in there, boy?" Matthew's question echoed Charlie's thoughts.

"Long enough," Paul said, not taking his eyes off Charlie. "We need to talk, and don't tell me there's nothing left to say because, honey, the anger Granddad felt is just the tip of the iceberg." He walked toward her, and she stepped back, looking to Matthew for support.

"Oh no," Matthew said, holding his hands up. "I'm not getting in the middle of this, little darlin', no way. This is one battle I'm afraid you'll have to fight on your own."

"But, Matthew," she said, taking another step backward when Paul took another toward her.

"See ya." He gave them a backward wave as he walked out the door.

Paul stepped closer. "Why didn't you tell me?"

"Tell you what?"

"Don't ask me what, you know what."

"You already know, obviously you were listening." She moved further back.

"I would have understood."

"How can you say that? You would have felt exactly the way Matthew felt and you know it."

"You still should have told me."

"Oh well." She backed up another few inches and came up against the television console.

"Oh well?" He echoed, and she flinched, not meaning it to come out quite so blasé, but he'd literally backed her into a corner.

"What are you going to do now, Charlie? You can't run anymore." He took another step and was standing directly in front of her. "You should have told me what was going on."

"I already got this lecture from Matthew." She glared up into his fierce green eyes, hating to be told the same things over and over again even if they were true. She'd gotten the point the first time, and she didn't need reminded of mistakes she'd made; she got enough of that from her stepfather.

"You have no idea of the hell you've put me through." His expression was unreadable, one she hadn't seen before, and she instinctively began to stutter when he reached out to brush a strand of hair from her eyes.

"I didn't, I couldn't have known—"

"I thought I'd lost you when I saw you lying in that hospital bed, Charlie, and now I find out that you've put yourself in danger again."

"But I'm not, I—"

He gently took her face into his hands and pulled her closer, using his thumbs to caress the soft smoothness of her neck and across her lips, sending little shivers through her body. She tried to look away, but he held her face and forced her to look at him. "Is this what I have to look forward to, you getting yourself mixed up in situations you can't get yourself out of?"

Held by the intense look in his eyes and the hypnotic deepness of his voice, their strange powers pulling her in and draining her of the desire to fight him anymore, Charlie couldn't answer. Right in the middle of things, her mind was drifting back to when she was a little girl dreaming of the day her knight in shining armor would ride up on his beautiful white stallion, sweep her up onto his mighty steed, and whisk her away to his enchanted castle where they would live happily ever after. And it was at that precise moment that she realized she just might have found him, except that her hero drove a red Blazer and wore tight jeans. She smiled up at him adoringly, wondering why it took him so long to find her when he suddenly burst her dream like a bubble and brought her back to the real world when she heard him say, "The next time you decide to take things into your own hands, you'd better think twice before you do because you'll have me to deal with, and trust me, Charlie, I won't be so forgiving."

Well, so much for happily ever after, she thought dismally coming back to earth with a crash and agitated as well because she didn't like ultimatums. "Now listen here, Paul—"

"No, you listen for a change, Charlie. I'm not fooling around. If you ever pull a stunt like that again, you'll answer to me, and Granddad won't be able to help you, do you understand?"

It wasn't a threat, it was a promise, and there was no mistaking his meaning or his anger, and she sensed that batting her eyelashes at him to make him lighten up was not an option.

To Charlie, the accident was over, a done deal, and she had survived, and in her mind, she reasoned that because she was standing safely before him and not lying in a grave under a headstone somewhere, there was no need of further reminders or reprimands for putting herself in jeopardy. Of course, in her heart she knew that if the roles had been reversed and he had been the one in the accident, the pain she would have felt was the kind of pain she couldn't treat lightly or ignore either. Right was right and knight in shining armor or man in a red blazer, she loved him and the thought of losing him overwhelmed her.

"I think I would have lost my mind if you had been in an accident like that, especially one that you could have possibly prevented, and I had no right to cause you that kind of pain. When you love somebody, you don't hurt them like that, and I can't tell you how sorry I am but—"

"No buts, Charlie." Paul's eyes grew darker.

"You don't understand, I'm just trying to—"

"And don't think for one minute that I won't walk out that door if you try justifying it. There was no excuse for what you did."

He was right and she knew it, but she was stubborn and bull-headed and was still trying to rationalize her actions. But she also knew he was dead serious and would walk out of her life permanently this time if she kept it up. And losing him wasn't worth it.

"Look," she said softly. "I can't promise you that I'll always make the right decisions or that you'll agree with everything I do, but I will promise to think before I act, okay?" She knew it was a kind of compromise, but she wasn't trying to give him conditions or ultimatums, she was just trying to be truthful and not make promises she couldn't keep, and Paul looked at her long and hard.

"I guess I can't ask for anything more than that." He kissed her then, reawakening her dream, and she quickly wrapped her arms around his neck and kissed him back, and it was several long minutes before she gently pulled away and looked up into his eyes again.

"I think I just may have found my knight in shining armor."

Sheriff Conley, on the other hand, was madder than hell that Charlie had held back so much information and hadn't come to him sooner, and though her story sounded beyond bizarre, he believed her. He also believed that someone had been following her because of the incident that had taken place at her house in addition to Braxton possibly being involved. Actually in thinking back, he should have realized something wasn't right the day he refused to allow the men from several neighboring counties to come into his town and help repair the covered bridge. Obviously, he was trying to keep everyone from knowing the truth, whatever it was, but at the time, he hadn't given it a whole lot of thought. Besides, it wasn't an easy thing to admit that a town official had gone bad, but stranger things have happened. And if he found out that Braxton was somehow involved in the death of the Caldwell boy as well, he would make damn sure he was put away for a very long time.

As unbelievable as it sounded, there was no doubt in his mind that someone wanted Charlie out of the way, but the problem was proving it was him and he immediately set up a surveillance team to keep a watchful eye on the mayor's office, his house, and anyone he came in contact with as well as putting a watch on Charlie. There was more than just a possibility that she was still in danger, and he wasn't about to leave anything to chance.

In the meantime, Simon Cartwright was already several steps ahead of the sheriff having set up his own one-man surveillance team in the parking lot of the savings and loan the week before, and while he hadn't seen anything out of the ordinary for days, his patience paid off when he saw the man in the business suit. He snapped a photo of him slipping inside the rear entrance of Braxton's office and continued snapping pictures in succession of the two men talking, Braxton reaching into a desk drawer and pulling out a rather large and bulky envelope, and then handing it to the man and shaking his hand. It was then that he came to the full realization that Braxton was most likely paying the man off for one or perhaps all of the many accidents that had occurred, and while he now suspected the mayor was behind it all, there was only one way to prove it, he had to confront him.

While he needed the pictures for a bargaining tool as proof of the mayor's association with the man in the business suit, he knew Braxton wouldn't have him killed until he had the pictures safely in his hands—and that was his ace in the hole. Although the pictures didn't reveal anything incriminating that would stand up in court because they didn't actually show money exchanging hands, Braxton had no way of knowing that, and that's when Simon then set the wheels of his plan in motion. He would drop off the film at a photo shop in Hectorville the next morning, leave them for safe keeping, and then call the mayor to set up an appointment in the guise of speaking to him about making a considerable contribution to the town which would enable Simon to tell him he wanted in on the deal. In turn, he would hopefully learn all he could about Braxton's involvement in the accidents, including the possibility that he was somehow connected to Boyd's death. If Braxton refused, Simon would threaten him with selling the photos along with the story behind it to the newspapers, as well as giving every bit of information he had to the authorities which would inevitably put him away for a very long time.

He called the mayor's office, and of course, because of the mayor's love of money, he didn't hesitate to instruct Hank to set up an appointment with Mr. Smith because as anyone could attest to, money was Braxton's middle name, and whoever offered it was always welcomed with open arms.

The appointment was set for three-thirty that afternoon, and because the mayor trusted no one, he told Hank and his secretary to take the rest of the day off, assuring that no one would listen in on their conversation, and when Simon arrived, Braxton bent over backward to make him welcome by immediately offering him cognac and a cigar.

"Thank you, Mayor, I don't smoke, but I would enjoy a cognac."
He noted the tall wooden cupboard in the far corner across from
the door as well as the size of the sparse but extravagantly decorated
room, noting no alcoves or possible hiding places.

"Certainly, certainly, and please call me John." The mayor
immediately poured a glass for both of them, and they each took a
sip. "Now, I understand that you would like to make a considerable
contribution to my little town, Mr. Smith." When it came to money,
John Braxton came right to the point and quickly.

"Well, actually, John, I would like to make a proposition to you."

"What kind of proposition?" The mayor took another sip of
brandy and nearly choked when he saw Simon retrieve a small
derringer from the inside pocket of his jacket and placed it on the
mayor's desk.

"What the hell do you think you're doing?"

"Actually, Mayor Braxton, my actual purpose for coming here
is two-fold in that I have something of value that you want in
exchange for something I want."

"And just what the hell is that?" the mayor snarled, his face
splotchy red with anger.

"I know what you have done, and quite simply, I want a piece of
the action."

Enraged, Braxton instantly jumped up out of his chair. "I don't
know what the hell you're talking about, but if you don't get the hell
out of this office in two minutes, I'll have you thrown out."

Simon picked up the gun from the desk and fondled it lovingly.
"Oh, I don't think you'll do that, Mayor, because you instructed
your assistant and secretary to take the rest of the day off, and there
is no one nearby to help you. Besides, if you do not do as you are
told, you will have some explaining to do to the sheriff as well as
the citizens, and I am quite sure you wouldn't want that. You aren't
very popular in this town as it is, now sit down, be quiet, and listen.
First of all, let me explain to you what I know so that you have no
misunderstanding about how very serious I am. You see, I have
proof that you hired someone, who shall remain nameless for the

moment, to destroy the covered bridge, burn down Mr. Freeman's barn, and attempt to kill Miss Faraday."

"You're completely out of your mind. I never—"

"Tut, tut, Mayor, I assure you I know these things for a fact, but just so we understand one another, do not be under the misconception that I will not shoot you where you sit if you if you interrupt me again or if you attempt to press the button under your desk to summon the authorities, do be kind enough to place both hands flat on the desk if you please."

Braxton sneered but did as he was told. "What good will it do you to kill me? You can't blackmail someone and then kill them and hope to collect your money. I'm not as stupid as you think."

Actually the fact that he took the bait and believed Simon said that he was. "Oh, I don't intend to kill you unless of course I must, but I can cause you immense pain, and shooting one's kneecaps can be excruciatingly painful, especially if left unattended and the victim is allowed to bleed to death in agony. Now please keep your unintelligent comments to yourself and allow me to finish." It took several minutes for the color to come back into the mayor's face and Simon smiled. "Now from this moment on, I really do need your complete attention and you must listen to my words carefully because I will not repeat them a second time. You see, I know exactly what you have been up to, and believe me when I tell you that I have ample enough proof to back up what I am about to tell you. Are we clear on that point?"

The mayor said nothing and merely glared at Simon, and when Simon aimed the little derringer under the mayor's desk and cocked the hammer back, the mayor immediately shoved back his chair and stood up. "You're insane!" he screamed. "You can't possibly think you'll get away with this, someone will hear the—"

Simon shot the gun into the floor, and Braxton's face drained of all color as beads of sweat instantly popped out on his forehead. He looked like he might pass out at any given moment until Simon slowly brought the gun back up in plain sight and placed it on the desk. "The next shot I fire will hit your right kneecap." His eyes never left Braxton's, and he slowly sat back down in his chair. "Unless of course I miss and hit your, well, to be delicate, shall I say a rather vital part of your lower anatomy? However, the chances of my missing are remote, I'm an excellent shot and there has never been a time that I have not hit my intended target. Now have I convinced you that I am quite serious?"

"Yes," the mayor answered in a begrudging tone.

"Good. Now as I was saying, I have ample proof that you did in fact hire someone to do your filthy bidding, including destroying all the hard work that was done to refurbish the bridge, burning Mr. Freeman's barn to the ground, and attempting to murder Miss Faraday on Pine Cone Hill. In addition, you instructed him to go to Miss Faraday's home with the intention of scaring her into perhaps giving up on her idea of a Christmas campaign, hence hoping to put a stop to her wish to use the pond as part of that campaign, thereby obliterating any chance of raising further suspicion regarding it because you see—and this is really quite good actually—I have more than just ample proof that you left young Boyd Caldwell to drown in that very same pond twenty years ago because I saw it happen. I watched you wait until he'd come within inches of retrieving his ball and then viciously kick it into the pond. I also saw you stand at the edge and watch him flounder in the water until it was nearly too late and he was going under for the third time, and it was only then that you finally made up your mind to possibly help him. But then after wading out only a short distance, you obviously changed your mind and turned around and came back without him and calmly walked to your long sleek limousine and drive away, leaving him to die in that watery grave." He watched the man's eyes widen, and his face turn a sickly gray. "And now you are wondering how I happen to know all these details, and I will quell your curiosity by telling you that I know all the sordid details because I was there. I was the friend with him that day. Surely, you remember the young boy whose parents would not allow his name to be revealed because of possible harassment from the fine citizens of your little town? Well, I am he and I saw it all." His sigh was heavy, as though he'd relived the entire incident all over again at that very moment. And though he did well to conceal the pain from showing on his face, the hatred in his eyes was all too real when the memory, suddenly provoked by reliving the day a third time in front of the very person his parents trusted to keep his secret, resurfaced and he remembered it all as plainly as if it happened two days ago. "And I revealed this to you when you came to my home not to ask my parents if I was affected by what had happened but to ask if I could possibly identify the person at the pond. You see no one knew my identity but the authorities and you, the mayor and paragon of the community." He let the surprising bit of information sink into his own brain as well as the mayor's for a several moments before going on, not only ensuring that the mayor fully believe he was indeed who he claimed, but to set it in stone in his own mind as well. Besides which, he wanted no doubt in the mayor's mind that he could prove every allegation. "Well," he said finally. "I believe that about covers it all—with the exception of a possible second attempt to dispose of Miss Faraday, of course, and perhaps that is where I may come in." He looked at the quivering coward before him and wanted to vomit, but instead, he smiled. "So what do you think, Mayor, do we have a deal? A deal that would be triple the amount you paid your hired killer of course—and just how much was that exactly?"

Braxton's throat was dry as a bone, and he swallowed, still trying to defend himself even though he knew now that it was useless. "I really don't know what you're—" He stopped when he saw Simon reach for the gun once again and quickly answered, "One hundred and fifty thousand dollars."

"Well, that's just fine, three hundred and fifty thousand dollars will do quite nicely. Now you are going to call your *friend* and you are going to tell him to meet you here on Sunday evening at eight o'clock. You are going to tell him that you need him to do another job for you and that you need to speak with him immediately. You will not try to signal him in any way because I will shoot your kneecaps one at a time and I will be forced to waylay my call to the authorities until you have had sufficient enough time to bleed profusely and come very near death, but I will allow just enough time for you to survive and spend the rest of your miserable life in prison with legs that are completely useless. Do we understand one another, Mayor Braxton?"

"Yes," the mayor answered, his eyes round with fear.

"Now merely out of curiosity, why did you decide to let that boy drown instead of rescuing him from the pond?"

The mayor strained his neck and nervously reached up to loosen his tie. "I, I thought the authorities would think I had something to do with his death."

"Now why would anyone think the town's honorable mayor had anything at all to do with the death of a child? Well, perhaps I could explain that for you. If you had rescued Boyd, he would have informed the authorities that you were the one to kick his ball into the pond, and though you could have found a way around that by saying it was simply an accident or that the boy was lying, they would still have questioned your reason for being there in the first place. It was a well-known fact that you hated that pond because the geese you despised so much left it a filthy mess with their droppings everywhere and since you fought with your father for years demanding that it be closed or filled in, it was certainly not due to the fact that you were there merely to enjoy the scenery. Perhaps in your devious and twisted mind, you thought if you were to put something in the water, it would kill the water fowl and the council and your father would finally agree that it was a polluted danger to the citizens and agree to do away with it. But then, quite by accident, Boyd and I appeared and put an end to your scheme. And while there was perhaps a slight bit of humanity that surfaced when you first attempted to rescue Boyd, the sick animal inside you surfaced as well, suggesting that if he were left there to die, it would substantiate your argument that the pond was far more dangerous than they had originally thought and they would have perhaps considered your opinions legitimate." Although Simon had no sound proof for his theory, Braxton's extreme pallor suggested that he wasn't far off the mark. "Whatever happened that day, you allowed an innocent young boy to drown for no reason, and eventually, you will pay for that crime with a power far higher than any court of law. Now you will do me the courtesy of calling your hired killer."

While Simon noted the entered numbers, the mayor made the call as directed, telling the man to meet him at his office on Sunday at eight p.m., there was an urgent matter which required his expertise for which he would again be compensated well, and of course, he readily agreed.

"My work here is done for the time being, and I will be on my way. However, should you make an attempt to warn him after I am gone, I will know it and will immediately go to the authorities with everything I have without one moment's hesitation, do you understand?"

Braxton gave a curt nod, and Simon stood up. "Contrary to popular belief, walls do have ears, so please do not disappoint me or cause me to do something you will regret."

Simon left through the front door, quickly disappearing from sight before anyone knew he'd been there, and while he hoped he'd succeeded in pulling off the biggest bluff he'd ever attempted, nothing was foolproof, which is why he had to move quickly before the man somehow realized he knew less than nothing for certain. However, he did have enough information to cause suspicion and a thorough investigation by the authorities providing Braxton didn't put two and two together and had him killed first, which is why he wanted to meet with the authorities before he had the chance to find out. Unfortunately, he needed Charlie to pave the way.

It was ten minutes after four when Simon left Braxton's office and called Charlie at work from a payphone. His conversation was brief, and he used no greeting or names.

"Be at the same place we last met in fifteen minutes but make very certain that you are not followed. This may well be the last chance I can meet with you."

"But—"

"Please just do as I ask."

The graveness of Simon's tone caused an alarm to go off in Charlie's head, and she immediately left the office and headed for the bridge site. She had no idea why he sounded so mysterious, but the fact that he had called her on the phone alerted her to be prepared. Prepared for what, she had no idea, but she did as he asked, making certain that she was not being followed by purposely turning down several wrong streets and, as though she'd made a mistake, turned around and went back to the main road again. She did this several times until she was certain that no one was behind her. When she arrived at the site, she didn't see Simon anywhere, but as usual, she didn't hear him approach until he laid a light hand on her shoulder.

"Let's walk across the meadow," he said, leading the way, and Charlie could do nothing more than follow.

"What's going on, Simon?" she demanded when they stopped just inside the perimeter of the trees. "You never call me to meet you."

"I needed to speak with you immediately, but I had to make certain you were not followed and that we met in a place where we could see if anyone was approaching."

"You're scaring me, Simon. I realize you don't want to be seen together but—"

"Especially now," he interrupted, and Charlie felt that familiar tingle at the back of her neck.

"Why?" she asked suspiciously. What's so important that you had to take a chance that—?"

"I met with the mayor today."

The color drained from Charlie's face, and she looked as though he'd just told her he was an ax murderer. "You did what?"

"I called the mayor's office and set up an appointment to meet with him," he explained patiently, and realizing the predicament he'd put himself into, Charlie spoke without thinking.

"Well, why in the hell did you go and do a stupid thing like that? I thought you wanted to keep your identity a secret and that we were going to wait until the time was right to confront him.

Everything was perfect, he didn't know who you were or anything about you and—"

"He does now." Simon smiled shrewdly.

"Oh God, Simon, what have you done?"

"Let me just say that I made him an offer he could not refuse."

Charlie was stupefied. "Offer? What do you mean an offer, what kind of an offer?"

"I simply told him that I wanted to make a rather large contribution to the town as a whole which in turn gave me the opportunity to tell him that I have proof that he was responsible for both fires, the attempt on your life, *and* Boyd's death."

"You did what?" Charlie's high-pitched voice echoed through the woods. "Are you completely out of your mind? Even if what we suspect is true, and there's no doubt in my mind that it is, why in heaven's name did you tell him something like that? Don't you realize the danger you're in? If he finds out you lied, he'll have you killed!"

"I think not, Miss Faraday. He admitted to me that he paid someone to commit those crimes and that alone will incriminate both of them, and I have the proof, in a manner of speaking."

"What do you mean, 'in a manner of speaking'?" She totally missed the comment that he paid someone to kill her. "You either have proof or you don't, there can be no overlaps."

"I did what had to be done," he said curtly. "The man needs to pay for his crimes, and I intend to see that he does. I have pictures of his henchman sneaking in the back entrance of his office, in addition to receiving a very fat envelope which is most likely his payoff."

"But you don't know that, the envelope could have contained anything. Besides, we don't even know who the man is. As a matter of fact, no one has really seen him or even knows he exists except what we've told them."

"Don't you worry about that. I have a friend who can enlarge the photographs to give us a clearer picture. I am also going to check out his license with the Department of Motor Vehicles. I assure you I have been in this business for a long time and I know what I am doing, and that includes bringing the sheriff in on this entire plan just as soon as I have the photos back and have them blown up. I did not go into this without a plan in mind, Miss Faraday, and I would never presume to involve you to the point of seeing you come to harm again. We must have proof to show the proper authorities, and this is the only way we obtain it as we are the only two people who know enough to help put him away for a very long time."

Charlie thought for a moment. "Simon, I know why you have such a strong interest in all this, and I also know you're trying to protect me and I'm grateful to you and can't thank you enough, but we need help now more than ever and I know someone we can trust explicitly and—"

"No, I am afraid I cannot do that, Miss Faraday. I do not want any more people involved in this than is absolutely necessary. As it is, I have already put your life in further peril by meeting you, but it was not something I wanted to do, it was something I felt I had to do. I do not want to put anyone else in jeopardy."

"But Matthew Torrance is a good man and he can help us, Simon. He is the most trustworthy man I have ever known and he knows people, a lot of people, people who could help us."

Simon seemed to consider it. "I don't know. I just think we are better off if—"

"Please, Simon, Matthew knows what he's doing and he knows a lot of influential people. Besides, in the beginning, you asked me to trust you, and I have without question throughout this entire thing. Now I'm asking you to trust me for once."

Simon was moved by the sincerity in her eyes. "Very well, Miss Faraday, you have made your point. We will do it your way. Call your Matthew, and try to arrange for a meeting as soon as possible. I told the mayor to meet me in his office on Sunday, which means you will have to talk to him as soon as possible. In the meantime, I have things I must attend to, but I will call you this evening and you can tell me if he is agreeable. I can only hope that you tell him what you are getting him into as I would not want it on my conscience if you or he would meet with foul play. We are taking a very big chance."

"I know that, Simon, but I promise you won't be sorry."

Although it appeared that the right hand didn't know exactly what the left hand was doing, everything seemed to be headed in the right direction. All everyone needed to do was end up at the same place at the same time, alive. And Charlie was smack in the middle trying to do just that when she called Matthew later that evening.

"Matthew? It's Charlie, and I need to talk to you right away—tonight."

"Well, that sounds a little desperate, darlin', but can't it wait until tomorrow? I'm—" "No, I'm afraid it can't. I don't mean to sound dramatic, but what I have to tell you is extremely important and very well could be a matter of life or death."

"Now come on, darlin', nothing could be that bad. I was just about to—"

"It could be that bad, Matthew. I'm not an alarmist, and this isn't something I would joke about, I really do need to see you. Can I come out?"

Matthew knew Charlie better than she knew herself, and he knew she wouldn't insist on seeing him if it wasn't vitally important. Besides, he had told her not to keep anything back from him. "Okay, little darlin', okay. I'll just jump in the shower, but Paul's here and he can let you in."

"Paul's there?" she asked, surprised.

"Yes, he's been working out here, is that a problem?"

Charlie thought about that for a minute, not sure if she wanted him involved, but she remembered his warning about doing something without thinking first, and she realized it would be better if he heard this from her firsthand. Besides, there was safety in numbers and she needed all the help she could get.

"Charlie?" Matthew broke into her thoughts. "If you'd rather, I can tell him to go—"

"No, no, it's fine if he's there, no problem. I'll see you shortly."

Fifteen minutes later, Charlie pulled into Matthew's driveway and was nearly at the top before she spied Paul sitting on the front step, and she instantly felt hot tears sting her eyes as well as her heart speed up and go into overdrive. She'd missed him more than she realized since he'd been away and was more than a little excited to see him; she only wished it didn't have to be under these circumstances. However, into each life, a little rain may fall. She only hoped it didn't turn into a monsoon.

If Charlie had any doubts that Paul missed her, they were gone when he appeared at the driver's side door, pulled it open, and reached inside to grab her, hauling her into his arms and kissing her as though he'd been gone a year rather than just two weeks. Several long minutes later, he reluctantly pulled away to look at her. "Jesus, you're sure a sight for sore eyes. I missed you like hell, woman." He kissed her again, gentler this time, raising her blood pressure sky-high while igniting fiery little sparks throughout her body, and she melted into his arms like hot taffy. When he pulled away the second time, her eyes were glazed, her eyelids heavy, and her cheeks were flushed. "Wow. Maybe you should go away more often, maybe a month," she said suggestively.

"You're putting on quite a show for the neighbors." A voice came out of the blue, and they both turned to see Matthew, leaning lazily against the doorframe, his arms crossed and his feet crossed at the ankles.

"You don't have any neighbors," Paul said, looking back at Charlie.

"No, but I'll have the entire town of Braxton standing in my front yard when they see the blazing inferno over here," he said sternly although they didn't catch the sly smile on his face. "You two wanna bring that inside? Besides, I believe Charlie has some important business to discuss."

Matthew held the screen door open for them, and they strolled in the house together arm in arm, staring into one another's eyes. "Do you two want anything before we get started, coffee, a beer, a cold shower?"

Charlie's face flamed red, and she looked up at Matthew, embarrassed. "Sorry, Matthew, I guess I just missed your grandson—a lot."

"Obviously. Now if you two can restrain yourselves —"

Embarrassed, Charlie sat down on the sofa, but before Paul could sit beside her, she waved him away. "You'd better sit over there, Paul, in the chair way over by the door." She blushed again.

"All right, Charlie." Matthew's face was stern. "Do you want to tell me what's going on? Contrary to what I just saw here, you had something else on your mind when you called me so out with it."

"Oh, right." Charlie realized in the heat of the moment that she'd forgotten what she originally wanted to talk to Matthew about and her expression immediately became somber. "Well, something has happened or may happen, and I need your help."

"I got that over the phone." He took a seat across from Charlie. "What kind of help?"

Charlie signed deeply. "I'm not sure I know where to start."

"Matthew frowned, becoming suspicious. "The beginning is always a good place."

"Well, Simon Cartwright, the man I told you about? He called me this morning around six a.m. and said he needed to talk to me and told me to meet him at the bridge site but to make absolutely sure I wasn't followed. He's always really careful about our not being seen together when we meet, but he seemed more than just a little cautious this morning, and while he normally just seems to appear wherever I am, for him to actually call me on the phone, well, it was the first time he'd ever contacted me that way and he seemed different."

"Different how?"

"I'm not sure exactly, more cautious that usual maybe? Not afraid but, oh, I don't know how to explain it, Matthew, he was just different. In any case, he apologized for being so cautious about me not being followed this time because, well, he told me he met with the mayor last night."

"I wasn't aware that he knew Braxton."

"That's part of the problem, he doesn't know him, he knows of him. Anyway, I was pretty upset with him for doing such a stupid thing, and when I asked him why he would put himself in that kind of situation, he told me it was because he had proof that he was the one who set the fires and caused my accident, well, that he hired someone to do it actually, *and* that he knew he had something to do with Boyd Caldwell's drowning."

"What? Why in the hell did he do something like that?"

"That's what I asked him. Matthew, you know as well as I do that Braxton wouldn't think twice about having him killed if he finds out he doesn't have any proof."

"You're damn right he wouldn't. What was he thinking?"

"Simon insists he has the proof, pictures of the man going into Braxton's office through the back entrance and Braxton handing him an envelope full of money, well, what Simon believes was money, and that it was the guy's payoff."

"How the hell does he know what was in that envelope?"

"I know, I know, he can't prove it was money, but Braxton apparently admitted paying him a hundred and fifty thousand dollars to do those jobs."

Matthew whistled. "That's a lot of money. And Braxton admitted it? What did he have, a gun to his head?"

"I don't know, but he insists he has the proof to back it up, sort of."

"Sort of?" Matthew echoed. "What the hell's that supposed to mean?"

"Well, like I said, he apparently got pictures."

"What is he, nuts? He doesn't know that for sure."

"No, he doesn't, but it does make sense when you think about it, Matthew. He did see them together several times, and it was usually before or after the fires and my accident." Charlie suddenly looked stricken upon the sudden realization that while her life meant nothing to Braxton, it was worth a hundred and fifty thousand dollars to see her dead. It was more than just a little disturbing.

"Apparently, he's a sick and evil man, darlin'," Matthew said lovingly. "And he's certainly not worth your tears."

Charlie smiled at Matthew through misty eyes. "You always know just the right thing to say, don't you, Matthew? And you're right as usual, he's not worth it at all." She swiped at the tear that slipped down her cheek with the back of her hand and took a deep breath. "But let's just say, argument's sake, that he was right and that it was a payoff. It doesn't do much good anyway because no one knows who the man is. The pictures were taken from quite a distance and they aren't very clear, but he knows someone who can blow them up. Oh, and he must have gotten his license plate number too because he mentioned possibly checking with the DMV. He says he wants to let the sheriff in on this as soon as he gets the film back, Matthew," she added, trying to alleviate any doubt about Simon's integrity. "He and I are the only ones who know enough to try and get them both put away, but since he set up a meeting with the mayor and his hired gun, so to speak, I knew we needed help and that's why I mentioned meeting with you. He didn't want to at first, but I convinced him that we needed all the help we could get and, well, that you knew people." Charlie looked at Matthew long and hard but failed to read his expression. "I'm so sorry, Matthew. I never meant to get you involved in this, and I should never have told him that you knew people. Above anything else, I don't want you hurt, but I didn't know what else to do."

"No, no, it's okay, you did the right thing coming to me, darlin'. I do know people who know how to get answers. When did you say he was meeting Braxton?"

"Sunday night at eight o'clock, the office is closed and no one will be around. He's supposed to call me tonight to find out if you agreed to meet."

"That doesn't give us much time, but I should be enough to get Bill in on this so he can set something up. In the meantime, I'll make a few phone calls to get things going on my end, and when Cartwright calls, tell him I'll meet him at the bridge site tomorrow afternoon at two o'clock. But this is it for you, darlin', once you make that phone call, you're out of it, do you understand?"

In the meantime, Carl had been doing some research of his own and had learned through an editor friend that Mrs. Caldwell had a sister living in the neighboring town of Hectorville and he and Matthew paid her a visit that same day. Upon learning that her sister had moved to Philadelphia, Pennsylvania, Matthew wasted no time purchasing a ticket for the next flight leaving at six a.m., Saturday morning.

Matthew arrived at Philadelphia International around seven-fifteen, stopped for breakfast, and with the address in hand, caught a cab and paid a visit to the Caldwell home in Piedmont, a small town about twenty minutes from the airport. And while her sister had called ahead saying Matthew would be coming and Melissa Caldwell did welcome him into her home, she was extremely nervous and very withdrawn.

A small woman nearing forty, Mrs. Caldwell looked closer to fifty-something and "quite frail" as her sister had pointed out, obviously never completely recovering from the loss of her little boy. Matthew was extremely gentle with her, her disturbingly sad eyes revealing the possibility that it would take very little to send her over the edge.

The house was small and nondescript and as unassuming as she was and had been chosen in a remote area, Matthew guessed, so as not to attract attention. She'd had a lot of heartache in her life, including the not too recent death of her husband, and now she had no one except her sister whom she hadn't seen for over fifteen years yet who continuously tried to get her to move back to Vermont to live with her. It was heartbreaking to watch her move about, quiet, inconspicuous, and practically nonexistent for so many years, but after some of Braxton's citizens practically accused her of leaving her young child alone in the backyard, it was understandable why she moved. It must have been hell for her living among neighbors she thought she could trust but who seemingly turned on her and blamed her for the loss of her own son.

"Mrs. Caldwell, I'm not here to hurt you by awakening the past, I promise you," Matthew told her after explaining why he'd come.

"But I need to know the name of the boy who was with your son that day. We know his identity was not revealed all those years ago, but we have reason to believe that he may be back in Braxton and we need to know why. You see, he knew things he could not possibly have known about your son unless he had been there, and we need to know if he is in fact the same person. The police are investigating this for reasons I can't reveal to you at the present time, but I can give you a number to verify it."

"That isn't necessary," the woman spoke for the first time. "I will cooperate in any way I can, but I'm afraid his name is all I can tell you."

"His name is all I need," Matthew said kindly, and she went to her address book.

"I kept in touch with his mother Candace for many years, but of course, her name changed when she remarried several years ago. I believe she moved, and though she sent me her new address, I'm afraid I simply stopped answering her letters. It was a difficult time for both of us. Here it is, Kingston, oh no, that is her married name. Her son kept his real father's name. Yes, here it is, Cartwright, Simon Cartwright."

"Simon Cartwright," Matthew repeated. "I should have known Charlie was right," he said more to himself than to the woman. Although he did suspect the man of lying about his identity, finding out he was actually who he said he was was rather a shock.

"Is that the name of the man you're talking about?" she asked, and Matthew nodded.

"Yes, that's him all right." His tone was strained, tired actually.

"You almost sound disappointed," she said sympathetically. "Have I helped you or merely hindered you?"

"You have no idea how much you've helped, Mrs. Caldwell, but in thinking back, although I know the police must have questioned you at length, do you recall anything that might help us to know who the man was at the pond that day? I realize it was a long time ago but—"

"Unfortunately, one does not forget such a tragedy as losing one's son. Although I have tried to put it from my mind, it replays itself over and over again nonstop day after day, just as though it happened yesterday." She stared off into space as though she reliving the day through her mind's eye. "I was quite hysterical and questioned Simon at length myself that day. I was so desperately seeking answers that I frightened him, I'm afraid."

"Was he able to give you any information besides what was said in the newspapers?"

"No, he wasn't, but I do recall Candace mentioning that the mayor's son stopped by his home several days later."

"Oh?" Matthew was taken aback. "Did he stop by to offer his condolences to you as well?"

"No. Candace told me that he had only stopped by and asked Simon many questions and that he intended to come by and pay his respects to us, but he never came. He was a rather odd man," she said reflectively. "But of course, I am wrongly comparing him to his father, who of course was very different. As a matter of fact, the mayor came by that very evening to ask if there was anything he could do and even offered to pay for Boyd's, for his funeral expenses, but we declined, deciding to have his services in Hectorville where my sister lives. We wanted to avoid the, the incessant questions and speculation in everyone's mind. Besides, we did not want nor did we need the town's unfelt charity," she said proudly.

While Matthew completely understood the woman's feelings, he couldn't help questioning the younger Braxton's ethics and, for the life of him, couldn't understand his cold and heartless actions.

"Well, I do apologize for taking up your time, Mrs. Caldwell, but you have been extremely helpful, and I can't thank you enough for agreeing to meet with me. I know how difficult this must be for you."

"You're quite welcome, Mr.—"

"Torrance, Matthew Torrance."

"Yes, Mr. Torrance. My sister did tell me your name, but I'm afraid my memory isn't quite what it used to be." To prove her point, she looked slightly confused as though she might be remembering something. "Wait, I may have, wait right here a moment."

She disappeared down the hall and was gone only a minute when she returned. "I've misplaced so many things when I moved as well as when I disposed of my husband's belongings," she said sadly. "But I did remember this." She handed him a photograph. "It was taken quite a long time ago, you understand, so I'm not sure it would be of any help to you. We had taken Boyd and Simon to the park that day and Ron, my late husband, took that picture when they were fishing together at the little creek nearby. They never caught anything but tiny little blue gills, but they had such fun. That was a wonderful day."

"This is Simon Cartwright?" The boy was of small stature, average height for his age, and looked to be about ten years old. His hair was dark, and though it was difficult to tell by the faded picture, his eyes appeared to be dark as well. "Yes. Though he was a bit older than my Boyd, he was a good friend to my son and was with him when—the day of the accident." She finished quietly. "I am sorry I have nothing more recent."

"That's quite all right. You did just fine, Mrs. Caldwell, and I can't thank you enough for all your help." He walked toward the door, then hesitated and turned around. "Pardon me for intruding, but I can't help thinking you might consider going back to live with your sister. It must be lonely living here by yourself, and your sister does miss you very much." He watched her eyes grow tearful and figured he'd said enough, but with any luck, she would at least think about it. "Take care of yourself, Mrs. Caldwell," he said, gently shaking her hand. "It has been a great pleasure meeting you."

"It was very nice meeting you as well, Mr. Torrance." She hung onto his hand a little longer. "And I may just take your advice about returning home. I do miss Cecelia terribly and it would be good to be with family. Goodbye, Mr. Torrance."

Matthew left the Caldwell home hopeful that the woman might consider moving back to Vermont. She deserved to have a little happiness after going through so much sorrow most of her life, and he made up his mind to stop by her sister's house soon with the hope of helping things along a bit.

He called Bill from the airport and alerted him to the fact that Mrs. Caldwell had identified Simon Cartwright as being her son's friend, although it didn't necessarily mean he was who he claimed to be. At the moment, there appeared to be no reason for him to lie about his identity, but if he had, there had to be a reason. Whatever the case, Matthew was even more suspicious of John Braxton's involvement especially after learning that he had questioned Simon just after Boyd's drowning. Although he hadn't mentioned that fact to Bill over the phone, he planned to tell him as well as show him the picture of Cartwright when he got back. For the time being, he would go on the assumption that Simon Cartwright was in fact a private investigator and Boyd's friend until or if he found out differently. And that meant that if Charlie was right and he was completely innocent of any wrongdoing and merely trying to find some closure to his past, someone else was responsible for all the accidents that had happened and he could think of only one person who fit that bill and that was John Braxton. And if he found out that he had anything at all to do with Charlie's accident or any of the other catastrophes that had happened including Boyd Caldwell's drowning, he would do his best to help see to it that he was behind bars for a very long time. In the meantime and to be on the safe side, he asked Bill to have someone to keep an eye on Charlie.

"No problem, Matt. I've already started the ball rolling and set up watches at her house as well as at Braxton's office and his home. The one thing in her favor is that Braxton doesn't know she knows anything about this or that she came to us, but it's only a matter of time before he figures it out, especially in view of what's going on. We have to move fast if we want to keep her out of harm's way, but we can't really make a move until we have something concrete on him and we don't have a whole lot of time. I can tell you that the check we did on this Cartwright character confirmed he's a private investigator just like he told Charlie and a pretty good one at that. He did live in Braxton for a time and the family did move away when he was pretty young, but we sure had to go through some hoops to find out, his parents did a good job of keeping his involvement under wraps. Just come by my office when you get here and we'll catch up before we go meet this guy. What time's your flight due in?"

"We're scheduled to land in Burlington around eleven-thirty. I'll grab a cab, and it'll take about an hour and barring anything unseen, I should be in your office by quarter to one latest so we should be good with the time."

"Okay, buddy, I'll see you then."

Matthew reached Bill's office just shy of one o'clock, and since they had an hour to kill and Matthew didn't want to have Bill make two trips out to his place and back again, they grabbed a quick bite at the diner and he would have Bill drop him off later or call Paul to pick him up.

"I talked to Mel Corey, the district attorney, and he's ready when we are. If Cartwright's telling the truth about the proof he claims he has and we can prove Braxton was the mastermind behind everything, he'll personally see to it that we have the warrants and whatever else we need in order."

"You know the weird part about this, Matt? John Sr. went by the book, but he had compassion for the people, he respected them and fought for their right to be heard, but his son took all that away and put himself so high up on a pedestal that no one wanted to even try to reach him and he was bound to fall off sooner or later." He shook his head slowly. "How far can the apple fall far from the tree? I can't believe a father and son could be so different, and for the life of me, I don't know how the hell he stayed in office so long. I know I didn't vote for him."

"I think people hoped he would turn out to be like his father, people have been known to change. It's unfortunately that his son didn't, he just got worse."

"Have you given anymore thought about running?" He took a sip of coffee, watching Matthew's reaction over the top of his cup, and he got the one he expected when Matthew's eyes darkened and the nerve in his jaw twitched. "Now don't go getting all agitated. You haven't mentioned it in a while, and I wondered if you changed your mind is all."

"You know damn well where I stand on that, Bill. It's all dirty politics—you see what's happened to Braxton."

"Yeah, and you aren't anything like him. You have to know how much you could do for this town and—"

"Drop it, Bill. There's no way in hell I'm getting into that playpen. I've told you that before."

"Yeah well, I'm just sayin'—" He took another gulp of coffee and Matthew glared at him.

"I know exactly what you're saying and the answer is still no, so how about we just change the subject?"

"Okay, okay, I get it." He signaled June for a refill. "You want another cup?"

"No thanks, I've had my quota for the day, but it's no wonder you're always on edge, that's your third cup already."

"It's my sixth, but who's countin? Besides, I need it to keep me going. Martha tells me the same thing, and I don't listen to her either."

They both laughed, and as usual, things were back to normal between them.

The two practically lifelong friends read each other like a book, and though they didn't always see eye to eye, it never got in the way of their friendship. They respected one another's space and avoided stepping over the line of friendship and position, but Bill knew what Matthew could do for the town, and it irked him that he refused to see what an asset he would be in a position of power. Similarly, Matthew respected Bill's proclivity for his neutral stance under the pressures of his job. He worked hard to stay balanced as far as injustice and excess of power were concerned, but John Braxton was like a raw and open sore: it needed tended to before infection set in but instead was left to fester and had become a dreaded disease that threatened to infect the entire town, and Bill felt helpless to prevent it from happening. However, he did believe that by getting rid of the cause, the wound would heal, and he was relentless in his determination to make Matthew the cure.

"You think this guy is on the level about Braxton?" Bill took a huge bite out of his hero sandwich "I think so. Charlie's a pretty good judge of character, and she hasn't been far off the mark about anyone yet. What I don't get is how he could think he had proof enough to confront Braxton. From what Charlie said, the pictures weren't clear, and he certainly doesn't have any real evidence that Braxton was the one at the pond when Boyd drowned."

"More coffee, guys?" the waitress innocently interrupted, and Bill glanced at his watch.

"No thanks, June, we're good." And then to Matt, "We have to be shoving off, it's quarter 'til."

Simon was already waiting when they arrived at the site although Bill used his truck instead of the squad car, but he knew Matthew from Charlie's description. "Mr. Torrance, I presume?" Simon reached out to shake his hand. "Miss Faraday's description was quite accurate."

"Yes, I'm Matthew Torrance, do you know Sheriff Conley?"

"I have never met him, but I know who he is." He shook Bill's hand. "I am sure you have questions, and I will be most happy to answer them."

Matthew looked at Bill as a head's up and took out the picture of Simon and handed it to him. "Do you know these people?"

Simon looked at the picture for several long moments. "I never saw this picture," he spoke softly while Bill carefully unsnapped his holster and made ready to pull out his gun. If he was in fact Simon Cartwright, he surely would have remembered his own face, let alone Boyd's which should have convinced both he and Matthew that he'd been lying to Charlie all along and Bill was ready to haul him in, but he soon changed their minds. "I was aware that his mother took several pictures, but I never saw them." Simon went on slowly as if in a daze. "This is a picture of Boyd and me at a little creek somewhere—Boyd's father took us both fishing." He stared at the photo for quite a while before finally looking up at

Matthew. "Would it be all right if I kept this? I don't mean to sound sentimental, but it's rather a nice picture of Boyd and that I do not have anything as a remembrance. This is quite a nice reminder of better days."

Matthew smiled and nodded as Bill closed the snap on his holster. "Sure, keep it. I'm sure his mother would like you to have it."

As they walked toward the bridge, Simon carefully slid the picture into his inside jacket pocket, patted it, and then was all business again. "First of all, gentlemen, I am sure Miss Faraday told you all about me, which precludes the necessity for going all over all of that, and we can get right to the point. I have been following the mayor since my arrival, although that was not my intention in the beginning. I was here merely to allay my mind of a past I knew very little about and had tried to put behind me when I heard of Miss Faraday's desire to use the pond in her quest to begin a yearly Christmas pageantry here, which of course, you already know. In any case, I began to realize that there was more to your mayor than met the eye when I noticed he had been meeting with another man either before or after and sometimes both, each time disaster struck your little town. Be that as it may and bringing things up to present, I managed to get pictures of the mayor and his henchman," he said for lack of a better word. "And though they were not very clear I did have them blown up, and thankfully, it was enough to show the man's face. I do believe he is a wanted man, although he is not from around here, I believe he is from Detroit." Simon handed the sheriff the pictures and he swore out loud.

"Well, I'll be damned! This is Eugene 'Wilbur' Spezak aka Chester Knoxx aka Manny Kardone, and whatever the hell else he calls himself now, and you're right, Cartwright, he's from Detroit. But what in hell is he doing in this neck of the woods?"

"This guy is wanted?" Matthew reached for the photo.

"He sure as hell is. He's been on the FBI's Most Wanted list in several states for robbery and extortion to name a few as well as attempted murder. They've been looking for this jerk for eight years, but he somehow manages to stay one step ahead of them.

How Braxton got mixed up with this piece of garbage is beyond me, but the FBI will be real interested to know he's around. But we've got to real careful with this one, he's as slippery as an eel and just as deadly. When did you say you're meeting with them?"

"I will meet with them in the mayor's office on Sunday evening at eight p.m. And though I warned Braxton not to try and warn this Spezak character until the meeting, I am not naive enough to believe he did not contact him after I left his office, therefore he may already know my intentions."

"And what were those intentions, Mr. Cartwright? How did you manage to get Braxton to listen to you in the first place? You have to know the man trusts no one."

"I simply made him an offer he could not refuse: money. You see, I went to your illustrious mayor under the guise of making a contribution to his town, which of course would allow me into his good graces and permit me to learn what information I could in regard to Miss Faraday's suspicions that he was involved with the fires as well as her accident. In addition, this of course would open the door for me to pursue certain information concerning the death of Boyd Caldwell, and needless to say, his greed got the better of him as I suspected it would, and he agreed to meet with me and I was welcomed with open arms. After securing his confidence, I then managed with a bit of gentle persuasion to convince him that I knew much more than I did about the incidences in addition to the actual fact that I was indeed the friend with Boyd the day he drowned in the pond. Hence, I eventually convinced him to notify his 'friend' to meet him in his office in order to discuss another 'loose end' that had surfaced that would require his expertise of course, intending that he would be amply compensated which would extend above and beyond the one hundred and fifty thousand already awarded him. This would make sense to the man because I am certain that he assumed he would most likely be asked to do away with Miss Faraday permanently since he had not succeeded the first time and he readily agreed."

"Braxton paid Spezak a hundred and fifty grand? Where in hell did he get that kind of money?" He looked at Matthew. "That SOB must have been skimming off the town's funds all along. It's no damn wonder he was so paranoid about strangers coming to Braxton, he didn't want anyone snooping around."

"It also explains why he's been after Charlie, she was getting way to close to exposing him and he couldn't take that chance, so he hired that scum to kill her. Fortunately, he didn't succeed, but it wasn't due to his lack of trying, she survived that crash only by way of a miracle."

"Precisely, Mr. Torrance, which is the reason I was so secretive about us meeting together. As I explained, they normally met before or after one of the incidents, but they did both after Miss Faraday's accident." Cartwright added. "Therefore, had they seen me with her at all, it would not have been long before they recognized some type of connection which is why I insisted she remain silent about our meetings and not inform anyone. I believe her life is still in danger which is the reason I moved so quickly to try and convince him that I knew far more than I did and in that way hoped to waylay the inevitable by buying time as it were."

"And now that he knows your identity, your life isn't worth a whole lot right now either, so you've got to have eyes in the back of your head. Okay, this is how it'll go and we have to work fast. I'll notify Agent Brody to set up everything on his end. In the meantime, I already have two men watching Charlie while more are on standby waiting for orders. So depending on what the FBI does, we'll be ready. But you should be wired in case something goes wrong."

"I am afraid there will be no time to prepare for that, and we cannot take the chance that I would be seen anywhere near your office. I did however leave a small wiring device under the right corner of the overhang of his desk which is connected to this remote and will enable to allow you to hear everything that is going on in his office as it is quite sensitive." He handed the device to Bill. "As a reassurance, I also have a small recorder that is quite reliable and small enough to fit inside the cuff of my sleeve, and of course, you will not be far should anything go awry. My plan is to be inside the building before the mayor arrives, which will allow me to see Spezak before his arrival as well so all should go as planned, although I am aware that there are no absolutes."

"I'm not so sure I like this, Cartwright, there are too many loose ends. Something is bound to go wrong, and if we're not here in time—"

"I have been in much worse situations than this, Sheriff Conley. I will be fine I assure you."

"Yeah, well, don't take any unnecessary chances, Cartwright. Spezak isn't known for his compassion nor is he known for his patience. He has a short fuse and a very itchy trigger finger and he'd just as soon shoot you as look at you. Hell! He'd shoot his own mother if she got in his way."

"Yes, but without sounding arrogant, I am an excellent shot, Sheriff Conley, and I never miss."

"Neither does he," Bill warned. "Just watch your back."

Simon arrived at Braxton's office about forty-five minutes early, and after making certain no one was around, he worked his tiny pick into the lock of his office door. After only a few seconds, it sprung it open, and he slipped inside and softly closed the door behind him and locked it. As he waited for his eyes to adjust to the darkened room, he silently looked about and then quickly checked the closet and under the desk and felt for the wire device. Finding it still intact where he left it and making certain that all was set, he walked to the tall cupboard in the far corner of the room. Although it was quite narrow, Simon was just able to fit and wedged himself inside. Although it was to be awhile before the men arrived, he took no chances of an early arrival and pulled the door tightly closed, and he peered through the louvered slats and waited. However, it was only minutes later that he heard a key in the lock and watched the door slowly open. As he suspected, Braxton appeared earlier than planned and he watched as he furtively gazed around the room, making certain no one was there before hitting the light switch and hearing the man's sigh of relief. He even smiled to himself as he watched Braxton nervously reach into his suit pocket and produce a handkerchief and wipe the sweat from his forehead. He was scared shitless, and Simon thought he just might pass out.

Braxton had a big mouth and talked a good story, but when it came right down to it, he was obviously an amateur at this type of thing and fully relied on his hired killer to pull the strings. And after what Simon had learned about Spezak from the sheriff, Braxton had no idea that if things didn't go his way, he would kill the unsuspecting mayor before he knew what hit him.

Having previously decided to wait until the two men were in the room together, Simon waited calmly but was instantly on full alert when he heard a light tap on the door. Braxton's eyes widened, and he didn't move a muscle for a few seconds as if frozen to his chair and then quietly moved his chair back and stood up. He approached the door cautiously, putting his ear against it listening before he spoke. "Who's there?" he whispered, and instantly, a gravelly voice came back.

"Who the hell do you think it is, you asshole? Open the goddam door for Chrissake!"

Braxton unlocked it, and Spezak strolled inside as the terrified mayor cautiously peeked out and scanned the hallway to the right and left before pulling his head back inside, closing the door and locking it.

"We can't be too careful, you know." Braxton wiped his forehead again.

"What the hell's your problem, you moron? There's no one around, I checked. Can't you at least try to act like a man for Chrissake? You disgust me." He flopped down in the chair in front of Braxton's desk, and Simon watched the timid mayor wince when the man lifted his feet and slam the backs of his sharp heels onto the luxurious cherry surface, but he wisely said nothing. "I get it that you're gonna pay me big bucks, and I do mean big bucks." He sneered. "But what the hell was so goddam important that you just had to see me now, couldn't it wait?"

"We've got problems, big problems."

"What kinds of problems, what, your mommy forget to wipe your ass?"

"Simon Cartwright came to see me."

"So who the hell's that and what's it got to do with me?" He picked at the filth under his fingernails, and Braxton almost gagged when he flicked the dirt onto the floor. "I don't know no Simon Cartwright."

"He knows I hired you to set the fires and get rid of that Faraday bitch—"

Spezak was up like a shot, his heels leaving a six-inch gouge in the desk where he dragged his heels when he dove over it and grabbed Braxton's lapels. "Shaddup, you stupid freak, do you want the whole goddam town to know? Why the hell'd you tell him anything?"

"He threatened to go to the police if I didn't bring him in on the deal. I had no choice!" He squealed his face reddening as Spezak squeezed tighter.

"Man, I oughta off you right here you dumb son-of-a-bitch!" He shoved him back into the chair, and Simon relaxed his grip on his gun. "Well, I got news for you, pal. I ain't goin to prison for you or nobody, you can take the fall for this. I'm gettin the hell outta here!" He walked toward the door when Simon suddenly pushed the cupboard door wide open, and Spezak spun around to see his gun aimed directly at his face.

"I would think twice about that if I were you," Simon said calmly. "This gun may be little, but it can do just as much damage as a Magnum .38, especially at this close range and if one is an excellent marksman as I am. Although it does not have near the velocity, it is capable of taking a life or, in your case, destroying a kneecap." He stepped out of the cupboard and motioned for Spezak to get away from the door. "Please remove the Colt .45 from inside the waistband of your suit pants, Mr. Spezak, and toss it across the floor to me, very slowly and carefully if you don't mind, and I would advise you not to move another muscle, Mayor." He warned as he watched Braxton move his chair a hairbreadth to the right out of the corner of his eye. "You would never reach it in time. You may slowly turn the chair to face me and sit down now, *Wilbur*," Simon said deliberately and watched his jaw clench at the mere mention of his given name and surprisingly he did as he was told and swaggered over to the chair to the chair and sat down.

"It's just a matter of time before I make my move, asshole, and you might get one of us, but there ain't no way you can get us both.'

"True, but you are the one I am aiming at, *Wilbur*. As you have shown, the illustrious mayor does not have the mental capacity to figure out what to do next nor, I am certain, does he have the capability or adeptness to use the weapon he had in his top right drawer, he is for the most part a coward and merely your boss." He exaggerated the last word, knowing it would provoke his adversary's anger.

"Nobody's my boss, Cartwright," he shouted, leaning forward in the chair. "And nobody, including you, tells me what I can or can't do, you got it?"

Simon smiled, the two of them reminding him of the characters in the movie *Dumb and Dumber*. The trouble was neither of them knew which was which apparently.

"Now, you are both aware that you will each spend pretty much the remainder of your useless lives in jail when the authorities are made aware of the fact that you hired Wilbur here to destroy the bridge and Mr. Freeman's barn as well as attempt to murder Miss Faraday because she knew your hands were dirty, not only."

"I don't have a clue what you're talking about, Cartwright. I never met Braxton before today when he called me to meet him here."

"Tsk, tsk, tsk, Mayor. You did not inform Wilbur that you needed him to do another job for you but then offered me triple the amount you paid him instead since he botched the job the first time? Well, Mayor, that does not seem at all fair. But of course, you had to stop her not only because she might you of the little matter of Boyd Caldwell."

Spezak glared at Braxton but said nothing, but the mayor insisted on trying to exonerate himself. "He's lying. I never offered to pay him anything. He threatened me if I didn't pay him triple for—"

"Shut up, Braxton, he's pulling your chain. We don't have any idea what he's talking about."

"Oh, have you forgotten already, Mayor? Why, that was a mere two days ago, and I distinctly remember you begging me to handle this for you before she had a chance to tell anyone about your meeting with Wilbur here after setting the fire on the bridge. She is quite smart that Miss Faraday, she even put two and two together after Mr. Freeman's barn burned down and he found that note warning him to not to become involved, remember? And you had to make certain she did not take that news to the sheriff, so you hired Wilbur here to cut her brake line, surely you remember that?"

"You dumb son-of-a-bitch!" Spezak jumped up and grabbed Braxton by the throat and started choking him. "You couldn't keep your mouth shut, could you? Well, I'm not goin' down for this, you miserable bastard. I shoulda shot her like I wanted to instead of cutting the stupid brake line. I told you it was a stupid idea!"

Braxton was beginning to turn blue, and Simon fired a warning shot into the ceiling. "The next one will shatter your kneecap, Spezak, let him go."

Spezak took his hands from around the mayor's neck, but before he moved away, he grabbed the paperweight from under him and swung around, threw it to Simon, hitting him square in the head, then dove for the floor to search for the gun.

Dazed and bleeding but knowing what Spezak had in mind, Simon had already crossed the room and dove to the floor beside Spezak just as he grabbed the gun, and Simon smashed his hand again and again against the desk leg until he let go and it flew out of his hand and skidded across the floor out of both of their reach. Spezak kicked Simon out of the way, but Simon grabbed at his legs and Spezak turned over, grabbing him and flipping him over in a chokehold. Simon was no match for the hefty man, but he was wiry and managed to slip out of the hold, but before he could turn and grab for the gun, Spezak dove for it, grabbed it, and turned and shot haphazardly, winging Simon in the shoulder and he went down but not before he swiftly grabbed the gun from the back of his pants and purposely shot the man in the kneecap, and still holding onto the gun, he instantly buckled to the floor, grabbing his knee and screaming in agony, but aiming at Simon's head just as Agent Brody broke through the door and stood pressing his semi-automatic against Spezak's head.

"I'd think twice about that if I were you," he said quietly, kicking the gun out of his hand. He rolled him over onto to his bad knee, and he screamed in agony.

"Watch my knee, you stupid bastard!"

"Well. Well, well! If it isn't the elusive Mr. Spezak, it certainly has been a while."

"Not long enough, you worthless piece of shit," Spezak snarled.

"Hey, you slipped up, *Wilbur*, what can I say? You're just not as good or as fast as you used to be."

In the meantime, Braxton tried to flee out the back door but was stopped by Sheriff Conley before he took two steps. "I don't think so, *Mayor.*" Bill actually smiled. "You have no idea how long I've been waiting to do this to you. Turn around." He snapped on the handcuffs and turned him around to face him and led him toward Brody who had just come out the front door, his men practically dragging the screaming Spezak behind him and shoved him toward the wagon. "This one's all yours too, Al, you can add him to the other pile of garbage, it's beginning to stink to high heaven around here."

CHAPTER X

———— ❋ ————

*C*harlie awakened Thanksgiving morning to the mouth-watering aroma of turkey roasting in the oven, along with the radio announcer's claim that it was the warmest day of the year so far, sixty degrees and still climbing with no sign of snow anytime soon. Although he did agree that it was peculiar for Northern Vermont this far into November, he added that it was his kind of weather, and Charlie threw a slipper at the radio and told him to move south.

Charlie always did love winter, especially the first snowfall—the snow pristine white and untouched, the air cold and biting. It was the time of year she wished she was a kid again making snowmen and sled riding until dark and your face was so cold your muscles didn't work so well and you felt like you were talking in slow motion. She still loved to get up at first dawn and take walks in snow so deep, you almost had to wear hip boots.

Winter was a special time, a new beginning according to Charlie, especially this year with the Bring Back Christmas campaign. She felt like a kid waiting for Santa Claus, but when she looked out the window at the sun shining like it was the middle of June, she was a little frustrated.

Although winter wasn't officially here, there was little time until Christmas with only three weeks left and there was still so much to do. And while most holidays were here and gone before you knew it and you were left wondering where it went, it was the main reason she'd planned the festivities to begin the day after Thanksgiving. Of course, the upside of the unexpected heat wave was that the townspeople could put up the fifty-foot tree in the town square along with the beautiful star at the top and string lights and hang wreaths on the lampposts along Main Street without forty-mile-an-hour winds howling in their faces and blowing tinsel, snow, and toupees into the next county.

The down side however, was that without snow and freezing temperatures for at least two weeks straight, there would be no ice skaters on the pond, and after what Charlie had been through to make it part of the Bring Back Christmas campaign, the thought that it might not happen after all was making her extremely anxious.

The five horse-and-carriage units on lend for the holiday season—including the extra one that Greystone had so generously offered without charge—were set to arrive on the thirtieth of November and would run every day until the second of January when the kids went back to school. Originally the horses were to be bedded down in Carl Freeman's barn, but because it had been destroyed they would now be housed in the old firehouse close to the Kissing Bridge which would actually give drivers easier access because it was much closer.

The cost for a ride would be one dollar for a trip around town to perhaps shop or simply ride along Main Street enjoying the brightly colored lights, the beautifully decorated tree, and the gazebo and the manger set up in the park in front of the courthouse. It was to be an old-fashioned sleigh-ride back in time, a reminiscence of days gone by, beginning at the entrance to the Kissing Bridge, traveling down Main Street South, and around the bend onto Main Street North and ending in front of the gazebo. The cost for a slow leisurely mile-long sleigh ride beginning at the park and traveling up Main Street North, over the Kissing Bridge, and out across the meadow through the beautifully scenic countryside would be two dollars—warm blanket and a man at the reins in a tall black hat and red waistcoat free of charge. It was to be something right out of the story books: a truly romantic ride of a lifetime that promised to one of the highpoints of the campaign, and while Charlie was guaranteed the very first trip in one of the beautiful horse-drawn carriages, she was having a difficult time picturing it with the sun shining and the sky devoid of snow clouds.

Still, even without the much-needed snow, Charlie's little town was fast beginning to resemble the beautiful Thomas Kinkaid paintings of Christmases past that Charlie always dreamed of: a time when life seemed simpler, unhurried, and when everyone seemed to be caught up in keeping families together rather than keeping up with the Joneses. Charlie loved that era and often wondered if she'd been born in the wrong time period which was the main reason she began the campaign in the first place. And part of that dream was bringing the old covered bridge back to life, which thanks to Jim McGuire who did such a magnificent job on the beautiful historic relic, that part of her dream was also resurrected. With Matthew's monetary help after selling the Circle C, much to Charlie's dismay, Jim had managed to refurbish the historic Kissing Bridge back to its former state with no blemish or sign that it had been nearly destroyed by fire. And though Charlie would be eternally grateful for Matthew's generosity, she had hoped he would sell the ranch to help enrich his own life rather than something like the Bring Back Christmas campaign, but he assured her that he had no regrets. He was happy with the young family complete with three little children who bought the beautiful ranch, and he was satisfied that they would care for it and enjoy it as much as he and Cherry had, telling her that his memories were all he needed. Although the house had been part of their lives for so many years, since Cherry was no longer there to share those memories with him or to make new ones, there was no point in hanging on to it. "Memories are not made of material things, Charlie, they're made from the love of the people who create them." And with prayers and a little magic, he fervently hoped Charlie and Paul could create new ones together.

Although the municipality would allow cars to be driven into and out of town, at Charlie's request they would have to enter Main

Street from the south and turn off at Second Street just before the park. While the Preservation Society made certain that the Kissing Bridge would be crossed over on horse-drawn carriages only; in keeping with the old-fashioned way of using only horse-and-carriage for travel through Braxton, an area just across the bridge and to the right had been made into a parking lot large enough to hold more than enough cars. And while not planned, the lot was conveniently concealed behind a natural row of tall pines and out of sight, though it would be cleared of snow and ice periodically as needed.

The day after Thanksgiving, November 26, 1998, just one month before Christmas, the entire town was out in full force hanging red bows and stringing lights from lamppost to lamppost, while business owners were busy hanging wreaths over their doors and setting up moving displays in store-front windows.

The gazebo, newly refurbished and trimmed with red and green tinsel intertwined with colored lights draped along the railings, wrapped around the posts and edging the rooftop, awaited its partner, a fifty-five-foot pine held down by guy wires to prevent the wind from toppling the massive beauty, stood proudly next to the gazebo waiting to be strung with lights and topped with the beautiful thirty-year-old star in anticipation of the annual Lighting of the Christmas Tree to be held on the twelfth of December while the manger that the Sunday school children created and worked on so lovingly waited to be placed outside the courthouse. The cardboard statues seemingly alive with brilliant colors and animals nestled in the hay next to baby Jesus's crib with flood lights illuminating it to life. While it would be moved inside the church and placed on the altar for two nights during the week before Christmas to be used for the children's play, it would then be returned to its original place outside the courthouse.

The entire town of Braxton had literally come alive, joining the festivities and giving so much of themselves, their time and much of their love in keeping up in the true Bring Back Christmas tradition. Neighbor now greeted neighbor as they shopped or while simply passed one another on their way to church or just a stroll around town. Carolers strolled along the sidewalks and even went house to house singing beautiful Christmas carols while actually stopping briefly at old Miss Caroline's for a steaming cup of hot cocoa.

For the first time since Charlie could remember, everyone had a smile on their face and attitudes seemed changed from worried and anxious to happy and cheerful. They had even loved the idea of visiting homes to share in their individual holiday festivities several nights before Christmas, and soon the children of Braxton, who had always talked about leaving the boring, old-fashioned town in Northern Vermont, were now talking about staying and perhaps raising a family in the very town they grew up hating. It was like a wish come true—as if the picture she'd created in her mind so long ago of a Thomas Kinkaid–type Christmas in her little town was really coming to life.

As far as the pond was concerned, everything was ready for the day it would officially open and come alive again with skaters. Benches had been built two together and placed at four places around the perimeter, and two small huts had been constructed on either side of the pond, one offering hot or cold drinks as well as light snacks and the other to be used as a first-aid station. And while safety classes for the pond had been offered free of charge by Clay Duggan, the fire department offered to perform daily ice checks and would be available as Braxton's emergency crew. Everything had been set in force. Now if only it would snow!

"I don't know, Charlie," Jean commiserated. "It's the end of November already and no sign of snow yet."

"Have faith, Jean, it'll come, we just have to be patient," Charlie said it, but she didn't believe it. The town was decorated and ready, the pond was good to go, and even the townspeople were anxious to get things started but still no snow. "Do you know any snow dances?" Her lame smile failed to bring a smile to Jean's face.

"I'm just worried we won't be able to use the pond after you worked and planned so hard to get it not to mention all the work that went into building the benches and the huts. And to top it off, the sleighs will be useless without snow. It just doesn't seem fair after all we've been through." It sounded strange coming from Jean, the optimistic one of the group "Well, we'll still have the rest of the campaign and everyone seems really excited, so how can we lose?" Charlie tried to sound positive. "All we can do at this point is keep our fingers crossed, hope for the best and think snow—the weatherman did say we would have flurries."

"Yes, but no accumulations and the temperatures aren't going very low, thirty-five at best."

"Well, if the nor'easter turns, we could get dumped on."

"It's headed toward Canada, Charlie, and it hasn't shown any signs of turning yet. You saw the radar, it already started to head north way back near Pennsylvania, it'll never reach Vermont."

"Well, don't give up hope, stranger things have happened."

Just as the weatherman predicted, it began snowing lightly just before rush-hour traffic around three in the afternoon but stopped around six. They barely got a dusting; it was pitiful.

Later that night when Charlie went to bed, she resigned herself to the simple truth that the chances of having her white Christmas after all were slim and next to none, as were her chances of having the first carriage ride over the Kissing Bridge through the white and drifting snow.

Actually the truth was she hadn't given a thought to the weather when she planned her Christmas campaign because in her dream to turn her little town into a yearly winter wonderland celebration, everything was perfect—from the glistening pure-white snow that fell as if on cue and continued for days on end keeping the entire town sheathed in a blanket of the magical white dust to the twinkling lights glowing like welcome beacons along Main Street transforming the bare undecorated storefronts and streets piled high at the curbs with dirty snow into a beautiful winter wonderland. She had never once thought about what would happen if it turned out to be the warmest winter in a hundred years because in her dream world, that simply could not happen. However, as she restlessly drifted off to sleep, her mind was at work thinking of a way to explain to the townspeople that they might need to unpack their swimsuits water shoes instead of their muck lucks and winter woolies.

Charlie awakened the next morning feeling like she'd been in a drinking contest the night before and lost. While she normally didn't feel so groggy unless she'd been dreaming all night or what perceived to be all night, she could only remember bits and pieces of each and they were all jumbled together. As she fought her way out of the fog, the dreams began to fade, and she could barely make out the time on the face of the clock on her radio. She pulled herself out of bed and stumbled to the window and pulled the drapes wide open and had to shield her eyes from the blinding brightness. Apparently, it had snowed through the night—a lot—and it was brighter than those annoying halogen headlights that often blinded her on the road at night. There was at least four inches or five inches out there, and it was still snowing heavily. And while she guessed the time to be about seven-thirty, she wondered why her alarm hadn't gone off and checked it only to realize that it was still set for six a.m., but the alarm had been shut off.

"Mom?" she yelled down from her bedroom. "Did you shut my alarm off?"

"Yes, dear, I did." She hollered up in answer. "School has been closed for the day as have many of the roads. Your boss called to tell you not to bother coming in today because we're expected to get at least four to six more inches before rush hour so I let you sleep in."

"You have got to be kidding?" She felt like she did when she back in school herself and just found out that it had been cancelled due to bad weather. She visualized the radar map in her mind that absolutely showed the storm moving north not east. Evidently, there were no absolutes. She'd told Jean things could change, she just hadn't believed it and she switched on the radio in the middle of Mr. Fairweather's spew of distaste over the debacle that had happened through the night.

"—was not in the cards for today, what a dirty trick! Well, folks, get out your boogie boards and snowsuits and hunker down for a while, this stuff is falling like manna and there's no sign of stoppage anytime soon. Radar promises at least eight more inches of the white stuff before this storm is over, so it looks like Braxton will be its home for a while. It's thirty degrees at six-forty this snowy Friday morning, and this is Bruce Shelton of KBSL 120 with another tune from—"

Charley switched off the radio and grinned. Poetic justice she'd call it.

"Do you believe this?" she asked Jean over the phone forty-five minutes later after she'd showered and was sipping her first hot chocolate of the season—hot chocolate was so winter. She was also watching Pete shovel the driveway although it was quickly becoming a lost cause. "See? I told you stranger things could happen."

"No, I don't believe this, are you a witch?"

"Some would say that," she ventured, grinning. "Actually, I knew it was going to do this."

"Oh, you did, huh?"

"Sure. My dreams always have happy endings."

"Good for you, wish mine did."

"They do. You're just too busy with your life to notice."

"Hmmm. Good point. So what are you planning today, just sit around and enjoy being snowed in?"

"Maybe and maybe I'll go out and make a snowman."

"How juvenile."

"You should know, how many are stacked up in your yard already?"

She could actually hear Jean's silent laughter. "Three and counting."

"And you didn't help?"

"Of course, I did, what kind of mother do you think I am? Besides, I had to supervise the stealing of carrots. I think they supplied them to everyone in the neighborhood. Anyway, it's a good thing tomorrow is Saturday, although we probably wouldn't have work anyway. Oops! The kids are back in for a fresh supply of carrots and black olives, talk to you later."

"See ya." Charlie hung up and took another sip of hot chocolate. Time was a-wasting, and she couldn't let all the glorious snow melt away before she made her imprint on it, not that it looked like it would stop anytime soon, thank goodness. Besides, Pete looked like he could use a breather. Ten minutes later and bundled up like a snow bunny in her heavy parka and boots, Charlie went outside to relieve Pete.

"This snow's pretty heavy." He was breathing was even heavier. "You don't have to do this, Charlie," he said when she grabbed the shovel.

"I'll take small shovels full, there's hot chocolate inside."

Pete succumbed to her offer, thinking there was no sense asking for a heart attack. "Take breaks in between and you'll do fine."

Charlie had been out about fifteen minutes and had only gotten a quarter of the sidewalk shoveled when she saw Paul's red Blazer come plowing through the snow literally—he had a plow attached to the front of his jeep.

"Need some help?"

Charlie's heart swelled as it always did when he showed up unannounced. He was so unbelievably good looking that it actually took her breath away, and the fact that he had the sexiest eyes she'd ever seen and was built like a brick *wall*, she thought properly, didn't hurt either. Although it wasn't just his looks because beauty was, after all, only skin deep; it never ceased to amaze her that no matter how many times she saw him, it was always like the first time, startling and heart-pumping, a feeling that went much deeper than just physical attraction.

"Sure." She flashed him a thankful smile. "But what are you doing out on a day like this?"

"This caused a work stoppage. It's too dangerous to work in weather like this, we can't take a chance that our guys will get hurt. So, get out of my way, woman, and I'll plow your driveway." He grinned boyishly, and again, her heart sped up. "Maybe when I'm done, we could go sled riding, what do you think?"

"Sled riding?" She hadn't gone sled riding in years, but it sounded like fun. "I'd love it!"

"Well, why don't you go in and get all layered up? I should be done in no time."

"What do you mean?" she said, looking down at her jeans, heavy parka, and boots. "I am layered up."

"In jeans? I don't think so, you'll need heavier clothes than that. Once I'm out, I plan on staying out for a while."

Charlie frowned. "How long is awhile?"

"Hours!" he said, laughing. "What's the matter, too much of a girlie-girl to run with the big boys?"

Charlie's eyes narrowed. He didn't know who he was dealing with. She was known as the champion of sled riding since she was a little kid and endurance was her middle name. "All right, we'll see who lasts the longest. Loser buys dinner."

"Oh, you're on, little girl," he said, taking the challenge. "But I get to pick the spoils." He grinned devilishly. "And you won't know what they are until the contest is over."

"Contest? I thought this was for fun."

"It is for fun, but you're the one who turned it into a contest by suggesting there was a winner and a loser so prepare to pay the piper."

"On second thought—" she began, but he drowned her out when he turned on the scraper.

"Too late for second thoughts," he yelled above the grinding noise. "Now go get ready."

He'd found a place called Willow Hill fairly close to his house, and though it wasn't a huge hill, it was a fairly steep and long ride, the path flattening out near the bottom, a plateau long enough to allow riders to come to a safe stop before crashing through the trees and ending up in the creek and soaking wet.

They rode his toboggan together and though the rides seemed much too short, they were exhilarating and Charlie hung on o him for dear life, believing if one fell off they would both go, although that wasn't necessarily the only reason she clung on so tight.

Charlie never laughed so hard as they skimmed over the well-packed snow—the uneven bumps along the way bouncing her up out of her seat like a roller coaster going from hill to valley and back up again. There were still a few of the die-hard younger kids who insisted on racing them to the bottom, and after reigning victorious, sang Rocky's theme song with arms raised and dancing his fancy footwork. Charlie couldn't remember having so much fun.

Hiking back up the hill at least twenty times, however, was exhausting and Charlie wasn't in as great a shape as she had been last year when she attended the spa, but she did well and Paul was impressed. But after several hours of climbing the hill, Charlie had had enough and cried uncle, totally disregarding the fact that he was to pick the spoils. Well, no matter, she would just have to bite the bullet and pay up.

"Come on, my place is just over the hill. We'll get warmed up and grab a bite to eat."

That sounded like heaven to Charlie as she carefully slid her aching thighs and tender derriere up into the seat of the Blazer.

"Have a good time?" he asked, finding her reddened cheeks and sparkling cold-induced eyes incredibly appealing, not to mention her little girl excitement.

"That was so much fun! And those kids, weren't they adorable?"

Actually *she* was adorable. And he'd thoroughly enjoyed having her behind him, hanging on so tight. "Yeah, it was all right. We'll have to do it again real soon."

She pulled off her cap and fluffed out her auburn mane, and he watched it cascade down over her shoulders like long strands of pure silk, feeling a lot more than just his heart stir. She was a knockout, no doubt about it, and she didn't even know it. He liked that. As a matter of fact, there was little about her he didn't like. At times, there was a childlike quality about her, uncomplicated and innocent yet flirty and devil-may-care. But there was also a no-nonsense level of maturity and intelligence that he admired. She loved kids, and he already knew she cared more about others than herself. Hell, she was damn-near perfect, and he found himself wondering what it would feel like to wake up to her beautiful smile each morning. He frowned then, realizing he'd subconsciously filled out a questionnaire for things you'd most want in a wife. He heard the word *marriage* bounce around in his brain like balls bouncing off bumpers in a pinball machine. He didn't remember even considering a life-long partner.

As they turned off the main highway onto a dirt road and began up a slightly steep driveway surrounded by woods on all sides, Charlie gazed around, intrigued by the fact that all signs of civilization disappeared, and much like Pine Cone Bluff which was just minutes from town, it was as if they'd entered another world. The driveway continued upward until it leveled off for about a hundred feet or so before ending in front of an attached garage to the right of an old but very well-kept two-story brick house, with the same type of wrap-around porch she had on her own new house, she noted, or what would be hers shortly if she decided to buy it, and she couldn't help smiling when she realized they actually had very much the same tastes.

Paul hit a button on the dashboard, and the garage door slowly opened revealing a spacious and very tidy garage. He hit the button again as he drove inside, and the door began to close behind them until they were engulfed in darkness. He shut off the motor and sat there quietly, and as her eyes became accustomed to the darkness, she turned to find him watching her.

"What?" she asked, smiling, and Paul gently grasped her face and leaned in to kiss her.

"What was that for?" she asked softly. "Not that I'm complaining."

"It just felt right." He opened the door and the interior car light immediately went on, and he noticed her face was a bit flushed. "Come on, let's go. I'm starved."

They walked through a door leading into a laundry area, and he flicked on a light switch. There, too, everything was neat and clean. She couldn't believe a guy could be so neat. She was neat, but this was beyond neat. He gave her a quick tour starting with the spacious but cozy eat-in kitchen complete with breakfast nook in the corner under a double window; through to the rather large dining room with built-in buffet and matching table; and on through wooden doors that actually moved on tracks embedded into the floor, allowing the doors to disappear into the walls, creating a continuous flow from dining room to living room. The living room itself, about one-and-a-half times larger than the dining room, was actually comfy and welcoming with two recliners, a huge leather sofa, a large roll-top desk, and even a fireplace and large bay window. Each room was mostly wood-trimmed, and it was definitely a man's home without all the frills, and Charlie fell in love with it.

He relit the fire and got it going while he talked. "There are three bedrooms upstairs with walk-in closets, along with a full bathroom with separate shower and bathtub." He led the way back to the kitchen and told her to have a seat.

"Your house is beautiful, Paul, it suits you. I looked for months and months to find one that was out of the way, but I saw nothing like this. However did you find it?"

"A friend of mine was moving to Seattle and offered it for a steal, and since I happened to be in the market, I couldn't pass it up. I had actually started out looking for a log cabin, but when I saw this, I knew it was the one. I'm glad you like it. Now, what are you hungry for—steak, chicken—what?"

"Mmmmm, I would love a steak." And as if on cue, her stomach growled.

"How would you like it?"

"Medium rare, please, a little scorched on the outside."

"Ahh, a woman after my own heart."

If you only knew, she thought, grateful he wasn't a mind-reader along with his other obvious talents. She leaned back against the booth, watching him amble easily around the kitchen, and within minutes, he'd grabbed a tomato and freshly bagged leaf lettuce from the fridge, thinly sliced an onion, and tossed a salad together, washed potatoes and placed them in the microwave setting the timer to bake for eight minutes, then placed the steaks in a preheated cast iron skillet on the stove and listened to them sizzle. He was a natural in the kitchen, a good thing to know.

Fifteen minutes later, both of them having ravenously devoured the unplanned dinner for two, Paul told her to make herself comfortable in the living room and he would join her after loading the dishwasher and putting on coffee. But upon finishing the small chore, he grabbed a bottle of Chianti and two glasses from the wine rack instead and found her lying on her stomach on the faux bear rug directly in front of the fire. Her slender legs were bent at the knees and crossed at her bare feet, and her chin rested on the head of the bear with her arms wrapped around his neck.

Charlie was a vision lying there, staring into the fire, seemingly mesmerized by the flames; her hair catching the glow of the blaze and shimmering with brilliant color as each new burst of flames transformed her silken mane into a glowing halo of fiery auburn and glittering gold while the crackling wood hissed every now and then as the moisture from the burning logs turned to steam and sent a shower of sparks and burning embers raining down on white-hot coals. She looked so natural lying there, as though she belonged. And she was so caught up in the calming peacefulness that she hadn't even noticed that he'd come in until after he'd placed the wine and glasses on the table near the sofa and joined her on the rug.

He reached out to gently sweep the hair back away from her face, and she leaned her head to the side, her elbow resting on the bear, her cheek resting on her palm, watching him with her eyes half-closed. She looked sexy as hell, and it was all he could do not to make love to her right there on top of Old Grizz.

"I wouldn't get a single thing done if I lived here, do you know that?" she asked dreamily. "How can you leave this place every day? If I were you, I would forget about work, forget about the world outside, just forget about everything and live right here for the rest of my life—no worries, no cares—just live in beautiful, peaceful serenity. Just give me a little white picket fence, a scad of kids and—" She stopped dead in the middle of the sentence, realizing what it must have sounded like. *Nice move, Charlie, why don't you just ask him if you can move in?* "Well anyway, I—"

"Would you like a white picket fence, Charlie?" Paul asked quietly and Charlie blinked.

"I didn't mean, well, I just, wow, look at the time! It's getting kind of late." She scrambled to her feet. "Mom and Pete are probably wondering where I am." She glanced around nervously. "Did you happen to put my coat somewhere? Oh! I guess I should ask if you mind taking me home first, shouldn't I? Well, if you could that would be great." She stopped talking, realizing she'd been babbling, and watched him raise his hand and point to the window.

"It's been snowing since we since we started sled riding and has been showing heavily ever since. We can try it if you want to, but we may not make it."

What's that supposed to mean? She wondered to herself. *Surely, he isn't suggesting I stay over, this could last for days.*" The thought of having to spend even one night with him was a little daunting. She wasn't sure she could keep her virtue intact for ten minutes at the rate she was going and the fault wouldn't necessarily lay with him.

"I think we should try, it's the safer thing to do."

"Well, I'm game if you are, but if we get stuck, it's an awful long walk depending on which way the crow flies."

Charlie frowned. Either he knew what he was talking about or was just trying to scare her into staying. Whichever way she looked at it, the choice apparently was hers.

"What do you think?"

"I can go either way." He wouldn't commit. She knew he wouldn't. He had the upper hand and he was either very astute or very sneaky. If she said she wanted to go, there was the possibility they could end up walking several miles in waist-high snow and giving him the answer to his unasked question. If she said she wanted to stay, she would also give him the answer to his unasked question.

He sat dispassionately with his long legs stretched out in front of him, his arms tucked behind his head lazily. "More than likely we can make it with the snowplow on the front of the jeep if that's what you're worried about." He was a gentleman after all and had given her an out. However, if by some act of God or even a misconception of conditions on his part, they could very well end up fighting their way through a blizzard or worse. She rolled her eyes in defeat.

"Okay, which bedroom is mine? The room farthest from yours preferably," she added mumbling.

"What was that?" He turned as he headed for the stairs.

"Nothing, I just wondered if I could borrow one of your shirts."

"I do have a pair of pajamas I've never worn if you prefer." She saw his eyes dance mischievously.

"That'll work." She'd have to roll up the sleeves ten times to Sunday and pull the bottoms up over her head in order for them not to drag on the floor, but she wouldn't look the least bit appealing—and that's exactly what she was shooting for. "Oh, where is your telephone? I'll need to call home."

"It's on the wall to your right as soon as you walk into the kitchen. In the meantime, I'll go up and get your jammies and throw on some clean sheets."

"Oh, had company recently, did you?" she asked cuttingly and then grimaced and rolled her eyes, wishing she had a knife to cut out her tongue. *Smooth, Charlie, real smooth.* She berated herself. *Just come right out ask him if he's been sleeping with anyone lately, why don't you?*

"If I had, I wouldn't need to be changing sheets in *your* room, would I?" he asked, continuing up the stairs.

She deserved that. She had no reason for asking something so personal and she got exactly what was coming to her.

The water under the Kissing Bridge was now still and quiet, frozen in time while the soft glow of white Christmas lights draped from portal to portal, danced across the ice like thousands of miniature twinkling stars.

The entire town turned out to watch the children's performances which were nothing less than spectacular as the little sheep, the three wise men, and Mary, Joseph, and Baby Jesus took center stage. Each child knew his part, and their voices rang out clear and true as they plundered through the cold and looked for a place for Mary to have her baby. As each individual child took their turn announcing their own greeting to welcome the Christ child and announce his birth, and there wasn't a dry eye in the church during the entire play.

On skates on a lazy Sunday afternoon, It was perfect skating weather, cold and brisk, and the pond had had almost two weeks of temperatures in the low tens and twenties, ensuring plenty of thick ice. The day of the pond opening to the public finally arrived, and the excitement in the air was like an electric charge.

Skaters could always be seen on the pond now on lazy Sunday afternoons; at least until school was out, and she still couldn't believe that her Christmas quest was becoming a reality.

She also wanted to set up a little hut for skate rental and hot chocolate.

When the countdown to the lighting of the tree began, everyone joined in, and when they finally reached one, someone plugged in the lights and the entire tree was instantly ablaze with thousands of tiny colored lights—all but the star at the top—and suddenly, the "oohs" and "aahs" died down to nothing.

"What happened, why isn't the star lit?" one person called out.

"I can't understand it," Lyle said. "It worked when we tried it this afternoon."

Soon the murmur of voices spread until the whole crowd was buzzing about it.

"Maybe it burned out," Miss Eleanor offered. "It is quite old, after all." But the disappointment in her voice echoed through everyone's mind.

"Oh, this isn't good," Grace Milford said, shaking her head. "This isn't good at all."

"Hush, Grace," Lyle ordered. "Quit trying to get everybody all riled up. It's probably just a burned-out bulb. We'll just have to climb up and change it. Hank, go grab a ladder, and Mildred, so if you can find some extra bulbs. We'll get that star lit."

"I'm telling you it's a bad omen, people. The last time I saw this happen, the light went on and then it sort of exploded and the whole darn tree caught fire and burned to the ground, burning Santa and his reindeer to a crisp—it was pitiful, just pitiful."

"And I'm telling you to—" Just as Lyle began to stop Grace again, someone pointed upward and yelled, "Look, a shooting star!"

Just as the entire crowd looked up, the shooting star streaked across the dark star-spotted sky, and as it passed over the tree, the star suddenly began to glow, lighting up the entire area with a brilliance unlike anyone had ever seen, and the bells in the church tower mysteriously began to ring.

A hush immediately fell over the crowd as they stood gazing in awe at the beautiful shining star nestled among the topmost branches of the tree, and then the bells suddenly stopped ringing and out of the stillness a solitary voice, that of Christina Noelle Braxton, began to sing "Silent Night." Her sweet melodic voice rang out so beautifully crystal clear and strong that it brought tears to the eyes of those who had forgotten the real meaning of Christmas and warmth to the hearts of those who had forgotten how to love.

So this is Christmas! Charlie thought, caught up in the love and the joy and the peace that had finally settled over her little town. Love in all its splendor and magnificence on that most blessed day of the year when all hearts are full of a sharing, giving spirit, and children were angels or at the very least as good as they could be, and all the hopes and dreams of every person standing went up as a prayer of wanting this joyous feeling to last forever.

It brought new life to a town that had forgotten how to live, mended hearts that had been broken, and rebuilt bridges that had been burned and left behind. It truly was a holy night with a peaceful calm in the air as a brilliant star shone from atop the tree, flooding its magnificence down onto the manger. It was as though the entire town had been reborn this Christmas night.

Then, right in the middle of everything, Paul tenderly took Charlie's face into his strong hands and looked lovingly into her eyes. He kissed her gently and then gently scooped her up into his arms and carried her up the steps and into the gazebo where he gently stood her on her feet. Without a word, he knelt down on one knee and, still holding her hand, asked, "Charlotte Lindsey Faraday, will you marry me?"

As Charlie stood looking down at the man she loved with all her heart and tears poured down her face, he stood up and she unexpectedly jumped up into his arms and wrapped her legs around his waist and threw her arms around his neck, shouting, "Yes, yes, yes!"

And among the cheers and screams from the crowd, he kissed her again, promising his love to her while she promised hers to him until they were old and gray and sitting in their rocking chairs together, gazing at the sunset.

EPILOGUE

———✦———

*P*aul and Charlie were married on March 25 of the following year, and just one month after the wedding, she was already busy planning next year's Christmas celebration—but with a special surprise added to the festivities, a brand new citizen would make his appearance on Christmas Day, bringing the population to a whopping one thousand!

Mary Forsythe got a marriage proposal from Tom Patterson on Easter Sunday. Jean O'Connell renewed her wedding vows with Henry. Helen Grouse won a good-sized lottery and opened her own little shop in the center of town where she displays her sailboats, trucks, and various other toys for tots. Matthew Torrance is elected mayor.

Printed in the USA
CPSIA information can be obtained
at www.ICGtesting.com
LVHW081647031223
765573LV00038B/616